The Cold Blast

Best wishes

Mary Easson

MaryEasson.

April '21

First published in 2021 by the author
Cockleroy Books

ISBN 978-1-8383530-0-1

Typesetting and cover design by
Raspberry Creative Type

Acknowledgements

Thank you to my family for their love and support. Thanks to my sister for reading the original transcript back in 2017 and for encouraging me to self-publish.

My grateful thanks to Kenneth for his assistance with proofreading and editing. However, any mistakes are mine and mine alone.

Thank you to the staff of the West Lothian Local History Library and the National Library of Scotland for their role in making the archive of the written word accessible to the public. Thank you to the historians of Scotland who, by their hard work and dedication, keep Scotland's story alive.

Thanks to everyone who read Black Rigg and who wanted to find out more. I hope you enjoy this story.

Thank you to the mining communities of Scotland whose story this is, and especially to my grandparents whose experiences are woven into the fabric of this book and make it real.

This book is dedicated to Mum and Granny, strong women both, each in their own way.

"O, wert thou in the cold blast
On yonder lea, on yonder lea,
My plaidie to the angry airt,
I'd shelter thee, I'd shelter thee,
And did Misfortune's bitter storm
Around thee blaw, around thee blaw,
Thy bield should be my bosom
To share it a', to share it a'. "

Robert Burns 1759-1796

List of Principal Characters

Rashiepark Estate

David Melville – Laird of Rashiepark, lives at Parkgate House with his extended family

Catherine Melville – wife of David and daughter of Charles Imrie, coalmaster

Isabelle Melville – elder sister of David

Phee (Euphemia) Melville – younger sister of David and friend of Elizabeth and Rose

Roger Stone – estate factor

Blackrigg and beyond

Murdo Maclean – farmer at Whinbank, stalwart of the Blackrigg community

Donald Maclean – nephew of Murdo

Rev Richard Fraser – minister at Blackrigg Kirk

Elizabeth Fraser – younger sister of Richard, lives at the manse

Dr Matheson – local doctor, assisted by Dr Lindsay

Rose Matheson – daughter of Dr Matheson, studying medicine in Edinburgh

Ernest Black – schoolmaster at Blackrigg Public School

Charles Imrie – widower and father of Catherine; coalmaster and owner of The Coal Company

Andrew Brownlee – son of the pit manager

Neil Tennant – blacksmith who left the village in 1910

Stoneyrigg

Alex Birse – coal miner, skilled face worker

Mary Birse – known as Highland Mary, wife of Alex and stalwart of the Stoneyrigg community

Davy Birse – coal miner, eldest adopted son of Alex and Mary

John Birse – colliery labourer, twin brother of Jim, also adopted by Alex and Mary

Ellen Broadley – wife of coalminer, Jimmy and mother of Eddie, Bert and Geordie

Peggy Duncan – widow of Robert, mother of Maggie, Lizzie, Rob and Sandy

Rob Duncan – coal face worker, left school after the death of his father in a pit accident in 1910

Sandy Duncan – brother of Rob, works in the pit office

Tom Graham – bricklayer, widower, father of five daughters, husband of second wife, Jean

Minn Graham – fourth daughter of Tom, a farm worker at Netherside Farm, later at Redburn

Sarah Graham – youngest daughter of Tom and domestic servant at the manse

Steenie Simpson – union official of the Mineworkers Federation, parish councillor

The Linlithgowshire County Courant

May 1914   Blackrigg News

ROYAL VISIT King George V and Queen Mary will be received by the Marquis on 11th July when they visit the county. A large number of Blackrigg folk is expected in Linlithgow as the royal party make their way through the town.

LABOUR PARTY Mr George Dallas has been chosen as the Labour Party candidate for the county in the event of a general election. Mr Dallas will address the Blackrigg community in the public hall on 20th inst at 7pm.

NEW RESERVOIR Work surveying the Black Moss has been completed and a report will be compiled for the council's perusal. The Rashiepark estate have been commended for their cooperation with the authorities regarding the development of this facility which is essential for improvements in public health and to meet increasing demands from mines and manufactories.

HOUSING SHORTAGE The shortage of housing in the county continues to worry the authorities. Blackrigg's housing stock, as elsewhere, is already insufficient and the growth in demand from new workers is exacerbating longstanding issues.

TRADE UNIONS Local workers and their representatives travelled to West Calder at the beginning of the month where an outdoor meeting was held at The Square to hear Mr Jim Larkin, Dublin Labour Leader, talk on the subject of Trade Unionism. There was a large turnout and the crowd showed their appreciation of Mr Larkin for his very informative talk in the usual manner.

SUFFRAGETTES A major meeting of suffragettes drew supporters from across the county. The leading militant, 'General' Drummond delighted her audience with her strident tones and call to action. The suffragette movement continues to press for the extension of the electoral franchise to the female members of the population. Regretfully, Linlithgowshire has not escaped the worst excesses of the militancy that is the mark of the struggle for Votes For Women.

PIPE BAND A pipe band has been founded in the village at long last. Contact the Pipe Major, Mr C MacLeod, 67 Stoneyrigg Rows for details.

HORTICULTURAL SOC. Exhibitors should note that the annual show will take place in the church hall on the first weekend in August. Details of classes TBC by the secretary.

PUBLIC SCHOOL BOARD Accounts for the year past were presented at a meeting of the Blackrigg Public School Board at the beginning of the month. Mr Brown took the chair and presented an overview of the many achievements of the school under the direction of the school master, Mr Ernest Black, supported by the lady teachers. The board chairman, Mr Murdo Maclean, was unable to attend due to continuing ill-health. Board member, Rev Fraser wished him a speedy recovery on behalf of all concerned. An abstract of the full accounts is provided on page 9.

TERRITORIAL ARMY 10th Coy (cyclists) Royal Scots. Local men have been involved in training, making regular patrols along the coastline, and taking classes in navigation, marching and shooting. Evening meets at the Drill Hall in Rowanhill have been well attended during the winter months but the recent turn in the weather has made outdoor manoeuvres equally enjoyable. 10th Coy will contest the Minto Cup in August once again hoping to repeat the success of previous years.

BATHGATE BRASS BAND Local man, Mr Victor Lawrie, trombonist, contributed to the success of the Bathgate Band in winning the Verdi Cup at the Scottish Central Amateur Brass Band Association Competition held in Lanarkshire last month.

Chapter 1

SPRING 1918

John

I am here.

Still.

Try as I might I cannot make sense of it.

And you are all here with me as much as you ever were. Though the night is dark as pitch I can see the shapes of your bodies all lying in rows, warm under your blankets.

Safe and warm.

Safe and warm and clean.

There's water by each bedside and, later, food might come.

Did we ever ask for more than this?

But oh, the price we paid for it.

What a cost and nobody but us will ever know how much.

Tears seep from my eyes till they sting, hot and grit-filled. Closing them makes it worse. Agony. But I must shut out the blackness. I need to escape into sleep. The sound of your breathing subsides at last. I feel a calmness descend from above like a cool, linen shroud and I drift.

Day breaks, the gift of another morning that has no need of explanation. Somewhere else the sun is already bright and, here, a grey glimmer is stealing along the valley from the east, alighting on rain-soaked window panes, touching the room in black shadow and shades of grey. No colour yet but it may return as in the past though I'm not counting on it. I've lost the certainty I had before, that unquestioning trust in the mundane, the ordinary routine of life that makes it fathomable. Life used to have an order. I could count on one thing following another, a kind of cause and effect I thought the world was built on and took for granted.

I see a chessboard being taken down from the shelf by one of my brothers. It might be Jim, my twin. The fire is flickering in the hearth and the light plays gently on my face. It's warm and comforting, like a cup of hot milk on a frosty morning before the walk to school and a day of humiliation at the hand of the teacher. He's spreading the board out on a table that's been scrubbed clean with disinfectant.

The pattern of squares has an order, 8 by 8; no two squares of the same colour touch except at the corners, which isn't touching in the true sense of the word. Each square is separate from the others, clearly defined, their difference expressed in colour. Black and white.

He, the one I take for Jim, empties a tin box of its contents: pieces of painted wood, chipped and worn, round and flat, easy to push around. Thirty-two men. He grabs the black ones knowing they're the ones I like and leaves me with the others. He's grinning and sniggering, intent on getting one over on me. It's always been like that. I feel the menace all around me. Fear begins to rise from the pit of my stomach. I want to stand up but my legs are weak.

I want to leave but he's drawn me into his trap and I'm stuck fast.

The draughts are lined up, two rows of men like armies facing each other across the battlefield of squares. Then I realise what's about to happen and it's already too late to save myself because I cannot run away. I'm pinned down unable to move.

The fire is blazing now, flames leap up from hot, white coals. My throat is parched, it feels like it's caught fire and I cannot swallow as panic engulfs me. The coals hiss and spit. There's a loud bang as the board flies up in the air and all the men with it, a fountain of men from each side, slowly rising and falling through the air, landing everywhere like clods of earth on muddy ground. In the midst of the shrieks and the shouting, he's laughing. A great big belly laugh. I see his face, his dirty yellow teeth, and it's not Jim after all. It's another one. But he isn't really my brother so what did I expect?

Elizabeth

Another winter over though it hardly feels so. These four years past have seemed endless, when the world has teetered on the edge of destruction and all that we know to be true and hold dear has been in doubt. How have we endured? I watch Sarah busy at her work as I sip my tea and take succour from her industry and quiet purpose. The kitchen is warm but it is quite dark even on a sunny morning. It is on the north side of the house and gives me a view of my garden: a long rig of gently sloping land that ends with a boundary wall of sandstone that is golden when the sun shines. During the winter months that wall brings welcome colour to cold Blackrigg.

The springtime has a foothold now. I love to see the snowdrops when they first appear. Even when the frost sets hard their delicate flower persists. They last longer here than in other places but this is not like anywhere else. The green shoots of daffodil have pushed through the heavy soil beneath the shrubs that are still bare, showing little sign of the foliage that will clothe them during the summer. The buds are only just beginning to swell. I have to remind myself that the garden will be a riot of colour and fruitfulness eventually. It is astonishing how a scene of desolation wrought by winter winds and icy rain can be transformed by the heat and light of the sun, and water and nutrient from the soil. Tiny seeds and roots hidden in the ground, quite forgotten about, will appear as if from nowhere to gladden the eye. It is the miracle of Nature and, God knows, we need a miracle right now. I know we must be patient, wait for Nature to take her course, and all will be well again with the world.

The sound of a small bell brings me back from faraway. It is benign at first, softly tinkling, faintly pleading then insistent, almost violent. It is ready to fall off its perch when I catch the look on Sarah's face as she steps backwards into the doorway from her chores at the scullery sink, wondering if I'm going to see to it as I usually do.

'Would you mind?' I ask. 'The minister will be wanting his tea.'

The girl wipes her hands on her apron, flattens out the wrinkles as best she can and tucks away a stray lock of fair hair, hoping she looks respectable enough for the master, before hurrying off to the study. I know she'll be wondering why I am sitting still. She'll be asking herself, *what have they been arguing about this time?* It's a fine state of affairs when a brother and sister cannot live under

4

the same roof without them going hammer and tongs about something every other day, unable to hide their differences from the servant. She must wonder why I find fault with so much of what he says or does. I must seem a heartless, ungrateful wretch to a girl from the Rows where people live cheek-by-jowl, sometimes ten or more to a room, whilst I live here in the manse in relative luxury – him a well-respected member of the community, with a fine house to prove it.

'It's as ye predicted, Miss Fraser,' she says brightly when she returns, advancing towards the kettle. 'Mr Fraser's needin' his tea.'

I reach for my hat and coat, kept on the hook behind the door. 'If you could see to it, Sarah, thank you.'

'Yes, Miss,' she replies, always happy to help. 'If he asks...?' She hesitates, not wanting to be forward though she has worked for me these four years past.

'Just tell him I had to go out.' I pick up a shopping basket as proof. 'I'll be dropping in on... Dr Matheson... so may be some time.'

I leave by the back door to avoid meeting my brother in the hall at the front of the house. Surely this is a state of affairs that cannot continue for much longer.

As soon as I shut the garden gate behind me I feel better. The narrow lane that leads to Main Street is obscured from the manse by a hedge and a notion close to subterfuge takes over, making me smile at the silliness of it. Not sure where I'm headed, I simply have to go somewhere, anywhere, out of the glare of Richard's disapproval.

Sarah may well wonder what latest dispute has come between me and my only living relative but, the truth is, the present situation has had a long gestation, some eight long years in the making. I fear I have become a shadow of the young and earnest girl I was when I first came to live with Richard in Blackrigg. I was filled with optimism back then, and the promise that God had a plan for me to be happy and fulfilled. It was what I was brought up to believe.

Inside the four walls of the manse nowadays, it is a constant struggle to retain any hint of myself.

Sometimes I simply walk away as I do now. Mostly, it is akin to a march and before I know it, I am taking the view from The Law or I am almost at Parkgate House or the bridge on the station road with a shopping basket and no money or food coupons to legitimise a visit to the shops for provisions. I stare at the basket in my hand and manage to stifle a giggle just in time: two parishioners, Mrs Gow and the Widow MacAuley are watching me from the other side of the street. I lift my basket in their direction and give a loud, 'Good morning', realising that I must seem a little too enthusiastic. These women have the eyes of hawks on the hunt – I'm sure they can read even my darkest thoughts from a mile away – and I do not care to hear their tittle-tattle today. I hurry on past the doors of the Cooperative Store leaving them to ponder the mystery of the minister's sister and the unused shopping basket. They see me bump into the righteous Miss Silver – on her way to dust the church pews no doubt – and they surely notice how I rush on nervously avoiding any chance of conversation with the good woman. They are still watching as I pass Smithy Cottage – their eyes are boring into the back of my head – so I hold my head up high, not too high, just enough to give the impression that the Tennant family are no longer of interest to me in the slightest.

Lord save us from the godly and the gossips!

I fix my gaze on the Stoneyrigg Rows and decide that is where I will go rather than taking the hill road which would take me past the forge and the glare of the blacksmith's wife. Mrs Tennant finds it difficult enough to acknowledge me when others are present though she makes an effort to be courteous for the sake of appearances. On an occasion such as this when I am alone, and vulnerable, she would not miss the opportunity to show her true feelings towards me by turning her back. To be ignored is surely the cruellest punishment of all! Her assessment of my character is so unfair! Though I have tried hard to put my position to her, it has been clear for a long time that her mind is made up against me.

I pass the Craigpark steading and the old ruined inn, leaving the village behind to be confronted by the stark reality of industrial life. The Stoneyrigg Rows are long and straight, imposed on the rural scene by the Coal Company with no thought given to the lie of the land, the curve of the hill or the legacy in the landscape of winding roadways and cosy cottages, productive farms and well-tended fields established by previous generations. There are no frills or fripperies here in the Rows, just grim shelters where the basic needs of the labouring classes are met, though even that is debatable. Thankfully, the ashpits and dry closets are located at the furthest extremity, downwind beside the wash house and the drying green. Nature is merciful today as the stench of humanity, some several hundred souls, dissipates on a stiff breeze.

A small group of infants appears as if from nowhere. They know me since I often visit to assist the doctor and the nurse; to help ailing mothers with large broods of children; to inquire after sons who are at the Front; to comfort the lonely and the bereft. Eager faces stare up at me, their hopeful eyes trained on my basket. I feel a sharp stab of guilt that it is empty. *Nothing today, I'm afraid.* So I lift the smallest up as compensation, rearranging the woollen scarf at her neck to keep out the cold. I wipe another's nose with my handkerchief and ask if she is feeling better after her bout of measles. *No sweets or apples to share, I'm sorry. Maybe next time.* It is me who is in need today. I have come for succour from these people who, on the face of it, have little but who give me so much.

'Highland Mary's at Mrs Duncan's,' says the eldest girl without prompting.

'Mrs Broadley's there tae,' adds a skinny boy with bare feet and a large jacket, several sizes too big for him.

'Oh, really? I might go and visit, in that case,' I say as if that hadn't been my plan all along. I prise myself away from their company, marvelling at the awareness of young children, somehow old before their time.

I knock hopefully on Peggy Duncan's door.

'Come awa' in, Miss Fraser,' she says giving me her broadest smile, one that lights up her eyes. She is a robust and good-looking woman who shines despite all of the misfortune life has thrown at her.

In the small room, I feel at home straight away. 'Elizabeth, please,' I beg, as I have done a hundred times before though it makes no difference.

She motions towards the table by the window where Mrs Birse and Mrs Broadley are sitting in mid-conversation. I wriggle out of my coat then remember what I have in my pocket. Their eyes light up.

'I'll put the kettle oan.' Peggy winks, accepting my gift- a twist of paper containing two spoonfuls of tea leaves, and another full of sugar.

'Are ye sure the minister willnae object, Miss Fraser?' asks Ellen Broadley.

'What the eye doesn't see the heart doesn't grieve over,' I reply. How I enjoy this moment at Richard's expense!

We snigger, me and my small coven of conspirators.

'Rationin',' says Ellen. 'Who would've thocht it?'

'As long as it's done richt,' says Mary Birse who is cradling Peggy's grandchild in her arms.

'An naebody's takin' advantage,' adds Ellen, squeezing the boy's hand.

Food rationing is making everyone's life difficult but we understand why it is necessary after four years of war, and as long as the men at the Front are well fed, we will thole it and make the best of it. It is one of our contributions to the war effort.

When the tea arrives the child is passed onto Peggy.

'Wee Archie here's been poorly thur twa-three days past,' she explains, 'But Mary assures me he's oan the mend.'

'I am glad,' I say, rewarding the boy's gaze with a smile. Peggy's daughter and grandchildren have been living with her since her son-in-law was killed at the Somme. The boy in her arms was born after his father left for the Front.

I try to hide the sorrow I feel for little Archie, named for the father he will never know. Pity is not welcome here.

'The bairns are a great comfort,' Peggy says when she sees me looking. 'Their Uncle Sandy fair dotes oan them.'

Ellen sighs at the mention of Sandy. She is thinking about her own boy, Bert, who is in France. 'I'm gled Geordie and Eddie are here still but it's hard oan them. They're wishin' they were awa' like the rest – it disnae get onie easier.' She looks at her friends for confirmation.

Peggy nods. 'Somebody's got tae bide an' win the coal.'

'Aye, though there's little thanks for it,' says Mary bristling. But her thoughts are with the twins, Jim and John, who like Bert are at the Front.

'Mind,' she adds, 'It's guid tae ken they're ootby the gither. They'll be watchin' each ither's backs, mark ma words.'

'They're guid lads,' says Ellen.

'Onie word?' asks Peggy.

Ellen and Mary shake their heads.

'Me neither,' she says.

I glance at the photograph in the metal frame high up on the mantelpiece. A dark-haired young man in a uniform stares back at me. He is serious, giving no hint of expression or thought. Rob Duncan, Peggy's elder son, has been posted missing these three months past.

'Still,' says Mary, refilling everyone's cup, 'Nae news is guid news, eh?'

Chapter 2

John

When I wake the room is filled with light and I try to sit up but to no avail. It must be time. I can't understand why nobody's called me. The hooter will have gone and all of the men with it. And here I am in my bed like a prince in a palace without urgency or purpose but to delight in the specks of dust dancing in sunbeams slanting in through high windows, the smell of beeswax and starched cotton sheets filling my head with memories of the meadow by the Red Burn. We called it the Meadie when we were boys and, more than anything, I want to be there.

I turn over onto my side to speak to the pals and pain shoots through my hip like a bullet from a sniper's rifle. When the focus in my eyes returns, I see them lying row on row down both sides of the room. I'm glad, knowing I'm not by myself, that they're with me and we will leave together when the time comes.

A woman's hastening towards me, almost running. She is all in white with an extravagant scarf covering her head. I wonder what colour her hair is and if it is long and black, like a girl I know from my village back home. The woman is talking to me and has a worried look akin to anger on her face. Maybe I've done something wrong. I fear my life has been full of scoldings because this is a familiar feeling though I do not understand what she's saying. Her words sound foreign just like the lassies who called to us from the roadsides as we marched past with our tails up – when we disembarked from the ship. I remember a great big ship and a grey fog and a feeling of excitement in my stomach that quickly turned to regret. The woman again, she might be a nurse – or a nun, God save us! She's holding my head so I can drink as she brings a cup to my lips. She's nodding, telling me to drink a wee bit more because I've only managed a few drops. The pain in my neck makes it hard and I feel I must have lost some of my swallow but the need to survive surpasses all. So I drink.

And it tastes sweet.

She tells me it is *Good, Good* then *Soup, Soup is good* and she hurries away. I wonder if she has gone to fetch some soup but as I watch her white figure disappear, the blackness of fatigue carries me far away from this place where there is sunlight and soft beds and water and women in white who hold my head in their arms and tell me to drink as if I matter, as if I am worthy of this day when the sun shines from a blue sky through the open window.

In my darkest dreams, shadows play on walls hewn from hard rock by men stripped half-naked in yellow lamplight. They lie on rough wet ground, pressed into bruising spaces too small for arms to swing through the dust-laden air. They mark time with hammer and pick. Ding, ding, ding. Wheels rumble past on metal rails, heavy wagons are pushed by skinny boys with large hands and dirty faces. This is the world I come from, my world of dark shadow and half-light, of rhythmic sounds, metal on stone, warnings called out against the constant racket of men and machines employed in the winning of coal. My shovel scrapes out dross to the railhead where others fill the hutches. The seam is coming away easily and the hewers are pleased. They remind me to pass on a message to the fillers.

Mak sure the hutches are tagged richt or we'll no get paid whit we're owed. Hoo mony thus faur? Three?! Fower surely?! Tell a lad tae follae them up tae the fit o' the shaft. Keep a tally, mind. There's plenty would be happy to tak what doesnae belong them, and no blush wi' the shame o' it. Folk that would call ye freen and ithers whau wouldnae bother tae pretend. Him frae the Back Row, new flitted frae Rowanhill wi' a wife and six weans, for instance. I kent his faither, somebody says.

We all know what that means, the seeds of suspicion have been sown.

And the Foreigner – the Russian – new on the payroll, him that lodges wi' Pretty Peggy Duncan. He's a funny wey o' lookin' at ye, has he no? Odd thon yin. As queer as his big moustache. A different breed, brocht up on black breid and sausage. No like us, no, us that're fed on guid Scotch breid, pure white bar the crust – weel-fired – an' raspberry jam frae the Co-operative Store.

At last, the noise subsides and hutches stand still. Pickaxes and shovels are abandoned as groups of men and boys collect, hunkering down, backs against the wall near the main underground road. It's cooler, almost fresh there. Thank Heaven for small mercies. Sweat's wiped from a dozen foreheads; pieces are retrieved from the pockets of jackets. A slurp of cool water from a bottle, or lukewarm tea out of a tinny slakes the thirst of a dusty throat. I see my comrades: the fillers, the drawers, and the colliers. We work together, winning the coal to earn a crust like the one in my hand. It tastes of the moist earth, the air, and the ripening sun; butter from a fat cow and a spread of jam made from berries, the taste of summer preserved in sugar. I want to make it last forever but it is gone in seconds, as usual. I'm famished. There's never enough or so it seems. I'll have to get back to work to earn another. Nothing else for it. On and on it goes, a never-ending cycle of work, rest and play. Food, sleep, and football with the pals but always with work at the heart of it. World without end.

Water is seeping from the stone above. Drip, drip, drip. Every drop merciless and slow, stinging my eyes with stone fragments. I feel a panic rising in my throat, from my stomach, in my heart. I smell fear, the smell of death or, worse, that which is beyond death, what we do not know. I hear the shrieking sounds of hell, a loud bang like a gun, and a curse in the black night. A hand is holding mine in a firm grip and I grasp even stronger as if holding onto life itself. A small light is coming towards me out of the darkness. It is carried by a man with moist eyes, red-rimmed in a black face. His teeth are rotting in his head but his smile is kind.

John? Are ye there, John?
Aye, I'm here.
I am John.
It is me.

Lying here, four years later, in a foreign place, I remember the days after that accident in the pit as if it was yesterday. I mind how I came to, opening my eyes and feeling the grit in them immediately, shaking my head and blowing down my nose like the old horse in MacCallum's hay field; how I raised a hand to brush away the coal dust only to

14

find I was safe at home in bed. I screwed up my face at the ceiling, seeing the familiar damp patch dried to a pattern of brown rings like mud round the edge of a pond after days of better weather. When I moved my head I could see a gap in the timbers, through the slates to the sky. Another flurry of plaster floated downwards. I raised my aching body onto an elbow and brushed away the debris from the pillow, too quickly, too late to save the injured hand. I mind how I held that hand out afore me, till the sickening ache subsided.

Blissfully unaware, Jim lay at my side. An earthquake could come and go, shaking our small cottage to its foundations, and he would sleep on. The sounds of morning came in through the open window: the gush of water from an outside tap into a tin pail and the swallows swooping in and out of the eaves as they built their nests of mud. Then a hacking cough and low muttering in the other room, followed by a loud bang of a door. Alex was up and about, off to the dry closets for his morning constitutional so I took my chance. I used the chamber pot, dressed as fast as my bruised body allowed and threw a shirt at my twin brother.

'Get up, Jim. Up.'

Groan. His usual reply.

'Davy.' I turned to the other bed. 'Davy. You an a'.'

I didn't wait for the stream of insults that would come from my elder brother when he surfaced, as always needing to apportion blame for the dawning of another day to be spent down the pit. Instead, I escaped into the front room where mother was busy. She nodded towards the bandaged hand.

'It's fine,' I said, settling in at the table where a basin of warm water and disinfectant was waiting. I tried to hide the pain as she eased the bandage off where it was stuck to the wound. She watched me put my hand in the water, said to let it soak for a bit. I swallowed hard and the pain soon subsided to a nauseating throb.

I remember studying her while she worked that morning, as if seeing her for the first time: how she made tea; ladled porridge into plates for the four men in her life; removed the cover from the milk jug; shooed away flies that appeared from nowhere. Her hair was mostly grey by then, kept in place at the back with a few pins, her blue eyes as bright as a bird's, her arms and hands strong because of the work she did. I thought she seemed slower than before, her body thicker round the middle where her cotton pinnie was tied. I realised I'd not noticed what had been happening right before my eyes. The passage of time and the changes it wrought. Strange how the loss of somebody can focus the mind, make you see what's round about you more clearly, in much brighter colours. Did I take her for granted like the rest of them? I couldn't imagine how bleak that place would be without her.

She made it home.

She lifted my hand out of the water and took a good look. It would heal just fine. The doctor had made a good job of it she told me – a clean cut with a big pair of shears and very little loss of blood. I'd soon get used to the loss of a finger, she assured me. I was lucky I hadn't lost a lot more in the accident. What sort of work could I have looked forward to with just the one hand?

I tried to feel blessed, pushing away thoughts of Charlie, the man who had died. I remembered his tight grip, how he'd held onto me there in the darkness, a slab of rock pinning us both down; how the hold had lessened as the man slipped away.

She took a towel to pat the wound dry then dabbed it with iodine, applied a fresh bandage and a big leather mitt that buttoned at the wrist to protect the hand while I was at work. She said I would be back to my normal place down below within a week or two, that the pain would lessen when I got it into my head that the crushed finger was gone for good. It was only a memory now and I'd to forget about it. *Get on with it,* she said. *It'll pass.* It did you no good to dwell on the past. I met her eyes to say thank you and she turned away, back to her work at the fire.

Then the peace was disrupted by the man I called father, Alex Birse, who came bursting in through the door with what could have been a smile on his face.

'Nice lookin' lassie, thon Minn Graham,' he said. 'She's gey...' he thought for a bit and settled for 'brazen.'

'Brazen? She's no brazen. She's a guid lass. Ay smilin', no like some folk I could mention.' Mother sounded exasperated. 'Whit kinna wurld would it be if we were a' like you?'

He washed his hands in the basin, scrubbing the skin and his nails like his life depended on it. 'She's ower auld tae be wavin' tae a grown man like me in the street,' he said at last. 'She's no a wean onie mair, if ye get ma drift.'

I kept my head down, stared at the spoon in my hand so that I wouldn't have to look at him.

He turned in my direction deciding, obviously, that I needed a stir. 'Ye could dae worse than Minn Graham.'

My heart beat loudly in my chest till I was sure he could hear it. I did not dare look up, just waited for the twist of the knife in my back.

'If she wid hae a scrawny specimen like yersel which I hae ma doubts aboot richt enough,' was what he came up with.

17

'Leave the lad alane, Alex. Yer no content bar yer gettin' at folk!' Mother said.

He sat in his usual place and his frown deepened as he liberally sprinkled salt on his porridge before adding some milk, then slurped it down whilst she poured tea into four cups. He tutted his displeasure loudly, rubbing his forearm where an invisible drop of tea had splashed, acting as if a gallon of scalding liquid had been poured onto his skin with malicious intent.

Mother saw me watching him, half-knowing what I was thinking.

'Drink yer tea, John,' she ordered.

I did what I was told. As usual, the atmosphere had changed since Alex had come in. You could cut it with a knife – a blunt one at that. Even the light coming in through the window had dimmed. He never missed a chance to put me down and it made me wonder why this man had opened up his house to me in the first place, giving a home to a poor abandoned orphan, with nowhere else to go but the poorhouse. I took his taunts as I had done my whole life, without a word, grateful for what I had in life and even more grateful for the life that I didn't have and which could have been so much worse. But something had changed that morning that surprised me, something about the way he had talked about Minn Graham cut deeper than anything he'd ever had to say about me, which was plenty. I stored it away for another time, tried to concentrate on my bowl of porridge. The milk was creamy, almost sweet against the saltiness of the oatmeal. I would have told mother how good it was, had we been on our own.

Jim appeared, radiating warmth, straight from a deep sleep; a tousled head; a clean work shirt half-tucked into baggy trousers. He murmured a sleepy greeting and I felt better for his arrival. Then loud cursing in the back room and the clatter of a chair on the hard floor had me on nettles again.

'Whit the...?!' Alex sprayed spit and porridge across the table. 'B'Jesus! Whit's he daen through by? Can he no find his breeks in thon wee room?' He pushed away his empty plate, ladled three large spoonfuls of sugar into his tea and stirred vigorously.

Eyes heavy, encrusted yellow with sleep, Davy entered the room at a run. He'd barely flopped into his chair before the spoon was in his mouth and porridge was surging down his throat. He grabbed some bread and applied a generous layer of jam.

Alex watched Davy stuff his mouth to overflowing. 'Fur the love o' God, whaurs yer manners? God forbid ye ever get an invitation for tea at the Big Hoose!'

I felt a little cheered as someone else felt the force of our father's ire.

'Got tae go,' muttered Davy, rising quickly. He emptied the contents of a cup of tea into his open mouth, grimaced through his yellow teeth.

'Yer lookin' the worse for wear,' barked Alex.

Mother pushed Davy's lunch into his pocket and pressed a tinny of tea into his hand.

'Yer needin' tae get in at a decent time,' Alex called after him as he made for the door.

There was no reply.

'Ye should be in yer bed, no roamin' aboot the place tae a' oors!' he bawled.

The door slammed shut.

When the windows stopped rattling in their frames, peace descended for which we were grateful. Mother plonked a piece tin and a tinny on the table in front of

Alex. I wondered if it was a hint for him to be on his own way. She fetched a piece for me and Jim, and an egg each in a twist of paper.

'Whit's this?' asked Alex, his frown deepening though it hardly seemed possible.

'Eggs, boiled,' she shot back.

'Eggs? Are we made o' money a' a sudden?' He looked as if the sky was about to fall in.

'There's fower wages comin' intae this hoose. The boys deserve a treat. Somethin' t' look furrit tae when they're hard at their work, tae keep them gaun.' She saw him looking at his piece tin. 'You've got yin tae, Alex, dinna fret.'

'Sounds kinda extravagant tae me. Ye niver ken when the work's gaunnae dry up. I've telt ye there's a stoppage oan the horizon, if the union disnae get its wey. Could last a while, like the last yin.' He shoved an arm into his jacket which he hefted up over his back as if it weighed a ton. Haversack over one shoulder, he thrust the tinny into a pocket. He could have left it at that – he'd already had the last word – but he felt compelled to give a parting shot from the doorway.

'Best get tae work then. Some folk have tae gang earn the cash for ithers' extravagances. Cannae hing aboot here a' day when there's work tae be done. No like some folk.'

'Aye...' She found she was talking to the back of the closed door then thought better of it, turned to me and Jim, straight-faced for a second or two before raising one eyebrow. We weren't sure what that meant but knew better than to test her loyalty to her man.

I remember watching her take the tin bath from under the box bed. She placed it in front of the fire, emptied boiling water into it then refilled the kettle before setting it back on the swey above the hot coals. The lodgers would be in from the night shift soon, in need of a wash. I saw her looking out of the window, examining the sky above the roofline of the next row. It was a fine summer's day, she announced, a good drying day and she had her usual Monday morning slot along at the wash house. She looked happy, as if she might burst into song at any moment. Jim and me made ready to leave for the pit, picking up the food she had prepared for us, including the eggs, feeling the warmth of the tea through the metal handle of the tinnies. By the time we'd opened the door, she already had a sweeping brush in her hand.

'See ye efter, Ma,' I said as I put on my bunnet.

'Aye, see ye efter,' she replied. 'Mind come hame in yin piece for a change? Tak tent. Ye niver can tell whit's roon the corner in this life, John.'

And as I lie here in this foreign land, far away from Blackrigg, examining the hand with the missing finger, I am reminded of her wisdom. I am grateful that it was Mary Birse who walked into the poorhouse that day and became my mother. She is wise in word and deed, and much respected in the community as nurse, as friend and neighbour. The world is a better place with her in it.

I cannot blink the tears away fast enough and they flow.

Elizabeth

I decide to take the longer route back to the manse so I turn up the hill road at the Smiddy. In doing so I am defying Mrs Tennant's wrongful judgement of me, asserting my right to walk past the forge. I will not allow her to determine my path in life no matter how remotely, not if

I can help it. I am also avoiding an early return to Richard's world and, before I know it, I am passed the top entrance to Manse Lane, have almost climbed to the place where the road levels off and I have a choice of routes. I can either climb to the top of The Law, or continue eastwards along the old coach road, go north towards Whinbank where the Macleans live, or meander along the edge of the muir towards Parkgate House and Redburn Farm. Oh, to have choices in this life! I decide the latter is the best option as I am welcome at both Parkgate and Redburn and, sheepishly I admit, that option gives me an excuse for having been absent for so long when I do eventually return to the manse.

I find the going hard over the open muir. It's not that it's heavy under foot but I do not seem to have the energy I set out with earlier in the morning. My anger often carries me further than I intend and when it dissipates, as it must, I can feel lethargic, weary of the struggle within myself. The wind has dropped and the sun is quite warm as I wander across a dip in the ground, so I settle beside an old wall to rest. The sky is a brilliant blue beyond the broken cloud above me. I can see that the lower cloud is stationary, completely still and unchanging, brightly lit by the sun which still has a while to climb to its highest point of the day. I love the patterns and shapes and colours in the clouds and watch them for a while, feeling more composed with every passing minute. I am not unhappy all of the time and I know that I have much to be grateful for – there have been many good times and opportunities these last four years. But as the higher cloud scuds past on faraway winds, I am fearful, almost panicked, that my sudden calm will be taken from me by forces that are great and overwhelming and everything will be beyond my reach

– as is the way of things. I often think of the summer four years ago and how much of a turning point it seemed to be at the time. But we had no idea what was ahead of us. How I ache for peace to return. We are all weary of the war and wish an end to it. I think of the women I have just visited in the village and the sons they yearn to have home, and all of the mothers and sons and sweethearts from across this land and beyond who pray for the same. Perhaps we will not have to wait too much longer before we can pick up the pieces of our lives and move on.

I often find solace here on the hill where I am all alone, listening to the wind in the grass and the birds' call, remembering people who are no longer here, hoping and praying for peace, dreaming of happier days that may lie ahead. If not here, I find succour in the garden at the manse. I have long had an interest in matters of a botanical nature and the garden has given me an outlet for my energy and creativity. It is also testament to my skills and determination, and what I can and have achieved when others conspire to control me.

Richard mocked my plans for the garden when I first took to it but I shut him out, letting his hateful words wash over me. I ignored his disapproving stare as he watched from the kitchen window, impatiently waiting for tea to be served, whilst I worked at the ground in all weathers. He would tut loudly when, finally, I returned to my household chores. He would chastise me as I sat by the doorstep easing off muddy boots, removing my soiled apron and wiping the sweat on my brow with the back of a dirty hand. Nothing he said could destroy the joy I felt from my time in the open air, digging over the heavy soil coloured black by peat, improving it with manure from the farm and with lime from the works on the hill. Nothing he said could remove that inner smile brought on by the product of hard work and a job well done, amongst the dirt, the flowers, and the bees.

In the first year, I moved mounds of earth by the barrow load from one corner to another, according to a plan drawn up in my notebook. I created levels and compartments, defining each small space with walls and little hedges that would afford protection from the worst of the weather. When the church warden appeared one day to give assistance, Richard could only manage a thin smile and take his leave, retreating into the manse to complete some very important work for the parish council. In the second year, much to his dismay, a greenhouse arrived to be positioned near the wall at the far end. Two labourers laid out a platform of red brick and returned the following day to erect the structure of wood and glass. Richard tackled me about the cost immediately, said it was a little too ornate for his taste. But when I explained that it was a gift from Parkgate House, salvaged from the reorganisation of the grounds by the new Mrs Melville, he acquiesced with pursed lips and a bow of his head in deference to the local gentry. In the third year, a succession of flowering plants and shrubs came into its own, drawing admiring looks from passers-by on their way up the lane. On leaving a Sunday service, I overheard a parishioner remarking about the wonderful transformation that had taken place in the manse garden under the minister's supervision, changing a rather plain space into a cornucopia of delights for the eye and the palate. Richard beamed and said that it had really been nothing at all. Gardening was such an innocent pleasure. It was down to God at the end of the day, and the many gifts he bestowed upon the world. After all, he asked enthusiastically, had the first garden not been planted by the Lord?

Until Sarah came to help in the manse in early June of 1914, I relished the tranquillity of the morning, especially in summer when the grey light of dawn slipped into that silent cavernous house and I could steal out into my precious garden once again. Although the morning was a busy time, with so much to do in the kitchen, I had hours of my own company to enjoy before Richard surfaced demanding breakfast, reminding me of the importance of his work as a minister of the church – attending to the spiritual needs of the local population. He might comment on the state of the brasses or the dust on the polished furniture, the need for a change of towel in his bedroom perhaps; or he would take an opportunity to scold me about the overuse of coals during the summer months; sometimes, he would offer help in the planning of my day, and remind me about who was coming for supper. He would test me on his guests' food preferences though the dinner menu varied little, being entirely dependent on the season and what was available at the Co-op, not to mention what he had allocated for housekeeping from his limited stipend.

I remember watching the silent house and planning that day as I anticipated Sarah's arrival. It was to be dominated by the funeral, of course. Richard was in a flap and would be until the whole thing was over and the man had been laid to rest. The deceased had been a pillar of the community, held in high esteem by all who knew him and respected by many he had never even met. A large attendance was expected. Proper procedures would have to be followed and appropriate things would need to be said. In his role as minister, Richard had spent hours visiting the family and writing the eulogy. It hadn't been easy: the amount of paper he wasted in the process was testimony to that. He had been in such a temper about it and that was not like him, I will admit. He does enjoy the limelight after all. In common with the other women, I was to have no role in the service or the committal. Unusually though, the mourners would be back in the church hall for a grand tea. The departed had insisted upon it apparently. That was where I came in, organising and overseeing a small troop of ladies who would descend on the place to set the tables, laying out a spread for the return of the men. After listening to one of the minister's long diatribes, they would be thirsty, gasping for a strong brew, and hungry for food and conversation.

I'd had no option but to join the other women on the Tea Committee, though I tried to avoid it for long enough. Somehow, along with my familial ties to the minister came responsibilities towards his parishioners. But as he was quick to point out, they paid for my keep at the end of the day. Richard rarely missed an opportunity to remind me that my position in this world was entirely dependent on his. My contribution as a Sabbath School teacher was not enough, even if I did keep house for him with all the hard labour that entailed. After my first year in the parish, back in 1910, my reticence to immerse myself in the work of the church was being noted, Richard insisted, and my diffidence could no longer be used as an excuse for hiding behind the walls of the manse. Besides, he added, being active in the community was a good way of moving on, putting the past behind me.

But I had not wanted to forget the past! In those first weeks and months after the scandal had broken and Neil Tennant had left the village, I had thought of him every waking minute of every day. I remembered our trysts at the shieling on the hill, of how he had taken me in his arms and told me how much he loved me. I wanted to go back there so many times but promised myself I would not return without him. When I was busy at my work I longed for his arrival, telling me he had come back for me at last. Every knock at the door brought a quickening of my heart. When I stepped out along Main Street to buy provisions from the shops or take letters to the Post Office, I would fix any stray locks of hair behind my ears, straightening my skirt in preparation. I would glance in the direction of the Smiddy, hoping to see him appear round the corner, dressed in the leather apron of his trade, holding me with his eyes as he walked to meet me, then offering to carry my basket back to the manse. When I was wet and cold from my labours in the garden, I prayed that the footsteps coming along Manse Lane would be his, and he would smile his beautiful smile as he came in through the gate to find me.

But he did not come, winter turned into spring, succeeding seasons came and went, one after the other. Long years passed without a word. In the quiet moments I wondered where he was and what he was doing. Always I hoped he was well: eating, sleeping, and working in the gentle places of my imagination where kindness and good fortune reigned. I prayed that bitterness had not entered his heart to cloud his memory of me, that he remembered me with fondness and with love.

Then came that fateful day in the early summer of 1914 and I remember every detail as if it was yesterday. I remember the warmth of the morning sun reaching out to me through the branches of a small rowan, its leaves young and fresh; how those delicate fronds shaded the bench where I lingered. I sat breathing in the morning air, and looked around at my beautiful garden, trying as usual to shake off the heavy burden of my loss. I had thrown myself into good works: committee work for the church and village organisations, visiting church members laid low with sickness. I worked from dawn till dusk in the house, cleaning and cooking, comforting parishioners as they waited to be seen by the minister, and serving the visitors invited to break bread with him. But none of it eased the ache deep inside me, the loneliness and the longing. Only there in that beautiful place of my creation did I find peace to think and remember the past, peace to reflect and to hope for the future. Hope and my garden were all I had to keep me going, I realised. But what I discovered later that day threw everything into a state of flux. Sometimes, as my late mother used to say, things had to get worse before they got better.

And they certainly did.

Chapter 3

John

It's dark except for a small lamp at the far end of this long room I find myself in. The ceiling is made of wood and is a fine construction the likes of which I have never seen before. The walls are a plain white plaster and quite high with no adornment of any kind save a simple wooden cross on the wall nearest to me. The windows are small but there are several and every second one is open day and night, weather permitting, for which we are grateful since the smell in the room would choke us all to death quicker than our wounds and infections could act against us. The delirium of recent days has gone. I no longer wake up in a pool of sweat, half aware that nurses are whispering at the foot of my bed about my chances of survival. The dressings on my hip, my right hand and on my neck wound are clean and fresh, devoid of the stench of death, unlike before. I no longer feel the heaviness in my limbs as if the life blood has been sucked out of them leaving me unable to raise a finger to help myself. I am reassured as I study the hand with the missing digit, that there are indeed only four fingers there, evidence that my memory has not been playing tricks. I am who I think I am and have begun to piece together the history of my short life, making sense of the rambling recollections that came with the fever.

The funeral for the man who died, Charlie Scobie, took place as quickly as possible after his demise when the roof collapsed in Broadrigg No. 1. As soon as the local joiner had knocked together a coffin and the lair had been dug, a send-off took place – a whip round funded the arrangements. It being the summer, and a warm one at that, the body would deteriorate fast in the back room of the but an' ben the deceased had occupied with his wife, three children and a couple of boarders. The lodgers were quickly decanted to another household for the time being. It was a frightful thing to put the Scobies through for any longer than necessary, knowing that a dead husband and father was lying prostrate through by wrapped in a sheet and covered in a mortcloth hired by the day. Still, that wasn't nearly as upsetting as the day of the accident when Mrs Scobie arrived home to find half a dozen men trying to pass her husband's dead and battered body through the open window and lay him out on the kitchen table. The door being locked, and no sign of her in the vicinity, they'd had no option but to deliver him through the window, they told her. But, no fear, Highland Mary was already on her way to dress the body, they explained.

I tried not to appear too affected by the accident, taking my mother's advice not to dwell on what couldn't be changed. Besides, it wasn't the way of it. Showing how you felt about such things would only open yourself up to ridicule and name calling. Sticks and stones and all that. But that bit about names never hurting? Fegs! Bruises can heal but names wound deep and leave their mark, in my experience. I managed a game of football of an evening and a daunder up the road to the moss with the lads but the day of the funeral was another matter entirely. It wasn't that I minded going but I knew all eyes would be on me, questioning, and so it proved. Mrs Scobie had insisted that I come into the house when she saw me standing with the crowd of men in the street, outside the door. They pushed me in through the mourners, into the front room where the relatives had gathered waiting for Mr Scoular of The Brethren to say a few words. There was Charlie Scobie lying dead in his cheap wooden coffin, on top of the table by the only window. The relatives stared at me, John Birse, the boy who had lived whilst Charlie had died.

'How close we are to death,' Mr Scoular said in the confident yet mournful tones of somebody who thinks often and deeply of such things. 'We never know the day nor the hour till it comes to pass. That is how it is meant to be. Only the Lord knows when it will be our time. It could so easily have been John who was crushed when the roof came in but Charlie had been chosen. It was Charlie's time, even though the man has a wife and three young children dependent upon him for food and shelter. It is part of the great mystery of life that a young lad of sixteen has been spared whilst the man has been taken.'

I stood with my head bowed, finding it easier to look at the bloodless corpse of Mr Scobie than the blank faces of the bereaved. Afterwards, the journey along the Rowanhill road seemed endless as I walked behind the cart carrying the coffin to its final resting place in the new cemetery – the kirkyard having no room for incomers. I felt my body quite detached from myself whilst I pondered the mysteries of life, especially the question of why Charlie Scobie who had so much to live for had died whilst me, unworthy John Birse whose very own mother had given him up at birth, had been spared.

When Charlie's body was about to be delivered home through the open window of his rented cottage, another funeral was taking place elsewhere in Blackrigg. I caught sight of it as I carried my bandaged hand in front of me up the pit road, having been released early from that fateful shift. Judging by the crowds, word had spread that the hearse carrying the deceased to his final resting place was well on its way along the road from Rowanhill. In recognition of his connection with Craigpark where his family had been innkeepers for many years in the distant past, the funeral procession was to stop in the road by the ruin of the old coaching inn for a minute's silence, before continuing along Main Street to the kirkyard. The street was lined on both sides with people from all walks of life who had come to pay their respects. Women with young children in tow had joined the old men already in place for a good view of the proceedings. Shopkeepers had left their places of business and the entire roll of Blackrigg School, some four hundred children, crowded the pavements close to the church. Numbers were swelled by workers from Blairha' and Back o' Moss Pits as they wound their weary way home after the early shift.

Murdo Maclean's final journey from his home at Whinbank to the village of Blackrigg for burial was slow and stately. His coffin lay in a glass-sided hearse, pulled by a black stallion, strong and sleek, its noble head adorned with a fine, white plume. A highly polished motor car followed on behind. It carried his widow, a nephew and the minister, Mr Fraser. The owner of the car, David Melville, sat in front beside the driver. As the local laird he'd have been pleased to be of service to the Maclean family at a difficult time, whilst publicly acknowledging Mr Maclean's long friendship with his own family, the

Melvilles of Rashiepark. A small number of open carriages followed. The first, drawn by a pale horse, was full of colourful flowers, sprays of summer blooms, floral tributes given by a variety of organisations and individuals to show their appreciation of his life's work as a stalwart of the community. The remaining carriages carried the select group of family and friends who'd attended the service that had already taken place in the privacy of Whinbank.

By the time the cortege pulled up in front of the old Craigpark Inn, a long line of smartly dressed, mainly elderly men had formed behind. Suited and booted, trussed up in black ties and stiff collars, they sweated under woollen coats more appropriate for a wild winter's day than sunny, summer skies. To add to their discomfort, all wore hats, either top hats or bowlers depending on their station in life, and most sported beards or moustaches. Even the local constabulary had sent two of their own, to pay their respects and take up the rear. Onlookers bowed their heads and mothers tried to keep infants quiet during the silence. This was a time for people to remember Murdo's long connection to this place they called Blackrigg, a place he'd devoted his life to and a place that he'd loved. With his passing had gone his memories of the coaching days on the Old Great Road that crossed the country and brought people and trade from far and near for business and pleasure. Gone were the images imprinted on his mind of his mother and father, of his sisters and brothers, children of a happy home by all accounts; gone too were his memories of the servants and the ostlers, and the old ways, long consigned to the past. They'd only be remembered in the stories he'd passed on, tales of olden times when life was simpler and more innocent no doubt, tales that would become less precise with every telling. But Murdo had left his mark on the place and that was why so many were present that day to give thanks and say goodbye. The village library, revived and invigorated by Murdo, carried his name into the future. His work on the parish council and on the school board would not be forgotten and would be continued by others. He had used the knowledge and experience of his long life, some eighty-five years by the end, for the greater good. True, his passing was a break with the past but the legacy of his long life, a life well-lived, lay in the way others had been influenced and encouraged by his knowledge and example.

I'd had no close encounters with Mr Maclean but had seen his portly figure striding through the village to his meetings or the Sunday morning service at the kirk. I'd heard his hearty laugh in the distance and bowed to his reputation as a good man. Death, the great leveller, had come for Murdo and Charlie at the same time. Why death had chosen to avoid Murdo for so long was another matter, giving him eighty years in which to leave a legacy that would live on after him. But who would remember thirty-year-old Charlie Scobie, the skilled hewer, bar his widow and children now facing eviction from their home? What would his legacy be?

At the end of the day, the two men were equal in death though they had not been equal in life.

Life, and the path it takes, is indeed hard to fathom.

I can still see the motor car suddenly purr back into life and follow the hearse when it moved off along Main Street towards the kirkyard. Like a wave breaking along a shore, men removed their caps as the procession passed. The widow (well catered for) and the heir (a nephew from faraway), the laird of Rashiepark, and the great and the good followed in the good man's wake and the rest of us, spellbound for a moment, turned back to our ordinary lives in the Rows.

Elizabeth

After an early luncheon, Richard sped off with David Melville for the private funeral service at Whinbank Farm, Murdo's family home. I was never so glad to see the back of my brother! There was no doubt he was in his element at the thought of a street packed with onlookers, hushed and respectful, as he took centre stage beside the deceased, amid a sea of silk top hats. He had lectured me a little too enthusiastically about how a funeral was a sad occasion for loved ones left behind but an occasion for rejoicing too. His faith told him that a man's passing marked the beginning of his journey from this earth to Eternal Life with God the Father in Heaven. It was also an opportunity to reflect on the achievements of the deceased, and to give thanks for their talents and virtues which in some cases, but not all, were many. Though good reason to rejoice, the changes wrought by the death of someone as influential as Murdo Maclean could be dislocating for those left behind. Murdo had been in charge of both the school board and the parish council, for example, and these positions would have to be filled soon.

As Richard had busied himself for his departure, he suddenly stopped short in the hallway, closed his eyes, seeking guidance from above. I watched as he quietly prayed that the void left by Murdo's passing might be filled for everyone's sake. He opened his eyes with a start and something approaching glee shone from his countenance. He had prepared a few uplifting words to say to the gathering in the family home and, later, to the multitude by the graveside and he seemed suddenly anxious to get them over with. It would be a tiring day, he told me, and there was a lot of talking to be done, conversing with mourners about local affairs, such as the state of the school and the use of the rates. He would press them for their priorities and impress them with his interest and knowledge of local matters. He hadn't realised that he had given himself away but I could read him like a book.

Who could fill Murdo Maclean's shoes? It was so obvious when he thought about it. Who better? He believed he had the authority and the bearing for it. He looked heavenward, convinced he was up to the task. And it wasn't vanity, it was his calling! Richard Fraser had turned the passing of a much loved champion of the community into an opportunity for himself. And the man wasn't even cold in his grave! Clutching his bible to his breast, with a flourish and a swish of his long black robes Richard left the manse at a rate of knots, impatient for the arrival of the motor vehicle from Parkgate House.

'Come along, come along,' he called out to no one in particular. 'Murdo wouldn't want to keep the Good Lord waiting, now would he?'

Later, in the church hall I joined the ladies of the tea committee who were crowded around the stool on which one of their own stood in order to get a clear view of proceedings in the small graveyard below. The hall was a bright airy space but the lower windows were frosted for the sake of privacy and only those brave enough to stand on tip-toe on a high stool were rewarded with sight of what went on in the world outside.

'Oh, my! Whit a sicht!' called out Mrs Gowans, revelling in the power her elevated situation gave her over the others who were clamouring to hear what was happening outside.

'Are there monie folk in attendance, Mrs Gowans?' asked the Widow MacAuley squinting upwards. 'Whau is there tae see?'

'Oh, there's a wheen o' them, richt enough, as ye micht expect. I hope we've enough cups for them a'.' Mrs Gowans stretched a little too far and wobbled precariously on her perch.

'Watch out!' I cautioned, feeling responsible for what was going on. 'Please don't fall. Perhaps we could look from the doorway instead?'

'Och, but it widnae be richt. Whaur's yer manners, Miss Fraser?' said Mrs Gowans from on high. 'A funeral's nae place for women.'

'Besides, ye get a better view frae up there,' added old Mrs Gow pointing a gnarled finger upwards.

'Be careful then. Please. Just tell us when they're about to finish so that we can get the tea brewing.' I knew there was no point in arguing.

'Can ye see Mrs Maclean at a'?' asked the Widow MacAuley. 'How's she lookin'?' Turning to her companions she said, 'It's a difficult time, as I fine ken masel.'

The ladies nodded. Mrs MacAuley had been a widow longer than anyone could remember.

'She's staunin' ower at the kirk, lettin' the men get oan wi' it. Respectfu' like,' Mrs Gowans explained.

'Respectful?! She should be in here with the women, not out there with the men,' lectured Miss Silver through thin lips.

'Whit's she got on?' Daisy Gowans called up to her mother.

'She's wearin' black,' Mrs Gowans called back.

'We ken siclike withoot lookin',' retorted Mrs Gow.

'A long frock and a wee jaicket. Silk an' brocade b' the looks o' things; a hat – no ower fancy, mind – an' a veil. Och, jist the ticket… fair braw. Gloves tae match… long yins… an' a string o' pearls.'

'Pearls? At a funeral?' tutted the Widow MacAuley.

'Mebbe her man gied her them,' snapped Mrs Gowans in defence of Mrs Maclean.

'We'll see her soon enough, ladies,' I interjected. It seemed immoral to be spying on Mrs Maclean at such an intimate moment, though it did feel strangely exciting at the same time. I held my hands up, ready to catch Mrs Gowans as she teetered once again.

'Is the nephew there, Mrs Gowans?' asked Miss Silver blushing. 'Just out of interest,' she added quickly. 'I believe his name is Donald.'

'Oh, aye. He's there,' came the reply. 'Richt next tae the minister, so he is. Haud oan, somethin's happenin'. Noo he's taen a cord. It's the yin at the heid. Aye, he's a handsome lad, noo I get a guid look at him.'

'He's a guid catch for somebody,' suggested the Widow MacAuley. 'Sic a shame I'm the wrang side o' twinty-five masel.'

'The wrang side o' twinty-five?' exclaimed Mrs Gow, her good friend and neighbour. 'Ye were the wrang side o' twinty-five when Adam was a boy!'

The Widow MacAuley gave a throaty cackle. 'I still ken a handsome lad when I see yin. Jist the dab fur yersel, Miss Fraser. Or young Daisy Gowans here, in a couple o' years time!'

Daisy's girlish protestations deflected attention from my embarrassment, surely evident in the blush spreading rapidly across my face. I have always felt cursed by blushing as it gives away my feelings for all to see.

'What else can you see, Mrs Gowans?' I asked, quickly moving the subject away from Donald Maclean and his eligibility.

'Some o' the ferm workers have been gien cords, Doctor Matheson tae.' Mrs Gowans steadied herself, clung evermore tightly to the window sill. 'His Lordship, David Melville's at the feet,' she continued. 'Nae show withoot Punch, I suppose.'

'Mrs Gowans! This is no time for disrespect,' chastised Miss Silver. 'Mr Melville and Mr Maclean were good friends.' She walked off in high dudgeon, casting an eye over the tables which were laden with sandwiches and home baking, all set for afternoon tea.

'The coffin's doon noo,' continued Mrs Gowans ignoring Miss Silver's rebuke. 'They'll be a while yet. Mr Fraser'll have plenty mair tae say, ye can be sure.' She glanced down at me. 'Nae offence, Miss Fraser.'

'None taken, Mrs Gowans,' I replied, hiding a smile. In my book, there was nothing wrong in speaking the truth and I was well aware of how much my brother liked the sound of his own voice. I joined Miss Silver in a review of the tables then made for the scullery where several large tea pots stood waiting to be filled.

'Weel, I'll be damned! Thon was quick! The meenister's in a hurry the day, for sure!' called out Mrs Gowans. 'They're feenished an' they're comin' this wey, like bats oot o' hell! Quick git me doon oot here, Daisy!'

A black tide of mourners clutching their hats swept into the hall just as Mrs Gowans was pulling herself together with Daisy's help. The crowd parted down the middle when Mrs Maclean entered to take her place at the top table, entreating everyone not to stand on ceremony and to tuck in. As soon as grace was said, of course. Her husband had left instructions for a tea to be laid on and they were to have their fill. According to Murdo, she informed the mourners, good conversation in good company over afternoon tea was one of life's joys, a delight to be savoured whenever possible.

'Enjoy,' she told them, so they did.

The tea committee was soon busy around the hall, filling cups and fetching more when required. I remained in the scullery, attending to matters there, supervising things from a distance, out of sight and away from the hubbub. I would make an appearance later, to give my condolences to Mrs Maclean, and to appease my brother who would be watching for me. Meantime though, Richard would be preoccupied, deep in conversation about important matters, currying favour with local worthies in the name of the church and for his own sake. I was busy at the sink when Mrs Gowans appeared at my back, pleading with me to lend a hand in the hall. Whilst Mrs Gow and the Widow MacAuley meant well, she explained, they were on the slow side. And they'd already scalded the undertaker twice and spilled milk into the stationmaster's lap. Could I come and lend a hand for a bit?

I entered the hall carrying a large teapot, scanning the hall looking for empty cups. A sea of faces, animated in conversation, looked up briefly in my direction. They were all male, or nearly so. At the far end, Mrs Maclean was surrounded by well-wishers offering their condolences. Catherine Melville had joined her husband at the top table and another woman sat by the door. I couldn't make out who she was at first. It was unusual for women to be in attendance, unless they were family or gentry. A hand went up for more tea so I made my way into the middle of the hall, making small talk and enquiring after someone's health on the way. I glanced around the room and noticed that the woman seemed to be looking in my direction. Perhaps she needed more tea. I was close to her before I realised who she was. Her bonnet sat forward on her head, shielding her eyes until she looked up, fixing me with a glare.

'Good day, Mrs Tennant.' I tried hard to hide my surprise. 'Would... would you like some tea?'

Stoney-faced, Mrs Tennant held out her cup. She glowered at me.

'What brings you here, Mrs Tennant?'

'A funeral, Miss Fraser.'

I remember how I wished the floor would open up. 'Yes, of course.'

'The Tennants have been smiths in Blackrigg from time immemorial, an' had a lang association wi' the Macleans o' Craigpark,' she lectured. 'It's oor place tae be here.'

'Of course it is. You've every right... It was just... that we haven't seen you here, at the church... for some time, Mrs Tennant. That's what I... was thinking.' I was trying to explain myself but was failing badly. I noticed Mr Tennant sitting beside his wife. He was looking in my direction, no hint of expression on his lined face, bright red from years at the forge.

How could the Tennants know that their son was rarely out of my mind? And the first thought that had come into my head, when I recognised them there in the church hall, was that they must have come to bring news of him? Wasn't it a reasonable conclusion to make? It had been nearly four years since the Tennant family had suddenly stopped attending church, not long after Neil had left the village. For all that time, unless there were witnesses, I'd been snubbed in the street by Mrs Tennant, more or less ignored by her in the store when I'd stood in the queue to buy provisions or had waited to be served in the post office, rubbing salt into the wound of my broken heart. I hadn't been able to understand his mother's treatment of me. I'd made it clear from the start how I felt about Neil, and how much I wanted him to return. I'd asked her to write to him and tell him how I felt, beseeched her to ask him to write back to me.

But he never did.

Now the Tennants were there in the hall, perhaps finally realising that they'd been wrong to blame me for Neil's decision to go away and not come back. Perhaps I was to be reprieved at long last. But it was none of that. Having prayed for his return for so long, it was only wishful thinking on my part that Mrs Tennant had come to bring news of her son after all this time. The Tennants were there for the funeral, to pay their respects. That was all.

I remember how Mrs Tennant began speaking then, her mouth animated, cruel, and her brow furrowed. I could see that the woman was talking at me, a torrent of words flowing out of her mouth. But I couldn't fathom it. It couldn't be true, could it? There was no sense to any of it. The babble from the crowd in the hall grew louder and it was suddenly hot. The room was whirling and I could hardly swallow. Mrs Tennant was in full flow, her eyes wild. I could hear her though my head was spinning. It was as clear as day and I understood. That was why I had to get away. I felt my knees go weak and made my excuses, gibbering like a fool. I made for the kitchen through a tide of raised hands. *More tea, dear lady! More tea!!* The tea pot left my hands and crashed across the floor.

In the kitchen, I clutched at the sink, relieved to have escaped the throng but feeling sick. I gulped in air, felt like I was drowning. My legs were giving way. The current was taking me down into the depths, the watery depths where daylight did not enter.

Miss Fraser, Miss Fraser! Elizabeth, is there anything wrong? People were there above me, looking down into the darkness where I lay. *What's the matter? Are you alright? Somebody fetch the doctor*, they were saying.

I could see them speaking as waves of consciousness swept and swirled over my listless body which lay still and cold on the floor, in the blackness of despair. I had entered a dark place where there was nothing, no light, no warmth, no hope, nothing.

Chapter 4

John

When I left the house with Jim the morning after the accident, I'd expected Alex to be well down the road but there he was just up ahead, keeping to the shaded side between the Rows as usual. Before he'd reached the rutted track that led to the pits, he'd had a long fit of coughing. I saw him lean against a fence post for support, fighting for air and choking on phlegm, his body shaking violently with every hack. He spat, adding his mark where others before him had patterned the gravelled surface of the road. A few shallow breaths later and he straightened his back. I was close enough to see him wipe his tear-stained face with the back of a shaking hand but I knew better than to run to his aid.

Alex was glad to be going to work, even though he complained loudly about the conditions he worked in. Mining was in his blood. It was what got him up in the morning, and made him who he was. He marched towards the pit, his eye fixed on the sheds up ahead and the pithead gear that turned back and forth as men in cages were delivered to the underground roads, way below ground. He walked with hunched shoulders, adopting the stoop that was his trademark, as if hiding his face from the sun. To his mind, there was little point in enjoying the delight of a summer's morning. In his experience it could only lead to a longing for something unattainable. He was inured to the day ahead: another long shift underground, in the feeble loom of the light on his leather cap.

Whilst the other men walked in groups, conversing about the weather and Saturday's football results, Alex walked alone. Me and Jim followed behind at a distance, knowing none of our friends would join us in his company. It wasn't that people disliked him, though that might have been true in the past. It was just that it was too early in the morning for one of his socialist harangues about justice for the working man. Everybody trooping down that road and lining up to wait their turn for the cage was resigned to their fate, more or less, and no amount of wishing otherwise could change things. It didn't make facing the day any easier being reminded by Alex Birse that the eight-hour-day, fought over for so long and enshrined in law these six years past, didn't actually start until the worker was at his place of work with tools in hand ready to strike the first blow. For the miners, and the younger lads like me who drew out the coal and filled the hutches, this meant they wouldn't be paid for time spent at the pithead waiting for the cages that took them down below, or when hurled in the bogies to the underground roads, nor for the journey on foot, often bent double, to the coalface. When the coal masters bickered over wage rates and whined about the difficulties of implementing the eight-hour-day in the mines, they had their opinions reported by their chums, the newspaper barons. The facts of the matter, Alex would rage, were never fully reported.

In the early years after our family's arrival in Stoneyrigg, Alex Birse had been viewed with suspicion. As a younger man he was known for his temper. He was quick with his fists. If someone crossed him their card was marked and, in time, Alex would have his revenge. And he liked the sound of his own voice. It grated on his workmates. All that anger and for what? His complaining had achieved nothing. At the end of the day, they had the same damp and overcrowded houses to live in, and the same poor pay that went up and down but never amounted to very much. Every worker in every community across the country was in the same boat. They might as well just get on with things and hope for the best. What could they do?

But after yet another mining accident, in Broadrigg No. 1 back in 1910, when three had died and others were injured, and the tale of Alex's survival had gone round, the strength of the man was acknowledged and his kindness towards the bereft was much admired. His efforts to make things better for the community and the truth of his words had started to dawn. He'd been right about the injustice of putting profit before people, of coal masters living in luxury whilst workers brought up their children in hovels. He had been right about the justice of fair pay for the hard work they did in the coal industry. It was the engine of the economy and the empire, after all. He had been right about the need for investment, reducing the risks underground and preventing pit accidents. The death of Charlie Scobie was further proof of that. Didn't they all risk their lives and their health every time they went underground? Alex had been at the heart of the dispute that had closed Stoneyrigg Pit for good, when everyone in the Rows had joined together, eventually, the men refusing to work for less than what had already been agreed. Then years of discontent across the country in all kinds of industry, not just in mining, had let the men see the bigger picture, the one that Alex Birse had been trying to paint. He was hard to listen to at times but the man had been right all along.

By the time me and Jim arrived at the winding shed, Alex was approaching the banksman in charge of the cage doors. They exchanged a few words above the tumult then watched the cage disappear down into the shaft, wheels whirring, chains clashing. The tumblers were going good style, wagons were rising up from below, feeding the shakers with coal from the previous shift. Beyond a metal screen, a small army were already working at the picking tables, removing the waste rock and sorting the coal. Old grey men, scrawny boys with staring eyes and women, mainly widows and unmarried girls not long out of school, stooped over mounds of rock at the start of a twelve hour shift.

Alex produced a roll of paper from his haversack, motioned to the banksman who nodded his approval. He pinned it to the noticeboard by the entrance then stood in line for the arrival of the cage.

*Miners Federation of Great Britain. Union Meeting. Public hall, Monday, 9*th *June 1914 at 7pm prompt.*

To discuss action proposed by the union in response to the Scottish Association of Coal Masters' proposal for a further cut in daily rates.

All members welcome.

S. Simpson, Union Official.

First one man then another left the line to read the notice. Back and forth the message was called out above the racket.

Nodding indicated their understanding and shaking heads spoke of disappointment. It was inevitable given the difficulties of recent times.

My stomach churned when the throb in my hand reminded me of my narrow escape the previous week. I had to fight hard to quell the panic rising in my throat as the metal cage rose out of the ground, settling into place with a clunk. A dozen men shuffled in and took up position like convicts in a cell, staring out into the bright light of the morning beyond the shadows of the winding shed. They stood motionless, waiting for the banksman to secure the chain that would hold them in. A shrill whistle cried out above the clamour and wheels turned to start the descent. Ropes and chains creaked as they took the strain and the cage was delivered downwards to the darkness beneath.

Later, the mineworkers of all five local pits crowded into Blackrigg public hall, eager for news about the national negotiations taking place on our behalf. Five union stalwarts sat at the front of the hall watching the men flood in. They were pleased to see a good turn-out. It meant there wasn't enough room for everybody but the large numbers spilling out onto the street and milling around open windows, trying to listen in to proceedings, served to show the masters that union membership was at an all-time high and the Blackrigg men meant business.

Steeny Simpson, union official and member of the parish council, took the chair. He was flanked by Alex and Davy with Joe McNab and John Doyle at either end of the table. The representatives watched as their caps were passed round the audience. Men fumbled in their pockets and gave something, a shilling here, a florin there, half a crown if they felt they could afford it though it might be all they had till pay day. Soon, the caps were returned full of coins to the altar of the union men. It was an offering from a compassionate congregation, mindful of sacrifice, given out of respect, to appease the Fates and ward off evil. It was a whip-round for Charlie Scobie's widow who had a man to bury and three weans to bring up on her own. In a ritual of shared understanding, eyes focused on the collection, a powerful symbol of their common purpose.

Joe brought the meeting to order, got ready to take the minutes. There was serious business to discuss and no time to be wasted. Steeny leaned forward.

'As you are aware, back in March, the coal owners approached the Scottish Coal Trade Conciliation Board for a reduction in wages from 7/6d to 6/6d, a one shilling reduction on oor daily rate, their argument bein' that the price o' coal had come doon while their ain costs had gone up. They succeeded in pairt', were granted a reduction of threepence on the daily rate by the Board. No content wi' this decision, hooever, they've approached the Board again, pressin' for a reduction o' yet anither threepence, tae bring the rate doon tae seven shillings.'

A murmur travelled around the hall. Steeny waited for silence to fall, sweeping a hand through a raft of thick, black hair and studying his notes before proceeding.

'In response, the Federation's Scottish Executive has met an' debated the matter. Gien the coal maisters' intransigence an' refusal tae negotiate, strike action has been threatened.'

A hundred animated discussions started up. Steeny held up a hand and Joe called for quiet.

'Noo, it micht no come tae pass. Let's hope it'll no.' Steeny could see how much the men dreaded a stoppage. He wanted to allay their fears, for the time being at least.

'But the union is askin' for yer support at this time, tae mak the maisters see sense an' change their tack. If we staun the gither, we've a chance o' success.' He watched until heads started to nod in agreement.

'Onie questions?'

'When will the union meet again? Hoo lang will they gie for the maisters tae see sense?'

'Aye, when will we ken whether we're gaun oan strike or no?'

Steeny replied, 'We'll ken in anither week. But mind, the maisters ken hoo strong the union is. We've a strike fund built up so they ken we could haud oot for a while.'

'Aye, but it would pey oot less than oor weekly wage. We dinnae want a strike if we can help it,' called a voice from the back of the hall.

'Of coorse we dinnae want a strike,' interjected Alex who couldn't keep quiet any longer. 'But is this oor fault? Naw, it's no,' answering his own question. 'Nane o' this is oor makin'! We didnae gang lookin' for a fecht, did we?'

'Yer richt there, Alex!' agreed two men in the front row. They sat with their arms crossed.

'The coal maisters are sae busy competin' wi' each ither for markets, haudin' supplies back tae put up the prices, floodin' the market at ither times when it suits them. They mak the prices gang up an doon theirsels,' explained Alex. 'An' syne if the price is doon jist noo, it'll be up afore we ken it, quick as a wink. Then whaur will we be? Will they gie us an eik tae oor wages as soon as?'

'Naw, they'll no!' Everybody agreed.

The mineworkers knew only too well how the mechanism by which their wage rates were decided worked against them. Although a minimum rate was guaranteed by law, actual wages were decided by a sliding scale linked to prices in the individual coalfields.

Steeny eyed up the audience. Things were becoming heated but he would let the discussion run for a bit.

'An' as for their costs gaun up,' continued Alex. 'Whit are they spendin' their money oan? Better hooses for you an' me? Naw! Are they makin' the pits safer tae work in? Nae chance!'

'It's a' aboot profit as faur as they're concerned,' interjected Davy. 'Mair profit for theirsels an' their investors.'

Everybody in the hall voiced their anger at the mining companies. Everybody was talking but nobody was listening.

'Thievin' bastards!' shouted a voice that spoke for everybody present.

Steeny Simpson stepped in, deciding that the Birses had fulfilled a purpose but that order had to be restored. 'We have oor opinion aboot the motives o' the owners, I'm sure. We'll be back here Monday week. Let's pray that good sense and fairness prevail in the meantime.'

The five union men remained in their seats and watched the assembly disperse. Some of the workers had their dander up, were ready for confrontation but others were subdued, worry etched on their faces. Whilst every one of them might agree that they had right on their side, not everyone agreed about how they should fight their cause. They had a roof to keep over their heads and mouths to feed. Responsibility weighed heavily on their shoulders. With knitted brows and many questions, wives would be waiting behind the door when they got home.

How were they expected to live on strike pay, twelve bob, if they were lucky? Did men no realise that the price of meal had gone up, and coal for the fire was gey dear, no matter what the pit owners said about prices being low? Did they no ken that the bairns needed boots for their feet and claes for their backs, forby? And hoo lang would it tak to recoup the money they'd lose because of the dispute? Wouldn't they lose more than they gained, at the end of the day?

Memories of the long stoppage of 1912 would be fresh in their minds, adding fuel to the fire of their invective. Two long months of conflict it had been, pitting man against man, family against family, depending on whether they supported the union cause or not. Even the bairns had fought about it in the playground, picking on the ones whose fathers were breaking the strike by continuing to work. Until, finally, they'd all downed tools and the wheels at the pithead had stopped turning.

'We need the men tae stick thegither,' Steeny said as the last man disappeared through the door. 'United we stand.'

'Divided we fa',' added Davy. At twenty-three years of age he was the youngest of the group at the top table.

'There's weys o' getting' folk tae staun thegither,' announced Alex, a hint of menace in his voice.

'Noo, haud oan,' interjected John Doyle, a thirty-something faceworker with a wife and five children to support. 'Yer gettin' aheid o' yersel. We're no lookin' fur bother, no if it can be helped.'

'Aye, it micht no come tae a stoppage,' added Joe McNab. At fifty years he was the eldest of the group and a union man through and through. 'The Executive'll meet wi' the maisters an' mak them see sense. The union's never been stronger.'

'But they maisters are a wily bunch,' said Alex. 'They're used tae getting' their wey. An' they work thegither whilst the workin' man has a hunder opinions aboot a'thing an hoo tae gang aboot it!'

'If the union says "strike", a'body should strike, every last yin o' them,' stated Davy prodding his finger into the table to emphasise his point. 'Or else.'

'Mind whau yer dealin' wi, lad,' warned Steeny. 'The men have their faimilies tae think aboot. It's no jist as simple as yer makin' oot. No tae mention the non-union men ready tae come in an' pick up the work.'

'Oftimes, ye've got tae staun up an' be coontit. Else nuthin gets done, nuthin gets onie better. Ye have tae say *enough is enough.*'

'Aye, ye have, Davy lad, an' is thon no whit we're daein'?' Steeny was calm. 'But there's weys o' daein' things. Reason aye prevails ower anger, in the long run.'

Davy snarled, 'But we're no dealin' wi' reasonable folk, are we? The coal maisters winnae see reason, an' whit's richt. We ay have tae get in line an' wait, cap in haun while THEY decide whit's reasonable. Some o' us is gettin' gey fed up waitin' fur the next wee bit crust tae come oor wey. We're gey hungert waitin' for *reason.*' He grabbed his bunnet and emptied the coins for the dead man's widow onto the table with a clatter.

'Easy does it, Davy,' cautioned Steeny. 'Keep the heid, eh? For yer ain sake.'

Davy stomped across the hall towards the exit.

'Keep the heid, son, eh? For a' oor sakes,' murmured Steeny after my brother had gone.

Me and Jim had been the first of our pals to arrive at the village hall for the union meeting. After a long day down the pit, union business was the last thing we needed when there were rabbits to snare and roads to walk in the fresh air. But our elders had stressed the importance of the meeting, so we'd felt compelled to attend, to show face. Deep in conversation about the political implications of a possible strike in the Scottish coalfield, Alex and Davy had stepped out manfully ahead of us. On arrival at the door of the hall, Alex had motioned with a toss of his head that we were not to come in but should find a suitable spot outside instead. At the age of sixteen we had to leave the limited space in the hall for our betters, the skilled hewers and the journeymen who'd earned their place after long years of hard work. We'd settled ourselves on the ground by the back door, reckoning that the discussion to come would be audible if we listened hard. Our friends and workmates would find us when they arrived.

It was a fine summer's evening and the warmth of the sun, still high in the sky, felt fine on our pale faces. We pulled up our shirt sleeves. As we often did, we compared our muscles and sinews which were identical, us being twins, and hadn't change since the last time we'd looked. I was glad no mention was made of my missing finger or the accident that had robbed me of it. Instead, Jim admired the long scar on my arm so I held it aloft, a badge of honour won in a battle against a runaway hutch full of coal. The wound had healed into a dark blue line because of the coal dust trapped in my skin. Alex said that the colour would fade a little but I would carry the scar with me to the grave. Mining was like that, he said, the scars never went away. They were always with you, no matter what. Every time I saw that scar, I remembered those words and believed he was right. Mining got under your skin till it was part of you.

After the meeting, we found the pals round the side of the hall under an open window. Rob Duncan had arranged his jacket on the grass and was lying back, an arm behind his head, eyes closed and deep in thought. Wee Geordie Broadley had been given the job of listening at the open window so that he could relay the bare bones of the discussion taking place inside the hall. Since it was a well-known fact that Geordie wasn't the brightest, this had been a mistake, leaving them none the wiser.

Mild mannered Dan Potts admitted, 'Even I was getting ready tae throttle him.'

They gave us an outline of what had been gleaned leaving Jim to add some detail where he could.

Geordie remembered: 'Steeny Simpson says there's tae be a strike ower wages.'

'There micht be,' corrected Jim. 'It's jist a warnin' shot. It'll mak the coal owners stop tryin' for anither reduction on the daily rates.'

Dan said, 'Accordin' tae Geordie, Somebody's lookin' for a fight, an' it was your faither!'

'That's aboot richt,' me and Jim agreed, pretending it was funny.

Bert added, 'But then Geordie says, *They're talkin' aboot the prophets. They're helluva concerned aboot the prophets.*'

Dan laughed, 'I was peerie-heidit! Whit dae the prophets have adae wi' it?'

Bert said, 'The penny dropped, "It's no PROPHETS. It's PROFITS,' I says, 'Dae ye no ken the King's English, Geordie?" Then the oracle fae the open windae says, *They're tellin' the men they're thievin' bastards.* An' we mair or less gied up.'

I remember how we all laughed, there in the shade of the public hall on that warm summer's evening. Everybody in the village agreed that Geordie was a tonic. Everybody except Rob, that is.

'They were talkin' aboot the maisters.' His voice was a growl, cold.

We watched as he slowly pulled himself up from the grass, turned his body and spat into the ground like a snake spitting venom. He calmly turned onto his back again and stared up at the sky which had all of us looking upwards to see what was there. We waited but no more was said. Something about his manner, or his tone, made me shudder. I think the others felt it as well.

Geordie piped up, 'We've tae pray for good sense. An' for fairness. Till next week.'

'Let us pray,' said Dan.

Rob was standing up, shaking his jacket clean of dust and dried grass. 'Whau's up for a gemm? Sandy said he'd be up at Mansefield.'

The mood suddenly changed for the better. I always marvelled at Rob's ability to do that, to change the atmosphere for good or bad.

'Can I come?' asked Geordie, hopeful.

There was a resounding *Yes* from the pals and a slap on the back from Rob. Wee Geordie Broadley would always be welcome, we told him, and he beamed.

Rob led us along Main Street and up Manse Lane towards the park, known as Mansefield. It was a plain green space, no trees or shrubbery, no seats or other structures, just a large swathe of grass with a fence on three sides. A brass plaque on the gate reminds everyone who goes there that the land had been gifted to the people of the village by Mr Imrie of the Coal Company, for the purpose of recreation. You can't miss it, the letters are burnished black into shiny brass, lest we forget how fortunate we are to have a kind benefactor in our midst.

When we arrived, a game of cricket was in full flow at the far end. A handful of boys sat in the shade by the gate waiting for more players to arrive for football. Rob's younger brother, fifteen-year-old Sandy, and Billy Tennant from the Smiddy stood tapping a leather football back and forward against the manse garden wall.

'Great! A new ba'!' shouted Rob. We marvelled at the brand new football. It was pumped up and shining.

Geordie signalled for a pass.

'It's Andra's ba'!' Sandy called out pointing towards the proud owner who sat by the wall. He flicked the ball up with his toe and it landed directly at Geordie's feet.

Andrew Brownlee, son of the pit manager, raised his hand in greeting. Rob cast a fleeting glance in his direction.

'Sure ye can spare the time, Andra? You no got hamework for the big school?' Rob asked.

Andrew laughed. 'Aye, but I thought I'd come along for a game.' He had been our classmate at the village school, staying on after the statutory leaving age of fourteen whilst we'd had to leave and seek employment. We rarely saw him now that he was attending the senior school in Bathgate.

'Nice tae see ye, Andra. This is a great ba',' said Bert as he intercepted a pass meant for me.

'Aye nice tae see ye, Andra. You an yer nice ba',' added Rob.

Sandy looked daggers at his brother.

'There's enough for twa teams,' said Geordie, carefully counting the numbers on his fingers. 'Twa teams, six-a-side,' he announced proudly, 'I'll be the ref!' Me and Jim took the initiative and two teams of seven were duly formed.

We soon got the measure of the ball, punting it back and forth. It was heavy, heavier than they were used to.

Andrew announced that it was of the best quality, equal to the kind used in professional games at the likes of Ibrox and Parkhead. This knowledge precipitated much discussion as we passed to our team mates and fought for possession once the game heated up. It made you feel like a real player, we agreed, on the park for one of the local teams, like Rowanhill United or the Blairha' Bluebells. Or the Scottish League teams that drew tens of thousands of spectators every Saturday. Andrew was in the middle of telling us about his frequent trips to Tynecastle with his father when he hit the floor clutching his shin. He fell onto his back, his knee bent up to his chest, groaning in agony.

'Sorry, Andra,' said Rob. He held up his hands in surrender as Andrew's team mates crowded round.

'Watch whit yer daein, Rob!' cried Sandy from where he was crouched beside the casualty.

'Fair tackle.' Rob was indifferent.

'It was a bit severe,' judged Bert who was worried that Andrew might have to go home, taking his football with him.

Rob stuck out the guilty foot in its size ten workman's boot for everybody to see.

'Look at the size o' yer feet! They're lethal weapons!' said Jim.

'Especially in tacketie boots,' added Sandy.

'Well, terribly sorry and all that,' retorted Rob in his best English. 'But we cannae a' afford fancy wee fitbae boots like His Nibs here. Nae fancy wee fitba' boots in oor hoose,' he growled at his brother.

Sandy turned his attention back to Andrew who, having decided that his shin might not be broken after all, suggested that if he could be helped over to the side of the park, he would assess the damage further. Everybody agreed this was a good idea. It meant we could get on with the game. Supported on either side, Andrew hirpled off and slumped against the wall. He encouraged us to play on. He'd be fine in a bit, and Geordie could take his place meantime.

'Fine then,' said Sandy, 'But first we'll tak aff oor boots.' He glared at Rob who gave him a sly smile.

It felt good to get the air about our feet. We wiggled our toes in the cool grass and remembered what it was like to go barefoot as children. How we had wished to be grown up back then, able to afford a stout pair of boots whenever we needed them. Now, here in the park, memories of childhood were returning as we ran about like urchins, the trials and tribulations of our working lives, including missing fingers and strike action, forgotten in the moment – until the ball came at us from the wrong angle or with too much force, slapping hard against a shin, or stubbing a toe and tripping us up. We persevered until, one by one, our energy spent and the sun sinking in the sky, we took a rest deciding to call time on the game.

As boys left the park in dribs and drabs, Andrew was thanked for bringing the ball and we wished him and his leg well. Bert and Dan got him to his feet then helped him along the road to his house on the hill. Geordie led the way carrying the ball. Me and Jim hung back with Sandy and Rob, enjoying the peace that had descended on the park. It was strange how a game with friends could lift the spirits, make you forget about everything going on in your world save the changing colours of the sky and the lark song still loud in the next field. I was sure the others felt it too though we said nothing, just sat quiet-like staring at the hills and the moss, before making our way home to Stoneyrigg where we wished each other goodnight.

Aye, see ye the morn we called back and forth. I was happy that we would.

Finally, the Duncan brothers thought they were out of earshot and Sandy could say what was on his mind.

'Whit's wrang wi' you?'

'Nuthin's wrang wi' me.'

'I'm no daft, Rob Duncan. Whit was a' thon aboot? Hackin' Andra Brownlee. He's mebbe no yer freen but he's no yer enemy either. Ye could've broke his leg.'

'He's got twa!' Rob's laughter came to nothing.

'I'm the yin that tells the jokes, an' yer no funny,' said Sandy.

'There's no much tae laugh aboot here, is there?' Rob fired back. 'But ye ken whit they say, if ye dinna laugh ye'll greet.'

Sandy shook his head. 'Whit's wrang, Rob? Sometimes ye're like a bear wi' a sare heid. Ye've a rare temper on ye. I haurdly ken ye whiles.'

'Leave it be, Sandy. Mind yer ain business. Mebbe if ye had tae gang doon the pit like I dae ye'd ken. You wi' yer fancy office job... keepin' the books and the ledgers in the pit office. Brewin' tea, a' day.' Rob gave a snort.

'I ken hoo lucky I was tae get thon job. I'm gled I'm no doon the pit. But dae we a' have tae suffer for Rob Duncan's discontent? Yer ower hard oan the bairn, an' Maw disnae deserve the snash ye gie her at times. Gie us a brek, eh?'

'Aye, mebbe,' agreed Rob. 'It's jist... och, nuthin... It'll be fine. I'll be fine.'

Sandy opened the door to the miner's cottage they shared with their widowed mother and three-year-old sister,

Maggie, and four lodgers besides. 'Mebbe ye should bide there a while an' think oan it, Rob. Mak it fine, fur Maw's sake, an' Maggie's tae.'

He stepped inside and closed the door, leaving his elder brother staring into the dirt as the light faded from the sky.

Chapter 5

Minn

I'm in the low field at Redburn, singling neeps, when I see Miss Fraser on the track that leads down from the muir. She's often out walking some place or other, either visiting some sick body or trying to get away from her brother, and who can blame her for that? She gives me a wave and I wave back, a big cheery wave with an even bigger smile though I know that it hides a huge sadness in her life. Each night I remember her in my prayers, that her kindness towards me and my sister will be rewarded in this life as well as the next. I'm glad that Sarah went to work in the manse and we got to know Miss Fraser. It's worked out well in so many ways. It's thanks to her that I have employment here at Redburn so close to my home in Stoneyrigg. I'm grateful even if Mr Gowans, the farmer, is a crabbit so-and-so, and is never pleased with the work I do no matter how hard I try. But he treats the other lassies the same so what does it matter? We're all he's got since the war took away his dairyman and the ploughman, and the old shepherd died and had to be replaced by a simpleton who, according to Mr Gowans, doesn't know one end of a sheep from the other which must be a problem at lambing time.

I haven't always worked at Redburn. Before the war I had a place at Netherside and was happy there. It wasn't just the folk and the work, or the Davidsons who treated me well, nor the place in general because Netherside is a fine big farm. It was me. I was different then. Everything was different before the war.

I was seventeen the day Sarah started work at the manse and I mind it like it was yesterday. I mind waking early and dressing, as usual, whilst the others slept on. It was a fine sunny morning and I couldn't wait to be on my way though I love my family dearly. I stood at the window weaving my long black hair into a single plait down my shoulder, studying the reflection of myself in the broken mirror on its rusty chain. I saw the bright blue eyes of the young woman I had become looking back at me like a stranger I sort of recognised but did not yet know. Little did I know what was ahead of me then and how my life would change.

When Sarah stirred, I whispered, 'Aye, its yon time.'

With a squeal, she disappeared under the covers of the box bed we shared when I was home on a visit.

'Shhhh. Ye'll wake the bairns,' I warned. 'I'll come through an see yer up in a bit. It widnae dae tae sleep in the day.'

Sarah's face was a picture of excitement and trepidation at the prospect of her first day at work.

Jean was already up and about, busy at the fire in the other room. She stirred fiercely at a pot of porridge that threatened to burn whilst the kettle whistled loud on its stand. All of a sudden, the porridge was abandoned as she grabbed a wet cloth to rescue the steaming kettle from the heat of the coals. Muttering, she filled the tea pot with scalding water that splashed hissing into the fire, sending a flurry of grey ash up into the air. Then she jumped like a jack-in-the-box out of harm's way, holding the tea pot at full stretch, set it down on the hearth with a clatter before turning her attention back to the porridge that was spluttering into a thick gloop more like fodder for beasts than folk. I watched like a body bewitched as the simple, daily ritual of breakfast was turned into a crisis by my father's new wife.

'Mornin', Minn,' she offered cheerily, aware of my presence when order of a kind had been restored. She wiped her brow with the back of a hand.

Through the steam, I stepped up onto a chair and opened the window as far as it would go, breathing in deeply, thankful for the cool air of early morning.

'Ye should've woke me,' I said. No matter how early I rose in the morning, it seemed, Jean always beat me to it.

'Och, ye've a hard week aheid o' ye, Minn,' she called up from where she was, hunched over the fire. 'An' ye jist get hame the yin nicht. The best I can dae is let ye lie oan an' mak ye a cup o' tea afore ye gang back tae Netherside.'

I took the jar of cutlery from the window sill to set the table for the workers – three places for the men, places for Jean and Sarah but just a cup for myself. I would eat later, in the kitchen at Netherside when the milking was done.

'Can I gie ye a hand?' I enquired.

Jean was busy at the fire and did not reply. She reached for the kettle to make the tea, forgetting she had already made it – I could see she was engrossed. It was hard to attract her attention at times, made worse because I didn't

64

know what to call her. It had never been discussed. *Mother?* Definitely not. Jean wasn't and never would be my mother. *Jean?* That was too familiar a name for my father's wife though she was only a few years older than me. *Mrs Graham?* Sounded too formal and brought attention to the fact that she wasn't being called *mother*. I reached for the empty tin pail in the corner and made for the door.

Jean looked up. 'Oh, aye. There's a guid lass.'

I was glad to be out of the confines of the house and into the street, heading for the communal tap between the rows, opening the spicket and water gushing into the pail, clean and fresh like a river in spate. I liked to go to the well to fetch water which was a task for women and girls. It was a place to meet and blether, to find out what was happening and swap stories. There were few folk about that morning. It was early yet but there were signs of life behind closed doors. A window rumbled open on squeaking sashes. A door slammed shut. Somebody coughed and voices talked about the weather. A pot clattered on a brick tile floor and a cat with a dead rat mewed on a doorstep. Jean hurried past on her way to the privies, careful with the chamber pot she carried, its contents concealed under a cloth and Alex Birse called out *Fine Day!* from the far end of the row, which wasn't like him and fair surprised me. I went back to the house and did what I could before Jean came back, including wiping the floor where porridge had splattered. The socks drying on a string suspended high above the fireplace were ready to be taken down so I put a pair each in the work boots by the door. Movement behind the curtains of the two box beds on either side of the room let me know the men were awake as I slipped away with a cup of tea for Sarah.

'Time tae get up, wee sis. Yer breakfast's near ready through by. Mrs Graham's got a fine pot o' parritch on the go.' I kept my voice low.

Sarah stifled a giggle at the thought of Jean's porridge. She propped herself up on an elbow to sip the hot tea. 'Dae ye think I'll like it up at the manse, Minn?'

'Miss Fraser's fair kind. Aye? She'll keep ye right and ye'll like it fine.'

'It's no Miss Fraser I'm frettin' aboot.' She burrowed her face into the safety of the bolster. 'It's the meenister. He's terrifyin'! He'll jist need tae look at me an' I'll drap the best cheenie.'

'Aye, he's a terror richt enough,' I teased.

'A holy terror!' Sarah snorted loudly and had to hide her head under the covers.

I cast an eye over the tousled heads of the children in the two other beds but none of them stirred.

'Ye'll be fine. Get up, get yer new claes oan an ye'll be jist the ticket.' I handed my younger sister a pile of work clothes. 'Dinna fret, an I'll see ye next week.'

Sarah wanted me to bide but knew that I couldn't.

'Mind tak yer letter,' she said.

'I near forgot,' I gasped forgetting to whisper. I reached under the bolster, took the envelope and examined the handwriting again, before holding it close. 'Mind keep this tae yersel. Promise?'

Sarah nodded. 'Promise.'

I pushed the letter into the pocket of my skirt then tip-toed across the room to the girls' bed and said cheerio, though all three were still sound asleep. I leaned over the boys and lifted a wee hand under the cover.

'Get back to sleep, Tommy.'

'Chap at the door!' he said. Only his big brown eyes

could be seen above the blanket but he was wide awake, ready for nonsense.

I pretended to knock on his forehead. 'Chap at the door!' I whispered.

'Keek in,' he said.

So I had a good look into his eyes.

'Lift the sneck.' I pinched his nose till he gasped for air. 'Walk in!' and I put a finger into his gaping mouth.

'Again! Chap at the door!' A wee lad ay up for nonsense.

'Get back tae sleep, rascal! I need tae get tae ma work.' I tucked him in firmly.

'Mind yer letter,' he taunted in a small boy sing-song voice.

I put a finger to my mouth and opened my eyes wide. Me and Tommy had a secret.

With a hug for Sarah, I went into the front room where breakfast was well under way. My father nodded, half smiling, his mouth full. Jean's porridge was going down a treat with the men. Conversation was limited as eating took precedence – everybody had a long day ahead of them. Jean's brothers – Peter and Gavin – said little, their eyes trained on the clock and the need to get to work on time. There was barely enough room for the two of them, sitting side by side in shirts and braces, hunched over the table, their big workmen's hands round cups of hot tea. At the allotted hour both gave a grunt then rose in unison to put on their jackets and bunnets. Jean told them to mind their heads. What else could she wish two coal miners on their way down the pit, way below ground in the dark and the damp? With her hands clasped tightly against her breast, she watched till the door closed and the brothers had joined the other workers heading along the terraced rows of Stoneyrigg to the local pits and quarries. She took

67

up the tea pot offering to top up my cup. *No thanks*, I had to refuse. I'd a long walk to Netherside and had to be there by six.

'Ye've forgotten somethin', lass,' came my father's voice as I took my leave.

My heart skipped a beat and my hand went straight to the pocket with the letter. I turned towards him, wondering. He held out my hat. It was made of straw with a wide brim pinned up at the front. It had been my mother's hat and now it belonged to me.

I took it and our eyes met. 'See you the next time, faither.'

'Aye, mind how ye go, lass.'

When I stepped into the road, most workers streamed past me heading east to the quarry and the Broadrigg Pits but I followed a group of men in the opposite direction to the crossroads at Craigpark where some took the station road for the mine at Blairha' and others continued straight ahead along Main Street to the Doctor's Brae, making for the coal pit at Back o' Moss on the far side of the burn. I ignored the hill road, the poor weather route to Netherside, and continued through the village then turned up Manse Lane for the short cut across the muir. I had the morning all to myself, just me and the birds of the air, and was glad of it. As was my habit, I strode out with purpose, thankful to be earning my keep, though sad to be leaving my family and friends behind for another week. I made my way across Mansefield and climbed the stile without looking back, followed the hedgerow upwards to the head dyke that marked the edge of the better land then scrambled over the wall onto the muir where sheep grazed peacefully in the early summer sunshine.

It was there that I put my pack down and put on my hat, as I always did. The wide brim brought welcome shade during long days in the fields. It was made of pale straw in the old-fashioned style of the bondagers, the female workers who had tended the fields and farms of lowland Scotland for generations past. My mother had worn the hat as a girl when her father – my grandfather – had been hired as a dairyman at Whinbank, and she was part of the bond. She'd been wearing it the day a handsome young builder called Tom Graham arrived on the scene, contracted to build a new stable block at The Mains. By Martinmas of the following year, she and Tom were married and five daughters arrived in quick succession. But soon after the death of their infant son, she succumbed to consumption and we were all left to grieve.

I adjusted my mother's hat against the sun as I looked across to the miners' rows of Stoneyrigg, and the small, two-roomed cottage where my family lived. My father would be getting ready to leave for his work, I surmised. He would be taking his bunnet from the nail by the door and donning the woollen jacket that he wore all year round, rain, hail or shine. Jean would give him a kiss on the cheek and say that she would see him when he returned for his dinner at midday and he would leave the house with a spring in his step. I was happy for him, happy that he had found a new wife to care for him and share his bed. But it had all happened so fast and it was hard to get used to, so unlike the days when Meg had been here.

As the eldest of five girls, Meg had left school at thirteen to nurse our mother and help in the house. Meg: our sister and second mother, who had cleaned and cooked and sewed for us all. She had watched her sisters, Marion and Nell, grow old enough to leave home for employment as domestic servants whilst the two youngest, Sarah and me, continued at school. Then, when it was announced that Meg was to marry Will Morton, I had assumed I would take over the reins from Meg, looking after our father and Sarah. But there was a shortage of housing in the village. No sooner had Meg married and got on the boat for Canada with her new husband but Jean had moved in as a lodger, keeping house for us Grahams in lieu of the rent. Not only that but she brought two brothers with her. And a young daughter of her own too. Then a whole series of children began to arrive: a niece and two nephews, the grandson of another brother who worked at sea, and several other waifs and strays who needed love and somewhere to bide. I smiled at the thought of them all sleeping soundly in their beds, tucked up together, soon to wake up to that beautiful morning and a cuddle from Jean.

The sun shone brightly on the moss spread out below the place where I stood that Monday morning, drinking in the view that I loved, enough to quench my thirst for another week. Snaking eastwards, through farmland and industry, the Red Burn carried spring rain out of the bog, a prospect of browns and greens interrupted by black, peaty hags, where the moorcocks rose in a flutter and the marsh birds gathered by dark pools. Great piles of waste rock rose up behind a maze of sheds and workshops, built beside the pits where a workforce travailed above and below ground made black by coal dust. Clouds of smoke and steam belched into the summer air from tall square chimneys, from the coke ovens and from the engines shuttling up and down the lines whilst a thin, grey pall of smoke seeped out of the chimneys of a hundred homes into the still air.

I looked for the church with its long rig of land where the manse was. Sarah would be up and about, ready for work, looking fine in her new clothes, bought specially for her first employment. I knew she would be nervous at first, in the company of her elders and betters, trying to do her best and not make any mistakes. At least she didn't have to bide in but could go home to her own bed at night, to be with our father and play with the children. She could see our friends and keep up with the comings and goings of the Stoneyrigg folk. I missed that. I had to bide at Netherside because it was too far to walk home each night, though I knew I was fortunate to be allowed to visit as often as once a week.

I reasoned that it wouldn't be long before the next Sunday evening and I'd be back in my own place, with my own folk, when I could walk up the rows to see friends and say hello to the women, enquiring after their children and their menfolk. And best of all, I would have the chance to pass the steading at Craigpark, where the men congregated for a blether. I would pray that the boys would be there, old friends from school but now working for a living just like me. I would feel butterflies in my stomach as I walked down Manse Lane heading for home with my bundle over my shoulder. I would take off my hat, and smooth down my hair, feel weak at the knees, an ache down my neck, and my mouth would go dry as each step took me along Main Street closer to where they might be. In vain I would try not to look when I passed them. I would hope that my rosy, red cheeks didn't give me away as I searched the faces for one in particular, the one who was never out of my thoughts, even when I was hard at work at Netherside. How my heart soared at the thought of him. Rob Duncan.

I pulled down my hat and picked up my bundle, a broad smile on my face. I ran up the hill, happy to be alive on that glorious summer's day, when the possibilities of life and love were all around, right there for the taking.

Singling turnips is the hardest job on the farm. Everybody agrees. My back is breaking with all the stooping and I have to lean on the hoe more and more as the morning wears on but I will not cry. There are worse things in this world as I know full well. I grit my teeth and keep going up the drill, removing turnips where they're overcrowded and will not thrive. The ones left behind will have space and light and nourishment from the land, and will grow strong. As I look back along the length of the rows I have singled and weeded, I am pleased with my work and soon forget about the ache in my back. I am fortunate to be here in this sunny field in the fresh air, able to go home in the evening and be with the children. There are many who are far away, at the Front, who must dream of the day when they will return to their homes and families and workplaces. There are many who will not return, too many. I can hardly bear to think of it.

As I soon found out, Sarah's first day at the manse was eventful to say the least. When she arrived, Miss Fraser had tried to put her at her ease by making a cup of tea, though this just served to unsettle her. Sarah had never been invited to take tea with a stranger before, far less drink from a bone china cup that might break in her hand if she wasn't careful. Miss Fraser explained what the scullery maid's duties entailed then she showed her around the house and the garden. It was such a great, enormous house, Sarah said, with different rooms for talking, eating and sleeping, a room called *the study* set aside for the minister to work at his sermons, a kitchen with a separate scullery for doing the washing and a walk-in pantry where food was stored in baskets and jars, though most were empty. There was even an indoor lavatory, and a bathroom with a huge bath, all for the comfort of the minister and his sister. Sarah marvelled at it all. She was used to domestic work along in the Rows and as soon as she got to know where everything in the manse was kept, and got used to Miss Fraser's ways of doing things, she knew she would enjoy her employment. Miss Fraser had been fair patient and helpful that morning, taking time to explain things more than once without being asked. She was a kind and understanding mistress, sensitive to other people's feelings, and ready to put them at their ease. Miss Fraser wasn't the type who needed to make you feel small so that she could look big herself – not like some folk Sarah could mention. And she was trusting too. After a morning's introduction to the ways of the manse and a meal taken together in the kitchen, Sarah's new mistress had set off for the church hall to organise the purvey for Murdo Maclean's funeral, leaving her young charge with a list of duties to complete by herself: the washing up, bringing in the laundry from the line, some vegetables to peel and the fire in the range to keep stoked.

I can picture Sarah singing to herself in light of her good fortune. But then later, as she came in from the coal shed with a full pail, she heard a commotion at the front door and all hell seemed to let loose. The door swung open and Miss Fraser was carried into the hall in the arms of a tall, fair-haired gentleman clothed in funeral attire. Sarah took one look at her, pale and insensible in the young man's arms and pointed upstairs to where the bedrooms were. She hurried up after them to open the bedroom door. The man deposited the mistress onto the bed and then held her hand in his, saying her name over and over again, kindly and tenderly, willing her to wake up whilst Sarah could only look on, her eyes out on stalks. At last, he pointed at the doorway and she heard the noises down below. She rushed to the top of the balustrade and was met by Dr Matheson who was taking the stairs two at a time in search of his patient. He disappeared into the room and the door closed behind him. Then, in a bit of a state, Mr Fraser appeared through the front door shouting *'Send for the nurse!'*, followed by Mrs Maclean who should have been at her husband's funeral tea, and Mrs Gowans who was babbling that Miss Elizabeth had been awful pale when she fainted but it was a common condition in young women of her age and she was sure she would be alright, nothing to worry about. Then Mr Fraser had begged Mrs Gowans to return to the funeral and tell everyone that his sister was perfectly fine, even though he couldn't have known that she was. She had only fainted, he said. She had been working too hard but everything was under control now that they had some help in the house. Mr Fraser glared at Sarah's coal-streaked face and hands – looking like *naebody's wean* in her dirty apron – and he ordered her to find Mrs Tough. Mrs Tough, who had been the cook at the manse at times in the past, was needed to fill in for a while until Miss Fraser got better. Sarah's heart was racing as she ran out the door.

She returned with news that the woman in question would be available for domestic duties from the following day. Sarah wasn't too enamoured with this sudden change in arrangements. She had taken an instant dislike to Mrs Tough and wasn't looking forward to her arrival at the manse. Mrs Tough had appeared at the door of her cottage with her arms crossed across her thin frame. It was the first time Sarah had been up close to the woman and she didn't take to her gaunt face with its sunken cheeks, nor to her thin mouth turned downwards in disapproval.

The house was quiet when she entered through the back door following her visit to Mrs Tough. She stood in the hall and listened for signs that people might be present but there was nothing. No one had waited for her to come back or to look after Miss Fraser in the meantime. She stood at the bottom of the stairs and gazed up at the closed bedroom door, wondering what she should do next. Was Miss Fraser alright? Did she need anything? Was it her place, as the scullery maid hired only that morning, to go up and enquire? What instructions had Dr Matheson left after his visit? And what had happened in the church hall?

Sarah's mind was in a whirl. The grandfather clock ticked loud in the corner, its big brass pendulum keeping time with her pounding heart. A portrait in a huge, gilt frame hung on patterned wallpaper by the parlour door. It was a painting of an elderly man of the cloth from an earlier age and it gave her the creeps, she said. The man fixed her with a cold, dour stare that was set in oils and frozen in time. His eyes seemed to follow her wherever she went. Sarah said that old man terrified her from beyond the grave – that day and every day. Sunlight filtered through a small stained-glass window beside the door and red carpeted stairs led up to the bedroom where Miss Fraser lay all alone, unattended. Sarah said she thought about our house in the Rows: two small rooms with brick-tiled floors and a fire for warmth and cooking; no carpets, no flushing lavatory or water tap; but full of people, young and old living together, getting along and looking out for each other. She shivered in the coldness of that huge house and contented herself that her mistress must be asleep. She decided to return to her place in the kitchen and keep busy – making soup, polishing the range – and see what transpired.

At length, the minister returned. Mrs Maclean had gone home in her carriage and the funeral tea had come to an end. The mourners had left with rosy cheeks no doubt, flushed from the lively conversations and laughter of an afternoon that had been a welcome break in the routine of daily lives that varied little outwith the Sabbath. Mr Fraser appeared in the kitchen to order tea. He towered over his new servant who cowered just as he intended. It had been a long day, he had a sermon to write, he proclaimed, before turning with a swish of his black coat and sweeping off through the house. The door to the study banged loud. That had Sarah fumbling with the china and she just managed to catch the sugar bowl as it rolled across the table. There was sugar everywhere and it was expensive so she swept it back into the bowl with her hand before anyone could see then set the tray just as she had been shown by her mistress that morning, and carried it to the door of the study at the bottom of the stairs. The china rattled whilst she waited. When the command to enter came, she laid the tray on the desk.

'That'll be all,' the minister said, examining her over his half-moon reading glasses.

Sarah had to pluck up the courage to ask, 'Miss Fraser? Is she..? Can I tak her somethin', sir?'

The minister tutted loud and looked up at the ceiling in the direction of his sister's room.

'Leave her,' he ordered. 'Dr Matheson prescribed rest. The nurse will look in on her in due course.'

Sarah wanted to know more but nothing more was forthcoming. She made to leave.

'Mrs Tough'll be here first thing in the mornin', Mr Fraser, sir.'

'Lord save us.' His eyes rolled upwards. 'Lord save us all,' was all he said.

Sarah ran across the hall, her head bowed so she wouldn't have to see the old man with the ill-faured eyes glower back at her. She closed the kitchen door and breathed a great sigh of relief.

Much later, the doorbell rang just as she had cleared the minister's table after supper. She opened the door to a well-dressed lady and Sarah recognised her straight away. Miss Melville had been a Sabbath School teacher in the past. All of the children loved her and adored her magnificent hats.

'I've come to visit the lady of the house. I hear she's rather poorly,' she said, stepping over the threshold into the gloom of the entrance hall. 'Can you tell her I'm here to see her?'

'She's not at all well, Miss Melville,' came the minister's dour voice from the doorway into the dining room. 'It might not be in her best interests.'

'Perhaps we should seek her opinion about that, Richard. Perhaps a visitor is just what she needs.' Miss Melville rarely took no for an answer. She was already taking off her gloves.

Sarah saw that the minister did not look happy.

'I really think it best if you return at another time. And let me know when you are coming in future. The doctor has ordered rest.'

He was watching the visitor close-like as she took off her hat – Miss Melville seemed to be taking her time, being careful not to disturb her hair. The minister's face was turning more and more red, as if he had decided she was deliberately trying to annoy him. Or maybe it was just that he hated vanity in a woman, him being a strict Presbyterian.

Miss Melville wasn't about to be rushed though. She was tall and confident in her light summer jacket and matching flowing skirt. She looked up to where her friend might be on the floor above and started to climb the stairs. 'Come on, Sarah,' she ordered. 'Go ahead of me and we'll see if Miss Fraser is receiving guests.'

Sarah sklent at Miss Melville then the minister and wasn't sure what to do. He looked as if his dog collar might choke him. She feared her employment was about to come to an end but she rushed up the stairs ahead of the visitor anyway.

They listened at the door, her and Miss Melville like a pair of schemers, before giving a knock. There was a rustle of covers and the faintest sound of someone turning over in bed.

'Come in,' said the mistress. And Miss Melville went in.

My sister stayed down in the hall waiting for news, staring up, looking worried. That's how Miss Melville found her when she finally reappeared after what seemed like an age.

She spoke in a whisper. 'She'll be fine in a couple of days with some rest, Sarah. You will look after her, won't you?'

'Oh, aye, Miss. I will,' Sarah whispered back.

'Let me know if you're worried about her meantime. If she doesn't want to get out of bed, or doesn't eat, send me a message and I'll come.'

'I will, Miss. I'll come for ye. I was fair worrit when I saw Mr Maclean cairryin' her intae the hoose in his airms earlier on. She looked sae.. pale an'.. an'..' She could hardly say what was on her mind. 'When he laid her doon gentle-like on her bed, and took her haun in his, strokin' her hair and speakin' her name ower an' ower again... I thoucht.... oh... I thoucht the worst!'

Miss Melville's ears pricked up at that. 'Mr Maclean, did you say? Mr Donald Maclean?'

'I believe it was, Miss. Sic a kind man.'

'Yes. Kind... mmm. You look after your mistress, Sarah. She needs your help. Send for me if needs be.' She lowered her voice further. 'I'll be back in a few days to see how she is.'

Miss Melville left the gloomy house for the late evening sunshine. According to Sarah, Miss Melville seemed to be deep in thought, miles away, as if a plan was forming in her head.

Elizabeth

When I see the women and girls working in the fields, I thank God for my good fortune that I do not have to undertake such back-breaking work in all weathers. But that does not mean to say that we do not have much in common. I take the opportunity to speak to Mr Gowans who is leaning on a gate, watching them labour, as I pass. I express my admiration for their hard work and remind him that women have kept the farms of Scotland going since time immemorial and point out how well they have turned their hands to those tasks traditionally done by the menfolk who are serving their country in foreign lands. He thinks twice about arguing with me, though I can tell that he would like to, but I reinforce my message by saying that the men might find they have to work harder when they return from the war to match what the woman have done in their absence. Perhaps I have been insensitive but increasingly I find that I must express my point of view without being asked.

I wave to Minn Graham, such a lovely young woman who shows great fortitude. Her smile hides huge sadness and a deep understanding of this world that is the privilege of those who see it through the prism of tears. Her sister has been a great help to me in the house these last few years that I cannot imagine how I would manage without her. Her work is done well and without complaint, and she is the soul of discretion. I am much blessed. I also have several very dear friends whom I am fortunate to know, who give me their love, their friendship, and their support in good times and in bad. Yes, I am much blessed.

When I awoke in my bed, not knowing how I'd got there, having been carried from the funeral tea, it was my good friend, Phee Melville's voice I heard at the door. I was never so glad to see her.

'What's all this, Beth? she asked, sounding worried. She sat on the bed and examined my ashen face. 'When she came home from the funeral, Catherine said you'd been taken ill.'

'I'll be fine. Don't worry,' I assured her though I must have looked pale against the white sheets and was glad to be lying down. 'I fainted, that's all. I'll be fine by tomorrow if I rest.'

'Been working too hard, I expect,' said Phee. 'Glad to see you've taken my advice and brought in some help.'

'Looks like she's come just in time,' I said.

Phee gave me a warm embrace and I had to fight back tears.

'It's lovely to see you,' I told her. 'Tell me your news, please. How are things? Are Catherine and Isabelle getting along any better these days?' I loved to hear Phee's tales of the goings on at Parkgate House. Besides, it took my mind off my own concerns.

Phee rolled her eyes and shook her head. Catherine was her sister-in law, married to David, head of the family and Laird of Rashiepark. At thirty-four, Isabelle was the eldest of three surviving siblings, several years older than her brother, and a formidable presence in the Melville household. She was set in her ways, with fixed views about most things.

'As you know, when Catherine Imrie married David, Isabelle thought her the perfect match,' began Phee. 'Not only would she inherit her father's considerable business interests, and pots of money to boot, but she seemed so... well, insipid! Isabelle's domination of household matters and influence over David, didn't seem threatened at all. But my! How wrong she's been!'

'So... fireworks... still?'

'You bet! My Goodness! They go at it with gusto! Isabelle's a stickler for tradition as you know. And Catherine seems determined to change everything... no matter what! Putting her mark on the place as if money was no object!'

I grimaced though I had gained a greenhouse thanks to Catherine's extravagance in the past and was grateful for it. I recalled some of the changes I had witnessed when I had visited Parkgate in recent months. 'Is the mine at Back o' Moss managing to pay for it all?' I ventured.

'Mmmm, more or less. As you know... Catherine's father handed over his share of the mine as a wedding gift... once

the pit had been sunk and was about to start producing....
making Rashiepark the majority shareholder. And the estate
already benefits from income coming from the lease of the
land to the mine. To be honest, I don't think David can
be bothered with it. He'd rather Rashiepark reverted to its
former glory, paying its way through agriculture, the fishing
beats, and shooting parties. He leaves a lot of the day-to-day
management of the estate to the factor now.'

'Does he still go away as much?' I asked.

'He's always off on some jaunt or other... visiting
friends... in the country... or Edinburgh – especially Edinburgh
– but anywhere, it would seem, except Rashiepark.'

Phee looked out of the window, at the hilly land that
rose up beyond the manse garden. Much of what she could
see was estate land. Melvilles had owned it for generations.
She sighed.

'He's off again at the weekend, in fact. Off to one of
his army camps. He's a captain in the reserves as you know.
Sometimes I think it's the only thing that really pleases
him these days.' She sighed again, 'Oh dear, I do miss the
old David.'

I had many more questions but kept them to myself,
deciding to change the subject to something less sombre
'And what about you, Phee? What's new? I haven't seen
you for ages.'

'Keep the second weekend in July free. Will you?' she
replied.

I was intrigued. Phee was always full of surprises.

'You're invited to a party!' Phee was hardly unable to
contain herself. 'An engagement party!'

'Who? When? You? You?!' My eyes went to Phee's left
hand and I gasped. 'Gosh! You're engaged!' I trilled. 'What
a beautiful ring!'

Phee held out her hand and admired the diamond and sapphire cluster in its 22ct gold setting.

'When did he propose?' I asked. 'Arthur, I mean. When did he finally get round to it?'

'Oh, it's not Arthur, Beth dear. I'd be in my grave waiting for Arthur Moffat to make a decision. No, it's a friend of David's... from the reserves. He's a captain too, from a Borders family. Such a wonderful horseman, you wouldn't believe! We've only known each other a matter of weeks.' She studied her ring again, smiling to herself. 'I can't wait for you to meet him. You will come to the party and give your seal of approval, won't you?'

I wished her every happiness and meant it. Phee Melville had been a good friend to me. She had been someone to confide in, someone who had lifted my spirits when I needed it most in the difficult weeks following Neil Tennant's departure from the village. Without daring and confident Phee, I wondered how I would have coped.

'Thanks, Beth. You'll receive a proper invitation through the post very soon. It's all happened so quickly. But one knows when the right man comes along. When it's the right one you just feel it, don't you think?'

I could see that Phee was happy and I was glad for her but I couldn't stop the film of tears that filled my eyes to overflowing.

She realised her mistake too late. 'Oh, Beth. I'm sorry, so sorry! I'm such a selfish, clumsy fool... coming here and crowing about finding love, wrapped up in my own world when you, my dearest friend, is so heartbroken. And you're lying here recuperating, not feeling at all well. I am sorry.'

Tears ran down my cheeks.

'You haven't mentioned Neil in ages. I thought you'd gotten over him at last. Is it still so hard to bear? Still so raw?'

I couldn't speak for a while. 'He's gone, Phee,' I said at last. 'Neil's gone forever. That's why I fainted and made such a fool of myself earlier. Mrs Tennant told me Neil is in Canada! He must have been there all this time. Whilst I've been wishing and praying for his return, he's been thousands of miles away.'

Phee could not believe what she was hearing. She sat with her mouth open, not knowing what to say. I knew she had prayed for long enough that Neil would return to Blackrigg to be reunited with me. It seemed logical, the only outcome that made any sense, according to her. We seemed so right for each other despite the differences in our backgrounds: me, a daughter of the manse and him a blacksmith, like his father and grandfather before him. If she was honest, Phee had been drawn to him herself. He was strong and handsome, kind and gentle with the most engaging smile. He was bookish and curious about the world, and wise. That was Neil Tennant, who was now in Canada and lost to me forever.

'I'm speechless, Beth. I really am. I would never have believed Neil could go away like that, without you. I thought he'd come back – was bound to – one day. But...' Then her whole demeanour changed. She was thinking hard, and finally blurted out what was on her mind.

'Perhaps we've been wrong about Mr Tennant. I know you won't want to hear this but... perhaps... he isn't who you... and I... thought he was.' Phee was finding it difficult to be so blunt. But she clearly felt it had to be said. 'This has got to stop, Beth. You've got to get over this!'

I sank back into the pillows, shaking my head from side to side, distraught. I didn't want to hear these words from my best friend.

'Forget about Neil Tennant, Beth. He hasn't so much as written to you in all this time! He isn't coming back and you need to start living your life again.' She could see how difficult it was for me but she persisted. Phee held me by the shoulders and made me look at her whilst she spoke.

'Stop living in the past and dreaming of what might have been. It's killing you, for the love of God!'

I nodded. It was destroying me and I knew it.

'Now listen,' Phee continued much more softly, 'I'll be back in a few days' time to see if you're feeling stronger. Rest tonight and try to get up for a bit tomorrow. Go and sit in that beautiful garden of yours and... and rest.' She walked over to the window and studied the garden laid out below: my garden, a living patchwork of colour, created by my hard work and with much love. 'You are such a wonderful, warm, talented human being, Elizabeth Fraser,' she declared then she turned to me, lying helpless and distraught in bed. 'You deserve better than this!'

I let the sobbing subside, took a deep breath, forced a weak smile. Phee always made me feel better, just by being there, and she was full of common sense too. But at that moment, as I lay staring at the ceiling thinking of Neil on the other side of the world where he couldn't be reached, I could not imagine being able to return to my old life, my busy life in the manse and in the community. In fact, I could not imagine any sort of life at all.

'You will get through this, Beth.' Phee hugged me hard. 'I'll be back soon and I expect to see you up and about.' She squeezed my hand. 'I will help you through this, I promise.' She waited until I had acknowledged what was being said. 'Now rest. See you soon, dearest Beth.'

As she closed the door behind her, I could tell her anger towards Neil was mounting though after the way he had been treated by Richard, who could blame him for staying away? I could see how much she empathised with my situation, could understand how awful it was for me but, also – she must have been thinking – was it really such a surprise after all this time?

Phee was true to her word and arrived for her end-of-the-week visit. I was sitting in the parlour reading a gardening book. I was wearing my blue skirt and a crisp blouse with a lace collar and mother-of pearl buttons down the front. My hair was pinned up in a fashionable style that, I thought, suited my face and accentuated my neck. I'd taken great care over my appearance, that much was obvious to Phee who was glad to see me greatly improved from the distraught and heartbroken, and frankly quite pathetic, waif-like creature she had left several days before.

Sarah entered with a tray – tea and cake for two – but she almost dropped it on the parlour floor when Mrs Tough bellowed from the kitchen. We looked at each other in horror as the poor girl ran from the room at full pelt.

'How awful!' said Phee. 'Can't something be done about the woman?'

'Richard's already had words with her,' I explained. 'But she's a law unto herself. Believe it or not, it was one of the reasons I finally got up out of bed and pulled myself together. I couldn't stand her shouting and abusing Sarah for no reason.'

'So, you're better?' asked Phee pointedly. Then after a pause, 'Are you better?'

'Much better, thank you,' I replied. 'I knew I couldn't go on like that, acting like a silly girl. I feel rather ashamed of myself, to be honest. I couldn't bear to think of life without Neil but you talked me into seeing sense. I began to realise that, although I've thought of him night and day, his perspective will be different. He's travelling the world and making a new life for himself. He has moved on from Blackrigg. I've got to get on with my life too. Mrs Tough can stay a few more days till I'm properly back on my feet then I'll be back at the helm here in the manse. Then… who knows what's ahead for me?'

'That's wonderful news, Beth! I wasn't sure what I'd find when I knocked on the door today!' She seemed mightily relieved for my sake.

'I've been resting in the garden, as you suggested, and even managed to walk along to the school last night. It was the monthly meeting of the Ladies Committee of the District Nursing Association and I didn't want to miss it.'

'Rather you than me,' she admitted.

'Like the Mrs Tough situation, it forced me to make a decision: either lie around wallowing and feeling sorry for myself or contribute to something worthwhile, something that makes a difference to people's lives.'

'Super. Well done, you.'

'Besides, I'm the chairwoman of the Committee now, and didn't want to miss my first meeting in charge,' I explained. 'When Miss Silver was in the chair, she caused all sorts of arguments and some of the women threatened to resign. She was altogether too dogmatic, wanting things done her way. She tended to take sides, rather than defusing conflict between people. So that's my role, to get things back on track, and have everyone working together so that we have a nursing service that all Blackrigg people can rely on.'

'But isn't that the role of the men... they make all of the big decisions, don't they? The Ladies Committee is there to see that the nurse's house is cleaned and report to the main committee, no?'

'On the face of it, yes. Eighteen men on the main committee make the big decisions about funding and spending. They make sure the nurse has accommodation and is properly equipped whilst we check the nurse's book every month and carry out any domestic duties at her accommodation in support of her work. But the Ladies Committee can also advise the men about how the service can be improved. Two women – that's me and Mrs Birse from the Rows – attend the Executive Committee every month and say our piece.'

'The nurse must be a great help to the doctor, I suppose. She'll do a lot of the work he doesn't have time for.'

'That's right. We've only had a nurse this past year as you know. The employers, mainly the Coal Company, pay the Nursing Association so that workers and their families can have nursing care at reduced cost. But we still have a lot of people who can't afford her. Perhaps they don't work for one of the big employers. Some can't even afford to send for the doctor never mind the nurse and, if they do, families run up debts. Even those in receipt of poor relief have to pay back – in instalments. It's often the main point for discussion by the Ladies Committee, and why Miss Silver had to be removed from the chair. She refused to discuss those who couldn't afford to pay, said that was outwith our remit. According to her, our only concern should be those who can afford nursing services.'

'She's right, in a way,' began Phee. 'You're there to support the work of the nurse, not to organise nursing for every Tom, Dick and Harry, especially those who can't or won't find the money for one.'

'You should have a word with some of our committee like Mrs Birse and Mrs Duncan from the Stoneyrigg Rows. They'll tell you how hard it is for some people to pay for these things, when they're unemployed or too old to work.'

'But there's insurance to cover that now, Elizabeth. Isabelle's always going on about the extra money Rashiepark has to pay in National Insurance to cover workers for sickness and so on. Old people get pensions now too.'

'But they don't pay out a fortune, Phee!' I was taken aback at my friend's lack of understanding but I persevered in trying to explain what ordinary people were up against. 'There's been a bit of friction between the nurse and Mrs Birse, ever since the nurse took up her post, in fact. Mrs Birse used to provide nursing services for the village, free of charge. But the nurse has argued against that. She says a nurse should be trained in the latest methods according to the rules laid down by Queen Victoria's Jubilee Nursing Association. Mrs Birse was the local midwife too. There are moves to ensure that all midwives are trained and certificated now – which is already the case south of the border.'

'And so they should be,' exclaimed Phee, crossing her legs. 'You don't want an untrained person bringing babies into the world, do you?'

'You want someone who knows what they're doing. And Mrs Birse is very experienced. She'll soon be barred from deliveries and poor women will have to pay for the nurse, which they can't afford! Understand?'

'Mmmmm. Sounds like Mrs Birse might be miffed that the nurse has come along and stolen her thunder.'

'On the contrary, Mrs Birse spoke out in favour of bringing a trained woman here in the first place,' I explained. 'But she speaks up for those who can't afford the nurse. And she thinks it shouldn't be left to one person, a trained person, to do it all. That person could work with the community to ensure everyone has the best care possible. When you think about it, it's the family that nurses a sick person back to health, don't you agree? Think of what could be achieved if all families had the support and advice of the nurse.'

'I wouldn't argue with that, Elizabeth. But I can see why you're cut out for committee work and I'm not,' admitted my friend.

I ignored her obvious lack of interest in committee matters. It did no harm to inform a member of the Melville family about community affairs. They had influence and might be of assistance in the future. 'So, getting back to what I was saying – as chairwoman, I believe it's my job to help everyone on the committee to work together to extend nursing services as far as possible – without upsetting the certificated nurses or the Miss Silvers of this world. Understand?'

'Totally,' lied Phee, who decided it was time to turn attention to more frivolous pursuits. 'Now can we go for a drive and get some air? My head hurts and you need some recreation after all that. You are such a serious young woman, Beth, and I'm not sure it's good for you. You must have been exhausted after the meeting last night, if the discussion was anything like you've just recounted!'

'Oh, it was tiring,' I recalled. 'I felt quite weak after an hour and a half of it. But as I was leaving, the schoolmaster was leaving too. He was coming this way and accompanied me on my way home.'

Incorrigible Phee had a twinkle in her eye. 'Do you mean *Mr Black*, Mr Ernest Black, by any chance?'

'Yes, of course. Who else? I felt quite weak and was glad of his arm.' I saw her grinning. 'Oh, stop it! He was coming to see Richard about school business, anyway.'

'Of course he was, Beth, of course!' She must have been thinking I was getting over Neil quicker than she had thought possible.

'Mr Black's been sweet on you ever since you came to live in this village, as you well know. But you've never given him the slightest indication that he might stand a chance. Yet still he holds out a candle for you, hoping that one day you might change your mind and he might, just might, be in with a chance. Last night he happened to be leaving the school at the same time as your meeting broke up... and happened to be going your way. A most fortunate coincidence!'

I blushed severely.

'Well, enough of Mr Black for the moment. Let's get into the motor car and go for a drive. We've been invited to drop in on Mrs Maclean at Whinbank. I'm sure she'd love to see you looking so well, Beth. And one never knows, if you're lucky, her nephew might be around to say *hello*!'

She grinned and I felt the heat rise in my cheeks once again.

Chapter 6

Elizabeth

A few days later, Phee arrived at the manse to take me out for a drive a second time. I protested that I was extremely busy in the house without Mrs Tough – thankfully the woman had gone – and it wasn't fair to leave a four-teen-year-old maid with so much to do. However, Phee was a difficult lady to put off and, besides, she insisted, Mrs Maclean was expecting us for afternoon tea. *Hadn't I remembered what we'd agreed the previous week? I couldn't let a poor grieving widow down, now could I? Not when Mrs Maclean needed tea and sympathy and a bit of company to cheer her up having only just buried her dear, departed husband.* I would like to believe that I needed to be persuaded but Mrs Maclean's grief was not, in truth, the motivation for my decision to acquiesce. I removed my apron and ran into the kitchen to have a quick word with Sarah before running past a delighted Phee and quickly dashing upstairs to change into something appropriate for the occasion.

'Do remember a bonnet!' she called up after me. 'The wind will play havoc with your hair otherwise!'

I soon reappeared in a fresh blouse, my hair brushed

neatly into place under a straw boater with a bright blue ribbon. A long flowing scarf, tied under my chin, anchored the bonnet into place.

'You needn't have taken such trouble,' she remarked looking me up and down. Then raising an eyebrow, 'I saw how Donald Maclean looked at you last week. You could be wearing sackcloth and he wouldn't mind.'

'You are incorrigible,' I whispered. 'Let's get out of here before someone hears and gets the wrong idea!'

'Or the right one...'

I hesitated at the door before running back into the kitchen, returning straight away with a neat bunch of flowers, already tied with white ribbon, for Mrs Maclean.

'Beth Fraser!' exclaimed Phee, 'You didn't need persuading at all! You were ready and waiting to visit Whinbank, you strumpet! ... Lovely flowers by the way!'

We hurried to the pale green soft-topped motor car parked by the church steps on Main Street.

'Let's take this top down for a better view!' she called. Gleefully, Phee pulled the roof back securing it with studs at the back. She handed me a waxed-cotton driving coat and indicated the woollen rug to cover my knees during the journey whilst she donned a pair of large gauntlets to protect her hands and a set of goggles for her eyes. She held out a pair for me but I declined the offer. Hopefully, the windscreen would offer enough protection. The first time we'd driven together, I'd hardly been able to see a thing through the goggles as we'd sped along the highways and byways. Besides, I thought as I climbed up into the red leather passenger seat, they gave the wearer all the allure of a demented bluebottle which was hardly the impression I wanted to convey. I carefully tucked the tartan blanket carefully around my legs ready for the off.

Although it was a dry, pleasant June day, with the car open to the elements, it might turn quite chilly, I reckoned. I watched her walk round to the front of the car with the starting handle in her hand and deftly tug till the motor started up.

'Your talents are many, Miss Melville!' I exclaimed as Phee climbed into the driving seat beside me.

'Got to keep up with the times, Miss Fraser!' she shouted back above the noise of the engine.

'I'm grateful you didn't arrive with two horses,' I called out, remembering Phee's attempts to teach me how to ride in the past.

'Not sure how many horses are under the bonnet of this beauty. Twin cylinder apparently. An Albion 16 out of Scotstoun. It doesn't get out as much since David bought the Rover 12 but I like it. The Rover has four cylinders but a smaller engine capacity and a different braking system. And room for more passengers. I'll see if I can bring it next time. You're completely enclosed in the Rover, windows all round so very comfortable and a lovely shade of blue.'

'I don't mind this little car at all,' I insisted, not being remotely interested in the technicalities. 'I'll leave the mechanical side of things, and the driving, to you!'

Phee smiled from behind her horn-rimmed goggles. She disengaged the brakes by operating a hand lever. 'Tally ho, Beth!' she called out. 'Hold onto your hat!'

The Albion 16 stuttered and spluttered for a few yards before taking to the road quite smoothly, puttering along Main Street in the direction of Rowanhill. We smiled back and forth at each other, enjoying the journey to Whinbank in our different ways – Phee because she was in control, learning all the while what the car would do under different circumstances as she operated the pedals controlling our speed, and me because I was racing away from Richard and the manse and memories of Neil, brought on by mere proximity to the Smiddy. But it was more than that. I was excited, I realised. It wasn't simply the thrill of being in the car, with the wind in my face and the countryside rushing by. For the first time in ages, I was excited by what the future might bring, by the unknown, by what joy might lie ahead, just around the corner. Perhaps Phee was right when she said I was too serious at times; perhaps I needed to let myself go a bit, grasp at life and its pleasures for a change.

'I loved that,' I called to her when the car drew onto the rutted track leading up to Whinbank. 'The countryside is so beautiful at this time of the year. Were you able to take any of it in?'

'Oh, yes!' replied Phee. The car bounced from bump to hump along the length of the farm road. 'Of, course, I have to concentrate hard on what the car's doing but every time I get into the thing, the easier it seems and the more relaxed I feel. It's exhilarating! And I'm glad you're enjoying it too, Beth, despite everything you're having to deal with. Actually, I think it's doing you the world of good, don't you?'

She slowed the car to a halt outside the house, a large mid-nineteenth century two-storey farmhouse built in the local style, with a slate roof and a large front door. Another door to one side led into the scullery, the dairy, and the byre where people were clearly hard at work, judging by the amount of clanging and clattering going on. Mrs Maclean appeared at the main door immediately. She welcomed us warmly with smiles and kisses, taking genuine pleasure in my gift of flowers. We struggled out of our driving gear, removed our bonnets, and followed our hostess inside.

Bookcases lined the walls and a patterned Persian rug in vivid colours brought warmth to the drawing room where tea and fancies awaited. Mrs Maclean poured, saying she was glad to see me restored to good health, and we remarked that she seemed to be bearing up very well under the circumstances, though we understood how deceptive appearances could be. She would not be drawn on the subject but instead asked dozens of questions about the manse and Parkgate House and the motor car, what it was like to drive, and what we had seen on our journey from Blackrigg. She didn't get visitors every day and she was determined to make the most of us, she explained. She grilled me about the flowers I'd brought, knowing I was well-read on the subject of garden history and all things botanical.

I explained, 'The pink rose buds represent *grace*. There's some periwinkle for *tender recollections* with a few sprigs of rosemary for *remembrance* and the bright green of feverfew with its white flowers for *warmth*. The bluebells are passed their best, I'm afraid, but I found some delicate harebells by the roadside for *constancy* and added some leaves of a particular pelargonium for *true friendship*. It's a bit of a mixture but I hope you like them.'

'You clever thing,' said Phee, speaking up for Mrs Maclean who was a little overcome by the message her visitor was delivering in her gift of flowers.

I asked about the books lining the walls. They were Murdo's confirmed his widow, and I was welcome to borrow any that took my fancy. There were quite a few on subjects that might appeal to someone like me who kept the garden at the manse. I nodded eagerly.

When tea was finished, and we agreed that we couldn't possibly consume another mouthful, Mrs Maclean invited us for a stroll in the garden at the back of the house.

'Just a short walk,' she insisted. 'Down the path to the riverbank and back.'

She took great delight in pointing out the landmarks, described the fields as we passed them, giving their names such as Witches' Hollow, The Neb and Shaw Park which gave a hint of their long history. We talked about the characteristics of the soil, their aspect and gradient and how it affected their potential, all factors to be taken into account when deciding the pattern of their use from year to year. She had learned it all from her father, she explained. She'd lived at Whinbank since childhood and had come to know every stone and tree, until they were part of her. When Murdo had bought the farm and come to live there, she had taken great delight in passing that knowledge onto him and it brought them close together, as he got to know Whinbank and to love it as she did. But now she was having to give Donald a lifetime's education in the quickest possible time. He was learning fast, she said, and he was taking to the place – she could tell – which gave her no end of comfort and satisfaction.

'And isn't young Mr Maclean in the vicinity today?' asked Phee, who had been dying to know where he was. 'We so enjoyed his company on our last visit. Didn't we just say that very thing as we were driving along, Elizabeth?'

'Yes, we did,' I replied blushing profusely, feeling that Phee was being less than subtle. 'I expect he's busy. He can't take tea with the ladies every day, I suppose.'

'Indeed, my dear,' Mrs Maclean replied patting my hand. 'But I'm sure he would have made a special effort to join us, knowing you were coming today. Work must be keeping him away.'

Phee stared at me from behind Mrs Maclean as we studied herons fishing from the riverbank. 'It must have been important work to keep Donald away,' she ventured, smiling broadly at me.

We retraced our steps back to the house from the river. Phee explained that she was due at Parkgate for a meeting to discuss the arrangements for her engagement party. She didn't want to be late but it was a shame to curtail our walk. We strolled in the shade of a line of tall beech trees, admiring the views and the wild flowers that carpeted the footpath, each of us caught up in our own thoughts about life, and the love of our lives. Mrs Maclean thanked us for our visit once we'd returned to the car, said it was kind of us to give our precious time to an old woman like her. She much appreciated it and hoped we'd return soon. Phee tied down her bonnet, adjusted her goggles promising that we'd be back very soon. She gave her personal guarantee and could assure Mrs Maclean that Miss Fraser would be delighted to join her. Phee looked pointedly at me and I nodded my agreement, I have to admit, delighted at the prospect of another visit. We made ourselves comfortable in the car, the engine purring ready to depart.

'You're leaving already?' came a deep voice from somewhere nearby.

Donald Maclean was striding towards us from the direction of the stable with a harness in his hand.

'I'm afraid so, Donald. My fault,' began Phee. She flashed a huge smile in his direction. 'I've an engagement party to plan. Remember I told you all about it last time? You will come, won't you? Invitations to follow soon,' she promised.

'We'd be delighted to attend, Miss Melville. Wouldn't we, Auntie?'

Mrs Maclean smiled broadly at her nephew.

'And you can tell us all about your plans for Whinbank,' I suggested, smiling at the dashing Mr Maclean. I looked towards the arable land, where the ground sloped gently towards the river. Green barley was already turning to gold in patches. It flowed in waves, nudged by a soft wind. 'Looks set for a fair summer... and an early harvest, Donald.'

'The corn's doing well,' he replied. 'But it's a little too early to tell.' He smiled and looked into my eyes. 'It doesn't do to assume anything in this life, Miss Fraser. The day you think you know how life's going to progress, well that's the day it can turn on a sixpence.'

'How true, Mr Maclean,' I replied, returning his smile. 'But we must always hope for the best.'

Minn

One of the great pleasures of life on a farm comes in the evening, when everything's redd up after a long day in the fields, the byre, and the house. When the weather allowed it, the Netherside farm servants would congregate on a bench out by the road. The farm was set on the side of a broad valley, and the views to the north seemed to go on forever in the gloaming of summer evenings. Sometimes we would sit quiet-like, just looking, listening to the lapwings and the larks, breathing in the scent of the flowers in the hedgerows and the ripening corn in the nearby fields. Then before you knew it, the lads were scrapping on the ground or daring each other to impossible feats that could not be denied though common sense begged otherwise.

One fine evening, the older men had retreated long since to their cottages where wives and children were waiting, leaving the youngsters to their games and endless chatter. Dochie, the stable lad, sat on his new bicycle, whilst the rest of us quizzed him about the make, the tyres and the apparent lack of brakes. It hadn't cost him a penny, he explained. He'd traded it for his late grandfather's waistcoat. The old man wouldn't be needing it any longer on account of him having passed away and, no, Dochie didn't think he had been robbed or that the bicycle had been stolen. It was in need of some attention, he conceded, but he'd do it up and it would be as good as new when he had finished with it. Even in its present condition, it got him around just the thing and as long as he remembered to avoid the steepest hills, it was perfectly safe. But my, it was fine, he said with glee, to see the sparks flying when he tried to slow down. He lifted his tacketie boots and everybody laughed when they realised that these were his brakes. He challenged the bothy lads to a backie and, one by one, they took their turn, swaying off down the Whinbank Brae with Dochie pedalling like mad, whilst their audience whooped and cheered them onto greater speeds. Then it was the girls' turn, Dochie insisted. Annie and me declined, running off to the safety of our bed under the stairs in the farmhouse, promising to consider the offer another time.

We got ready for bed with smiles on our faces. Giggling, we recounted the adventures of the lads on the bicycle; how it snaked its way down the brae, catapulting them into a bank or a ditch by the side of the road when Dochie's desperate efforts to slow them down with his tacketie boots came to nothing. Annie brushed out my long black hair and confessed that she would like to have a go on the bike but only if I'd do it too. She didn't want to appear forward but if both of us did it then it would be fine. I said I would think about it, though it looked dangerous. But it looked like great fun as well. Maybe I would have a go, next time.

We'd known each other for ages, Annie and me. We were in the same class at school and we'd worked as servants together at Netherside for three years by then. Annie worked mainly in the house, helping the farmer's wife with domestic duties but she could turn her hand to the outside work at busy times in the farming year. I was employed to work in the fields and assist with the milking but I could work in the house when required, especially when somebody was ill. Since we lived away from home, it was good to have a friend to talk to. We talked about most things, me and Annie, and stood up for each other in the company of Dochie and the bothy lads who were always out for fun and pleasure.

Rays of evening sun came in through a tiny window, lighting up the small space where we slept. A wooden platform with a straw-stuffed tyke served as our bed. There wasn't room for much else, just a single chair, and nails on the back of the door to hang up our clothes. I reached up to my dress and retrieved the letter from its place in my pocket then studied the writing, the stamp, and the postmark. Annie had turned over in bed and was watching me.

'It's frae ma sister,' I said.

'I wish I had a sister,' said Annie. 'Or a brither. it was ay jist me an' ma mither.'

I turned to her and smiled. Annie never mentioned her father, an evil man who had come to a bad end and not before time.

'It's frae Meg, in Canada,' I explained.

'I can see the stamp,' remarked Annie. 'Jist think, thon letter's come hauf wey roon the world tae get here. It's a lang wey.'

'Aye, it is and it taks a lang time tae get there. But this letter brings that world, and Meg, close.' I held the letter against my breast with both hands and closed my eyes. 'I miss Meg,' I said at last. 'I wish she was still here, still livin' wi' me and Sarah and ma faither.'

'It's hard when things change, Minn. But oftimes it's for the better.... in the end.'

I knew she was thinking of her own situation. When her father had died, Annie and her mother were free of him and their lives improved, once they got over the shock.

'I'd gang tae Canada wi' ye if I could, Minn,' said Annie. 'We'd be a fine pair, lookin' oot for each ither. We could get employment in a fine shop in a big toun. It'd be rare!' She stopped and thought for a moment. 'But I couldnae gang 'cause o' ma mither. I couldnae leave her by hersel.'

I squeezed her hand, knowing that she would love to go to Canada if only her circumstances were different. I snuggled under the sheet and lay on my back to open the letter. I had read it a dozen times already but I had to do it again, before I went to sleep.

c/o Central Post Office
Calgary, Alberta
20th April, 1914

Dear Minn,

Thank you for your letter of 6th November with all the news of home and family. I hope that Sarah is recovered from her illness and is back on her feet, long before this letter arrives. Give my regards to father, Jean and the bairns. I must apologise for taking so long to write back to you, perhaps you have been thinking the worst, but now you will know I am alright and still in the land of the living. Will is also fine and he sends his love to you all. He asks that you convey his best to any of his family that you might come across. He would be especially grateful if you could visit his mother and father and let them know he is well. Thank you in anticipation.

As you can see from the address, we do not have one at the present time! We are no longer living in Hamilton, Ontario with Will's cousins. At long last, we are making the journey, long anticipated, to the west where we hope to settle for good. We have heard of the many opportunities there are in the west and, although we were happy in Hamilton, we decided some time ago that we would try our luck in 'the new country' so to speak, hopefully finding some land and starting a business with our savings. God willing. Will has some temporary work with the railway company at the moment but we will travel north soon, when the ice has melted and the spring is here. When you next write, address your letter as above and I will arrange for any mail to be sent on to me.

I was excited to read of your proposal to come to Canada in the future, Minn. I would love to have my sister(s) living near me as I miss you all very much, as you know. When Will and I are settled I will write to you again and let you know where we are. It is much easier to settle in Canada if you have family or friends to support you in the early days, as we had with the cousins, John and Louise. I would be very happy to see you and your young man if you decide to come, and Will says he would be delighted to help find work for both of you. It has become harder for people with trades to find employment but there are still jobs on the farms and for domestic servants. I assure you of our discretion in this matter until I hear different from you.

I often think of you all back home in Scotland. I miss the neighbours and the 'characters' in the village. Give my regards to any of the Stoneyrigg women who remember me, especially Peggy Duncan, Mary Birse and Ellen Broadley. I hope they are well and their families too. There are many Scots in Canada. And every time we strike up a conversation together, we say how much we miss the old country. At times, it makes me wonder why we are all here, we have such fond memories of home. Will and I have met people from all over: Glasgow, Dumfriesshire, Aberdeen, the Highlands and the islands especially. We have even met Blackrigg people. Do you remember the Wilsons from the Back Row and John Baxter, an apprentice of father's? They lived near us in Hamilton. Will and I bumped into Neil Tennant from the Blackrigg smiddy in Calgary when we first arrived here from the east. He has been working for the railway company as an engineer and is doing very well for himself. He said that he would be making his way back to Blackrigg at the end of the summer before the winter sets in, as he has business to attend to, so you may bump into him one of these days.

I must go now, Minn. Please write soon with all news of the family.

With kind regards,
Your loving sister,
Meg

I closed up the letter and held it close. Perhaps I would see Meg again. Sooner rather than later, I hoped. I inhaled the smell of the paper and placed it carefully under my pillow. It was still light outside but I turned over and closed my eyes. Tomorrow was a new day. Who knew what it might bring?

Chapter 7

John

The second meeting of the Miners' Federation was a noisy affair. We sat outside like the last time, doing our best to follow the discussion taking place inside. When Steeny announced that the union was having second thoughts about calling for strike action, the men were relieved – at first. The worries and fears of the previous week were gone in a flash, only to be replaced by consternation that the union might be giving into demands from the coal masters for another reduction in the daily rates. Though a strike wasn't welcome, they didn't want to appear weak either. *Where would it end*, somebody shouted? *We have to mak a stand!*

Steeny was able to make himself heard – eventually. He explained that the Union had come up with a much better plan, one that would avoid a stoppage. Nobody wanted the financial hardship brought on by a strike. Nor did they want their community torn apart, family set against family for years to come. The new idea was a stroke of genius, in his opinion. The union was proposing a four-day week. This meant that the work would be shared out equally amongst the workers and the pits wouldn't have to close.

Aye, there'd be a drop in income for everybody but it would be bearable. We could thole it for long enough. And the really clever part about it, he explained, was that the mineworkers would be controlling the price of coal by reducing output. The price of coal would rise and that would up the minimum wage which was determined by the sliding scale that linked wages with prices.

The hall erupted once again as the men debated the merits of a four-day week versus strike action. Steeny called for attention, heartened by the many supportive comments being made around the room whilst sensing the disappointment that here was another consultation, another delay in resolving the dispute. There would be another week of uncertainty when the consequences of the new proposal would be debated at home and at work, another week for anger and fear to mix in equal measure, impacting on family life. He took a few questions and answered them swiftly, emphasising the need for the workforce to unite behind the union. Steeny sensed the men's impatience and their need for reassurance. He had kept his trump card up his sleeve and chose that moment to play it.

The Miners Federation was consulting the other trade unions at national level, he revealed. They were being asked for their support in order to achieve a favourable outcome for the miners. The railway workers were close to making a decision in our favour. If the railway workers cooperated by refusing to move coal supplies across the country, and if the dockworkers could be persuaded to join in and prevent the import of foreign coal, then industry would be starved of its most important resource. The pressure on the coal masters to capitulate would be huge. The economy could be brought to a standstill and everybody in the country would be forced to see what everybody there in the hall knew to be true – that the work of the mineworker was fundamental to the prosperity of the country, and that he should be paid accordingly.

Amid the cheer that went up Alex shouted, 'United we stand, boys! We're no oan oor ain!'

Me and Jim flushed red at the sound of our father's voice.

More cheering inside the hall.

'It's time some o' thon prosperity cam oor wey! The wey o' the workin' man!' shouted Davy in a voice as hard as nails. 'An' since they're no keen tae gie us whit we're due, we'll tak it for oorsels!'

Me and Jim looked at each other. Did the coal masters realise who they were up against when there were folk like Davy Birse shouting the odds?

Steeny said he would call another meeting as soon as there was new information to pass on and applause rang out in the hall. Workers began flooding out into the street, leaving on a tide of hope, with news for waiting wives that the signs were good, that justice would prevail and they had nothing to worry about after all. Even the sight of Constable Mackay and his cronies – who liked to put in an appearance when men congregated in large numbers – didn't threaten the optimistic mood.

We stood up with the pals to move on. None of us had anything to say about what we had heard though we understood the barebones of what was happening. A lot had been explained at the meeting, about wages and prices, supply and demand, but it was complicated. Nothing was straightforward when you didn't have all the facts. It was a matter of waiting for others to make the decisions and determine the outcome. None of us wanted to ask a question since nobody seemed to have any answers. We would hear our fate shortly, like everybody else, but it sounded as if things would be resolved soon enough. So we made our way through the multitude, weaving this way and that, caught up in the river of humanity streaming out onto the road.

Right on time, Geordie came running towards us.

'Are ye comin' for a gemm?' he shouted. 'They're waitin' up at the park.'

'Aye, we're comin',' we replied in unison, the weight of union affairs suddenly lifting.

'Try an' haud us back,' called Jim enthusiastically pulling at my arm.

'Andra's brocht his new ba' again!' said Geordie. 'Come oan, hurry up.'

We marched towards Manse Lane with Geordie leading the way, a small general ahead of his men. He looked back proudly as we fell in behind him.

'Come oan, Rob! Keep up!' he called back. Rob was almost lost in the crowd.

'Gang yersels,' called Rob. 'Get sterted withoot me!'

'Sandy says ye've tae hurry!' shouted Geordie.

There was no reply.

I saw Geordie staring into the crowd, confused. Where was Rob going? He was always with the gang.

We all stopped at the bottom of the lane and looked back for him, studied the crowd of workmen making their way in the opposite direction, towards Stoneyrigg. But Rob had disappeared from sight. 'It's no like Rob tae miss a gemm,' somebody said.

'Mebbe he's got tae be some place and forgot tae say'.

'Mebbe he'll join us later oan, when he's able.'

'Aye, that's it, he's awa' a message or somethin',' we agreed.

'Mebbe he's meetin' a lassie and hadnae wanted to say'.

'Aye, mebbe.'

As we searched the crowds for any sign of our friend, I spotted a small group of men passing on the other side of the road, heading for the Doctor's Brae. If the rest had been looking in that direction, they would have seen Davy and his gang striding out. And Rob slinking past in their midst, his collar up and his head down. Something about the look on Rob's face and the mere fact he was with Davy and his cronies worried me severely.

At each of the five pits, impromptu meetings were held at the end of the day shift the following week. When the men came up in the cages, they collected round their respective union men wanting to hear the latest news about how national negotiations were proceeding on their behalf. The need for good news and a favourable outcome subdued them. They stood wondering, anxiety showing in their bloodshot eyes, faces pale beneath black coal dust.

Alex stood in the middle of the group gathering outside the winding shed at Broadrigg Number1. A question was shouted at him from the back of the crowd but he urged them to be patient, to give the others a few more minutes to reach the pit head and join them. The paper containing the latest bulletin from the Federation was clutched tightly in his hand as he succumbed to another of his coughing fits. He held it up for all to see as the air filled his lungs once again, and he was ready to speak. The pit head gear and the machinery inside the shed rumbled and clashed, delivering coal from below for sorting and washing and the men stood in silence, whilst Alex delivered the news they had hoped not to hear.

The District Board had consented to the coal masters' request for a drop in the miners' daily rates. Forthwith, their wages would be cut to 7 shillings and the ancillary workers' rates would be reduced accordingly. Disbelief rumbled round the men like thunder on a low horizon. *How had it been possible to push through such a reduction? It went against all that was decent and fair.* Alex was as perplexed as the next man but, he pointed out, when they reflected on who they were dealing with maybe they shouldn't be surprised. A groan went up. Everybody agreed with Alex's sentiment. In a more hopeful vein, he continued, the Federation had applied for an increase in the minimum wage from its present level of 5/10d and he confirmed earlier speculation that every district in the Scottish coalfield had backed the proposal for a four-day week. The Union was strong, shouted Alex through another bout of coughing. They weren't finished yet. The dispute had a long way to go and had the backing of the other big trade unions, he reminded them. The situation was changing by the day and he would keep them abreast of developments as and when the Branch was notified.

Me and Jim followed the men up the pit road. We were joined by others who'd been too late to hear the news first hand and a wave of revulsion moved up and down the line. The workforce from Broadrigg Numbers 2 and 3 had joined us by the time we reached the outskirts of Stoneyrigg on the Rowanhill Road. They shouted back and forth when they spotted their neighbours or particular friends whose views they respected. The men from Blairha' and Back o' Moss Pits appeared from the opposite direction to join the throng. Small groups formed around the union men, listening intently as their situation was analysed and the anger and humiliation that everybody felt was put into words.

Steeny Simpson reminded those within earshot that the Union south of the border was supportive of the Scottish miners. Joe McNab stated that other trade unions were ready to back them up, and that workers in all industries were becoming more organised, mindful of the need to support each other in order to achieve a fair settlement both for themselves and for others. John Doyle described the Triple Alliance of railwaymen, dockers and miners, a formidable force that the owners would be hard pushed to break if the men stood resolutely together. Alex spoke about the struggle facing labour across the entire continent of Europe at that very moment. From St Petersburg to France, through Germany and Italy to the miners of Blackrigg, working people were standing up to the tyranny of capital. If the workers of the world could unite, he proclaimed using the metaphors and epithets of the Socialist press, they had nothing to lose but the chains that bound them. In spite of everything I endured from Alex at home, I had to admit that what he said made perfect sense. I found the idea of workers, in many places at home and abroad, engaged in the same struggle at the same time, comforting. It made me hopeful that justice could and would prevail one day.

From my place in the throng I caught sight of Davy standing at the side of the road leaning back against a dry-stone wall with his ankles crossed. He rolled some tobacco for a smoke as he watched the men discuss the latest developments. A small group of his pals had gathered round him, saying nothing, just waiting for his lead. When I realised who was there I moved in closer but stayed out of sight as best I could.

'Sheep,' said Davy, spitting a thread of tobacco onto the road.

'Aye, sheep,' said Malky Moran. 'Waitin' tae be telt whit tae dae.'

'Fearties,' added Jimmy Grubb.

'Great, big fearties,' said Huey Bone.

My friend, Rob, the youngest of the group by far, was surveying the crowd of men who were his workmates and his neighbours. He knew their names and he knew their families. He knew that they were probably afraid, afraid they could lose everything, afraid that they wouldn't have a job and couldn't put bread on the table or might find themselves evicted because of any action they might take to improve their working conditions. He knew the work that they did and the conditions that they worked in. *Fearty* was surely not a word he would use to describe them but he was keeping his thoughts to himself.

Huey Bone gave Rob a stare. 'Ye've no ower muckle tae say fur yersel, Rab. No got an opinion aboot it a'?'

'Rob,' came the reply. 'Ma name's Rob.'

'Oh aye, R-o-b,' replied Huey loudly sounding out the name with a prolonged roll of the 'R'. 'Rob.'

Rob said nothing. Just glowered at Huey.

'If we wait on thon lot daein' somethin' tae help theirsels, we'll be here tae Kingdom come,' said Davy. The rest of the group turned to him, waiting for the punchline. Eventually he said, 'There's things could be done.' He paused again for effect. 'Mebbe the workin' man could hurry things up a bit. Ye ken, show folk we're no gaunnae tak their snash onie longer.'

'Aye, we'll let folk ken we're no gaunnae tak their snash onie longer. Thon's whit we could dae, Davy,' agreed Malky Moran.

'They've got awa' wi' it lang enough,' said Jimmy Grubb.

'Ower lang, aye,' agreed Huey Bone. Huey was staring at Rob, daring him not to express an opinion.

'Whau dae ye have in mind?' asked Rob after a while. 'Whit folk?'

Davy nodded along the road in the direction of Rowanhill. A pale green motor car was speeding towards them. Its fender glinted in the sunshine. Two women in fancy bonnets sat in the front seats, long scarves billowing out behind them.

'Folk like yon,' said Davy, screwing up his eyes for a better look.

The others followed his gaze, studied the vehicle as it got closer to the crowd spread out across the road.

Davy turned his attention to the last of his tobacco, drawing the smoke into the depth of his lungs. 'They kinna folk is whau I've got in mind.' He flicked away the butt of his cigarette before it burned his dirty fingers then ground it into the dirt with the heel of a large boot.

The gang of five took several paces into the crowd of animated men who were unwittingly blocking the road to vehicular traffic. They sidestepped a particularly large group, and pretended to be looking elsewhere, listening to the discourse around them whilst intent on emerging on the Rowanhill side of the throng. I moved through within earshot for a better look. The pale green car came ever closer. It was hard to see the reaction on the driver's face because of her goggles but the car was slowing down, that much was certain. Then it rolled forward and came to a stop.

Davy said nothing from his position directly in front of the vehicle. He stood with his arms folded, cast his gaze across the highly polished bonnet.

'Nice motor,' he pronounced at last.

'Why thank you, young sir,' replied the driver. 'Would you mind standing aside so that I might proceed?'

Malky and Huey formed in beside Davy. They stared back at the woman and her passenger. Jimmy slowly circled the car, examining it in great detail. He pulled at something here and pushed something else there. He slapped the bodywork a couple of times like a bad-tempered ploughman might treat a lazy horse.

'If you don't mind, young man,' the driver began, concerned to be hemmed in by such a large gathering of workmen whilst one manhandled her vehicle.

The passenger jumped a foot in the air when Jimmy kicked at the offside tyre, directly behind where she sat. Then she gave a yelp when the driver sounded the horn.

'Phee, I really don't think that will help...'

But the driver was losing patience. 'Could you move to one side? And leave the tyre alone if you please.' She was glaring at Jimmy who just grinned back at her. So she honked the horn again, fiercely this time.

The passenger sank into her red leather seat as the noise of the horn had many heads turning.

'If you don't mind!' called the driver. She waited, unsure. 'Are you going to move out of the way?!'

Then her passenger – who I could now see was Miss Fraser from the kirk – stood up holding onto the top of the windscreen.

'Hello, all! Would you mind clearing a path?' she cried out. She held out her kid-gloved hand like a road sign showing the way forward.

'Thank you very much,' she said, though nobody'd moved out of the way in the least. Their pleas had fallen on deaf ears since the men were still caught up in their own affairs.

The women were looking nervously at each other, wondering what to do next. They had been polite. They had used the horn but to no effect. Miss Fraser, I supposed, knew the mood within the community through her acquaintance with local women like my mother, and she looked worried. Her friend, one of the Melville sisters, would be much more worried though. She was used to folk doing exactly what she told them, and wouldn't know how to react when they didn't.

It might have occurred to me to help them had I been older and wiser. But I was just a young lad then and was not about to interfere in Davy's business. It was more than my life was worth to do that so I watched intently, caught up in the drama in front of me.

Davy stepped forward just then and caressed a dirty, calloused hand across the bonnet of the car. The sneer on his face caught Miss Melville by surprise as he came close.

'Nice motor,' he repeated, leaning in towards her ear. 'Wouldnae mind a wee shot in her masel. If yer willin' that is.'

Malky and Huey sniggered with delight. Only Davy Birse could be that bold.

The women stared back at him in alarm. They watched as he continued along the driver's side of the vehicle only to melt away into the crowd. His companions did likewise.

Relieved but flummoxed, the women soon saw the reason for the sudden change in their circumstance. Two officers of the local constabulary had appeared.

'Yous ladies a'richt?' enquired Constable Mackay, touching the peak of his cap.

'Yes, perfectly,' replied Miss Melville. 'We're fine now that you are here, constables!'

She watched and waited as the second police officer urged the workmen to clear a path and be on their way.

'Ye can never be too careful, ladies,' warned Mackay, hovering around the motor and its female occupants whilst his colleague ensured safe passage up ahead.

'It was rather alarming,' Miss Melville continued. 'It felt... well... threatening actually.'

'I'm not sure we would have come to any particular harm, Phee,' said Miss Fraser. 'It was just unfortunate that we came upon the men on their way home and we got stuck in the road for a bit.'

'Dinnae underestimate this lot,' continued Mackay. 'There's some bad eggs amongst them, an ithers daft enough would dae their biddin'. Oftimes it's the followers ye've tae watch, ladies. No the Big Man whau cries the shots, if ye get ma drift.'

'Thank you, officer. I think you came along just in time.' Miss Melville relaxed back and let the motor roll forward.

'Mind yersels, ladies,' he warned. 'There's trouble brewin' in this neck o' the woods, mark ma words. But if ye get onie further bother, Constable Archibald Fergus MacKay is at yer service. Noo, safe hame. Mind how ye gang.'

From the safety of the far side of the throng, Davy Birse was watching the motor car and its occupants move off towards the village. He followed it through narrowed eyes.

'Thon was gallus, Davy,' said Malky in admiration.

'Aye, gallus,' said Jimmy and Huey together.

Huey stared at Rob, challenging him to say otherwise.

'Ye best hope they dinnae ken ye again,' said Rob. 'They got a guid look at ye.'

Malky, Jimmy and Huey sniggered in unison as they thought about how bold Davy had been and at the consternation on the driver's face, her from the Big Hoose.

117

'Ken me again?' said Davy. He stood back with his arms outstretched. 'Hae a look, lads. Whit dae ye see, eh?'

He proceeded to tell them.

'No big, no wee, an' a bit oan the scrawny side. Mug? Black as the ace o' spades,' he pointed to his grinning face, disguised under a layer of coal dust that emphasised his thick, pink lips and tobacco-stained teeth, several of which were missing. 'Hair? Black an' a' but maistly hidden unner a bunnet.' He doffed his cap as if to a lady, eliciting laughter from his gang. 'An' auld jackit an' troosers, mair patches than oniethin' else, covered in coal frae the pit. An' a pair o' big boots.' He looked down at his feet, lifted his trouser legs a shade. 'Dae ye see onie body else like this roon aboot here, I'm wonderin'?' He moved his hand round in a broad sweep indicating the crowd of workers who were all dressed exactly like him.

Malky, Jimmy and Huey laughed. Davy Birse was bold AND clever.

'We a' look the same tae the Miss Melvilles o' this world,' declared Davy through gritted teeth. 'She widnae ken me fae Adam if she seen me again.'

Rob nodded. During their encounter on the road, I had noticed how he'd stayed in the background, fearful of being identified with the others. But Miss Fraser had stared him straight in the face from where she had been sitting in the braw green motor with the smart leather seats. She had been his Sabbath School teacher when he was a boy yet she had given no hint that she knew him. What did Rob make of that? Like Davy and the others, was he just one of the masses, one of the great unwashed who went down the pit and mined the coal? They were all the same to people like her. Was it making his blood boil by any chance?

'We meetin' at the usual place? asked Rob.

'Aye, same place. Back o' nine,' ordered Davy. 'An' mind naebody kens whaur yer gaun.'

But I knew where Rob would be going and wished that I didn't. Whatever was going on, I didn't like the sound of it and I feared for my friend. I felt that I barely knew Davy, the man I called *brother*. But I knew enough and it filled me with dread.

Chapter 8

Minn

After the second milking, I herded the last of the kye out of the byre whilst two of the lads mucked out, telling me to hurry home or I'd be caught with another job to do. There was always more work to be done on the farm. And I wasn't to worry, they jested, they'd see to the calves that were making a racket in the small byre. The terrible noise of them, distraught and confused, tugged at my heart strings. They were newly separated from their mothers. I wanted to go to them, taking comfort in pails of fresh, warm milk as I normally did after the milking was done. But I wanted to get home even more. It was the Sabbath and I hadn't been able to get away for a couple of weeks on account of a lurgy that had kept some of us low so the work had taken longer than usual. I thanked the lads promising I'd make it up to them one of these days, and ran off, removing my apron for quickness as I crossed the yard, ignoring their quips about how I could best make it up to them. Dochie shouted if only I would meet him in the hay barn one night when the moon was up! It wasn't the first time I'd had such an offer but there was only one lad I wanted to meet on a moonlit night and he didn't bide at Netherside.

In the small sleeping space under the stairs, I made up my bundle making sure I had Meg's letter with me. I took it everywhere in my apron pocket as if my future depended on it. I was soon joined by Annie who had washed and dried the supper dishes at lightning speed. She picked up two bags of eggs, one for her and one for me, to be taken home as a kindness from the farmer's wife who said we had worked especially hard. We shouted our cheerios, leaving by the back door. Mrs Davidson called out after us, *Remember to shut in the hens in the hut below High Field,* and we said that we would, on our way along the hill path together.

A shower of summer rain moved along the valley behind us, far to the north. Grey clouds that had been building all day parted, pierced by shafts of yellow sunshine from the blue sky high above. We hurried over the stile onto the high pasture hoping the rain wouldn't come our way so we would get home dry. Cresting the hill, we caught sight of the village and relaxed, the threat of rain and the worst of the climb over. It was a good sign we agreed – we were always looking for good signs, Annie and me. She took the right fork towards Parkgate House where her mother lived in an estate cottage on the edge of the wood. I made haste, scrambled over the wall and ran down the hill towards Mansefield, delighted to be back where I belonged after another week.

Despite my constant longing to be back in the village and the chance of a glimpse of Rob, I was relieved to see that the steading was abandoned, devoid of men and boys, though I found my relief hard to fathom. Maybe my need for Rob was so great that I preferred not to see him at all, when the alternative might be cold rejection and shattered dreams. It didn't bear thinking about. Pigeons fluttered and cooed in and out of the empty shell of the old inn, its shattered windows like cold, dark eyes looking out on the sunlit world and at me, the Graham lassie with a secret letter in her pocket, hurrying by on her way home.

Jean was all by herself when I opened the door expecting to see the house teeming with children. She explained that the men were at the allotment and Sarah had taken the bairns for a walk, giving Jean a few precious minutes to herself – time to make supper and have the bath ready for their return. A plate of jam pieces, a jug of milk and twelve cups were waiting on the table. The tin bath sat on the hearth rug and was already part-full of hot water. A kettle and a pot were coming to the boil on the fire. I put my mother's hat on the nail behind the door and saw her glance up at it – just a brief glimpse – but no words went between us.

Would I like a cup of tea after my walk from Netherside? Perhaps Jean needed it more.

Jean sat by a small sewing machine that burst into life at intervals through the application of pedal power. For somebody who couldn't make a pot of porridge without leaving chaos in her wake, she was a dab-hand with a machine. She was getting clothes ready for the children to wear on Fair Day, now known as the Gala Day, and only two weeks hence. The bairns would have to look their best and, if possible, boots would have to be found for their feet. There would be a bit of borrowing back and forth between friends and a lot of sewing by Jean to ensure the large Graham brood was well turned out. I asked if there was anything I could do and Jean said that the tea was enough but if I could see my way to emptying the kettle into the bath and putting on some more water to boil then that would be much appreciated.

We sat without talking.

'Will you get time aff for the Gala Day?' Jean enquired after a bit.

'Mrs Davidson says Annie and me can lowse a bit early oan the Seturday an' come ower fur the dance, if we like.' I looked out of the window at a small group of people passing between the Rows.

'An' are ye gaun tae the dance?' Jean asked, testing a newly sewn seam, pulling it taught.

I shrugged. 'I've niver been afore.'

'Thon's no whit I asked. Here's a better question. Would ye like tae gang tae the Gala Day dance, Minn?'

'I suppose. But naebody's asked me.'

Jean persisted, 'Are yer pals gaun? At seventeen, near-enough eighteen, yer age tae gang.'

'Sadie cannae, oan accoont o' her work. She cannae get awa'. But Jenny's been at me for weeks.' I had assumed I couldn't go to the dance and hadn't pursued the matter.

'Ye'd like tae gang but ye've nuthin' tae put oan. Is that it?'

I shrugged again. 'It disnae matter.'

'Aye, it matters. It matters a lot,' she insisted. She left her machine, went into the other room and came back holding up clothes on a hanger for me to see – a narrow, grey skirt with three large buttons down the front and a white blouse, plain but hardly worn.

'But they're yours.' I recognised the outfit as the one Jean had worn when she had married my father.

'They're a wee bit big for ye but I can soon tak them in. Try them and we'll see what we can do, mak them right for a young lass like yersel.'

I wasn't keen but I didn't want to offend Jean who was full of enthusiasm for the idea of me going to the dance.

'But they're yer Sunday Best. What will ye wear in their place?'

'Och, niver mind me,' she replied. 'Who's gaunnae look at me at ma age? I can mak dae. But you, Minn Graham! There's plenty wants a look at you! Noo, get ben the hoose an' try this oan till I see what's what.'

I obliged and disappeared into the back room, returning minutes later feeling swamped. The blouse was two or three sizes too big and the skirt too wide around the waist and the hips by a fair margin. The look on my face must have said I wasn't hopeful of a flattering outcome. Jean, however, thought otherwise. She took the skirt fabric in each hand, first at the waist then down the side seams where it slumped over my hips then she turned her attention to the blouse, pinching the cloth under the arms and in at the waist.

'That's fine,' she said at last. 'I'll get tae work on them in yer absence and we'll have another look at ye in a week's time. Ye micht be surprised at the difference. Noo, get yersel changed an awa' see whaur yer sister's got tae wi' the bairns. Else we'll be up tae yon time getting' them intae their beds. Some have school the morn.'

I returned from the back room to find Jean hard at work once again, altering a small white smock for one of the younger children. She had unpicked a seam to let the material out as far as it would go, sufficient for a growing child. I studied this hard working woman who devoted her life to looking after others, including children who were not her own. Jean Graham took great delight in giving them all a happy home.

'Just when I mind,' she called after me as I went out the door. 'Tak this roon tae Peggy Duncan, would ye?' She held out a small white chemise. 'It's for Maggie but, if it's ower big, she can bring it back next time she's passin' an' I'll tak it in a bit mair.'

I took the chemise from Jean. My hands trembled and I hoped it didn't show. Suddenly I had an excuse to visit the Duncans and I wondered if Annie would agree that this was a good sign.

At Peggy's place a small face appeared at the window before the door was opened a chink.

'Good evening, Miss Margaret Duncan,' I said in an affected voice worthy of Daisy Gowans at her elocution lesson. 'Could you tell your mother that Miss Thomasina Graham is here to see her?'

In a fit of giggles, Maggie opened the door wide.

'Come in, Miss Graham,' she ordered, in the voice of somebody ten times her age. 'Mither, we've a visitor!'

I held out the chemise for Peggy and passed on Jean's message. Peggy asked after the Grahams, inviting me to take a seat for a moment. I would've been happy to stay, hoping for a glimpse of Rob had there been room for me at the table. But two of Peggy's boarders – the Fifer and the foreigner with the big moustache – sat finishing off their supper and the only other chair, over by the fire, was occupied by Peggy's knitting.

'I'll no bide,' I said hovering by the door.

'Weel, I'll no keep ye,' replied Peggy. 'It goes like a fair in here whiles! Just as weel Sandy an' Rob are alang at Rowanhill wi' their freens.'

I tried hard to hide my disappointment but I'm sure I saw a wee smile on her lips.

The door to the back room opened just then and two aged figures shauchled forward.

'Here's Mr and Mrs Pow, ma ither lodgers,' said Peggy taking a few paces across the room towards them with her arms outstretched, ready to catch whosoever fell first. The old woman grimaced and turned her head to hear what Peggy was saying.

'Whit ye sayin'?' asked Mrs Pow. 'Sit doon an' I'll mak a cup o' tea, hen.'

'Naw, Jess, naw,' insisted her husband who'd hobbled into a better position to hold up his wife. 'Mind this isnae oor hoose. This is Peggy Duncan's bit. We're bidin' here a while. Peggy maks the tea in this hoose.'

'Does she?' replied old Jess Pow, looking confused. 'Whau gied her permission? Was it yersel, Tam?'

He shook his head.

'Three cups o' tea, dear,' ordered Mrs Pow, smiling at Peggy. 'Milk and sugar.'

'Ye mean, twa cups, Jess,' corrected her husband.

Mrs Pow stopped their advance across the room and glared at him. 'Three,' she repeated. 'Yin for yersel, yin for me, an' yin for Jamie.'

Old Tam glanced briefly at Peggy. He encouraged his wife to take a few more shuffling steps then plonked her down in Peggy's chair, more by accident than design but with great tenderness.

'Jist the twa cups, Jess,' he said to her, kindly. 'Mind, Jamie's gone, lass. Jamie's gone.'

'He's gone? Awa'?'

'Aye. Awa'.'

Mrs Pow frowned. 'Oh, aye,' she said, remembering. 'Jamie's awa'.'

Peggy turned to me. 'As ye can see, Minn. Never a dull moment here at the Duncans'.'

I watched as Peggy turned back to Mrs Pow, telling her she would get her a cup of tea straight away. The foreigner with the big moustache grabbed a cup and poured thick black liquid from the tea pot. The Fifer ladled in two heaped spoonfuls of sugar and stirred, adding a splash of milk from a jug. Maggie reached up and took it, carrying it carefully across the floor to old Jess, without spilling a drop. I closed the door quietly behind me thinking how kind it was of Peggy to take in Mr and Mrs Pow and save them from the poorhouse. Peggy, whose husband had died in the same pit accident as Jamie Pow, had a heart of gold.

I was pleased to find that my friend, Jenny Campbell, was at home when I knocked on her door. She called to her mother that she would be back in a minute to help bath her younger brother and sisters. We whispered hurried plans to attend the dance. Jenny would talk to the other girls in the village about who was going and she would see about tickets for the two of us, if there were any left. She had something she could wear and she liked the sound of what Jean had in mind for me. We wondered what boys would be there, boys that we knew and maybe some that we didn't know, boys who might be nice and ask us to dance. Jenny hoped that Rob would be there for my sake and I listed the names of all the young men I could think of for Jenny's appraisal. Wasn't there somebody she had her eye on? Jenny just smiled. Her mother had told her never to wear her heart on her sleeve and she was taking her advice. It brought you nothing but trouble, Jenny warned. And she wasn't a shameless hussy like Minn Graham. Everybody knew I was mad about Rob Duncan, she teased, Rob of the dark, brooding looks who rarely smiled these days, especially at girls. *Still waters run deep* was another of Jenny's mother's wise sayings. You'd to watch the quiet ones, according to Mrs Campbell. I took my friend's teasing in good spirit because I knew that Jenny was a good friend and didn't mean anything by it. I'd tried to hide my feelings about Rob and only Sarah, Jenny, and Annie knew how I felt about him. I'd felt that way for years, ever since I'd been in the same class as him at school, stealing glances as he sat in the back row, giving all the right answers. In my book, Rob was top of the class in more ways than one and always would be.

We were soon brought back down to earth with a thump, reminded of our responsibilities, when Mrs Campbell appeared on the doorstep, hands on hips, bawling at the top of her voice even though Jenny was barely two feet away. There was too much work to be done before bedtime for us to be standing there gabbing, she called out in her Irish brogue. And who cared if it was the Sabbath?! She would say her piece. The Lord seemed to have forgotten about women when he made that particular rule, the one about resting on the Seventh Day, she declared for all and sundry to hear. Sure it was proof, if proof was needed, that the Good Lord, God Almighty, was most definitely a man and not a woman! Mrs Campbell hauled Jenny away before I could make plans to see her the following week and I prayed that it wasn't a bad sign when the door slammed in my face.

I decided that Sarah must have returned with the children by now and that I'd better hurry back to help with bathtime before the men returned. They were at the allotment, taking advantage of the fair weather and the long daylight hours of summer to tend their crops. The good weather of recent days, interspersed with showers, was bringing everything on a treat, including the weeds, so there'd be plenty to keep them occupied – as I knew fine well from my own work at Netherside. Leeks and cabbage were well established and the onions were starting to swell. The potato shaws were well through and the soil wasn't needing to be heaped up anymore to protect from frosts which were surely past now that it was well into June. Even the peas were flourishing, sending out tendrils and showing signs of flowering, which was surprising when you considered the altitude hereabouts. Surely, a triumph of hope over experience! But on this side of the ridge, the slope faced south and that helped. There would be vegetables aplenty in late summer and into the autumn, and supply enough to keep the family going in broth well into the winter months. The allotment was also an excuse for the men to be out of the house in the fresh air after long days at work. It was a place where they could stop for a blether and a pipe of tobacco at a time of their choosing for a change. They could take a rest on a makeshift bench, survey the peat moss in peace, hearing nothing but the sound of the curlew and the soft summer wind.

Meanwhile, down in the Rows, the Grahams' place was a hive of activity. Sarah was in charge of heating the water for bathing the eight younger children. Some mothers bathed their bairns on a Friday night, dunking the entire brood in the wash house boiler with the fire heating the water from below then everyone hurtling through the Scottish weather in their night clothes back to the warmth of the house. But that wasn't Jean's way. The Sabbath was bath night in her household. It was a special time when all of the children were given their supper then bathed in turn by the hearth and sent to bed for a good night's sleep before school the next day. I sat at the table with the older ones, made sure they had done their homework then took the family Bible from the shelf above my father's bed and the children read a short piece in turn, to practise their reading skills among other things. In the back room, Jean laid out clothes for the following day. Sarah, set up the clothes-horse, draped with some towels to give the children privacy from each other and from anyone who might walk in the door. When she said that the bath was about ready for the younger children, a line of five formed.

Eight year old Jenny read aloud.

'The Lord is my light and my salvation: whom shall I fear?

The Lord is the strength of my life; of whom shall I be afraid?'

Jean hushed the two girls in the bath; told everyone to listen carefully. She loved the Psalms, she told them. The Psalms never let you down.

'When the wicked, even mine enemies and my foes, came upon me to eat up my flesh, they stumbled and fell,' continued Jenny.

With wide eyes, the children hung onto every word.

'Though my host should encamp against me, my heart shall not fear: though war should rise against me, in this will I be confident.'

'Weel done, Jenny dear. Angus, your turn, you have a go,' ordered Jean.

I helped Angus spell out the difficult words like 'trouble', 'sacrifices' and 'tabernacle' whilst Sarah bathed each of the smaller children in turn, keeping them quiet as she soaped their soft skin and their hair. They were passed onto Jean for drying. Then their hair was inspected with a bone comb. Jean declared each one free of nits, *Thank the Lord*, and handed them their night attire to put on by themselves. Even the wee ones were old enough to learn.

Felix read out the last verse of Psalm 27. *'Wait on the Lord: be of good courage, and he shall strengthen thine heart: wait, I say, on the Lord.'*

'Weel done, Felix. Yer readin's comin' oan. An' yon's guid advice, boys and girls,' said Jean, repeating the words which she knew off by heart.

I went with Sarah and the wee ones through to the back room. We supervised the ritual of potty, prayers, and getting into bed: the two youngest girls under the window leaving room for Jenny, and the three boys side-by-side at the bottom of the big bed. Angus and Felix would get in at the top when they came through. There was a commotion in the boys' bed so Sarah reminded them that they had to go in order, an order which they knew very well but which they chose to ignore every night.

'Stop yer nonsense, Tommy,' I said.

'Read me a story,' he pleaded.

'No the night, no oan the Sabbath. Sarah'll read tae ye the morn's night.'

'Read me yer letter,' said Tommy, his sing-song voice letting me know he had remembered the letter was a secret and he wasn't supposed to know.

'Aye, read us yer letter,' said everyone else in unison.

'Niver you mind aboot ma letter,' I said, exasperated that virtually the entire family now knew about it.

I tucked Tommy in and tried to placate him with a rhyme.

'Tommy Graham is a noun

Parse him up and parse him down

Pronoun, gender, hopeless case

Subject to his funny face!'

Tommy erupted in peals of laughter. 'Again!' I ruffled his dark hair and told him to settle down.

Each of the bairns had to be told the rhyme in turn with their own names inserted into the first line instead of Tommy's. They giggled and roared and Tommy took a fit of the hiccups that caused even more laughter. Jean appeared with the three eldest, astonished at the raucous carrying-on. So Sarah and me left her to it, taking our chance to slip out into the evening air, using the excuse of having to empty the bath tub.

Outside, we tipped the dirty water into the syver along the middle of the street then propped the bath up against the wall of the cottage to dry.

'It's no as if there's much in Meg's letter,' ventured Sarah. 'Jist the bit aboot ye havin' a young man.'

'Which isnae true at the present time,' I said, looking round to see if anybody was about. 'But it gies me awa', Sarah.' I started to walk to the end of the rows, beckoned my sister to follow. I didn't want to be overheard through an open window.

'Ye ken whit it's like roon here. News spreads like wildfire. Even if it's no true.'

We wandered along the street for a bit, talking about Rob and whether he could possibly feel the same about me as I did about him. I told her about Jean altering some clothes to let me go to the dance. We wondered if, in preparing to go to the dance in clothes that made me look nice, I was influencing my future and, therefore, tempting Fate. Surely there couldn't be anything wrong with it? If there wasn't, why did I feel that there might be? Some might say it was too forward, too gallus. We agreed that our father might think it wasn't right. What would he have to say about my plans to go to the Gala Day dance with Jenny and the other girls? Would he put his foot down when he found out?

'Be of good courage and wait on the Lord,' said Sarah, remembering Psalm 27.

'WAIT on the Lord?!'

'Aye, so the psalm says. The Lord's plan will be revealed in guid time.'

'Is thon whit it means? Dae ye think? WAIT for the Lord... tae mak' somethin' happen?'

Sarah didn't know what to say. She could see I was in torment.

I ventured, 'Is it no sayin', Follow the Lord or Serve the Lord... like when a servant *waits* on a master. It's nothin' adae wi' bidin' yer time till the Lord's ready.'

Sarah thought hard. Another silence followed and, at length, she felt compelled to fill it.

'Miss Fraser's waited a lang time for the Lord tae bring Neil Tennant back tae her.' She knew straight away she'd said the wrong thing but persisted.

We talked about the scandal surrounding the minister's sister and her illicit affair with the village blacksmith. The gossips had had a field day four years before and he'd left for distant lands, leaving her heartbroken in the process.

'I hope I dinnae have tae wait as lang fur the Lord tae bring me an' Rob the gither,' I said looking off into the distance.

'Och, I didnae mean you'd have tae wait sic a while.' Sarah was working hard to make amends. 'It's jist that Neil was mentioned in the letter fae Meg. You and Rob bide in the same village. Yer bound tae get thegither, whaur as Neil Tennant's on the ither side o' the world fae Miss Fraser!'

My stomach churned.

Sarah recalled Meg's account of her chance meeting with Neil in Calgary. 'Miss Fraser an' Neil micht meet up again when he comes back at the end o' the summer.'

That made me feel better. I felt a connection with Miss Fraser who, like me, had been pining for her true love for a long time.

That was when Sarah told me the story about Miss Fraser fainting at Murdo Maclean's funeral and how his nephew had carried her up to her bed in his arms, saying her name over and over again to her, willing her to wake up and get better. Everybody was saying that Miss Fraser had fainted when Mrs Tennant told her that Neil was in Canada, that he wasn't coming back and it was all her fault. Sarah said that Miss Fraser had stayed in her bed for days. Everybody feared the worst, even Miss Melville, but she had done a sterling job and had brought her good friend back from the brink.

'Should we tell her Neil's comin' back?'

Sarah looked worried. 'I'm no sae sure we should. Miss Melville's taen Miss Fraser tae Whinbank, tae visit Mrs Maclean... and Donald Maclean an a'. She's been lookin' fair cheered up thur last twa-three weeks.'

'Ye're thinkin' she's forgot aboot Neil at last?'

'Aye... mebbe...'

'So how come we were appraised o' the news aboot Neil comin' back tae Blackrigg then? Mebbe its God's plan and we're meant tae gie the guid news tae Miss Fraser.'

I thought Fate might be at work in the event of Meg bumping into Neil thousands of miles away in Canada then her writing to tell me about it. On the surface, it could be seen as a coincidence but maybe it was more than that, and I was all for helping to reunite the star-crossed lovers. I looked at Sarah hoping she felt the same.

'Maybe we found out aboot Neil comin' back fae Canada cause Meg happened tae mention in her letter that she'd seen Neil in the passin', an it's naethin' adae wi' the Lord or oniebody else forby.' Sarah had concern written all over her face. She was fourteen and the daughter of a bricklayer so she didn't feel she had the authority to meddle in anybody's life, especially in her employer's life. And she didn't want to incur the wrath of the minister. Everybody said that he hated Neil Tennant and had driven him out of Blackrigg.

'Aye, I suppose. We'll keep quate... for noo.'

Sarah nodded, relieved that I had chosen to see things her way, for the time being at least, and that I wasn't expecting my wee sister to do anything heroic. Up at the manse, Sarah didn't feel very brave, she said.

We soon reached the railway bridge on the station road where we stared up and down the track. There was no movement of rolling stock. Everything was quiet. No trains to see, no people at work, no activity of any kind. Although the sun was shining and the evening was pleasant, we felt deflated after our long discussion about love, loss, and longing. We gazed along the railway lines that curved off into the distance, glinting in the sun and never meeting at any point along the way. It was a desolate sight. Then we retraced our steps, slowly.

We came to the small bridge across the burn and looked down at the water, watching the way it gurgled and splashed over the stones as it flowed downstream. Sarah picked up a small piece of wood and threw it in. It disappeared under the road so we hurried to wait for it to reappear on the other side. There it was and it hadn't taken very long.

We searched the hedgerow for small sticks, got ready to throw them into the water at the same time. I decided that if my stick was first through it would be a good sign. Neither of our sticks reappeared. They must've got stuck on the way. *Just like real life*. Sarah nearly fell in the next time, desperate to see the re-emergence of the sticks.

'Mine won!' called Sarah.

I was sorely disappointed. 'Best o' three?'

My next stick was first through and I was elated. But, as I made a wish, my entire future happiness now depended on that last small piece of wood.

I studied that stick which was smooth to the touch and bleached by the sun. A small knot near one end resembled an eye, maybe the slanted eye of a lizard, or a large newt. Newts lived in the water most of the time and were good swimmers. That it had the eye of a newt etched on its side could be a sign of the stick's prowess in the water, I decided. At the agreed moment, I dropped the newt-stick into the stream and made a wish, ran to the other side and watched. My stick emerged first, way ahead of Sarah's. The newt-stick had won and I was ecstatic.

Sarah looked puzzled. It was only a silly game and I wasn't normally so competitive. Oblivious to my younger sister's feelings, I walked up the road as if in a dream, light as air. Surely it was a sign, a sign that I was destined to spend my life with Rob. The message in the sticks was that what I hoped for in life might take a while but I'd be successful in the end. The sun shone brighter and the sound of the birds in the hedgerows was suddenly sweeter. Red campion and cow parsley mingled softly in the grass by the roadside. Blue cushions of low-growing speedwell and forget-me-nots spilled out of the green by my feet. Fair weather clouds decorated the horizon. Good signs were everywhere, I realised. But I wouldn't be able to tell Sarah what I was thinking. That would break the spell. I'd have to keep to myself the knowledge that Rob Duncan and Minn Graham were going to be together for all time. It was a secret I would keep for as long as was necessary in order to make it happen. I was almost running with excitement when I heard Sarah's voice calling out to me.

'Minn, wait! Haud oan. It's Rob! He's comin' up the Station Road!'

I looked round and my heart almost missed a beat. Was it true? Was my future to be revealed as quickly as this? I focused on the lone figure making his way towards me. It was Rob! Even though I was now at the top of the road, I recognised his dark hair and his gait, strong and determined but with his head down as if he was thinking deeply about something, which was typical of him. I would recognise him anywhere, even from a hundred miles. I stopped and waited whilst Sarah walked towards me, a wide smile on her face, happy that she had spotted Rob for me. Then her face darkened as if a cloud had passed overhead. Her mouth turned downwards. She was looking past me, over my shoulder. I looked round.

'Oh! Hello, faither,' I said, faltering. He was striding down the hill road flanked by Peter and Gavin, fresh from their visit to the allotment.

'There's a bit o' luck,' he said. 'Ma bonnie lassies come tae walk me hame. Come oan you twa, it's gettin' ower late tae be oot on the Sabbath. We'll have a cup o' tea afore bedtime.'

I took his arm and he led me past the steading, towards Stoneyrigg. Longingly, I looked back down the Station Road.

Rob was nowhere to be seen.

Elizabeth

As part of my rehabilitation – though by then I had almost recovered to full strength – I arranged to visit Phee at Parkgate House, insisting that I could get there under my own steam. It was only a mile or so along the road and I would enjoy the exercise. In fact, I enjoyed the walk so much that I entered the grounds by a side gate and ambled slowly through the shrubbery, extending my time out-of-doors and, perhaps if I'm honest, delaying my arrival at the imposing seat of the Melvilles of Rashiepark.

Isabelle sat alone in the small parlour when Jameson, the old retainer, showed me in. The room had been known as the *Ladies' Room* for generations and the decor reflected its use by the women of the house for quiet reflection, reading, sewing, and the occasional bridge party. This was also where they took tea with close friends, or with visitors who did not merit the use of the drawing room. Isabelle occupied a chair at the circular table by the French window which gave views of the terrace and the lawn. Unfortunately, I chose to admire the new painting that hung above the fireplace – an arrangement of fruit and flowers in highly coloured oils by one of the new Scottish artists favoured by Catherine. Thinking of the portrait it had replaced, Isabelle could have cried, she told me. Society beauty and great grandmother, Charlotte Agnes had once graced the room but was now gathering dust in the attic. What an affront to the family line, Isabelle wailed, to be replaced by splodges and swirls representing apples and carnations! She had remonstrated with David about it but he had meekly supported his wife's choice explaining that carnations represented true love and the apples... well, apples told their own story. How vulgar, Isabelle had exclaimed at the time! And didn't I agree with her? As I studied the painting, I confessed that I probably would never eat another apple in the same way again. Isabelle was not one who understood humour readily and her scowl made it clear that I had not responded appropriately, in other words, by openly agreeing with her point of view.

There was a time when I would have moved heaven and earth to work out what she expected me to say, in order to comply, but those days were long gone and, instead, I complemented Catherine's choice, saying that the painting did wonders for the room. Sometimes, I could surprise even myself with my pluck.

Dressed in tasteful grey silk, Catherine Melville entered the small parlour and gave me a kiss on the cheek before taking her place at the table opposite Isabelle who acknowledged her with a virtually imperceptible nod of the head. They did not speak as we waited for Phee to arrive. Absentmindedly, Catherine tapped the small timepiece she kept on a long chain round her neck. Isabelle sighed in irritation before turning her ire on her absent younger sister who was always late, who always kept her waiting, apparently. *Confound the girl*, she muttered under her breath.

I wondered how long it might be before she would be forced to make small talk with Catherine, the daughter of a man who had made his money in trade, and the coal trade to boot. Isabelle did not approve of *new money* and I noticed how she bristled in her sister-in-law's company. Unexpectedly, after her marriage to David, Catherine had established herself as the woman of the house straight away, as if she was born to it. Isabelle seethed that the interloper dared to sit in her presence with such confidence, ready to argue about every detail of household management, among other things. And now Catherine was pregnant with David's child, a possible heir to the Rashiepark estate. Their first child, a sickly daughter, had lived only a few hours. Isabelle had famously told Catherine that she was praying for a better outcome this time, for the sake of the family name.

139

'Any news of David, my dear?' asked Isabelle at last. She patted her auburn hair, perfectly coiled and pinned on top of her head.

'No, I hadn't expected to hear from him. They have so much to do now that the reserve battalions have responsibility for coastal defences.' Catherine was doing her best to hide the hurt she felt at yet another of her husband's frequent absences from the family home.

'He seems to relish his little jaunts to play at soldiers with his friends,' said Isabelle, nonchalantly studying her perfect fingernails. 'It sounds to me like a jolly good wheeze with the chums rather than serious business,' she continued, twisting the knife a little further.

'They're training hard: artillery practice, lectures in strategy, navigation, and communications. The situation in Europe has everyone's wind up. But David assures me the army will be ready for whatever comes their way.'

'He should be here at Rashiepark with the family not playing his army games, my dear,' Isabelle said with exaggerated – and unconvincing – kindness. 'These are difficult times, economically speaking, as you are well aware. He should be planning for the future.' She nodded awkwardly, acknowledging her sister-in-law's advanced stage of pregnancy. 'He should be taking more interest in his investments... at home and abroad. The markets are so volatile and there's more trouble brewing in the coalfields.... the Back o' Moss Pit cannot afford another stoppage like the last one.'

'I can assure you that David has everything under control,' said Catherine standing up to the onslaught against her husband's good name. 'He has a good and loyal manager in Roger Stone with whom I meet regularly when David is absent. I am my father's daughter and am well versed in matters of business.' Charles Imrie was the main shareholder in the Coal Company which had a dozen coal mines in its portfolio, as well as considerable business interests in related industries.

Isabelle seemed deflated. However much Catherine's interference in Parkgate House matters irritated isabelle, her sister-in-law's money and business acumen were proving essential to the future of Rashiepark.

'Well, I suppose we have David's army connections to thank for Phee finding a suitable husband at long last,' she said, changing tack away from the insufferable Catherine, and looking on the bright side. 'Eric Hyslop seems a fine young man from a good family and he's mad about horses just like Phee. That's always an advantage, I find. When two people have similar interests, it can make for a happy marriage. Of course, I'd hoped that Arthur Moffat would have proposed to my sister long ago. Phee and Arthur have known each other forever. And Lady Moffat has been such a good friend of the family.' Isabelle sighed. 'A Melville-Moffat marriage would have been quite an affair!'

What an inveterate snob you are, I thought. I much admired Catherine's dignity in holding her tongue. It would have been easy enough to steal a march on Isabelle by asking if she had any offers of marriage in the offing. No dukes or earls waiting in the wings for Isabelle Melville's hand? But Catherine wouldn't dream of it. She wouldn't stoop that low. It wasn't her way and Isabelle, though she didn't realise it herself, would have been far too easy to squash. Instead, Catherine rose laboriously from her chair and rang the bell for Jameson.

'Let's have some tea while we're waiting for Phee. Shall we?' she said.

'Coffee for me, if you please,' replied Isabelle, though as everyone knew, she hated its bitter taste with a vengeance.

After luncheon at Parkgate, I returned to the village where I bumped into Mrs Birse outside the post office. She seemed pleased to see me, as if she had been actively looking for me, which I soon realised was the case. Our recent discussions at the meeting of the Ladies Committee of the District Nursing Association had set her thinking, she explained. Would I like to accompany her to the Rows where she was planning some visits? I could learn first-hand about the difficulties facing the families living there, people we had considered at our meetings, especially those who could not afford nursing care. I knew straight away that she was attempting to recruit me as an ally but I determined, as chair of the committee, to keep an open mind. As we walked together, a feeling of trepidation descended. In all the years I had lived in Blackrigg, I had never ventured into the Rows and I wondered what Richard would say when he found out I had been there, as inevitably he would.

Mrs Birse waved in at the window of the first cottage we came to. A grateful mother greeted her anxiously on the doorstep, thanking her for calling in so promptly. She ushered us in to a small child, wrapped up in a shawl in the box bed whilst several others looked on. Rosy cheeks and a fever had convinced the mother of scarletina, the scarlet fever. Had the child been vomiting at all, Mary asked? Was there a rash? No, replied the mother to both questions, but she was having trouble with her breathing at times. Mary heard it at once, the rasping in the child's throat then the rolling eyes. She had a good look at the other children in the room, told them to go out into the street but not to go far, to stay away from the other bairns in the village till the doctor had seen them, to check them for symptoms. It could be diphtheria, she said, quite sure that it was. The doctor would come and have her removed to the hospital. It was what had to be done, for the sake of the patient, and every other child.

Next, with me trailing after her, Mary knocked on a door further along the row. We were welcomed in by a work-weary woman, her sleeves rolled up and her face etched with worry. She could see that her husband was getting worse instead of better, she explained, just as an outbreak of ferocious coughing erupted in the back room. Mary had described to me before we came to the cottage that the husband hadn't worked for nigh on a year. The family's only income came from the rent paid by three boarders and an occasional hand-out from the Parish. Eviction was always on the horizon – she was lucky it hadn't happened already since they occupied a Company cottage. With four children and another on the way, the wife didn't know how she was going to manage. I smiled meekly at two young girls who sat at a table with a small cloth doll. They looked back in silence.

The woman led Mary into the back room where the patient lay. She asked him questions. For a long time, he had assumed it was just the effects of working underground. Everybody reacted to it in different ways, he claimed, speaking through another bout of coughing. He had returned to work a couple of times in the previous year but hadn't been able to continue, even though the responsibilities of putting food on the table weighed heavily on his shoulders. He had taken to his bed these several weeks past, barely able to eat or get himself to the dry closet at the back of the house. And now there was blood in his spit and he feared the worst. He looked deep into Highland

Mary's eyes and said he was done. She patted his hand and told him the doctor would need to be informed.

The women returned to where I stood with the girls in that airless, cramped, nauseating front room. In whispering tones, the wife asked if it was consumption, as she feared. Mary said it was likely, but the doctor was the one who would know for certain. Would it help if she got in touch with him on her behalf? The woman nodded. Mary stroked the girls' hair and asked for the name of their doll. *Bella,* they told her, and Mary said that it was the prettiest name she had ever heard. She told the girls to play outside, shooing them out of the fetid air of their home though the stench of the dry closets was foul after days of warm weather. The woman followed us into the street and thanked Mary for visiting. She felt the need to explain. Even if the news was bad, she couldn't afford to send for the nurse or the doctor, not unless it was absolutely necessary. Mary said that it was but she would look in on the family from time to time and told her to take care of herself. She looked down at the woman's pregnant belly, said to send for her if she could help, if she could help in any way whatsoever. The woman thanked her profusely before going back inside.

The next visit was to old Mrs Pow who lived with Peggy Duncan. She had hurt her leg in a fall, it transpired. I could see that her wound was healing thanks to the care she was receiving from both Mary and Peggy. Mr and Mrs Pow were pensioners and their small pension paid for their keep. Old Tom Pow was picking coal from the bings at that very moment, to earn a few pence extra.

Afterwards, I remember standing outside the door of Peggy's cottage feeling as if I had spent my entire life until then in a dream, sleepwalking through life, occupying a very different world from this. And I had. Of course, I had seen the Stoneyrigg Rows from a distance, from the top of The Law or the window of Phee's small motor car. I thought I had understood the difficulties of life in the Rows when I argued with Miss Silver during the meetings of the Ladies' Committee but now I realised how very little I had actually grasped about the realities of life. It wasn't just the weariness in the women's faces or the tiredness in their overworked bodies, the stench from the dry closets or the sound of the man's racking cough; it wasn't only the smell in the tiny room where two children played listlessly with a homemade doll, where the fire burned constantly even though it was summertime or the lack of air and light and space I now knew lay behind every door of every row in Stoneyrigg. Of course, it was all of those things together but, more than all of that, it was the look in the eyes of those women that I would remember. The way they looked at Mary Birse as they cried out for help. I would remember the fire burning inside of them, that sustained them in their battle against dirt and disease for the sake of their families. I would never forget their plea for help, just a little help then they would see to the rest. When Miss Silver got on her high horse next time, arguing that the Nursing committee should only discuss those people who help themselves, I would be ready for her.

I declined Mrs Birse's offer of refreshment – she could see how moved I was – and I bid her farewell offering to visit the doctor on behalf of the families. I walked away from the Rows in a daze, a fire slowly kindling inside of me. I thought about my scullery maid who was brought up in the Rows. She was hardworking, helpful, and happy. Then I remembered the comfortable women with whom I'd sat down to luncheon earlier and I wondered if they

145

had even the slightest inkling of what lay beyond the boundary walls of the Rashiepark estate where a dozen servants kept them in a style to which they had become accustomed.

Everything was in order on my return to the manse. The kitchen was spotless and the tea tray had been set for later in the afternoon. The clock on the wall ticked away the seconds and the minutes, whilst the coals settled in the range. I remember how bright the colours seemed in the manse compared to the cottages I'd visited and I thanked God for my good fortune.

Sarah had been waiting for me to come home. The look on her face suggested all was not well – Richard had wanted to see me. Apparently, he had been into the kitchen several times and appeared quite agitated so I ventured into the hall immediately and stared at the closed door of the study, composing myself. An all-out confrontation with him was not for the feint hearted. In all likelihood, he had spent hours, perhaps days, preparing his latest argument against me. I soon found out that Constable Mackay had been speaking to him with my *best interests* in mind.

'If you didn't go gallivanting around the countryside with Euphemia Melville you wouldn't find yourself in such precarious circumstances, Elizabeth.' His voice was scolding, censorious, and superior though that was nothing new.

'I was not in any difficulty, Richard,' I retorted, recalling my recent journey home in Phee's car from Whinbank. 'We found the road blocked by workmen at the end of the early shift. I expect they had important matters to discuss and didn't realise they were blocking the road. They soon moved on.'

'That's not what Constable MacKay tells me. Had he not arrived precisely when he did, God only knows what might have happened! I shudder to think!' He was shouting uncontrollably. Sarah must have been wondering what on earth was going on.

'There was no problem whatsoever, Richard. The men moved on as soon as they realised they were blocking our way.' I remembered the small menacing group that had surrounded the vehicle but dismissed the thought immediately. I was not about to discuss the point with someone who wasn't prepared to listen.

'Constable MacKay thinks otherwise and I'm inclined to believe him more than you, Elizabeth. You did not even think to tell me of the incident.' He sounded wounded, like a petulant child denied a secret.

'I didn't tell you because it was unimportant and of no consequence. AND because of your present reaction! Why should I invite such a response from you, if I can avoid it by not telling you?' I could not help but raise my voice at him. He could be so exasperating at times.

'Remember that your behaviour reflects on my position as a minister of the church. I cannot gain their respect if I have a harlot, who is my sister, living in the manse!'

I gasped in disbelief. Where did such a remark come from and where on earth was he going with this line of thought? Was that how he viewed all women? The Reverend was well-known for the strictness of his sermons, full of fire and fury at the temptations of the flesh.

'Your concern in this is not for me and my welfare as you pretend,' I began when I'd gathered my thoughts, 'It is for the scandal that might erupt from some imagined outcome of the incident in question. Your imagination has been sparked by the wild fancies of the local constabulary who are on tenterhooks at the possibility of some future confrontation with the miners, in the dispute over their pay and conditions.'

'My concern is for you, of course, my dear. Your well-being is uppermost in my mind at all times, though you refuse to believe it. You are naive when it comes to people and misunderstand their motives, Elizabeth. They are not all as good-hearted as yourself.' He sounded extremely patronising.

'The people of Stoneyrigg are good people, in the main, Richard. Many do not come to your church but they have their reasons for that, I'm sure. They only want reasonable recompense for the hard work they do... and a decent home... to bring up their children in good health.' Images of life in the Rows flooded my mind. My visit with Highland Mary had left its mark.

'And you know the Stoneyrigg people very well, do you?' A sly smile crept over his face. 'I am not happy with your foray into the Rows, Elizabeth. I forbid it in future.'

How could he have known that I had only just returned from the Rows? My first and only visit! The knowledge that he might know my every move gripped like a vice around my chest.

'You cannot forbid it!' My voice was raised just as my brother intended. 'I visited in connection with my position as chairwoman of the Ladies Committee, of the District Nursing Association.'

'You are only required to oversee the work of the nurse IN COMMITTEE. You do not have to supervise her when she is actually making visits to her patients!'

'I know that, Richard. But it would be useful to know what the problems actually are. And by attending with her occasionally. Thereby, ways might be found of extending nursing services to all, not only those who can afford them or those employers pay on their behalf. In future, I hope to visit one or two of those in need of support. I will take my turn with the other women. Today I met Mrs Pow who forgets that her grandson was killed in the pit and still wanders down to the pit head looking for him. I could sit with her or take her for short walks and help with her toilet. It will be a great help to Mrs Duncan, who has opened up her home to the Pows to save them from the Combination Poorhouse.'

'And that's exactly where they should be,' he retorted. 'The ratepayers have made perfectly adequate provision for them. In the Poorhouse!' He stopped and looked at me, his younger sister and only sibling, who riled him so. 'I forbid you to go anywhere near the Stoneyrigg Rows in future. Or Whinbank for that matter.' He folded his arms and turned his back.

'You are forbidding me from doing good works? Forbidding me from visiting the sick and the elderly in need? And even Mrs Maclean? You do not wish me to visit Murdo's widow in her hour of greatest need and loneliness?'

He turned on me with fury in his eyes. 'Do not pretend that you go visiting Mrs Maclean when you go to Whinbank!' His voice was harsh. 'You go running after Donald Maclean while you only pretend to be doing *good works*. You don't fool me, Elizabeth Fraser. A leopard never changes its spots!'

'And would you be so good as to explain what is in your mind when you make that remark?' Though I knew perfectly well.

'You know what is in my mind, sister. The scandal of you and that... that workman has only just died down.

And now you go chasing another... openly... flagrantly... for everyone to see. You are without shame.'

'How cruel you are,' I said at last, trying to keep my voice even. 'You have a mind like a cesspit and call yourself a man of God.'

We became aware that Sarah had been knocking at the study door, perhaps for some time, and I prayed she hadn't heard too much. The girl hurried away as soon as I appeared, leaving a visitor in our care.

'Good afternoon, Ernest,' I said cordially. 'Richard is expecting you. Do come in and I'll bring some tea.'

'Don't rush away just yet, Miss Fraser,' urged the schoolmaster who looked with concern at the two of us in turn. 'I've only this moment been appraised of some disconcerting news.'

I called out to Sarah, asking if she would mind preparing the tea. The tray was already set and she could go home immediately afterwards. It seemed a good idea to have the house to ourselves in case our tempers flared again, after Mr Black had gone.

Ernest closed the study door whilst Richard and I waited, wondering what was afoot.

'There's been some trouble along at Parkgate House, by all accounts,' he began. 'The factor, Roger Stone's been seriously injured in a fall.'

'Oh dear,' said Richard. 'What happened?' Ernest Black's demeanour suggested there was more to come.

'He went off this afternoon on horseback, heading through the woods to the fishing station on the loch. A trip wire had been set up across the path to the higher land, on the edge of the wood. The horse went down and rolled onto poor Roger.'

I asked if he had been badly injured.

'Fairly. Broken ribs, a fractured collar bone, and extensive bruising. But he came off better than the horse which had to be put down. Broken leg I'm afraid.'

'How awful,' I said, shocked that such a thing could have happened at Parkgate. And only a short while after my visit earlier in the day when everything had seemed calm and ordered.

'Such dreadful news.'

'A trip wire, you say?' asked Richard.

'Mmm. Set up deliberately to catch whosoever was going that way on Rashiepark business, it would seem. But that's not the end of it.' Ernest looked at us both in turn. 'Another had been set up at the gates to Parkgate House and caught the doctor unawares. When he arrived to see to the patient, he drove straight into it.'

'Is he alright?' I gasped.

'He's fine. By good fortune, the wire gave way on one side when his car drove through.'

'Thank God,' Richard declared. 'He could've been...' Unable to say the words, he held his throat with two hands, swallowing hard.

'But who would do such a dreadful thing?' I asked.

'Who indeed?' My brother glared back at me as if he already knew where the authorities might start looking for the culprit.

Chapter 9

Elizabeth

I was in two minds about accepting Phee's offer to join her family for dinner on the evening of the Gala Day but I decided that the tripwire incident had probably left the family shaken, and that I should show my support by accepting their invitation. Similarly, when she suggested that another visit to Whinbank was due, I agreed to accompany her in spite of Richard's protestations. As we whizzed along in the Albion 16, Phee described the mood at the house, and it did not sound cheerful. Catherine had been confiding in her how much she missed David and, although she appreciated how important his role in the Army Reserves was, all she wanted was for him to return and spend some time with her before the birth of their child. Phee reckoned that Catherine had been especially upset by events and who could blame her? Over the noise of the engine and the rumble of the wheels on the road I shouted back that I could understand how Catherine must be feeling.

Phee described how everyone at Parkgate was interviewed by the local constabulary whilst the grounds were searched for evidence. Officers studied the tripwires, showing particular interest in the choice of materials and the method of attachment of the wire, and looking for any possible clues that might have been left behind unwittingly by the perpetrators. At the front of the house there was much pointing of fingers back and forth along the main road that led from the house to the mining villages located east and west. When the stone wall into the field on the far side of the road was inspected, a section where stones had tumbled forward onto the grassy verge drew interest. So that was how they had approached the house, Constable Mackay decided. They must have crept along, under the cover of the hedgerow, all the way up from the burn at the bottom of the hill, in the still of the night.

Phee brought the vehicle to a halt by the roadside, about a mile from Whinbank. Normally so confident and headstrong, she admitted that she was as relieved as Catherine when Mr Imrie appeared that evening for dinner. Isabelle greeted him with the same affection she might lavish on a much-loved uncle bringing him a glass of his favourite sherry as he settled himself into a chair, concern all over his fifty-year-old face. He listened intently to Catherine's resumé of the situation, beginning with a description of Roger Stone's condition. Though his injuries were bad enough, he was fortunate not to have been more seriously hurt. He had lain still, unable to move, but knowing that if he tried to roll over, a lung might have been pierced by his damaged ribs. Indeed, he could have lain undetected for long enough had the gillie not decided to go up to the loch, a day earlier than he intended. Roger, she explained further, was now comfortable in one of the beds upstairs, where he would remain until he was much improved, the doctor was satisfied that the injuries to his collar bone and ribs were healed, and there were no complications. Catherine had been unable to contemplate the patient all alone in his estate cottage without anyone to care for him and, as Isabelle had been quick to point out, there was always the possibility that the motive for the attack was personal, towards the factor himself, so he was probably safer at Parkgate. The police were given a list of employees, past and present, and would no doubt question Roger about the matter later when he was well enough to speak to them. Phee said that, according to the police, the attack could have been directed at Roger Stone personally. In fact, it could have been aimed at anyone involved in estate matters, and might have been concerned with causing harm to members of the Melville family directly.

'Bear in mind our recent encounter with the local riff-raff,' she reminded me.

In her opinion, the fact that a second trip wire had been constructed across the main entrance to the house was surely proof that the perpetrators were out to hurt the family. It was only by great good fortune that she had decided to postpone a visit to a friend in Torphichen, planned for that very morning. Otherwise, she would have been the first person to drive through the gates and not, as it transpired, the good doctor coming to treat poor Roger. In fact, when she thought about it, she often went riding through the woods and up to the loch. Someone could have seen her in the past. Perhaps it should have been her lying injured upstairs and not the factor. She confessed to being very upset at that day's events, even when Catherine explained that the constabulary were sending a constable round later to patrol the grounds overnight. They were bound to find the perpetrator soon, said Catherine, and Phee was much too loveable to have been the target.

'But after we were held up by those ruffians, Elizabeth, how can I be sure?'

Sitting beside me, she looked so vulnerable in her ridiculous goggles. Phee shook her head vigorously as if shaking off her fears and she apologised for her over-reaction. 'Anyway,' she continued, 'Mr Imrie sounded confident the constabulary would have things in hand. As soon as he had returned to Rowanhill after dinner, he would organise a man or two to assist the police during the hours of darkness. Parkgate's a big house and we can't be too careful.'

'Has the constabulary come up with anything new?' I asked tentatively.

Phee almost sniggered – which I was very glad of but it left me intrigued. 'One thing they've ruled out right from the start, apparently, is the possibility that it's linked with Suffragette activity!'

Such a thought hadn't crossed my mind in the least though there had been incidents across the county in recent months. 'Glad to hear it! But if your telephone wires are cut, you'll know who it is straight away!' I giggled.

Phee became serious again. 'Constable Mackay has shown Mr Imrie the wire used in the crime. It's the kind used at the mines operated by the Coal Company but it's a common enough type. However, the stores at all the local pits are to be inspected and he'll report to the police if there are any signs of a break-in or loss of stock.'

'Do they think this affair could be linked to the present dispute between the men and the coal masters?' I asked, knowing that feelings were running high. 'The men seem determined to have their way.'

'That's exactly what Isabelle thinks... some might see a direct attack on the owners of Back o' Moss Pit as legitimate activity in accomplishing their ends. Such is the warped logic of undisciplined minds! ...according to my dear sister.'

She continued, 'Mr Imrie agreed that there are individuals who see such behaviour as justified but they're few and far between. As far as the dispute is concerned, he thinks most of the workforce will see reason, given time. The pit owners have to get costs down if those same pits that provide work for the men are going to survive in the current climate. The market for coal is low presently, hence prices are low. Wages have to come down in line with prices. That's how pay's been determined in the mines for long enough. Low prices... low pay. The owners have been hit hard with extra costs resulting from new laws... the Insurance Act and the Mines Act... and they've got to set capital aside for future investment. Am I making sense, Beth? Are you still with me?'

I nodded, impressed by how much detail Phee had remembered. Her interests didn't normally extend to industrial matters, as far as I was aware.

'I pointed out that everyone needs coal,' she went on. 'Surely we can't get enough of it, both here and abroad? Why is the market so low? Charles agreed that coal fuels the economy, nothing's truer, but when supply is greater than demand, the price comes down. You see the home market is depressed at the moment. Iron and steel output is reduced and Germany is undercutting us left, right, and centre. Then Catherine explained that our export market is reduced too. Scottish companies have lost some big contracts recently to Westphalian coal.'

I had read in the press that the Lothian and Fife pit owners had lost lucrative contracts with Swedish, Finnish and Danish Rail and even the London Gas Works to German suppliers. No wonder they were so keen to see the current dispute through to a suitable conclusion, from their point of view.

'Isabelle said it would be difficult for the miners to understand but they would eventually come to realise that their jobs are on the line, and the future of the country is at stake,' added Phee.

I could imagine how quickly Isabelle would conclude that the coalmasters had right on their side.

Phee looked out at the countryside for a while then thanked me for being with her that afternoon. It had been good to get out of the house, away from thoughts of disputes and conflict and the dread of assassins lurking in the garden. The relationship between Isabelle and Catherine was getting her down too since she always felt like piggy-in-the-middle and didn't want to upset either by taking sides. She couldn't stand the way Isabelle always dwelt on the news these days and brought up a new problem at every available opportunity. If it wasn't the continuing situation in Venice – which was closed to visitors because of striking railway workers – it was protests in Germany and Paris; if it wasn't Germany or Paris, it was Turkish atrocities against the Greeks; if it wasn't Greece it was fifty thousand protesting workers, shot at by Cossacks in St Petersburg at the start of the month; if it wasn't Russia, it was the Balkans or Scandinavia or rebellious Ireland.

I could not imagine what it was like to live at Parkgate at that moment. To have every luxury available and yet not be happy. Perhaps the possibility, however remote, of losing it all might be too hard to bear.

'Let's go,' I said, squeezing Phee's hand.

She put the vehicle into gear, 'I'd love to go to Venice!' she called to me.

'Perhaps Eric will take you! On honeymoon!'

We sped off much faster than I anticipated, our heads suddenly full of happy thoughts of weddings and love and foreign travel to romantic destinations.

Dinner at Parkgate House on the night of the Blackrigg Gala Day was a rather uncomfortable affair, though the tension of the past week, according to Phee, had dissipated both with the passing days and the presence of Imrie's men in the grounds during the hours from dusk till dawn. David's return from army camp the previous day had been warmly welcomed but everyone seemed tired from lack of sleep, leaving them fractious.

Isabelle held court at the dinner table treating the family to a précis of the week's events and a list of the perpetrators' possible motives. The constables, she reminded everyone, had concluded that four, possibly five, men had been involved in the trip wire incident and the materials they'd used had been stolen from the stores at Back o' Moss Pit. Several sets of footprints had been discovered in the muddy ground beside the burn and in a boggy part of the field opposite the entrance to the house. The perpetrators wore boots similar to those worn by the majority of working men in the area, so the evidence hardly helped to narrow down the list of culprits. Only two sets of similar footprints had been found on the path out of the wood onto the moss where the second trip wire had been set up, suggesting that the perpetrators had split up in order to carry out their dastardly deeds. The break-in at Back o' Moss Pit was, perhaps, more helpful in narrowing down the field, according to Constable Mackay. Due to the central location of the stores within the complex of buildings around the pithead, and the presence of two nightwatchmen, detailed local knowledge had been essential in the execution of that particular crime. Unfortunately, it was unclear exactly what else might have been stolen from the stores during the break-in except that the head storeman was able to confirm that one coil of wire, two containers of paraffin, and a variety of tools were unaccounted for.

David nodded, agreeing with Isabelle for the tenth time that security at the pit would have to be tightened up. He would have a word with the manager first thing on Monday morning. He understood her concern for the safety of the family, wanted to indulge her. He was less inclined to agree that the incident was a sign of orchestrated insurrection against the Melvilles. He reminded her of the constabulary's view that a small group of wastrels had probably taken it upon themselves to cause trouble, capitalising on the present discontent within the mines and using it as a distraction, or an excuse for bad behaviour. Constable Mackay knew the miners well and knew them to be a peaceable lot, in the main. There were bad apples in every barrel, however, but Mackay knew who they were and had his eyes on them.

'The culprits would be laughing their heads off at this very moment, Isabelle, if they knew how upset they'd made you,' declared David 'That's probably been their intention all along!'

'I'm not upset,' she countered. 'Not upset, at all. I'm angry, outraged and livid. But not at all upset. You make me sound like some whimpering idiot.' She hated the idea of people seeing her as anything other than a considerable force.

'Let's try to put it behind us, eh?' said David. 'Going over it again and again, well... it just serves to bring us all down. If the motive of the culprits was to unsettle us then they're succeeding. Let's talk about something more positive, shall we? Like the weather... or... Phee's engagement party... or, better still, the arrival of my son and heir.' He stretched across the table towards Catherine and put his hand on hers.

Catherine smiled back at him, shyly. She looked tired.

'Oh, alright,' said Isabelle abruptly, looking like she'd been told off. She glanced around the table at the small gathering, a muted echo of the grand dinners and parties her parents had held on the last Saturday in June, in years gone by. 'Don't you just hate how the miners have stolen the Blackrigg Fair Day from us?'

'Meaning?' asked David glumly. Was this his elder sister's idea of a happier topic of conversation?

'In the past the village held a fair on the last day in June and people came from all around. The children did their hill walk. There were stalls, sports, and a tea at Mansefield – before it was a park. Father would go along to present the sports prizes to the children. Don't you remember? And guests would gather here at the house to celebrate the arrival of mid-summer.'

'Isn't that what happens at the moment?' asked Catherine wearily, wondering what point Isabelle was trying to make. 'We would have organised a 'grand' dinner at Parkgate as before, had Phee's engagement party not been imminent, scheduled for next weekend.'

'Of course it's what happens, more or less. But they call it a *Gala Day* now rather than a *Fair*, don't you see?' Isabelle emphasised the operative words as if we were stupid. 'Now, it's a *Gala* to celebrate the eight-hour day in the mines. They're supplanting village history with a tradition of their own.'

'Isn't it the same thing? They're simply giving it a new name,' I ventured, feeling that I had been silent for too long. 'It's the same old local celebration.'

'An excuse for a party!' added Phee.

'It's a step towards a change in... in culture. Unless one had been here for a long time, one would think it had always been a *Gala Day* and that nothing else ever went before,' explained Isabelle.

'I don't think that's so bad,' said Catherine. 'The miners are taking an old tradition into a new age. They make up the majority of the population here nowadays, after all.'

Isabelle glared at her sister-in-law and I guessed what she was probably thinking. Why couldn't Catherine simply agree with her point of view? Why did she always have to argue, as if trying to score points against her?

'Everything's changing. And we have to learn to adapt,' said David in support of his wife, sensing Isabelle's animosity. 'Now what happened to my suggestion that we look forward, and with optimism?' He squeezed Catherine's hand again.

She smiled at her husband. 'I think I'll go upstairs to lie down for a bit. I'm rather tired.' She pushed back her chair and rose slowly to her feet. David rushed to help her. 'I'll be fine,' she assured him. 'Honestly, I'm fine. Finish your dessert, please. I'll see you when you retire if I'm still awake.'

'Goodnight,' said Phee. 'I hope you manage to get some sleep.' She watched her sister-in-law leave and must have wondered, as I did, what it was like to carry a child. At times, Catherine looked wonderful – calm and serene and contented – but tonight she looked heavy and slow, as if carrying a great burden. She had passed that middle stage of pregnancy when she had glowed with happiness, after the morning sickness had disappeared and when the difficulties of childbirth were still far off in the future. Now she seemed tired and quiet, sometimes remote, wrapped up in her own world with her unborn child.

When the door closed David turned to Phee. 'Has she been well when I've been away?'

'She's been well,' replied Phee gently.

'Of course, she's been well,' declared Isabelle. 'It's what women are made for. Nothing out of the ordinary there. Mother had five of us, no trouble at all.'

'She misses you, David,' continued Phee, ignoring her sister. 'Do you have to go away as often?'

'Of course, he has,' interrupted Isabelle before David could speak. 'The Melville men have always been warriors!'

Neither looked in her direction. Trust Isabelle to miss the point.

Isabelle threw down her napkin, got up from the table. If no one was going to listen to her, she wasn't about to hang around and listen to conversation about her brother's wife. 'I'll look in on Roger upstairs, shall I? See if he's on the mend.'

David and Phee waited until she had left the room.

'Do you?' Phee repeated her question. 'Do you have to be away so much?'

'When you join the army, there's no half measures,' he explained. 'Even when you're not with the colours and simply a reservist, like me. When the army says *jump,* you jump. And at the moment they're saying *jump* rather a lot.'

'Why is that, David?' asked Phee quietly. 'Is it true what they're saying? That there might be trouble in Europe?' I knew she was thinking of Eric, her fiancé, presently on manoeuvres at Hawick with the Lowland Mounted Brigade.

'There is trouble in Europe, Phee. There's trouble all over Europe at the moment if you think about it.'

Phee looked worried. The papers often carried stories about the fleet and the need to strengthen coastal defences.

'There may be trouble of the kind you're thinking about, in the future, but not now. That's what they're saying in army circles and that's why we're training. If and when there is trouble, we'll be ready for it. Don't worry.'

Phee nodded and smiled. 'Perhaps this business with the trip wires and poor Roger coming off his horse has put me on edge.'

I saw how she squeezed her brother's hand. They had always been close and she missed him when he went away. She couldn't bear it if anything happened to him.

'Let's take a drink through to the study before Elizabeth goes home,' suggested David. He pulled back her chair and helped her to her feet. 'We'll go through the list of guests for your celebration next week and I'll make sure you haven't missed any of my friends. I don't want anyone's nose to be out of joint!'

He seemed much more relaxed out of Isabelle's company and Phee always cheered him up.

'I'm so looking forward to your party. And you'll be glad to know I won't have to be away again for a while. No more playing at soldiers for a bit. Summer camp's over and, apart from a church parade in a couple of weeks, I should be here all summer with you... and Catherine.'

I followed behind when they walked through to the study. He seemed like the old David, the one Phee had described to me. The one who would hold his little sister's hand when they had been children at play, in the garden or on the beach. All this talk of trouble and trip wires and army reserves was unsettling, a reminder of how precarious life was. When you cared about something very much, you realised how easily it might be taken away from you, snatching away your happiness in one fell swoop. I could see how deeply Phee felt about Eric Hyslop. She wasn't

163

blinded by the whirlwind of their romance – it was more than that. She'd had time to reflect upon their future together.

'Thinking about someone nice?' asked David.

I caught her eye.

She giggled, realising she had given herself away. 'Yes. Very nice, actually.'

When I left to go home later that evening, I prayed for Eric and Phee, my dear friend and confidante, hoping they would enjoy a long and happy life together. I hoped that she would regain her usual happy, carefree, spirited demeanour quickly, in time for her engagement party and that nothing could spoil her happiness on that special day and all the days of her life to come. Although I had not met Eric, I believed that he must have been exceptional. He was certainly much blessed to have captured Phee Melville's heart and to be setting out on life's wonderful journey with her. When people find true love, surely there is nothing that can stand in their way. But as I was driven home through the glow of the summer night, that thought made me feel very sad.

John

I found out today they're not here – not one of them – and I have to say, it shook me to the core. An orderly got me up out of bed and said I had to start walking. My fever's gone and my wounds are healing so I've no excuse for lying here feeling sorry for myself.

Besides, the bed is needed for other folk.

There's more wounded to come, he told me in his foreign accent, plenty more.

That's why I'm here – humanitarian reasons.

My legs were like jelly at first but I made it to the lavatory without his support. It gave me a chance to look at the faces as I passed. Not one was familiar. I wondered if it was just that I couldn't remember their faces outside my dreams.

I spoke their names, hoarsely because of my wound. Jim...? Bert...? Dan...? Rob?

But nobody answered.

The orderly told me they might be in another camp, another hospital if they were wounded. An officer would come and see me soon, to find out how I was bearing up, and to take some particulars. They already had my details though; my family would be informed as soon as possible but the number of men in my position meant it was taking a while to process the information and get word back. I'll be moved into a regulation dormitory in a few days' time, as soon as the doctors are happy the infection is gone and won't come back. As soon as I'm strong enough.

I press my hand against the clean white bandage around my neck and feel the place on my hip where a dressing covers a wound. My hand is aching – not the left one with the missing finger but my right hand under its dressing. I have no recollection of what happened and how I've come to this place with its white walls and its clean sheets and a big cross of Jesus up on the wall.

I stare at the faces of the other men here, all in various states of disrepair, and repeat the names.

Jim? Bert? Dan? Rob?

I ask if anybody knows me.

Does anybody remember me, I ask?

Do you know where my pals are? Royal Scots...

Where have they gone?

Did somebody take them away?

Only one man replied. What's your name, son?

I say *I am John.*

My name is John, I say, and I cry like a bairn for my mother.

When I say their names to myself, a rush of panic comes at me, rising from my chest, choking, taking me off down a long tunnel, rushing, rushing, the blackness of the tunnel rushing past and my body hurtling down, ever downwards like I've stepped into a shaft at the pit and the cage isn't there. Last night I woke up in a sweat. I was about to scream and had to stop myself, managed to stop the sound coming out of my mouth just in time. They don't look kindly on lunatics here and I don't want to be tied to my bed, to be taken off somewhere by the orderlies. I've had the same dream a few of times now but when I wake it goes out of my head. I want to reach out with my aching hand and grasp at the images, drawing them back so I can piece them all together but no matter how hard I try, the dream disappears with the night.

I know that Andrew is in my dream and we're all around him. He's injured. His face is a mess and he's moaning in pain. He's clutching his belly and he's covered in blood and bruises. We gather round him and carry him, telling him he will soon see his mother. We stumble along. There are other folk as well, people with faces I can't quite make out; they're hovering in the background as if they don't want to be seen.

There's menace in the air, crowds of people moving together against the enemy.

They've had enough.

They didn't want a fight but they've no option because the people who could put an end to the misery wouldn't listen, thought they could have it all their own way. They take it all, never giving an inch. It's better to give than to receive but only if you have little to give in the first place, it seems. They could have stopped it before it began. They had it in their power. It was their job to make the decisions. They were born to it – they told us so often enough. But now we're in this big mess that's not of our making and we have to make it better. Men, women, and children are suffering. Their hearts are breaking, knowing they've been led down the garden path, knowing that it didn't have to be this way but it's the only way out.

We have to keep going.

Stick together.

For all our sakes.

It is sunny and warm in my dream, not cold with pissing rain lashing our faces. There's no mud or shrieking of artillery shells or rattling of guns, just the sound of the birds on the moss and music, soft lilting music like a band is playing far, far away.

Chapter 10

Minn

I spent nearly every waking minute of the week before the Gala Day dance looking for signs that I was going to find love in the arms of my chosen one. In my mind, I listed every superstition I had ever heard. The weather was fair apart from an evening thunderstorm – and everybody saw fine weather as a good sign. I looked around for bird mess on windows, stared upward in the hope that a passing bird might bless me as I moved about the farmyard and the fields. Regardless of the large numbers of swallows swooping around the yard, I was out of luck. But it didn't mean bad luck either, I reckoned. I warned the bothy lads to take their boots off the table when I saw them scraping off the mud from the fields at the end of a day's work because that was bad luck. And shut my ears to the talk of a fox being seen in the stackyard. A fox was the worst possible sign according to Annie. It was a sign of..... d-e-a-t-h. I prayed that a black cat lay in wait around every corner, ready to walk across my path and bestow lasting good fortune on me, simply because I was there, in the right place at the right time. All week I hoped and prayed that the black stray with the white socks would put in an appearance. But I was sorely disappointed. Dochie claimed to have seen her in the wood by the burn the day before, said she was running wild with the ginger tom and probably wouldn't come back until she needed a place to have her kittens.

What a silly, silly, innocent girl I was back then. Naive and hopeful, and so unprepared for the real world outside the romantic notions of my childish dreams.

On the night of the dance, I sat in the back room at home wearing Jean's clothes, skilfully altered to accommodate my tall, slender figure, with a trim of lace around the collar of the blouse. Sarah brushed out my hair and told me about the awful life Miss Fraser had with the tyrannical minister in the manse. She related the story of an argument between them earlier in the week and how they were going nineteen to the dozen until Mr Black had appeared on the scene. Mr Fraser always calmed down in company. We agreed that Miss Fraser deserved to find a beau, someone she could truly love and who would love her in return. Then she would be shot of her horrible brother who didn't seem to like women in the slightest. We reckoned he was lucky to have his sister to look after him but he would probably only realise how fortunate he'd been when she was married to somebody and living elsewhere. And that would serve him right.

Sarah pinned up my hair then I stood up and twirled around, waiting for her verdict. I looked grand, she told me, elegant and feminine for a change, but it was a pity about the boots. I stuck out one foot and looked down, hands on hips. It was a shame about the boots right enough, sticking out below the skirt, but there was no alternative. I'd always worn boots, ever since I'd learned to walk. But at least they were clean and polished and laced up the front to just above the ankle, so they didn't look too bad. Not as bad as the tacketie boots I wore on the farm. Sarah howled with laughter and had to hold her sides at the thought of me in my workboots, covered in mud and dung from the fields, clod-hopping around the public hall at the Gala Day dance.

Our shenanigans drew Jean through from the other room, wondering how things were progressing. Her eyes lit up and she smiled at the sight of me.

'Yer quite the lady,' she began. 'Turn roon till I see the back.'

I turned round and waited.

'Ye'll turn a few heids at the dancin', so ye will,' she said. 'Shame aboot the boots.'

'They're fine.' I was starting to think that my footwear might spoil the entire evening.

'It's the style o' the skirt,' said Jean with a loud tut. 'Ye can see yer feet and ankles ablow it.'

'Longer an' it would look auld-fashioned,' I argued. 'I'm happy wi' the skirt the wey it is.'

Jean shook her head.

'They're fine!' I was afraid Jean was about to perform major surgery on the skirt and make me late for the dance and a possible meeting with Rob. 'The boots are fine, the skirt's fine, the blouse is fine an' I'm fine tae.'

A smile crept over Jean's face and I wondered if she'd been teasing me.

'Aye, yer fine,' agreed Jean. 'But there's somethin' here ye might like.' She reached under the boys' bed, drew out a box which she handed over.

I looked at it in amazement, hardly able to speak. It was a shoe box.

'Open it up then,' she ordered. 'Let's see whit they look like.'

I took off the lid and carefully parted the tissue paper inside. Slowly, I removed a black shoe marvelling at the suppleness of the leather and the perfect, tiny button that secured a single strap across the front. I held it up, examining the small heel and the slightly pointed toe, so feminine compared to anything I had worn on my feet in the past.

'Dae ye like them, then?'

I nodded, lost for words. 'A.... a... are they for me?'

'Aye! They're yours. Let's see them oan.'

'They're braw so they are. Jist... braw.'

'Can ye walk in them?' asked Sarah.

I took a step. 'They're a wee bit big.' My heart missed a beat at the thought that I might have to wear my boots after all.

'That's nae bother,' said Jean. 'I thocht they micht be on the big side. But ye'll grow a bit yet, at yer age. They'll last ye for years.'

She reached into the box and tore off a piece of tissue paper, scrunching it up into a ball. I knew exactly what to do, taking each shoe off in turn and wedging a wad in the toes before putting them back on. I walked a few paces back and forward.

'The very dab!' I declared. 'Cinders can go to the ball!'

Sarah clapped her hands in delight and dashed off to answer a knock at the door. It was probably Jenny. She would let her know that I was ready.

I gave Jean a hug and was about to tell her how grateful I was for the clothes and the shoes, and for being so good to me. I was suddenly sorry that I'd taken so long to warm to my father's new wife and, when I thought about it, I hadn't been as welcoming as I could have been. And here Jean was, spending some of the family's limited income on a pair of shoes, a frivolous pair of shoes just for me.

But before I could say a word, Jean grabbed my wrist hard and looked me straight in the eye.

I was taken aback.

'Afore ye go, Minn Graham. Sit doon a meenit,' she said, suddenly serious.

I waited. What was coming? I looked upward at Jean, towering over me.

'I hope sincerely that ye have a guid time at the dance, young lady.'

I nodded. She didn't sound as if she meant it. Her voice was gruff and her eyes were piercing.

'But mind this!' Her finger was pointing straight at my face. 'Ye mak yer bed ye hiv tae lie in it!'

'Pardon me?'

'Ye ken whit I'm talkin' aboot, Minn Graham.'

I must have blushed a brighter shade of crimson. Could Jean possibly be talking about what I thought she was talking about?

'If ye mak yer bed ye've got tae lie in it, Minn,' she repeated, a wee bit softer this time.

'Aye, Jean. I'll mind.' I nodded, my heart thumping in my chest. Suddenly there was great responsibility attached to my attendance at the Gala Day dance.

'Ye need tae think aboot these kinna things,' she explained, guessing that nothing of the sort had occurred to me before. That was exactly why she'd had to bring the subject up. 'Itherwise, ye can get caught unawares. Ye need tae be prepared, in yer mind... 'specially... a guid lass like yersel.'

I gave her a smile as best I could. I knew Jean meant well and, although she wasn't my real mother, she was doing her best to give advice before I went off to my first dance. One day I would come to realise how important that advice had been. I gave her a cuddle and assured her I would be careful.

'Guid, lass,' Jean said. 'Noo, oan yer wey and enjoy yersel, the ither lassies are waitin'. Peter's gaun tae the dance tae. He's awa' tae meet his pairtner and he'll meet ye alang at the steadin'.'

'Peter? Is Uncle Peter gaun tae the dance?'

'Aye, an' I've telt him tae look oot for ye an' mak sure ye dinna come tae onie herm.'

'Oh, thanks... thanks very much.'

The bairns watched open-mouthed as I made my way through the front room to join my friends who were waiting with Sarah by the door. My father had a richt dour look about him, kept his head down as I passed. He wasn't too happy that I was going out to the dance with the other girls at such a young age. He thought I should wait to be asked by a young man but Jean had persuaded him to let me go.

Jean had said there was no shame in it and I was a guid lass.

And I had assured him, I'd be fine.

I was mightily relieved when I saw my friends blethering excitedly in the street but any brightening of my mood soon dulled as we got near the steading where Uncle Peter was waiting. Beside him stood his dancing partner, Bessie Morrison, who worked in the Cooperative store. She half-smiled as we approached then led Peter off to the dance at a fair lick, leaving us to follow in their wake.

The hall was already busy when we took our seats, arranged in double rows around three sides of the hall to fit in as many people as possible and still give a good view of the dance floor. As the seats filled up, groups of revellers congregated at both ends of the hall: at the main entrance from the street and beside another door in the top corner by the small stage where the band was setting up.

Jenny said I was looking braw in my outfit but I was being very quiet. Was everything alright? I said I was fine, just a bit nervous to be dressed up for a change. It made me feel conspicuous, especially wearing new shoes which would take a bit of getting used to. In truth, I was weighed down by Jean's words of warning. Doubly so knowing that my father had had to be persuaded to let his seventeen-year-old daughter go to the dance with friends of the same age, rather than with a young man who could have been entrusted with my care and instructed to return me to the family home by a particular time, in the same condition as I'd left the house. I glanced along at Uncle Peter, there as my chaperone. The signs weren't good, I thought, and hoped things would improve.

The band started up. We watched the dancers take to the floor, including Peter and Bessie who stood ready for a waltz. He glanced over in my direction to let me know he still had his eye on me. Meanwhile, we chatted about what the women were wearing and tried to name the young men we were less familiar with. It was thrilling to hear the music and to see who was dancing with who. But several dances later, we were still sitting. At the start of every new dance, when the band played a chord to signal for attention and the caller told everybody to take their partners, we sat up straight in hopeful expectation of being asked up but each time we were disappointed. The excitement of the event, anticipated for such a long time, was beginning to wane. I wondered if my father had been right. Maybe young women should only attend dances when they're accompanied by a young man.

Just as the dancers were leaving the floor, breathing hard after a vigorous reel, an argument erupted on the other side of the hall from where we sat. Two of the organisers had confronted a small group of men. Unlike everybody else, they still wore their bunnets and had brought attention to themselves. Jenny said they probably didn't have tickets and had sneaked in by the back door. I asked if anybody recognised who they were. It was hard to make out their faces under their caps but wasn't the smaller one Davy Birse, elder brother of John and Jim who had been in our class at school? The men were moving away towards the exit by the stage so it was hard to see them clearly. We agreed it wasn't right that people got in without a ticket. It hadn't been easy to get one and if people were able just to walk in then that wasn't fair.

A loud chord from the accordion drew our attention back to the caller. It was a barn dance, he said, for those who still had some puff left after the reel. Bessie dragged Peter from his seat. She seemed to have plenty of energy and wouldn't take *no* for an answer. Jenny elbowed me in the side at the sight of them, and we laughed. Poor Uncle Peter wouldn't be able to get out of his bed in the morning, not after Bessie Morrison was finished with him. Our laughter was interrupted by a voice from behind asking me if I would like to dance. I turned round to see who it was. Where had he come from? He was hunkered down behind me, almost hiding. I had no time to reply, never mind recover from the shock of seeing Rob's serious face over my shoulder. He whisked me out of my seat and onto the dance floor, telling me to hurry up, the dance was about to begin.

I stood facing him, hardly able to believe it was true, unable to speak. Butterflies fluttered inside me – not just my stomach but my chest, my throat, my head, and other places I shouldn't mention. It was a feeling I liked. He was the only person in the room as far as I was concerned. I placed my hand gently on his shoulder as if too much pressure might break the spell and have him disappear in a puff of smoke. He took my other hand in his and I felt the strength of him, for the first time. A quick glance at the other couples to see what to do next and he placed his right hand on my back, pulling me towards him. I closed my eyes and prayed I wouldn't faint.

The music started up and the caller shouted out the instructions till the dancers got used to the steps. Most had done it before but me and Rob were beginners. I had to guide him round for the jig at the end of each refrain but he got the hang of it eventually. We faltered now and again but he remained serious, staring deep into my eyes without saying a word. He spun me round and I floated somewhere between here and the moon, wishing it would go on forever. The music soon stopped and I lingered. There was always a second set. He returned my gaze for a moment. Then his eyes darted round, back and forth across the hall and to the exit by the stage, near where we stood. The band started up for the second phase of the barn dance but Rob didn't respond. Instead, he yanked at my hand and quickly pulled me out of the back door. I gave a small yelp but I went with him.

In the dappled shade of the tree-lined lane that ran down to the road, Rob pressed me up against the wall of the public hall. I felt his body against mine when he put his arm around my waist and drew me to him. He looked deep into my eyes and said not a thing. Then he bent his head and kissed me full on the mouth. He looked along the lane, back and forth, and kissed me again, quicker and harder this time, before running off towards the road. I was left quivering like a jelly.

'Get awa' wi' ye, ye tike!' called a voice.

I steadied myself, looking in the direction he had taken off in. He was gone. A strong hand grabbed my arm, marched me back into the hall where the dance was carrying on as if nothing whatsoever had happened out in the lane.

'Whit dae ye think ye're up tae?' asked Uncle Peter. 'Yer faither'll gie me whit for if he hears aboot this. Get in here an' content yersel.'

I was speechless as he led me back to my seat and told me to stay put, OR ELSE. He was going back to Bessie, to finish the dance, but he would have his eye on me. I could be sure of that.

I came to, slowly, out of the dream-like state brought on by Rob Duncan's kisses. Jenny was all ears but I wasn't making sense. What was it like to dance with Rob? And why was my uncle so angry with me? Where was Rob, by the way? Where had he gone?

'Jenny,' I said eventually, swallowing hard. 'It was a barn dance, a CANADIAN barn dance!'

Jenny waited for more information but nothing else was forthcoming.

'A CANADIAN barn dance,' was all I could say. It was a sign. I was convinced of it. But I couldn't explain it to Jenny. Nobody but me – and maybe Annie – could understand its significance.

The tea interval didn't come a moment too soon for the dancers. The hall was hot, despite every window being open, and the number of fast and furious reels greatly outnumbered the slower, more sedate waltzes. We lined up to collect a cup of tea, lamenting the lack of partners

177

fighting over themselves to ask us to dance. The younger men seemed to prefer staring at the goings on, sizing up the single girls on the opposite side of the hall from where they sat, hunched up with long faces. Perhaps they were too shy to come and ask, one of my friends suggested. Another said it was a waste of a good dance, and good money, if we were just going to sit there all night. Jenny said that the men would soon find their nerve and there would be a queue of lads asking us to dance in the second half.

'Dinna fash, quines,' she whispered. 'Yince the penny draps they micht be gaun hame b' theirsels, they'll be ower, as ma mother would say, like bees roon a honeypot!'

Peter gave her a stare – he was beside us in the queue – and I reckoned if Jenny had been his daughter, he would have given her a clout round the ear into the bargain. He seemed to have taken upon himself the welfare of, not only me, but that of my friends as well. With Uncle Peter riding shotgun like he was, it was probably just as well Rob had disappeared. I scanned the hall and the queues of people but he was nowhere to be seen.

Bessie led the way outside and we followed with our own cup of tea, and a plate of buttered pancakes between us. A big gathering of revellers had collected under the chestnut trees and along the walls on either side of the main entrance to the hall. Merry chatter and raucous laughter rang out in the evening air. We watched the comings and goings of couples and bigger groups of friends and relations, who were enjoying good company and tall tales out in the open air. There was still plenty of light around but the shadows lengthened as the sun sank lower in the west. The night of the Gala Day dance was one of the few nights of the year when such revelry was allowed to disturb the peace and quiet of Blackrigg life well into the wee sma' 'oors. We took it all in. Glad to be part of it, we looked forward excitedly to the second half. We looked forward to many more Gala Day dances in the future, imagining the dresses we'd wear and the young men we might meet there. Little did we realise, and nobody could have told us, that it would be several long years before Blackrigg public hall saw another Gala Day dance.

After a while I spoke up. 'Uncle Peter? Can we gang ower for a blether wi' the lads oan the ither side o' the street. Dae ye mind?'

Five lads sat on the pavement, diagonally opposite from where he and Bessie were perched close together on the wall, enjoying the last of their tea.

'They were in oor class at the school, Mr Logie,' explained Jenny. 'They're no at the dance but can we gang speak wi' them? Till the dance sterts up again?'

Peter wasn't convinced that it was a good idea to let us go, even though the boys were only twenty yards or so up the road. But a dig in the ribs from Bessie helped him make up his mind.

'Aye, fair enough. Five meenits then back in the hall or I'll be oot lookin' for ye mind!'

Dan, Bert, Sandy, and the twins sat with their backs against the wall in front of the village school.

'Hello,' said Jenny on our behalf.

'Hello,' said Bert.

'Yous no been at the dance then?' asked Jenny knowing full well they hadn't been.

'Naw,' replied John. 'We've been havin' a gemm up at the park.' He blushed. We were old friends and we'd played together in the street or down at the Meadie by the burn often enough in the past. But in the three years since we had all left school to take up employment, a gulf as wide as an ocean seemed to have opened up between us.

'Yous no gonnae staun up?' asked Jenny who certainly wasn't going to sit down beside them on the ground.

'Naw,' they replied in unison.

'We're fine here,' explained Bert.

'Whau else was at the park?' I asked, unable to stop myself.

'Jist some o' the younger lads,' said Sandy.

'An' Andra Brownlee,' said John.

'An' Geordie,' added Bert. 'He's walkin' Andra hame. He likes tae cairry the ba'!'

Then right on cue, Geordie appeared from the direction of the Smiddy at the bottom of the hill road.

'Here's the man himself,' announced Sandy.

Geordie was running as fast as he could. He was smaller than might be expected for a lad of fourteen years and this endeared him to everybody in the village. His small stature was emphasised by the substantial football he carried under his arm. His face was flushed and he looked upset.

'Smile, Geordie,' shouted Sandy when he was near enough to hear. 'Ye left the school yesterday. Miss Foulkes an' her strap are a thing o' the past! Cheer up!'

Geordie didn't reply. He wasn't happy, everyone could see that he was crying once he was close enough.

'Whit's wrang, Geordie?' asked his brother. 'Whit's up?'

Geordie arrived and we gathered round him. He made a few loud whoops as he tried to get his breath back. Geordie had a weak chest, everybody said so. He held up the ball for us to see.

'Calm doon, calm doon, Geordie,' said Bert. He took the ball from his brother. It was Andrew Brownlee's ball.

'Is it the ba', Geordie?' asked Sandy.

Geordie shook his head.

'Is it Andra?' asked the twins together.

Geordie nodded.

'Is Andra a'richt?'

Geordie shook his head.

'Has somethin' happened tae Andra?'

Geordie nodded again. He bent double and pointed in the direction from where he had come.

'Bad yins!' he said at last. 'Bad boys jumped us. They're giein' Andra a hammerin'....' He pointed again. 'Up the hill road! Ye need tae help him!'

I put my arm round Geordie's shoulder as the five pals ran full pelt along Main Street towards the steading. They turned the corner at the Smiddy and disappeared up the hill road.

'Did ye see who it was, Geordie?' I asked him, horrified that something so terrible could have happened to well-mannered Andrew Brownlee, son of the manager at the Broadrigg Pits.

Geordie didn't take time to answer my question. He wrestled from my grasp and ran after his brother and his friends. I wanted to go too but a stern voice rang out from across the street, reminding me that the second half of the dance was about to start and our five minutes was up. We wandered slowly across the road, our gaze fixed on the place by Smiddy Cottage where the lads had disappeared from view. Jenny said she hoped Andrew would be alright. Maybe Geordie had been exaggerating. He was a well-known character, famous for his stories, so maybe it had just been a scuffle with lads who wanted a kick of the ball. Maybe, we all agreed. But Geordie had looked distressed and we didn't think he would make up

181

such a tale, not now that he was growing up, and had left the school.

John

I remember sitting in the dirt by the roadside with the pals. The sweat ran down my back, out of my hair, into my eyes. I was still catching my breath from the game but gradually the sound of the music inside the hall came to me on the evening air.

Da dee, da dee, da dee, dum. Da dee, da dee, da dee, dumm.........

I can hear it yet and it soothes me to sleep.

Laughter and chatter and clapping, people flowing out onto the street, laughing and talking and couples hand-in-hand.

Then suddenly she was there in the street with the others. They came towards us and we sat there like fools, looking up at them as if we had been looking at the clouds and seen angels instead. If we'd stood beside them, the gulf between us would have been stark. Not only would our scruffiness be shown up beside their finery but the difference in maturity would be obvious and too embarrassing – we were still boys but they seemed, somehow, transformed. Better to pretend to have no manners than to be shown up for the immature specimens that we were. All five of us sat in silent admiration, seeing how braw they looked in their special dresses – completely out of our reach – though if somebody had asked us at the time, we would have protested no interest in the opposite sex.

The pals whispered that Minn Graham was barely recognisable but I'd noticed her immediately. Her eyes blue and bright and kind, her lips full and smiling. The lace at the collar of her blouse touched milky white skin just below her neck and her dark hair spilled out of the pins that held it up at the back. She was wearing shoes that showed off her slender feet and legs clad in black stockings. She was only a few yards away, close enough to touch, and everything a sixteen-year-old boy could wish for. I could have stayed there forever drinking her in but the world turned on its head with Geordie's arrival and I was running like the rest of them, running full pelt up the hill road to Andrew Brownlee's aid.

Fleet-of-foot, Dan ran ahead with Bert in close pursuit. Me, Jim, and Sandy took up the rear. The hill road was steep but nobody seemed to notice, our minds focused on a friend in need of assistance. Dan and Bert arrived at the end of the lane that led to Mansefield where we'd been playing football only half an hour earlier, then sprinted between the hedgerows, expecting to find trouble at any moment. They scanned the park but Andrew was nowhere to be seen. By the time they returned to the road just below Kaim Farm, we three were making a final push up the hill. Dan and Bert shook their heads and pointed to the other side of the road. Jim leapt the stile first then held up his hand for all to see. There was blood on his hand. Was it Andrew's blood? We crossed the stile and ran along the path, the short cut to Bankhead Cottage where Andrew lived, but we didn't go far before we found him.

Andrew lay on his side curled into a ball on the ground. His head was covered in blood and he held one arm across his middle. He didn't flinch as we crowded round. His eyes were closed and he didn't make a sound. He was perfectly still.

'Is he a'right?' asked Jim.

'Coorse he's no a'right,' replied Sandy. 'He's been beaten tae a pulp!'

'I mean... is he... breathin'?' replied Jim.

Dan knelt down beside Andrew for a better look. 'Andra, are ye a'right?'

Bert joined him on the ground. 'He's had a richt doin',' he concluded. 'Andra. Speak tae us, Andra.'

Bert and Dan looked at each other then cast their eyes up at the rest of us standing over them, deeply concerned.

'Is he deid?' asked Jim.

I gave him a dig in the ribs.

A silence followed, a profound heart-thumping, stomach-churning silence when the possibility that the world had changed forever hit home; the possibility that our friend, Andrew Brownlee, was no longer of this world, and nothing would ever be the same again because of it. Football games without him in the park – quiet moments when he would come into your mind for no reason – the possibility of heading down the pit road knowing that Andrew wasn't going to the big school anymore and would never attend the technical college in Edinburgh as he'd intended, that we would never hear of his future life because there wouldn't be one, not anymore. He would be a memory, something only of the past, not of the future or even the present.

We were shocked beyond belief.

Andrew's still, battered body lay in our midst, glistening crimson blood oozing from his broken nose, congealing in his brown hair, and smeared across his white football shirt. I remember how I knelt down in the grass and lifted one of his lily-white hands, now dirty with soil and covered in blood. I groped around the wrist for a pulse but couldn't find one. Jim gulped when he saw me gently place Andrew's hand back on the ground. I felt around the base of Andrew's neck, where the muscle and tendon disappeared into the collar bone then beside his throat and up towards his chin.

I could feel the tiny throb of life beneath my fingers. 'He's no deid!' I gasped. 'He's alive!'

'Thanks be,' whispered Dan.

'Jim, go for yer Ma,' ordered Bert. 'We'll get Andra hame tae Bankheid.'

Jim ran off towards the hill road, the quickest route to Stoneyrigg.

Andrew gave a low moan, making us gulp with relief. Between us, Bert and me did our best to work out the extent of our friend's injuries and the likelihood of him being able to walk the half mile to Bankhead Cottage. He was wearing only one football boot, the other presumably lost in the fray, but that was the least of his problems. The worst of his injuries were to his head and his stomach. He had scrapes and bruises on his knuckles and lower arms gained, no doubt, when defending himself from the onslaught, and his knees were grazed and full of grit from being pushed to the ground. Andrew clutched at his hip and the top of his leg when we tried to move him. He was probably bruised in that area too, we agreed, but nothing seemed to be broken.

'We'll need tae cairry him,' I said. 'Watch how ye move him.'

Between us, there were three jackets which we laid on the ground. We rolled and cajoled Andrew onto the makeshift stretcher and, clutching the material in strong hands, did our best to raise him from the ground. It was hard going. The path was narrow, uneven, and the woollen fabric kept slipping through our fingers. Besides, Andrew was a ton weight.

'The feedin' must be guid at Bankheid,' declared Sandy.

Andrew gave a groan and clutched at his middle. He was trying to say something but we couldn't make out what it was.

'At least ye've still got yer teeth, Andra. Ye'll be back tae yer guid-lookin' self in a couple o' weeks when the swellin's gaun doon,' said Sandy trying to throw his injured friend a lifeline.

Soon, we discovered a better way. We slipped our arms under Andrew's body and gripped each other's wrists. We moved as one after that, an eight-legged creature with Andrew at its centre, stumbling and staggering all the way across the hill.

We were almost at Bankhead when Geordie caught us up, the leather football still firmly wedged under his arm.

'I'm sorry, Andra,' he sniffled. 'I'm sorry I ran awa' an' left ye.' He drew in a loud suck of air and almost turned purple before breathing out. Tide marks of tears patterned Geordie's dirty face and a white bubble of snot blew out of his nose with every breath.

'I'm sorry,' he repeated. 'I should've helped ye!'

'Ye did help him,' said Dan. 'Ye came an' got us.'

'Whit else could ye've done?' said a new voice. We looked back in surprise at the arrival of Rob. 'There were ower monie for ye tae mak a difference, Geordie,' he added.

'An' hoo would you ken?' asked Sandy, studying his brother's face, almost losing his footing in the process.

'Oniebody can see there was mair than yin,' replied Rob quickly. 'Look at the boy!' He nodded at Andrew who moaned loudly whenever we stumbled over a stone or a clump of grass.

'Did ye see who it was, Geordie?' asked Rob. 'Did ye see who jumped Andra? Afore ye ran for help, hoo monie were there? Hoo monie lads?'

Geordie thought for a moment, sniffing. 'Three. There was three o' them. But I dinnae ken whau it was. They had their faces covered.' He bubbled again. 'They were big. They were... they were men, no boys. They were men!'

'Whit aboot Andra? Has he said oniethin?' Rob asked. 'Did he see whau it was?'

'He's no got ower muckle tae say at this precise meenit, as ye can see for yersel,' replied Bert puffing, red in the face.

'Mebbe he kent them an' mebbe he didnae,' added Sandy, recovering from another stumble. 'He'll tell the polis a' aboot it, nae doobt.' I could see how suspiciously he was eyeing his brother. 'Nice o' ye tae ask efter the casualty b' the wey.'

Rob did seem very interested in whether or not the culprits had been recognised by either Geordie or Andrew, and not at all concerned about the victim's condition. It made me wonder where he had been all evening, how he had found out there had been trouble in the first place, and why he had made the effort to find us on the short cut to Bankhead. He hadn't been that keen on our company these past two or three weeks yet suddenly he had gone out of his way to seek us out.

We nudged open a gate, carried Andrew into the garden at the back of his house. He wretched a mixture of bile and blood onto his father's vegetable patch before starting to cry. I'll never forget that sound of him bleating for his mother like a newborn lamb.

'Ye'll be fine,' we all said to him, more or less together. 'Yer hame noo.'

'There's Highland Mary runnin' alang the road. She'll see tae ye. We'll gang for the polis an' let them ken whit's happened, Andra.' Sandy glared at Rob. 'They'll sin get tae the bottom o' this,' he said.

In the middle of the following week, my family sat around the small table in the front room of the end cottage in the Back Row finishing our supper: a plate of broth made with a bone and a hunk of bread, followed by homemade pancakes and strawberry jam. Mrs Cherrie – Mags – had appeared at the door with the jam in return for my mother's help during her latest confinement. Mags was now a proud mother of ten bairns and could ill-afford so much as a pot of jam but she had insisted that Highland Mary take it. She was grateful for her presence during the birth, she explained, as she craned her head into our cottage from the doorway. I hadn't given such matters much thought before then and the knowledge that my mother had assisted during her confinement would have been sufficient information for a young man of my tender years but Mags was not one to hold back on the details. Whilst the nurse officiated and dealt with the technicalities of childbirth in the back room, it was Highland Mary who had organised the older Cherrie children so that the youngest were fed, watered and comforted in the front room to the sounds of their mother roaring in pain. Eventually, it had all become too overpowering and upsetting for the wee ones, apparently, so she'd hunted them out to play on the washing green, even though it was late in the evening and long past their bedtime. It was Mary who chastised Bobby Cherrie when he came in from the Village Inn reeking of drink whilst his wife gave birth to his tenth child through by. It was Mary who cleared up afterwards, washing the floor, and making sure Mags had a cup of tea and something to eat to restore her strength, before promising to look in on subsequent days to check that the elder Cherrie girls were coping with the rest of the brood. By the time Mags had said her piece and departed, even my father was wondering if he could bring himself to consume her strawberry jam.

I admired my mother as she sat watching her family tucking in to what she had made for us. It pleased her to see us enjoying our food after a hard day's work down the pit and, for once, the place wasn't crowded out with boarders – people who helped pay the rent but were strangers nevertheless. There was only Alex, Davy, Jim and me. Her twin boys were still growing fast, almost young men working hard in the Broadrigg Pits and paying our way. I could see how that pleased her and, in return, it pleased me.

It was unusual for Davy to join the rest of us. He kept his own hours and pleased himself as a rule. Alex had been overjoyed when Davy had become the union man at Back o' Moss Pit at such a tender age, still in his early twenties. It had given him a focus for his anger and his energy, too often misdirected in his younger days and aggravated by strong drink until he had taken the pledge at my father's insistence. Yet there was still something about Davy that worried my mother, I could tell. He was sullen and quick to anger where me and Jim were concerned, something he had probably learned from Alex. She never knew what was going on in Davy's head and it grieved her. He was so unlike me and Jim, she would say, which wasn't surprising considering we had been adopted separately, in infancy. It had simply been a matter of walking into the Combination Poorhouse in Leith and showing willing, promising to take good care of the child and signing a paper. She didn't know much, if anything, about our respective parents and she'd taken a chance that she'd chosen well. It was a matter of luck at the end of the day what you got. Davy, it transpired, had a temper – reinforced and nurtured by a childhood witnessing Alex's outbursts. Me and Jim, on the other hand, were more placid and restrained, subdued by our father's hand rather than riled by it.

She was making a fresh pot of tea when another knock came to the door. She glanced at the rest of us but no one gave any indication they were expecting a visitor. Davy peeked out of the window and relaxed, too obviously relieved for it not to go unnoticed. It was Jimmy White, the grocer. Nothing to worry about. My mother opened the door and was presented with a box.

'Courtesy of the Brownlees along at Bankheid,' said Jimmy cheerfully. He leaned into the room, doffed his cap, and smiled at us sitting round the table. 'Whit wid we dae withoot Highland Mary, eh boys?'

She thanked Jimmy before closing the door then placed the box on the table and we craned our necks to see what it contained.

'They shouldnae have bothered,' she said as she inspected the contents: various jars of jams and pickles, biscuits and dried fruits, and a big side of cooked ham the likes of which had never graced her table before. She retrieved a folded piece of paper from the bottom of the box. It was a note from Mrs Brownlee, thanking her for caring for Andrew after he had been attacked when there was no one at home to look after him. Andrew was still in hospital in Edinburgh but he wasn't as badly injured as they'd first feared. He was going to make a full recovery in due course. My mother had tears in her eyes as she folded up the note, tucking it behind an empty tin on the mantelpiece.

'I dinnae ken hoo some folk can be sae rotten,' she said remembering the state she had found the boy in when she'd arrived at Bankhead Cottage that evening. 'Just as weel you laddies were there tae help him,' she said proudly, turning to me and Jim.

'Some folk have plenty,' said Davy grudgingly, referring to the box of groceries. He lifted up one or two items our family could never have afforded in a month of Sundays. 'Mair than enough, they can gie it awa'.'

'Ye'll no be havin' onie then,' said Alex. 'In case ye choke oan it.'

'The world's ill-divided is a' I'm sayin',' countered Davy through a mouthful of pancake and strawberry jam. 'The rich have got whit's comin' tae them.'

Alex shook his head. Our mother gasped.

'Andra Broonlee niver did oniebody onie herm. He didnae deserve the hammerin' he got the ither nicht,' she said, horrified.

'Folk are sayin' Andra was battered 'cause o' whau his faither is,' said Jim.

Alex shrugged and shook his head. In common with the rest of the community, he didn't know but he had his suspicions. It was a reasonable conclusion to draw.

'I've plenty time for the likes o' Mr Broonlee,' he said. 'If it wasnae for him, I would be deid an awa' b' noo. He kept up the rescue when the roof came in ablow ground and killed three ither boys. But he kept it gaun as lang as he could, an' risked his ain life an a'.'

'He toadies tae Imrie an' does his biddin',' retorted Davy as he leaned back on his chair and spat a large blob of phlegm and venom into the fire. Sneering, he quoted scripture in support of his point of view, 'The sins o' the faithers shall be visited upon the sons.'

My mother glared at him like she hardly knew him at all. He was a hard case with a hard heart. He had a big mouth with several teeth missing, a scar down one cheek and a squint nose, all evidence of a hard life and the many fights he had gotten into. He had a permanently torn face that only a mother could love and, if she was honest, even she must have found that difficult at times.

'Onieweys, whit are they sayin' aboot yon business?' continued Davy, biting into another pancake, sounding casual. 'Has the laddie spoke up aboot whau jumped him? Have they got whau done it?'

'No yet, no as faur as I ken,' said Alex. 'The wee laddie Broadley says there were three but he didnae ken them, they'd their faces covered. A' the polis have got tae gang oan is that yin o' the Broonlee lad's fitba' boots is missin' – alang wi' his bunnet.'

'Yin boot's missin'? Jist the yin? Are they're lookin' for somebody wi' the yin leg!? No monie yin-legged criminals aboot here!' Davy roared and laughed at his own joke but nobody joined in.

'Yin leg or twa, I'd like tae gang a couple o' roonds wi' them when they're caught.' Alex glared at him.

'Dinnae look at me!' he said, showing offence. 'Nuthin adae wi' me, yon.'

Alex lifted his spoon and pointed it at Davy's face. 'Gled tae hear it.'

Davy nodded. He thought he was a hard man but his father was still a force to be reckoned with. It was time to change the subject.

'Onie word fae the union aboot the dispute, faither?'

'Naw, no yet. They're still waitin' oan the coal owners makin' the next move. A fower day week tae control supply an' put up prices is still oan the cards but the owners've no indicated yin wey or the ither whit they're gaunnae dae aboot it. I expect they'll be haudin oan till Friday afore they speak up – when the pits gang oan holiday fur the summer. It's an auld ploy, tried and tested. They'll haud oan till the last meenit an' the men cannae git the gither the same, tae discuss their response.'

'Whit we need is Robert the Bruce,' I said like a fool. I could have kicked myself but I loved the stories of Scottish history.

'Robert the Bruce?!' said Alex loudly. He didn't try to hide his contempt for me.

'Robert the friggin' Bruce?!' exclaimed Davy half-laughing.

Mother told them to leave me alone. Maybe I had a point.

'Aye, it was his anniversary the ither day. Five hunder year. Folk've been celebratin' *the triumph o' the oppressed ower the oppressor*.' I was convinced of The Bruce's relevance and pushed on. 'There's been celebrations in Stirlin' an' Edinburgh. Dan Potts says they had a special service in the kirk here in Blackrigg.'

'Oh, aye. They've been celebratin' *freedom fae the Yoke o' Tyranny*, I hear,' said Alex, 'and their *love o' Liberty*.'

'Aye, folk are fair taen oan wi' the story.' I was pleased that my father had heard about the celebrations too and was glad I'd made a contribution deemed worthwhile to the discussion.

'The same folk that were hingin' aboot the station the ither day, waitin' for His Majesty tae gang by on his wey tae Glesgae? Waitin' tae see whit colour frock the Queen had oan? Was it gonnae be white or was it gonnae be yella? Hopin' she'd catch a glimpse o' them an' mak their day. They same folk?'

'Aye...' I was suddenly unsure, my heart sinking. I knew when I was about to be ambushed by my father's cynicism.

'The same folk that had tae be moved oan efter an oor when they kent the royal train had went by oan the Breich line an' wasnae gaun through Blackrigg at a'?'

Davy and Jim started to laugh. Mother was trying hard but she couldn't control a snigger. She had heard about the disappointment in the Co-op earlier in the week, she said. Mrs Gow and the Widow MacAuley had been in high dudgeon at the back of the bread queue.

'The same folk that've hired yin o' Brogan's charabangs tae gang ogle at the oppressors when they visit their auld palace in Lithgae, in a week's time?' continued Alex.

Davy was bent double. He could hardly control himself.

My face must have been puce and I felt yon size.

'So much for freedom an' liberty, eh? The triumph o' the oppressor ower the oppressed, mair like. In a white frock an a'! Victory complete!' Alex slapped his hand down on the table.

'Leave John alane,' ordered my mother. 'It's no his fault folk are sae stupid.'

Davy got up, reached for his bunnet to go out. Before I knew it, he'd walloped me round the ears with it.

Mother gave a loud tut.

'See thon, laddie,' said Davy, pointing his bunnet in my direction as he opened the door. 'When thon laddie was born, they threw the wrang bit awa'!' He slammed the door and his laughter could be heard all the way down the street.

And I hear it yet all these years later, and I feel his scorn like a knife twisting in my stomach, even after all that has happened in between.

Chapter 11

Elizabeth

As a frequent visitor to the manse, Ernest Black became a fixture in my life soon after my arrival in the village. We did not spend much time in each other's company because he was there to speak with my brother about matters pertaining to the school. But even without the insight that lengthy conversation brings, I soon decided that I much admired his wisdom, brought on by years of careful study and contemplation. From time to time, he would leave a text for me to read and it was through these readings more than any other method of communication that I came to know Ernest Black as a man of honour and independent mind. I would have liked to spend more time in his company, debating points of principle and philosophy but any discussion we had was limited to a brief interaction at the door or when I served him tea or supper in Richard's company. In great part, I looked forward to his visits because I felt he might be a positive and ameliorating influence on my brother's dour, unwavering interpretation of the Scriptures. I suppose I hoped he could turn him into a much kinder, more forgiving soul though I hoped in vain. I expect Ernest must have relished the opportunity for debate about theology, morality, and educational matters but I am sure he wondered at times whether Richard had ever read further than the end of the Old Testament.

On one such occasion – a few days before the engagement party – when I took tea into the study, the schoolmaster's glum face spoke of his disappointment at the minister's intransigence over the important matter he had just raised with him. As I discovered – though the detail was only made clear to me later – he had approached Richard, the newly appointed Chairman of the School Board, to enlist support in asking the parish council to agree to the provision of school meals for the children of striking miners should the latest dispute escalate, as it would in all likelihood by the end of the summer. Ernest had reminded him that the council's support of the children during the 1912 strike had been essential for their welfare, especially since the dispute had lasted two long months. Several families had been close to destitution by the time the men had returned to work and the children's suffering had been minimised by the kindness of the ratepayers on that occasion. However, Richard had argued vehemently against the proposal this time round. In his opinion, the previous strike had been prolonged by such misplaced charity and he did not believe it was the job of either the school board or the parish council to support one side of the dispute against the other since it smacked of political bias and favouritism. Ernest had been unable to demolish the minister's strongly constructed defence against the forces of dissent and anarchy that, he had claimed, were at work all around, at home and abroad. When he had started to quote from the Bible, specifically *Suffer the children to come unto me*, Ernest must have closed his eyes in despair, realising that he was on a hiding to nothing and would be better to approach other members of the board and the parish council in support of his proposal.

When I showed him to the door, he seemed quite down-hearted and I could not help but apologise on my brother's behalf. I encouraged him to pursue his mission and not to give up, and I resolved to find a way to help bring matters to a successful conclusion if I could. That instance sticks in my mind as a seminal moment, not only because of the impact my resolution would have much later on Ernest and myself, but also because of the way Richard looked at me from the study once his visitor had gone.

Such anger!

I had picked up the morning's mail from the mat – something he liked to do himself – and he grabbed the letters out of my hand with indescribable malice. Without thinking I swiped them back, selected the envelope addressed to me, and threw the rest at him before marching into the parlour where I wept like a child – but only briefly. Though every confrontation cost me dear at the time, it was another small step forward in the battle for myself.

I leaned with my back against the parlour door and opened the long-awaited invitation to Phee's garden party. As I placed the card behind the carriage clock on the mantelpiece, I swithered about whether to keep it to myself and have Richard guessing who had written to me but, since he wasn't being invited, it gave me considerable satisfaction to place it in full view. He had already grilled me for information about the celebration, clearly expecting to receive a personal invitation, so he would be upset at being excluded from one of the main events in the Blackrigg social calendar. But what did he expect? He wasn't exactly welcoming when Phee came to see me at the manse. Did he really think that being a minister of the church brought an entitlement to loyalty from those he treated badly?

When I think back to that time, I realise how much Sarah's happy disposition and down to earth outlook kept my own view of life on track. Somehow, without knowing the detail of her employers' differences, she always said the right thing and helped me keep my troubles in perspective when Richard was at his worst and I was at my lowest, about to fall into the abyss. For all the material poverty of her circumstances, Sarah was gentle, kind and constant; her hopeful outlook was firmly rooted in her upbringing, it seemed, and I understood something of where this came from when I made my next visit to the Rows – to meet Sarah's stepmother who happened to be a skilled dressmaker.

That morning the Graham home was devoid of children. The older ones had been tasked with looking after the infants and had taken them for a walk. Jean Graham had only just finished scrubbing the floor of her small home and was sitting on a wooden chair at the door, unaware of my approach in the company of Sarah. She sat with a cup of water, wiping the sweat from her brow, engaged in a shouted conversation with several other women up and down the row. The fine weather permitted the mid-morning break from their labours to be taken in the open air, and the gentle southerly wind had temporarily removed the stench from the closets. Sarah claimed you got used to the smell, when you had stayed in the Rows long enough, but when the wind blew in the right direction you were always aware of the difference it made.

The women seemed taken aback when they realised I was there in their midst but not a toothless Mags Cherrie who stood in the middle of the street, her baby of one week wrapped in a tartan shawl and secured firmly to her ample bosom. She cackled loudly as she related the details of her latest confinement. It was like shelling peas, she reckoned, the more practice you had the quicker you got. But, God, the pain never lessened! She looked down at the tiny bundle strapped to her chest, her eyes brimming over with love for the child. Another mouth to feed and prices going up all the time. Still, there might be more to come in the future, she confessed, winking in my direction. Who could tell? She counted herself blessed, however, much blessed by a large and happy family and wouldn't wish for things to be otherwise. Then she picked up her washing basket and bid good day to her neighbours. There were floors to sweep and windows to wash, she announced. Couldn't sit about gossiping all day. Her man brought home more dirt than all of her children put together, she declared, waddling off, laughing all the while.

Inside the Graham home, Jean agreed to take on the challenge of transforming an old-fashioned dress of mine – an extravagant purchase made in haste – into something worthy of a grand affair at the Big House. She ordered me through to the back room to put it on. Sarah went ahead of me, proudly pointing out the built-in bed she shared with her elder sister, and the other beds where the boys slept top-to-tail and the girls kept each other warm under the window. She saw me looking around the cramped space she shared with eight children and an elder sister when she was home from the farm where she worked.

'This is ma hame, Miss. This is where I bide.'

'It's a happy home, Sarah,' I told her. I could tell.

When she left the room, I put on the dress but I could hardly bear the feel of the fabric as soon as it touched my skin. The tiny glass beads, sown delicately into the bodice and across the arms, glinted in the daylight penetrating through the small window. I gently lifted the tiers of soft tulle that made up the overskirt to examine the intricate pattern of embroidery around the edges. I deeply regretted visiting the Rows with such a fine garment but here I was, and there was nothing that could be done about it now. How thoughtless I'd been, to bring the dress here and rub their noses in it.

Jean appeared at the door with a box of pins in her hand, wondering what was taking me so long. She found me close to tears.

I looked down at the dress and then at Jean. 'I'm sorry. I shouldn't have come.'

'Nothin' tae be sorry aboot, Miss. I'll charge ye the goin' rate.'

Jean Graham was a cup-half-full kind of person, happy with her lot. She did not resent what others had just because she didn't have the same. She had more than enough to compensate for the lack of a pretty gown.

On the day of the party, I stood at the kitchen table wrapping my engagement present to Phee: a botanical drawing of honeysuckle created by my own fair hand. I did not have funds at my disposal to compete with the expensive gifts that she would no doubt receive from her family and old school friends so I had opted for a very personal and unique present of my own making. With professional framing the drawing had been shown to good effect and, as it disappeared into the white and silver wrapping paper, I hoped that Phee would appreciate it and understand its significance. Richard, of course, criticised my choice, saying that I was vain to think that a sketch from my own hand made a suitable gift – even if it was coloured and labelled with great care and accuracy to the same standard as any of the drawings he had seen in libraries and botanical gardens.

Sarah, on the other hand, praised it to the hilt, marvelling over my rendering of the pink and yellow flowers in various stages of maturity along a slender, winding stem embellished with rich green leaves. She read the labels out loud, *Lonicera or Honeysuckle; leaves opposite: oval to elliptical; five long stamens; round, twining stems; red berry, poisonous.*

Then she whispered, 'Honeysuckle... *the bonds of love...* in the secret language o' flooers, Miss.'

Sarah had remembered that day by the Avon, the day of the Sabbath School Trip four years before, when I had told the girls about the secret language of flowers used by the Victorians. The girls, in turn, had told Neil Tennant, much to his amusement and my embarrassment. I smiled at the memory, glancing out at my garden as I reminisced. It looked wonderful in the heat of that sunny afternoon.

The doorbell clanged. Sarah rushed to open it. I patted my hair at the back where she had swept it up into a tortoiseshell clasp for me, then I took a quick look at my dress. Mrs Graham had made an excellent job of the alterations. It fitted perfectly at the top and was exactly the right length. I lifted the hem a fraction and examined my grey shoes and stockings before putting on a pair of summer gloves in matching lace. I decided to carry my hat rather than wear it and made my way into the hall where Donald Maclean stood waiting.

'You look beautiful, Elizabeth,' he said with a warm smile. He held out his arm for me to take.

'It's kind of you to collect me, Donald,' I said, nervously slipping my hand into the crook of his arm.

'It's a pleasure, Miss Fraser, truly a pleasure,' he replied. 'Auntie's waiting outside. And we picked up Dr Matheson and his daughter on the way.'

'Rose?'

'Yes, Miss Rose Matheson. I believe you are good friends.'

'How wonderful!' I said. 'I think I'm going to enjoy today even more than I realised!'

I gave Sarah a huge smile as I left the manse on the arm of Donald Maclean.

It was a pity that Richard had been too busy to wish me well or even to greet Donald and show him some common courtesy.

Judging by the laughter we could hear on arrival at Parkgate, the party was already in full swing in the gardens on the far side of the house. Donald helped Mrs Maclean out of the front passenger seat then drove off to park the car by the stable block at the back, as instructed by a servant. The elderly butler, Jameson, stood in pole position to greet guests and relieve us of the gifts we had brought for the happy couple. He led us into the drawing room where Isabelle was busy welcoming everyone on behalf of the family. She had done her best to persuade family members to assist her in meeting guests as they arrived but, evidently, they had flown the coop, leaving her to soldier on and keep up appearances which she was only too delighted to do. She encouraged us to help ourselves to some champagne from the silver trays set out on the sideboard and explained that we would find everyone in the garden if we cared to go out through the French doors onto the terrace.

A large white marquee had been set up on the south lawn, providing a base for the musicians and shade, if required, for the partygoers. Garlands of flowers trimmed the entrance, lines of bunting stretched out in all directions, and large urns overflowed with summer blooms. Parkgate House, the seat of the Melville family, looked splendid and Isabelle was well pleased with the results of a few short weeks of fervent planning.

In the run-up to the day of the party, she had fretted that the weather might soon deteriorate back to its normal state. The cold, dreich grey of an average Blackrigg summer never showed the Melville estates off to good effect, in her opinion. Situated at a relatively high altitude, the lands of Rashiepark were testimony to the toil of generations of farmers who had dug away the peat and made soil where none had existed before, planting shelter belts against the winds, to eke a living out of a harsh landscape. Acres of bog and moss had proved impossible to tame, however, and the bleak wastes of the Black Moss, held in check by Paddy's Wood, remained a highly visible landmark that was not to everyone's taste. However, the pleasant weather that had greeted the house guests when they alighted at the railway station persuaded even those who'd visited in the past that this was a delightful place of green fields and pleasant woods; the wild romantic wilderness kept at bay, far off and shimmering in the sunshine. The Perthshire cousins from the land of mountain and flood found Rashiepark tranquil – the moorland soft and gentle compared to the rocky precipices and tumbling streams of home. The London-based family were glad to be out of the smoky city, leaving behind the frantic bustle of shops and traffic, for a short period of rejuvenation in the countryside. And the Hyslops, used to the high rolling hills and fertile plains of a Border landscape, admired the fishing beats and the shooting butts, and the productive pits which were carefully hidden from the house by the judicious planting of trees.

A vision in black and grey silk with a large feather clamped onto the side of her head by a jewelled clasp, Isabelle strolled the grounds, firmly attached to Charles Imrie. She introduced him as David's father-in-law, the owner of the highly successful Coal Company, drawing admiring glances from those in the know. From her position on his arm, she surveyed the partygoers who were conversing and laughing in small groups on the lawn or strolling in pairs along the network of garden walkways as they sipped their drinks whilst admiring the flower borders. When Phee and Eric were married later in the year, as they planned, the celebrations would need to be held in Edinburgh, Isabelle had decided. Probably St George's for the ceremony, and the North British for the wedding breakfast. Parkgate House could never look as good again as it did that sunny afternoon, and it would be a shame to spoil everyone's memory of a perfect day by trying to bring the same guests back there at the onset of a Scottish winter.

I settled with my good friend Rose Matheson into an arbour by the garden wall, enjoying the shade and relative peace and quiet away from the music and the constant chattering of voices. Rose had admired my dress earlier, reminding me of the day we had spent shopping together. I said that I was glad I had taken the plunge and made the purchase when I had, even though it had taken a substantial chunk out of my limited savings. It had saved me a great deal of trouble when it came to choosing something to wear. I glanced at Rose's plain attire: a simple black ankle-length skirt and a pale-pink cotton blouse with long mutton-sleeves and high necked, without frills or embellishments of any kind apart from a neat tie of grey striped fabric held at the neck with a gold pin. Rose saw me looking.

'I know what you're thinking,' she said. 'No frills or flounces, even on an occasion such as this?'

'Yes. But I'm not criticising you for it,' I replied.

'I don't have the time, or the inclination these days. Another year or so and I'll be fully qualified – a practising doctor. I spend most of my time on my studies, and at the hospital. And I volunteer once a week supporting Dr Inglis and Dr MacDougall who do great work, offering care to poor women. I so admire what they do.'

'You found your vocation then, Rose?'

'Funny how things turn out, isn't it, Beth? The last time I was here, I was quite a different person altogether.'

I studied my friend as she stared off across the garden to the house. Was she reliving previous visits she had made there in her younger, less experienced days? Her long dark hair wound down her back in a loose plait and a straw boater shaded her grey eyes from the brightness of the sun. I could still see that younger Rose – her pink cheeks and full mouth with its ever-present, pleasant smile – but there was also a hint of sadness in the shadows around her eyes. I followed her gaze across the lawn to where David Melville stood conversing, his heavily pregnant wife on his arm.

'You don't regret the path your life's taken then?' I asked, guessing what the answer was going to be regardless of the truth of the matter.

'Hardly! Can you see me in Catherine's shoes? No, she's welcome to her role as wife and mother-to-be.'

I could have seen you in that role at one time, I thought, remembering when Rose and David had been romantically linked. I had seen something in David Melville's face when he had greeted Rose earlier, something that he had found impossible to hide; whilst Rose had responded cordially, unwilling or unable to look at him directly.

'Things often turn out for the better,' she mused, still following David with her eyes as he mingled with the guests. 'Eventually,' she conceded after a long pause.

'Phee's life took a sudden turn,' I began, changing the subject. 'She seems very happy with Eric, or *Captain Hyslop,* as she calls him.'

'They're well suited... and he seems to adore her... which is a good start,' agreed Rose. 'I suppose something told her he was the one. All those years waiting for Arthur Moffat and suddenly she takes the plunge with the dashing Eric. Good for her, I say. Following her heart... in a completely different way from me, of course... but she's made a choice and she's following it through.'

'I hope they'll be happy together. It's funny though, I never ever saw Phee as the marrying kind, to be honest. Too high spirited and wilful. But there you go.'

Rose turned to look at me directly. 'And you, Miss Fraser? What about you? I've seen how the delectable Donald Maclean's been following you around all afternoon! Do you have something to tell me?'

I blushed severely. 'Absolutely not!'

'Do you see him, Beth? Up on the terrace?' she teased. 'He's looking over in your direction right now, even whilst pursued by voluptuous Violet from Perthshire. Look!' She gave a wave and Donald waved back. 'Look, Beth! Look!'

I couldn't look. 'Stop it,' I pleaded. Then after a long pause, 'But he is very nice, I have to admit.'

We gave each other a hug.

'Let's go and find Phee, shall we?' Rose suggested. 'She's been stuck to her captain like glue, all afternoon. Let's prise her away from him for a bit. They've got their whole lives ahead of them, after all. Surely she can spare her old friends a few minutes of her time!'

An afternoon of canapés and drinks on the lawn merged seamlessly into a light supper buffet served in the marquee as the shadows lengthened. Isabelle, no doubt, prayed that the subject of the recent security scare around Parkgate would not raise its ugly head to spoil the day. However, it was inevitable when Roger Stone arrived on the scene, bandaged and wheelchair bound, and pushed onto the terrace for all to see by David who had decided that his factor should come down from his room to join the party. Mr Imrie assured everyone that there was nothing to worry about. He had personally appointed several good men to see to security around the grounds.

As the guests tucked into the magnificent spread provided, washed down by fine wine, thoughts of the criminal classes couldn't have been further from their minds. Conversations revolved around the frivolous: fashions, travel, mishaps of all kinds (especially relating to fashion and travel); motor cars and trivial pursuits such as bridge and tennis; and more serious topics, namely farming matters, politics, industrial relations, and the rise and (especially in the current climate) fall of share prices in rubber and other commodities.

'Talking of fashion misadventure, Isabelle,' called out a London cousin, twice removed, after an afternoon of too much fruit punch, 'Where on earth did you acquire your get-up?'

Conversation ceased and many heads turned in Isabelle's direction.

'I said,' continued the cousin, much more loudly this time, 'Where the hell did you get that bloody disaster of a frock you're wearing, Isabelle?! And what's that on your head? Something dead by the looks of it!'

No amount of shooshing could turn back the clock. The words were out and Isabelle had heard. She looked hurt but drew herself up to her full height as she patted the feathered concoction in her hair.

'Are you going to a funeral, my dear?' slurred the cousin before Isabelle could cut the woman dead. 'I've seen less black silk on a horse-drawn hearse, for the Love of God! It's supposed to be a bloody party!'

'This garment,' began Isabelle, hiding her fury as best she could, 'has come straight from Paris, I'll have you know, Maud! This season BLACK is in vogue. Don't think we don't know anything about fashion up here in the sticks when we have the finest of department stores and emporia on our doorstep, only a train ride away from here in Glasgow, second city of the Empire.'

No one quite knew where to look and toyed instead with the salmon mousse. Maud was being very rude but, given the severity of Isabelle's costume, she possibly did have a point.

Maud blew a drunken raspberry and several guests couldn't help but snigger.

'You may laugh,' retorted Isabelle, holding her head high like a ruffled black swan, 'But according to Miss Fitt of Les Modes de Paris in Sauchiehall Street you'll all be wearing black by the end of the summer! Mark my words!'

The more superstitious in the audience looked horrified, as if someone had walked over their grave. Phee gave a small squeal, rolled her eyes upwards then hurried over to the musicians who had paused between sets.

'Do start up again soon,' she pleaded. 'Before they start throwing the jelly at each other!'

Eating, drinking, and conversation soon got underway again and the spat between Maud and Isabelle was put to one side. Phee and Eric took time to work their way around the assembly, thanking everyone for their good wishes and kind gifts, and for gracing the occasion with their company. It had been such a lovely day, one they promised never to forget. When asked if they had set a date, they remained coy but admitted that they hoped to be married before the year was up. People would find out in due course! They hoped everyone had enjoyed themselves at the party and explained that dancing in the marquee would begin in about an hour, leaving time to freshen up in preparation for the marathon ahead.

Mrs Maclean wished Phee every happiness in her future life with handsome Captain Hyslop. He looked like such a nice young man, reminding her of her younger days when she had first met her own husband. All at once, she became quiet and confessed she was rather tired. She gently patted Phee's hand, said she didn't want to spoil the party but hoped that Donald might take her home quite soon. Dr Matheson agreed that old age didn't come itself, and if he could be dropped off in Rowanhill after Mrs Maclean had been returned to Whinbank then he would be most grateful. Donald got up to leave, courteous as ever, saying that he would fetch the car round to the main door in a few minutes, reassuring Rose and myself that he would be back promptly and we could dance the night away for as long as we wished. He would make sure to take us both home at the end of the night.

No one could have missed the fact that he was smiling at me as he said it.

Chapter 12

John

In a fankle of black scrub, the ruined mill stood silhouetted against the gloaming like a solitary jagged tooth in an old crone's mouth. Dark shadows lengthened around the fringe of stunted trees and bushes by the burn. Rob was walking up ahead into the brilliant orange glow that was melting outwards across the sky but I hung back. He slowed down, looked round, back and forward along the path. He squinted through the wind-hewn hedgerow below the cottages up on the ridge, seemed to be scouting the riverbank for folk who might be about.

The loud calls of startled birds above the rush of the stream were the only sounds.

Then I saw him part an opening in a dense curtain of bramble, duck low and disappear out of sight.

So that was their hidey-hole, I guessed, more sure than ever that my friend had been drawn into something beyond his control. I decided to return later and have a look for myself.

Though the days were warm, the nights could be cold with no cloud to keep in the heat of the daylight hours. And so it proved. I sat shivering under the bridge to Back o' Moss with the sounds of the burn loud in my ears, grating on my nerves while I waited. From my place on the opposite bank, I had a good view of the mill. My mind filled with the surge of the river, a hundred rushing thoughts and questions till I could wait no longer, praying it was late enough to enter without being seen.

Dipping through the veil of bramble, I was confronted with a stone wall that offered no obvious way in. It towered above my head towards the starlit sky. I had no option but to wrap an arm round the end of the wall and dig my fingers into a slot between two blocks of stone, taking all my weight in my hands before swinging round over the flowing water whilst hoping for the best. Momentum pulled me into the ruined building where shadow and damp emptiness awaited. I crouched on the ground, stared into the blackness, letting my eyes adjust, listening to the squeal of the bats in the broken rafters. Though I worked in similar conditions, I was half-scared to death without the closeness of my workmates and the familiar sounds of the pit. When I was sure nobody else was about, I scrambled over a tumble of stone into the small dark lair that was concealed from the outside world. Only then did I dare light the inch of candle I had brought in my pocket. I could only imagine the scene when Rob had visited earlier, the failing light of the setting sun penetrating the holes in the roof, down into the dank depths where Davy and his cronies must have been waiting; each face a skull, gaunt and pale in the shadows, staring back at him.

I moved around the inner sanctum of their den, shadows circling me and my small light. No sign of a fire – the smoke would alert passers-by; cigarette ends ground into the floor; an empty bottle of whisky and the broken glass from countless others smashed in fury and intoxication.

High up in a recess in one wall was a single leather boot. It sat like an ornament on a mantelpiece, a trophy awarded for some sporting triumph maybe, or something more sinister. I held it, touched the studs along the sole, felt the softness of the leather. On the ground, half hidden among the dirt and the pigeon droppings, lay a cap. I picked it up, sensed the love of the mother who had bought it for her son, and saw the name sewn into the crown: *Andrew Brownlee*.

Andra. Brother, son, scholar, right back with two left feet, and good friend. Patient of the Royal Infirmary.

I knew exactly what Davy would have said about the boot. *Braw leather. Fine for them that's got the money tae pey for sic things.*

Did they give the boy a second thought? *Broken jaw, broken nose an' ribs, bleedin' in his belly – internal. Severe bruisin' near enough a' place an' a broken wrist. Gey near lost the sicht in yin e'e but it'll come back, they're sayin'.*

Had they meant to go that far? Maybe a bit of roughing up had gone further than intended.

Aye, mebbe.

And what had Rob to say about it? I couldn't believe he'd been part of the violence. But he seemed to be involved, somehow. And he had been there in the mill earlier so he knew something of what the gang were up to.

What did my brother want with somebody like Rob Duncan who surely wasn't like the rest, had a mind of his own. Davy would have enjoyed bringing him into the fold, I decided, more than he had done with any of the others for whom crime brought its own reward. Corrupting the boy would have been sweet, sullying an innocent whose only flaw was... what? Frustration... or anger... wanting more out of life than the pit had to offer?

Was that it, Rob? I mouthed my question into the same darkness where he had been with the gang, as if he was still there.

I reflected on how the dispute over pay and conditions was continuing to simmer. Earlier, Steeny Simpson had dropped into the house for a word with my father. As predicted, the coal masters had waited until the pits went on holiday before announcing their response to the union's proposal.

'Whit have they said?' asked Davy, impatient as ever.

'They're no havin' it,' Steeny replied. 'But wait for it... They've put in anither request tae the Board... for a FURTHER reduction in the daily rates... this time doon fae seven bob tae 6/6d. Can ye believe it?'

'I can believe it a' right. Evil bastards,' Davy had said.

'Has the union had time tae respond?' Alex asked.

'No. But I think they'll want tae proceed wi' the fower day week, wi' the threat o' a strike as a back up.'

Alex said, 'It'll drag oan a' summer. It's the stert o' the holidays. We'll no ken whaur we are for ages. Coorse, it's whit they want, tae keep us guessin' an put the fear o' God intae a'body.'

As I sat there in the foul smelling ruin, a monument to a time and a life that was long past, I recalled Davy's reaction to my father's words, the shadow that had fallen across his face, the anger that had burned in his eyes. I wondered how long he would wait for matters to be resolved.

And as I soon guessed, not long at all.

I ducked under the lintel of a doorway in the opposite direction from where I'd entered the mill. In the narrow space beyond, I edged past a stash of materials assembled by the gang, no doubt, during their robberies at various farms and industrial premises in recent weeks: a bolt of hessian, coils of rope and wire suitable for making tripwires, cans of paraffin and mineral oil, a hammer or two, a mallet, and a spade. I got down on all fours then pushed through a hole in the outer wall of the mill where others had gone before. I crawled under the low branches of scrub hiding me from the track that ran between the Doctor's Brae and the bridge to Back o' Moss, coming out like a fox from its den, making sure I wasn't seen. I walked smartly towards the brae in the darkness. Only then did I realise that my heart was thumping in my chest, like it was fit to burst.

I came across Rob by himself the following evening – Saturday it was. He was walking along Main Street with his hands in his pockets, looking bored. I stopped further along the street as he kicked a stray stone ahead of him, lifting it into the air with the toe of his boot. He was watching as it arched upwards, a leather football of his imagination that dropped precisely between fictional posts for another goal. *Goal!* he shouted at the deserted street, raising his clenched fists in the air. What was he thinking? That one day he might make it to a big game at Ibrox? Just now he had to content himself, make do with a local match because money was tight. The weekly Saturday fixture at Rowanhill was more than he could afford at times.

It wasn't fair to spy on him but he barely acknowledged me as I came into view. He made another shot at goal before he started his rant. One day he would have money in his pocket, he told me. Then he would have choices and the world would open up. Presently, his mother took all his wages, gave him a shilling or two to himself. She did the same to Sandy right enough so maybe he shouldn't feel so ill done by. She had rent to pay and food to put on the table. She was always complaining about the price of things, even coal. Yet the coal masters were arguing that the price of coal was low and that was why mineworkers' wages had to come down. How did that work? Eh? It was all relative, he supposed. When you lived near the breadline, small increases in the price of a loaf or the daily rates going down by as much as a threepenny-bit could have dire consequences for ordinary folk. But the masters hadn't a clue about what it was like to live like him and his family. The owners had more than enough but thought they needed more. Maggie needed clothes and boots at regular intervals; him and Sandy had to wait till there were a few shillings saved before they got anything so much as a new pair of drawers. Somehow, he fumed, as the elder son of a widowed mother, he'd acquired all of the disadvantages of marriage and none of the compensations. And he'd just about had enough of it!

Then he seemed to calm down for a bit as he told me how he'd thought about going to the Continuation Classes, held in the evening up at the school. But they had to be paid for up front and, anyway, he knew that he wouldn't be able to concentrate if he went. His heart wouldn't be in it. Not right then. Maybe later, when he felt more settled in his head. He'd been top of the class as a boy but had to leave the school when his father was killed down the pit. His mother had been broken hearted, not just about the death of her husband but about what it meant for her children who'd lost any chance to stay on in education and better themselves. She'd often told him and Sandy that they should strive for a better life, better than an existence in the damp, cramped Stoneyrigg Rows; going down the pit every day and never having anything extra at the end of the week. She'd told him often as a child there was something better out there and he'd believed her. Of course he knew it was true, she hadn't been lying, but the accident had taken away any chance of it coming his way. As the elder son he had to leave school, go down the pit to support the family, and it hadn't helped that his mother had just given birth to Maggie. Maybe that was why he resented the child so much, and his Ma as well – proud Peggy Duncan who got herself in the family way late in life and needed her sons to pay for her keep. It was her fault that he felt the way he did! She deserved the snash he gave her, barking at her, biting her head off when she tried to be nice to him which she ay was. He hated her for being so kind to him. Why couldn't she turn round and give him a thump like he deserved?

I stood with my hands in my pockets wondering how long Rob's anger had been simmering, yet I'd hardly noticed until recently. I understood some of it but not the way he blamed his mother and his sister for the life he had to live. They were hostages to fortune like the rest of us. Besides, I'd found myself quietly envious of Rob at times. He had a lot going for him and his family was well-liked in the village. It wasn't his mother's fault he'd gotten mixed up with Davy Birse and his motley crew. That was entirely his own doing, his own choice and, if I wasn't mistaken, he was deeply regretting it now.

Rob paused at the top of the Doctor's Brae, took another shot at goal, the Ibrox crowd chanting his name over and over in his mind. *Rob Duncan! Rob Duncan!* He missed completely the first time, tried again to no avail. The stone sat there, stubbornly unmoving, whilst the toe of his boot hit the ground hard, jarring his leg in the process. Tears filled his eyes. He bent over double, holding his hip, staring into the road.

He knew they were waiting for him – the gang – down by the river in the ruined mill with a new plan hatched out of Davy's anger and impatience, desperate to make a difference and bring about change, and what was called *justice for the working man*. That's how my brother would explain it, making virtue out of sin. The others were ne'er-do-weels, followers, content to make mischief at somebody else's direction, just for the hell of it.

Mischief?

Malevolence more like.

I pitied Rob for the torment I saw in his eyes. Did the image of Andrew Brownlee's broken body ever leave his mind? The broken nose oozing blood and wheezing snot; a swollen purple slit for an eye; lip bursting outwards like a piece of meat on a butcher's slab; brown hair congealed with blood; bruised limbs, red and blue and brown, the imprint of boots on Andrew's leg and on the downy softness of his innocent cheek.

'It haunts me,' he said, reading my mind. 'It's the first thing I see when I wake up in the mornin' an' the last afore I get tae sleep at night. If I sleep at a' that is. *He wasnae my freen but he wasnae my enemy either.* I hear they words in ma dreams an' when I wake up in a sweat, they're there in the pitch-black night.'

I knew he was walking down the brae towards a rendezvous with evil. Rob knew it too. Whatever Davy had next in mind could not be justified, even though the coal masters had upped the ante, looking for a confrontation. Maybe the owners wanted bother, an excuse to make them look whiter than white to the public. The ball was in their court because the pits belonged to them and they had the money to see out a strike. Their tails were up. Successful in their last request now they were looking for a further sixpence off the daily pay. No hint of a compromise to end the dispute, far from it! They had rejected the union's four-day week proposal but hadn't said what that might mean in practice. What would they do to stop the men implementing it? They were keeping everybody waiting because it suited their purpose. That way, the men would know and understand the power the owners wielded over their lives: the lives of ordinary folk like Rob and Davy, Alex, Steeny Simpson, the pals, and thousands of others. No wonder many were angry, hungry for a new order.

'Dinnae gang, Rob,' I called to him from where I stood at the top of the brae.

He stared back at me. He'd known all along, deep down, that Davy Birse's way was not Rob Duncan's way. He'd made a mistake when he'd let himself get drawn in with him. But there would be consequences if he didn't turn up at the mill to help with the latest plan.

'Whit dae you ken?' More a statement than a question.

'Dinnae gang,' I said again, knowing more than folk gave me credit for.

And in an instant, to my complete surprise, he turned tail and was marching back up the brae. He would have no more of it. Rob Duncan was better than that, he'd decided. Whatever the gang planned to do that night, they would have to do it on their own.

I followed him across Main Street, up Manse Lane and into the park. He leapt the stile and hurried up the path by the hedgerow to the head dyke. He climbed the wall before he looked back, casting his eye across the bog and the peat, the fields and the pits far below from where he'd come. The Red Burn snaked through the moss, the mill a dark blot by the deepest pool.

He had to hurry, he told me just as I came up beside him, breathing hard from the climb. He ran ahead through the sheep on the muir to where the hill curved downwards on the other side. He seemed to know the path well, as if he'd walked that way many times in the past.

'Gang hame, John,' he called back to me.

'Rob! Wait,' I shouted, the truth dawning at last.

But he wouldn't wait. He wasn't for listening. He was running down the top field to find her. He knew what he wanted. He wanted to make everything better. It would all be fine again, if only he could see her.

I sank into the grass and watched him run to her. He was going to find Minn and it made my heart sore.

Elizabeth

I became rather sombre after Donald left the party along with his aunt and Dr Matheson. That confused me, sitting there dressed up to the nines with laughter and good cheer all around. I decided perhaps I was missing Donald already but I knew, deep down, it was more than that.

'Shall we have another dance, Beth?' asked Rose as the music started up again. 'Donald seems to be taking rather a long time.'

'No thanks,' I replied, trying not to sound too melancholic. 'I like you very much, Rose, and you do a fabulous foxtrot but I don't relish dancing a waltz with you, thank you very much.'

Rose took the rejection in the spirit it was intended and laughed out loud.

'Glad you haven't lost your sense of humour,' she quipped.

I wandered away from the lights and noise of the marquee for a wicker armchair, one of several arranged in the middle of the lawn. I soon found myself staring at the place where a doorway in the beech hedge connected with the front of the house and the tree-lined avenue that led in from the main gate. When Donald Maclean returned, he would emerge from that same doorway, having parked the motor car at the back of the house. I stared at the shadows for what seemed like an age, willing him to reappear. The terrace was bright with electric light from the drawing room. Older guests who were feeling the cold had gathered there but there was no sign of Donald. My gaze returned to the corner of the house. The sky had darkened and the stars were coming through. I stared upwards, searching for the milky way – so vast and mysterious that butterflies fluttered inside me. It all seemed so fixed and permanent till a shooting star flashed across my vision and disappeared over the horizon.

Someone opened the wooden door in the hedge and my heart skipped a beat. As my eyes strained to see who it was, I asked myself if it truly was Donald that I hoped to see. Or someone else entirely.

Rose emerged from the marquee and joined me on the lawn. We didn't speak for a while.

'It's lovely to be here, don't you think?' I said at last. 'But I keep thinking about what's out there beyond the gates.'

Rose was listening.

'The food, the music, the house, the pleasant chatter about nothing of any consequence is... well, jolly good fun. I've loved being here in my nice dress... but how can I enjoy myself when I know that my scullery maid lives in two damp rooms with a dozen members of her family? And old Mrs Pow, half deranged because of the loss of her grandson, is only a step away from the poorhouse?'

'I know lots of Mrs Pows, Beth,' began Rose. 'You should see the living conditions in parts of our capital city. Huge change is coming, you can be sure of that. People like you and me will see to it... because our eyes have been opened and they won't be closed again. Yes, it is lovely to be here and celebrate with Phee but you can't turn your back on what's out there, beyond the boundary wall. There's a lot of work to be done and we'll do our bit.'

'If we get the chance.'

'We will take the chance. We have to make our own choices in life. No one else should do it for us.'

I smiled in admiration at my good friend: purposeful, intelligent Rose who would soon be a practising doctor in her own right. Strong women like Rose were showing the world what women were capable of. They were an inspiration to others, not just in what they were achieving but that they were achieving it in the face of centuries of opposition and entrenched opinion against women having choices and making their own decisions. I felt privileged to be Rose's friend, resolved to meet up with her again in the near future to learn from her, and gather ideas to benefit the people of the village. Perhaps Rose could take me to the Hospice where she volunteered, and I could see the good work being done there for myself. But right at that moment, I felt it would be an imposition to grill her about her experiences. She deserved a break and time to relax. Besides, the music was soft, the stars were bright and the night was still young.

I gazed across the lawn at the large dark edifice of Parkgate House, the ground floor and the terrace lit up and alive with partygoers; servants hurrying back and forth with trays of food and drinks to keep them happy; laughter rippling outward from the marquee.

Then suddenly, 'Fireworks!' called a voice. 'Look, fireworks!'

We stared at the roof of the house as the sky exploded with colour. Emerging from the marquee, curious dancers stared upwards in awe. They showed their appreciation in a chorus of ooing and aahing accompanied by a flutter of applause.

David Melville barged through the small crowd followed by Phee and Isabelle. They stared upwards too, mouths open in horror.

'It's not fireworks!' called David. 'Keep back everyone! Eric! Eric! Come with me!'

The gathering stood stunned by what they were seeing. The bright colour had become a flickering orange glow and thick smoke billowed upwards from somewhere at the back of the house. Something was seriously amiss. Several men ran after David and Eric who quickly disappeared around the corner, heading to the back of the house.

'Oh dear,' whimpered Isabelle. 'Nothing to fret about, I'm sure. Let's go back in! Please!' she urged, trying to regain control. 'Maestro! Play on!'

Rose turned to me. 'Stay here, Beth. Look after Phee. I'd better see what's up, in case someone's been hurt!'

I stood helpless in the middle of the lawn, the well-planned order of the celebration evaporating into chaos around me. No one seemed sure about the best course of action – to stay on the grass or hide in the house which might well be about to go up in flames. Suddenly, I could only think of Donald. Had he been caught up in what was amiss? How selfish I had been to let him go off without warning him about the dangers he might meet, especially when he drove back through the night all alone. And for my sake!

I ran off after Rose, around the side of the house, through the rowans and the rhododendrons. The sounds of panic and confusion reverberated through the night.

A number of figures, silhouetted against the brightness of burning vehicles, were dashing around in the mayhem. Thick, acrid smoke billowed out from the gaping hole that had been the garage and a car was still burning in the middle of the yard. I barely recognised it as the one that had brought me there earlier in the evening. Now the seats were on fire, the soft leather top had melted away and it was fast becoming a burned-out shell.

But where was Donald?

David and Eric were taking control of the situation, organising servants into a line to pass buckets of water from the pump across the yard to where they were needed. A shocked-looking Billy Dodds, the family chauffeur, operated the handle of the pump, his mouth and his eyes open wide as he took in the enormity of what had transpired. Eric quickly joined a young man who was busy at the stables, leading each horse one by one, away from the noise and the smoke, and releasing them into the lower paddock, out of harm's way. Panicked with fear, a mare with a foal, her motherly instincts spiked out of control, was making difficult work of it.

Rose, I saw, was standing back surveying the scene for casualties, trying not to add to the difficulties faced by the rescuers. At first, there didn't appear to be anyone in need of assistance but she was waiting in any case. It was touch and go whether the fire would spread to the house or not, and any one of the vehicles lined up round the yard could explode into flames if the heat of the fire wasn't dowsed and brought under control. Then Rose caught sight of a figure lying on the ground near the paddock. He lay still, holding his arm, looking shocked.

'Donald? It's me – Rose,' I heard her say. 'What on earth happened here?'

She kneeled down to take a look at his injuries, adjusting her position to see better by the light from the flames behind her. She looked into his eyes. 'How are you feeling? Does anything hurt?'

My heart leapt with a relief close to joy when I heard him speak.

'Just a bit stunned, I think. There was an explosion then I found myself on the ground. It happened in an instant. I can't believe what......' He lay back and closed his eyes.

Rose felt carefully along the length of Donald's arm, the one he held awkwardly across his body. 'Looks like you've broken your fore arm. But that's easily fixed. Move your fingers for me.' She quickly felt along the length of his legs asking if he had pain anywhere else. His chest? His neck or head? 'Can you move your legs for me?'

Donald moved each leg in turn. He said his neck felt a bit stiff but he could move his head around without too much difficulty. Rose continued her examination, gently pressing the vertebrae along the length of his neck and spine.

At last, she decided that his arm had taken the worst of it.

'When things die down, I'll have you moved to somewhere with a better light and we'll fix the arm. You've a few grazes and a nasty cut on your brow. No burns of any great significance, not that I can see at the moment. A little singeing of your lovely locks but nothing that'll cause you any real difficulty.' She took another look at his eyes.

'Thank you, Rose. Thank you so much. I feel so much better just having you here.' He lifted his good arm and grasped her hand.

'I'm glad to hear it,' she quipped, replacing his hand where it helped to support his broken arm. 'All that medical training hasn't been for nothing then?'

Donald sank back into the grass and glanced across at the fire fighting. Pails of water sloshed along the line to David and Eric who aimed the water at the heart of the fire, as best they could.

'How did you get all the way over here, Donald?' Rose asked, concerned. 'Did you crawl on that arm?'

He shook his head then grimaced. 'Nope. A lad came along and dragged me out of harm's way, just in time by the looks of things.'

The fire in Murdo's car had finally burned out. It stood, a smoking metal frame and little else, where Donald had driven to a halt only minutes before. He looked upwards, remembering what had happened in those few seconds when he had braked by the open garage before Armageddon had erupted. Two men had been lurking in the undergrowth, he said. It was coming back to him. He would let the constabulary know when the time came but he hadn't had a good enough look at them to be able to describe them, he was sure.

Just then, a call went up and there seemed to be a commotion of some kind. Rose promised to be right back and ran to see what it was.

I had watched in admiration as she examined her patient. How level-headed she had been, how clinical yet... kind. I had stood back in the darkness letting her do her work, praying Donald would be alright and wasn't suffering. I took Rose's place beside him and held his hand, brushed my fingers through his sandy-blond hair and looked deep into his eyes.

'I'm here, Donald. Don't worry,' I said. 'I'll look after you.'

I could see he was in pain. I kissed his hand and held it tight.

The yard was a scene of carnage – flames and smoke – and a hive of activity. Eric had erected a ladder against the wall, called for water to be sent up to him in order to douse the low roof of the stable block and prevent the fire from spreading to the main building.

David led from the front. 'Keep going, we'll get there!' he shouted. 'Faster at the pump, men!'

'More water up here,' shouted Eric from the top of the ladder.

'Keep it up at the pump!' shouted David. 'We've got to keep going!'

'Get me an axe!' ordered Eric.

An axe was thrown up at him on the ladder. He hacked at the smoking roof, hurled pieces of wood down into the yard below. One or two burst into flame momentarily but were soon dowsed and made safe.

Then David was shouting, 'Get it off him! Hurry up for God's sake!"

Rose was standing by: a calm, slender figure outlined against the glow of the flames. Four or five men surrounded one of the stout garage doors, splintered down one edge by the blast. They lifted it upwards, out of the way.

A blackened body lay perfectly still on the ground.

I craned my neck to see what was what. Whispered enquiries went back and forth. Rose was crouched low beside the body but she was shaking her head.

Who was it, people were saying? Did anybody know who it was?

It took a further thirty minutes of dowsing before they were satisfied that the fire was out and would not reignite, to spread to the rest of the house where it could cause unspeakable devastation. The roof of the stable block – the part that housed the garage – had been destroyed but the buildings around about had been saved, and there was no obvious damage to the house itself beyond the black soot on the walls of the older part of the house where tongues of flame and clouds of smoke had licked upwards at the height of the blaze. It was fortunate that so many people had been on hand to contribute to the fire fighting. David expressed his heartfelt thanks to all in attendance. Several servants sat on the grass recovering from their considerable efforts, eyes wide as the enormity of the calamity that had just been averted hit home. Billy Dodds lay prostrate and inconsolable on the ground, sweat marks down his sooty face and patterning his uniform. All he could say was that it was his fault; it might not have happened if he hadn't taken so long over his supper and had been on hand to keep an eye on things.

Burly members of the security staff soon put in an appearance saying the constabulary had arrived at the front gate. They had ordered a sweep of the grounds. No one was allowed to leave until everyone present had accounted for their movements.

As I knelt on the ground holding Donald's hand, I saw a young man who looked familiar walk across to the charred body lying on the gravel. He stood looking at the dead man's burnt face and soot-covered limbs. Blood glistened from wounds to the hands and forehead, and a foot had been blown off in the explosion. The young man altered his position this way and that, and eventually hunkered down for a better look.

'Do you know who he is?' David asked.

'Aye,' he replied, his voice hoarse.

Constable Mackay and a colleague appeared. 'Weel then, Rob Duncan. Can we have a name?'

'Grubb. His name's Jimmy Grubb.'

'A freen o' yours, is he?' asked Mackay.

'Naw. He's nae freen o' mine,' Rob replied.

'So how come ye ken 'im?'

'Cause he works in the same pit as me. He's a lodger in the Middle Raw, close-by whaur I bide.'

Mackay was sceptical. 'Nae ither reason? Like ye mebbe cam here thegither, tae cause bother.'

'Naw. Nae ither reason.'

'So, what are you doing here in any case, young man?' asked David, becoming suspicious, realising this was a pit worker rather than a member of his staff.

Rob Duncan didn't have time to reply. The two security men sweeping the grounds at the back of the house had returned, shoving two others ahead of them. They were pushed forward, their heads bowed, unable to look at the body on the ground. Mackay asked for their names saying they looked familiar though they hadn't come to his attention previously for the wrong reasons, as far as he could remember.

'Hugh Bone.'

'Malky Moran.'

'Dae ye ken the deceased?' Mackay braced himself

'Aye. It's James Grubb.'

'Did ye come wi' him... wi' the intention o' committin' arson?'

'Naw,' the two said together. They were indignant.

Bone began. 'We cam tae see whit we could lift... ye ken, thieve. We had a quick look then hid in the bushes, waitin' oor chance. But Jimmy went richt in b' hissel. Next thing we ken, Woosh! The place is in flames.'

'Thievin'? No arson?' asked Mackay.

'Naw, thievin' jist. It's been an accident but no oan oor pairt, oan Jimmy's.'

In horror, Bone turned his face from the body on the ground.

Mackay studied the two accomplices and then Rob Duncan. His eyes narrowed.

Rob bristled.

'An' are ye acquainted wi' Mr Duncan here, the pair o' ye?'

'We ken whau he is,' replied Moran. 'Bides in Staney.'

'An' did he come wi' yer wee gang, tae rob the Melvilles?'

'Naw, he didnae. Ye'll need tae ask him why he's here. But he didnae come wi' us.' Bone gave Rob Duncan a black look, a look that could kill in other circumstances.

'This is a gey funny business this,' said the police officer smoothing down his moustache with a big hand. 'We'll tak the three o' ye in fur questionin'. Bone, Moran, an' Duncan. Ye can spend the nicht in the cells, till we're feenished here. We'll tak a guid look in case there's onie mair o' yer pals lurkin' aboot.'

The suspects were marched off to a vehicle waiting on the road, by the gates to the house. Mackay turned to the laird and a discussion ensued about the possibilities of the men having been involved in a deliberate arson attack, in the light of the laying of tripwires on Rashiepark land back in June. The police officer assured David that he would get to the bottom of the matter when he interviewed the threesome at the police station later that night. It could be that the deceased had indeed had an unfortunate accident with flammable materials stored in the garage. The presence

229

of Mr Duncan was something of a mystery, however. Either his accomplices were covering for him, or he had been up to no good on his own. Perhaps it had just been a coincidence that Grubb, Moran, and Bone were there at the time, though it seemed unlikely. Mr Mackay declared himself not to be a great believer in coincidences.

As Rob Duncan disappeared through the trees ahead of his captors, I thought of his mother and what this would mean to her. I knew her to be a good woman who worked hard for her family in unfortunate circumstances. How would she take the news that her boy was spending the night in police custody? Surely Peggy's son could not be mixed up in something so insidious?

David thanked Mackay for his prompt attendance, asked for reassurance that the constabulary would be thorough in its investigations but, to his credit, he also asked that the earlier behaviour of Mr Duncan be borne in mind when his character and motives were being assessed. The Duncan lad had been helping to rescue the horses from their stables when the fire first took hold, and had done a sterling job on the pump when Billy Dodds had flagged. It seemed unlikely that a guilty man would hang around at the scene of the crime, only to be apprehended later. To which Mackay gave a snort. In his opinion that was exactly what a guilty man would do, having been seen by witnesses. Had he run off, it would have looked suspicious whereas this way he could play the hero.

Either way, he assured the laird, Constable Archibald Fergus Mackay would get to the truth, no matter what.

Chapter 13

Minn

I've been sent inside from the fields to help in the farmhouse. Mrs Gowans doesn't keep awful well, not since the start of the war. She takes to her bed without warning, doctor's orders, and it's usually me who's sent in by to help out. I can turn my hand to most things and it's good to get out of the wind and the rain when it's lashing but I prefer to be in the open air if I can help it. I feel like it's where I belong, where I'm happiest. More than a day being cooped up like an old hen is too much for me. I could go doolally.

I get on fine with Maisie, the maid. She knows I'm a good worker. It's baking day so I've left her to get on with making tea bread in the kitchen while I do the work in the house. I've stoked the fires and filled the coal scuttles, and I've taken the carpets out for a beating. I'll give them an extra twa-three minutes just because it keeps me outside for a bit longer. I have to say I always feel a bit nervous when I'm sent inside but as long as Daisy Gowans isn't at home I get on with the work no bother. Daisy is Mrs Gowans' second daughter. She's the same age as me. In fact, we were at the school thegither. If I'm honest, I was a wee bit jealous of Daisy when we were younger because

I thought she had her eye on Rob – well she did for a while – but that was before he had to leave the school to support his family.

When I was working at Netherside, I didn't see her for long enough until the day of the big party when I was sent to the Big House to help out. It was a fine morning and I was glad to be going to Parkgate for a change from my normal routine. It always seemed an exciting place to me. My big sister, Nell, was in service there and I loved to hear her stories. Anyway, I was walking through the wood – Paddy's Wood – between Netherside and Redburn and that's when I caught up with Daisy and her mother on the path. They were taking eggs from the farm to help feed all the guests who had descended on the Melvilles. The guests had come with enormous cases and appetites to match, apparently. I knew Daisy straight away though she was taller than I'd remembered. Her hair was in a prefect blond pigtail down her back and she wore a braw grey pinafore and a white shirt with lacy cuffs. She walked like she had half a dozen books on her head, like the papers and journals say you should if you want to be a lady, and she acted as if she had never laid eyes on me. Mrs Gowans reminded her though.

'It's Minn Graham fae the Rows,' she said. 'You were at the school thegither and had the same teacher at the Sabbath School. Mind?'

Daisy was having none of it. She walked on with her head high. I suppose that was when I realised how much had changed in the short time since we had left the school – me to work as a farm servant over at Netherside and Daisy attending the big school in Bathgate with a view to becoming a schoolteacher in the future. Nothing had changed as far as I was concerned. For me, we would always be the girls we were but plenty had changed about Daisy.

At the time, I was in turmoil about Rob and it crossed my mind that I was being punished for feeling jealous about Daisy when we were younger. One of my mother's sayings came to mind. *Careful what ye wish for.* I had wished for Rob for so long and it wasn't turning out as I expected.

It felt like torture to relive his two kisses over and over again. When I'd headed back up the hill path for Netherside again, at the start of the working week after the Gala Day, I knew I wasn't that earnest and innocent girl anymore, the one who had walked home by the same route only two days before, looking forward to my first dance. The years of wishing and wondering what it would feel like to be with him had come to an end. The very thought of him started the same breathlessness, the same fluttering inside that I'd felt when he'd pushed up against me in the lane behind the hall, and pressed his mouth to mine, eager and hard.

Annie found me fickle. I seemed far away, she said. It took some time before I could reply to Annie's questions right enough. I heard them alright but it felt like they were being said in the distance or in another room. I had to swallow hard before I could answer, remembering Rob's dark eyes staring into mine, and how they'd seemed to penetrate further, deep inside me.

Rob was one thing but what happened after the dance when I'd returned home was another. I came in the door to find Uncle Peter spilling the beans to my father who had already been told by Tommy and the other children about my secret letter.

My father's disappointment weighed more heavily than his fury. In time, he could have forgiven two kisses from a young man, even if they had been delivered furtively in a back lane, but the revelation made in Meg's letter that I was scheming and secretive was harder for a father to bear. When he confronted me, a huge strong hand gripping the letter, I was no longer his gentle, sweet Minn who had skipped along the road with her sisters and rushed to make him tea when he came home from his work in the past. He might call me a daft lassie to my face but I was now an altogether different creature in his eyes – one with all the cunning and guile of a grown woman.

Despite my assurances that Rob knew nothing of what was in the letter, we'd made no plans of any kind and we'd had nothing at all to do with each other until that evening, my father made me promise to have no more to do with him. It all sounded a might unsavoury as far as he was concerned.

When lassies go ahint their mither and faithers' backs thon's when ye've tae worry.

At Netherside, Mrs Davidson asked if I was feeling alright. I didn't seem to be quite myself and she was wondering if anything ailed me. I said I was fine but I fooled nobody. Even Dochie and the bothy lads said I didn't seem my usual happy self. That was why, when the decision was made about who was to help at Parkgate House, I was told to go rather than Annie. Mrs Davidson thought that a change of scene would do me good. In my absence, Annie would be grilled for what she knew about me. Was all well back at home with the Graham family? Did Minn have a sweetheart? What did Annie think could have put even-tempered, hard-working Minn so out of sorts?

My mood did lift a little at the thought of a few days at the Big House with Nell. I hoped to snatch a blether or two with her at the dinner table in the servants' quarters or on the washing green. If the opportunity came along, I might even confide in her. But I would have to think about that. It might be too soon to speak about what was going through my head, about what was in my heart. Nell might offer advice that I didn't want to hear and I could end up feeling worse than ever. I was trying my best to be cheerful and activity of any kind helped but new activities in a new place might help even more so I set off. *A change was as good as a rest*, as my late mother used to say, and the tears rolled down my face at the memory of her.

The days at Parkgate were hectic. On the day of the grand affair, I had duties in the kitchen and was dispatched out the back door into the stable yard with a mountain of potatoes and other vegetables to scrub and peel. As ever, it was Rob that I saw in my mind's eye and I wished he could have been there with me, laughing and blethering in the fresh air. I knew that he couldn't, not right at that moment, but one day he might. It was a possibility, something to wish for the future. I tried to forget Uncle Peter's assertion that Rob had been seen in bad company, gate-crashing the dance without a ticket whilst everybody else had paid. That wasn't the Rob I knew – or thought I knew – and I convinced myself that it wasn't true, just idle gossip from wagging tongues with nothing better to do than spread malicious tales. My father might change his mind in time, when he got used to the idea that I was growing up and once he realised that Rob was a fine upstanding young man and not a rogue after all. It was something to dream about and hope for, and I scrubbed those tatties with such determination, they were the cleanest that had ever been served up at a Parkgate dinner.

The kitchens and pantries went like a fair through Saturday. I washed an endless stream of dishes, at the same time watching the production-line turn out trays of comestibles, as if food was about to go out of fashion. The maids came back and forth from their forays upstairs with tales of the beautiful dresses worn by the female guests and accounts of the handsome, and other not so handsome, men who were in attendance. Opinion came down heavily in favour of sandy-haired Captain Hyslop with his neat moustache and infectious laugh, tall and gallant, just right for Miss Phee whom he doted on. In the midst of a panic about the burnt meringues, the cook let slip that the good captain might have a brother hidden away who could take Miss Isabelle off their hands, then life at Parkgate would be more amenable for all concerned, especially poor Mrs Melville who didn't have the life of a dog thanks to her sharp-tongued sister-in-law. The sudden silence caused by Cook's disloyal words brought panic to her flushed face, until she was sure no one of note had been present – just Jameson, the butler, looking on from behind his half-moon glasses. Then everyone fell about and Maggie Lennox had to fetch the cook a glass of water and a seat to recover. As I joined in the sport, I wondered if working at Parkgate was always this rare. The hours flew by at a pace.

Late on, Maggie joined Nell and me on the steps at the back door for a rest. After the heat of the kitchen, the evening was cool and still, barely disturbed by the sounds of the party on the front lawn. The cawing of the crows, settling in their rookeries in the darkness of the wood, seemed far away from where we drank tea and ate bread and cheese, watching the stars appear in the sky above the ridge. We admired the motor cars arranged across the stable yard, gleaming and glinting in the light of the moon. The muffled voices of a courting couple looking for privacy at the back of the house made us hush, eagerly searching the shadows for the lovers. We had to be quiet and not be seen. Miss Isabelle would have frowned upon three serving girls brazenly drinking tea on the back step, being spotted by the guests. Our place was inside, out of sight, as if all the cooking and cleaning and washing up was done by itself and not by real folk at all.

Maggie was first to decide it was time to get back to work. It sounded as if Cook and the housekeeper were having a heck of a to-do in the kitchen. I brushed the crumbs from my apron before taking a last long breath of fresh air under the starry sky. The lovers were nowhere in evidence but somebody was about. My heart pounded and I swallowed hard. In the shadows by the stable block, a man lurked, staring at the house. I could only see his outline: lean, young, quite tall. I couldn't make out the colour of his hair or the details of his clothing beyond the lightness of his shirt and the dark hue of his trousers. He was standing out of the circle of light coming from the garage. Rob came to mind but I banished the thought immediately. There was no reason for him to be there in the grounds of the big house. Maybe the mystery man was a stable lad or one of Mr Imrie's security detachment.

But there was something familiar about him.

I only realised what it was when I went back inside. The set of his shoulders and the angle of his head as he stared across in my direction, the way his arms were folded across his chest. I nearly dropped the plates I was carrying. Rob! He definitely looked like Rob! I ran back into the yard and peered into the darkness beyond the stable block. But he was away, nowhere to be seen. I plunged into a pit of sadness. My imagination had been playing up, I guessed. He hadn't been there after all. Why should he be? I had only wished it to be so.

Yet barely ten minutes later, I was back in the yard and the place was on fire. Sweating and red-faced, Billy Dodds pressed the handle of the water pump with all his might. As I took each pail from him, I urged him on with frantic words, telling him to keep going for everybody's sake. Soon he was joined by another who took his turn, a young man with strong arms in a light-coloured shirt, a bruised face and knuckles and a nasty cut across his cheek. I looked into his dark eyes as I took the pail from him. Rob stared back at me, his eyes glinting in the firelight under a fop of dark hair. He was the same young man I had seen leading the horses to safety with Captain Hyslop, and the same one who'd been standing in the shadows beside the stable earlier. He was there at Parkgate in the middle of the chaos, pumping the handle of the water pump for all his worth, putting his back into it, handing me pail after pail to pass on to Maggie and down the line. His presence confused me beyond belief, there in the panic and danger of the moment, when the future of Parkgate House lay in the balance, ready to go up in flames if our efforts weren't enough to save it.

But we did save the house and soon Nell and Maggie were pulling me back inside. There was work to be done. Of course, I tried to resist, unable to take my eyes off Rob. I watched him go over to the dead man and my heart froze. He glanced across at me and I wondered if, somehow, Rob had a connection with the awful calamity that had happened that night.

John

Me and Jim looked forward to the summer holiday that year like no other. There'd been a rare day out to the toun one-year past – a fish tea in a fine establishment after a walk in the gardens and down the Royal Mile from the castle to Holyrood. And a trip on a steamer the year afore – *doon the watter* to Rothesay on a day when the smirr barely gave sight of land two minutes after leaving the Broomielaw though we didn't care. The salt air filled our lungs and the breeze blew away the cobwebs of daily life in the Rows. But the thrill of a week under canvas in the Highlands with the pals? That had us talking and planning for hours on end! These trips had come about courtesy of my mother's determination to save on our behalf. She insisted that things were looking up, were getting better with all of us working, but I knew the sacrifices she made to put away the odd shilling here and there to give her boys a holiday.

When it came to the bit, only me and Jim, Bert, Dan, and Sandy got on the train for the camp. Rob was noticeable by his absence – the seat next to his brother stayed empty all the way to our destination in the hills. There hadn't been enough time to find out the detail of what had happened along at the Big House on the Saturday night in question, even the Blackrigg rumour mill didn't work that fast. There'd been an explosion and a man had been killed, that much we knew for sure. We also knew that Rob and two others were being held in police cells and Constable Mackay wasn't about to let them out in a hurry. Had we not left the village when we did, tales of a planned insurrection or even revolution, and a train load of Glasgow polis on its way to quell the riots, would have come to us on the grape vine, for sure.

As we crowded onto the station platform, we wondered whether Sandy would be joining us but, true to form, he appeared on the horizon just in time, shadowed by his mother. I guessed she was making sure her younger son was packed off and wasn't going to reappear at her door. With Rob locked up, the waste of one holiday would be more than enough in her eyes. Besides, why should one son suffer because of the actions of another? As the train departed, I imagined her setting off for the police station to enquire about Rob's situation. His two hands pressed against the window, Sandy looked for a glimpse of her for as long as he could then he slumped in his seat, his head against the glass, and he didn't speak for the first hour. We knew to leave him be and hoped that, in time, he would reveal something about his brother's predicament.

Our week at the camp was everything I thought it would be and more. It was every football match we had ever played at Mansefield or down on the Meadie like we did when we were bairns; every daunder up the road looking for bird's nests; every foray onto Melville land to poach rabbits and hares, taking a fish or a turnip home in our breeks for the pot. It was all of that rolled into one – times a hundred – and I hoped it would never end. We met lads from all over who worked for a living just like us, all liberated from mines, manufactories and shops for a week and, though I liked them all well enough, the kinship I felt for Dan, Bert, Sandy, and Jim grew stronger than ever as the days passed. On the football field, in the queue for meals in the catering tent, and even in quiet times before bed, we stuck together and stuck up for each other. On the morning of the Sabbath, when we were walked to the local kirk for the service, a group of lads from the west decided to take exception to Dan, not for any particular reason as so often happens with bullies and bangsters. The Staney lads got into formation around Dan and the ne'er-do-weels got the message.

We had no option about going to the kirk on the Sabbath. I felt that I should protest but after a sideways glance from Jim, I kept my mouth shut. We joined in with the rest as we had done years before in the school but we wouldn't mention it to Alex when we went home.

Knowing how much he would disapprove, it felt strangely rebellious to be walking up the gravel footpath to the doors of that country church. I had spent my lifetime listening to my father's invective towards the established church which – according to him – toadied to the lairds and turned a blind eye to inequality and poverty. So, I sat there in that cold place with its whitewashed walls, my mind full of scepticism. I marvelled at the minister's honeyed words, at their power to subdue the hardest of hearts and the illest of thoughts, the clype and spin of the sharpest tongue silenced for the duration of his sermon. Though the full meaning of those words was surely beyond my ken, known only to the learned and the wise, I sensed enough of the sentiment to be drawn into the maze of language and felt that I was being offered a key to the door of understanding.

I remembered back to a time as a young lad when I'd sat at the table by the window at home, my mother busy with her darning whilst I studied the blood vessels in my wrist, fascinated by their blueness and the way they snaked down into my hand.

'What's life, Mither?' I asked her.

She took my hand and said, 'That's what it is, John.'

'Blood?' I said staring even harder at my wrist.

'Aye,' she sighed, 'Its whit's in there wi' yer blood.'

'Blood?' I said.

'Aye, blood. And this.' She held out her open palms to the small warm room where the fire crackled and the light through the window was grey as the snow fell softly outside, covering the Rows in silence.

'This is life,' she said. 'You and me, here, the now. This is what life is.'

'Oh, blood,' I said again, following the blue lines up my arm as far as I could, hoping they would reappear somewhere. 'Blood and bein' here.'

But I wasn't satisfied.

'And whit's it for then, this life, Mither?' I asked in the way that only a small child can ask an impossible question and expect an answer.

'Thon's something ye have tae find oot for yersel, John. Yin day ye'll find oot. Ye'll jist have tae wait an' see.'

She could see I was disappointed and wasn't inclined to wait and see.

'Yin thing I can tell ye,' she said putting her hand on my shoulder. 'Life is precious, John. Whitever it's for, an' hoover it turns oot, life is precious.'

Sometimes I feel her hand on my shoulder just like it felt that day when I was small, and I did feel it that morning in the church as we stood to sing Psalm 23. I stared up at the bearded man in his robes, walking on water so impossibly blue in the stained-glass window. I saw the nodding branches of the yew tree in the sunny churchyard outside and the rows of young men like me, crowded into the pews at the back of that church, and I remembered her words.

Life is precious, John.

For all the stories, and allegories and strange words, and the lesson spoken by the minister and all of the ministers that there ever were, those words of my mother were the key to my understanding of that great mystery that was my life back then.

Towards the end of our week at the camp, Sandy received a letter from his mother. He went off into the woods below the crags to read it. The rest of us were on nettles about what it said but we didn't dare ask. After a hike that afternoon, when it was our team's turn to go down to the shop in the village, Sandy revealed the contents of the letter. Rob had been released without charge. Apparently, the other two had been adamant that he hadn't been with them. They'd been charged with robbery but not with arson. The authorities seemed satisfied that Jimmy Grubb had died as the result of an unfortunate accident. I thought of the stash of materials I'd seen in the mill and remembered Rob's torment about meeting the gang that Saturday night. I knew in my bones that they'd been planning something big and it wasn't theft. My elder brother was the instigator but his name hadn't been brought into it, as far as I knew. Maybe that was why Moran and Bone were keen not to implicate Rob who might crack easily under pressure from Mackay. What had Rob been doing at the Big House if not meeting them? I'd left him on the hill behind the steading at Netherside. He said he was on his way to see Minn. Had she turned him away or had he changed his mind and met up with the gang after all? Either way, although I called him my friend, I was glad that he hadn't gone to Minn. But I couldn't be sure if I was more glad for her sake or for mine.

Bert, Dan, and Jim were soon clapping Sandy's back, congratulating him on the good news about Rob. They said they had known all along that he couldn't have been mixed up with a bad lot, not Rob Duncan, son of Peggy and top of the class. Sandy noticed me watching from the sidelines. I quickly grinned but not quick enough. We both knew there was more to Rob than met the eye but we would keep it to ourselves for now.

'Dae ye ken whit this place is lackin'?' said Sandy, suddenly breezy and cheerful.

We were all ready to be cheerful.

'Lassies!' he said, quickening his pace in the direction of the wee grocer at the far end of the village. 'I hear tell the hotel's fu' o' them, scullery maids and chamber maids galore. Get a move oan an' we'll have a look.'

Seeing Dan, Bert and even my dear brother, Jim, almost trip over each other to get along the road made me realise that I was not alone in my fascination with girls – or in my case, a particular girl. The opposite sex, it seemed, was another key to our understanding of the great mystery of life back then and we were definitely ready to find out more.

Chapter 14

Elizabeth

One sunny afternoon, and there were many in that summer of 1914, I was pedalling along the road to Whinbank on a bicycle that belonged to one of the lady schoolteachers. Miss Foulkes had offered me the use of it during the school summer holiday whilst she was off on her travels. Much to Richard's annoyance, I had jumped at the chance of learning to cycle but he had been unable to prevent it, since out of the blue, Miss Foulkes appeared at the door of the manse ready to give me a lesson there and then. He'd had no option but to allow me to depart in her company though he got his own back later by sulking in his study until supper time.

I hadn't taken easily to cycling. It required a great deal of nerve and bravado but my determination to get back onto the contraption after my first, rather shaky attempt was soon rewarded. My confidence grew with each and every outing. I revelled in the freedom cycling was bringing, a new independence that let me escape from the close confines of village life, to enjoy the countryside further afield than walking and my limited free time allowed. I could easily visit Rose and the Macleans whenever I had time to spare without having to rely on Phee.

In the days since Phee's engagement party, I had already visited the Macleans several times and Richard was threatening to put his foot down. He had begun to complain about the quality of Sarah's work in the manse. As he drew his finger across the furniture, bemoaning the imaginary dust, or when he pointed to invisible tide marks on the crockery, he blamed me for inadequately supervising a servant who clearly, in his opinion, required careful watching. I had been shocked but not surprised at the lengths he would go to in order to keep me in line and I knew that I would have to be careful that loyal, hard-working Sarah would not fall victim to his petulant power games.

In truth though, as Richard's behaviour got worse I grew stronger and more determined in my resolve to stand up to him and make my own decisions about how I would live my life. I had become very fond of Donald and looked forward to seeing him on my visits to the farm. Even if he couldn't join me when I dropped by, the sight of him in the distance or a wave across the stackyard when he was supervising in the stable, gave me no end of happiness. Regardless of Richard's complaints about how my visits to Whinbank were being perceived, I dug in my heels, ignoring his protestations about my reputation and how it reflected on the church.

One Friday, I turned north out of Rowanhill and let the bicycle take off down the steep slope of the drove road towards the river several miles off in the distance. I loved to feel the wind in my hair and against my skin as I sped along, whirring past the hedgerows and the fields, a blur of green and gold. In no time at all, I reached the rutted track that led up to the farmhouse where I knew Mrs

Maclean and Donald would be waiting for my visit: Mrs Maclean in the kitchen making drop scones on a girdle, and Donald in the parlour, his arm in a sling, with one eye on a book and another on the view from the window, waiting for me. When I dismounted, not wishing to endure the bumpy road ahead, I had started to push the heavy bicycle along the track and was surprised to see Rose coming towards me.

'I got back from town yesterday, sooner than expected,' Rose said anticipating my first question. 'And I thought I'd visit my patient to see how his arm was doing,' she added, accurately predicting my second.

'And is Donald's arm healing well?'

'Everything seems to be in the correct place and, with some careful exercise, he'll be as good as new in a few weeks. His recovery is testimony to the excellence of your nursing skills, Miss Fraser.'

I brushed off her compliment. 'He can't bear to be out of action. Though I think he's out and about a lot of the time, watching everybody at work and joining in as best he can, one-handed.' I looked around for a place to sit in the shade of the trees that lined the track.

'Shall we sit for a minute? I'm quite out of breath.'

Rose sat on the grassy verge beside me. She picked a stem of forget-me not and studied the tiny, delicate flower, as blue as the sky that day and pierced by a bright yellow centre. She reached for some daisies, added a sprig or two of speedwell and some white clover, constructing a tiny posy in her fingers. She held it out for me to admire.

'*Forget-me-not* speaks for itself,' I told her, 'And goes perfectly with the clover: *think of me*; the daisy means *innocence* and the speedwell is *fidelity*. All in all, quite appropriate, I'd say.'

'For you or me?' Abruptly, Rose threw the flowers into the long grass.

She stared after them, unblinking, thoughtful, almost frowning.

'About a month.' She studied my puzzled face. 'Wasn't that your next question? How long will I be staying in Rowanhill?'

I nodded.

'Until mid August or thereabouts, then I'll go back to finish my training. I've asked father if I can follow him on his rounds and sit in on his surgery while I'm here. Why miss an opportunity to learn from an old hand?'

I agreed. 'Judging by how you conducted yourself on the night of Phee's party, you already know what you're doing. Will you be visiting your other patient? Or should I say *patients*?'

I watched Rose for a reaction but there was none.

'I mean Mrs Melville, of course... and the new baby.'

Rose looked away. 'I'd like to. Do you think I should?'

'Of course you should. You'd be welcomed with open arms after what you did, delivering the baby when there wasn't time to send for the nurse. Catherine had such a hard time of it, all hell let loose at the back of the house, the guests in a state of shock, and the baby intent on making its way into the world. Poor Catherine!'

'And the child's doing well, is he? Have you heard? My father seems to think so but it's a few days since he called on them.'

'According to Miss Shanks at the post office, he's thriving. And very little passes her by.' I studied my friend. 'David Melville was grateful for what you did, Rose. I'm sure he'd like to thank you properly, having got over the shock of the moment.'

'It was quite a surprise for him. Covered in soot from the fire, walking into the ladies' parlour, only to find his wife in the latter stages of labour on the floor, and me of all people in attendance. I'll never forget the look on his face.'

'I saw how he looked at you, Rose... earlier in the day. Did you notice?'

Rose gave a sigh. She picked a long piece of grass and put it into her mouth. In the distant past, a brief liason between Rose and David had promised much but delivered little, in the end.

'It was four years ago, Rose... you and David. You've had time to move on and you have... with your studying, being busy in the hospital.'

'Yes, it was a long time ago. But you of all people should appreciate how hard it is to forget.'

I gave a start, swallowed hard, remembering Neil.

'But you said you were happy with your life as it was, soon to qualify. You said...'

'I know what I said, Beth.'

She looked me straight in the eye.

'I've seen David many times since I moved away. I was determined to forget him but he was equally determined not to let me.'

Rose registered my confusion.

'After about a year – just before Christmas 1911 it was – we bumped into each other several times... in the street or around the university... he has friends there from his student days... then, when I finally agreed to have tea with him, he admitted it hadn't been a coincidence. He'd orchestrated it. I was angry with him, said he wasn't being fair on me or on Catherine. But he would turn up out of the blue and... well, eventually, I couldn't turn him away.'

Rose saw the disbelief in my face.

'But I haven't seen him for over a year now. When I heard about the death of their first child, somehow I found the strength to say no. And he didn't come back. Perhaps guilt kept him away, perhaps he felt he was being punished.'

'Divine retribution for his...' I hesitated, my mouth dry. 'Deceit?'

Rose nodded, blushing red at the sound of the word. *Yes, deceit.* Hers as well as David's.

'And you saw each other again for the first time... at the garden party?'

'I should have stayed away but had to go because of Phee.' She picked at the grass then tossed it aside. 'No, I wanted to go..... because of Phee.'

'You know he still loves you.'

'Love? Yes, I suppose you could call it that. But that's why I don't think it will be a good idea if I visit Parkgate House.' Rose stood up, brushed down her skirt. Without a hint of emotion, she looked down at me and I could only stare back not knowing what to say.

'Come and visit, Beth, please. Don't judge me. Try to understand.' She paused before making up her mind not to say any more. She had said more than enough already.

I got up and hugged my friend. Of course I would visit her and soon, very soon.

I retrieved the bicycle from the hedgerow. What an extraordinary encounter, I realised, as I followed her progress back along the track to the road. My good friend, the medical student, devoting her life to the care and treatment of the sick; the same determined and focused professional woman who had conversed with me at the garden party, conveying an air of quiet control over her life. Yet beneath the calm exterior she had shown that night, when treating the injured and during the birth of Catherine Melville's child, Rose hid a secret she had kept to herself for nigh on three years. How difficult had it been to conceal the truth from her friends, pretending that she had moved on with her life and consigned her feelings for David to the past, when the opposite was true? I felt deeply disappointed. I realised how much I had wanted to believe that Rose had forgotten about him, that she had become an independent woman who would not be restrained by romantic notions of love. Had I seen only what I wanted to see in my friend or had Rose been particularly skilful in her deception?

I walked on, shoving the heavy bicycle along the bumpy track towards Whinbank where Mrs Maclean and Donald waited for me: Miss Fraser, the minister's diffident sister who spent her life keeping house at the manse, contributing to church life and looking after others; kindly, smiling, innocent Elizabeth who, like her good friend Rose, might not be all she appeared on the outside.

Minn

A couple of weeks after the fire, Mrs Davidson told me to go home for my Sabbath night visit straight after the mid-day meal was over because I had worked hard in the fields all week and given extra help in the house, in the absence of Annie whose mother had been ill. As she often did, Mrs Davidson told me that, had she been blessed with a daughter, she would've been happy to have one just like me. But it was high time I paid a visit to see my family. The Grahams would be missing me and wondering if something was amiss. It had been a while since I'd been home to see them.

Though my employer's kind words brought a smile to my face, my spirit remained lukewarm. I'd returned from Parkgate with my thoughts tapsalteerie and I needed time to think it all out. Sure, hard work in the byre and in the house, and long afternoons in the fields, harvesting corn and hay with the men, had made the days fly by. Warm evenings sitting on the bench at the roadside, in the company of Dochie and the bothy lads, had been cheerful. Games of quoits using horseshoes gave an excuse for feigned disagreement and horseplay which was good fun. I liked listening to their blethers, laughing at their pranks, grateful for their company in the absence of Annie. In bed, I had slept alone for the first time in my life and each night rejuvenating sleep, after the long days of hard labour, had washed over me like a gentle wave on the shore. But loneliness and confusion returned each morning with the greyness of dawn. I left the farm that Sunday afternoon in two minds, and without enthusiasm.

I took the Whinbank road, instead of my usual route, the hill path. Yet again, I felt like a change to my usual routine would do me good. A different direction might give me a new way of looking at things, another view in more ways than one.

At the junction with the road that crossed the muir, the ruin of Eppie's Mill was almost hidden from view by alder and birch. The roof had lost many slates and gaping holes in the timbers were pierced by tall saplings growing out of the dark interior towards the daylight. Against an outer wall, the mill wheel sat motionless, the frame rusty, its timbers broken. The trickling waters from the lade continued to spill over the top of the wheel but lacked enough energy to push against the corrosive power of age. Like most of the old mills in the area, Eppie's Mill had been abandoned by the miller and his family a long time ago, when ancient ways had been left behind by newer developments in the towns. Once a hub of activity that drew farmers and carters from all around, the dilapidated building was now a lonely place, visited only by bats and crows, and the ghosts of the past. I took a fleeting glance at the empty windows and quickened my pace, till I was soon running to be free of whatever might be there. The place was cursed – I was sure of it.

All at once, a flight of black crows erupted from the midst of the ruin. Their cawing and fluttering gave me the shakers till I got a sense of them and their noise faded away. I hated how they could scare me like that, as if they had been lying in wait, planning the moment together. I hurried on as fast as I could, my eyes on the light at the far end of the long tunnel of trees lining that part of the road home.

'Good day,' came a man's voice from the shadows.

I can hardly put into words the fright I got! I jumped backwards, drawing my arms up to protect myself. The brightness of the faraway light and the dimness beneath the trees combined to near blind me.

'Good day to you, Miss,' he repeated in an accent that wasn't local. When he came nearer and my eyes adjusted, I got a better look at him. He had fair hair beneath his hat, and was smartly dressed in a tweed suit.

I stepped to the side, putting what distance I could between me and the man. As he came into focus in the semi-darkness, I recognised him. 'Mr Maclean? Oh, Mr Maclean! Is it you? Guid day, sir.'

He smiled broadly when he doffed his hat and apologised for making me start. One of his arms was held in a sling, tight against his chest and was partly hidden, just visible beneath his jacket held shut by a single button. I think he was quite amused, as I took to my heels.

I hurried away, hoping I wasn't being rude. Sic a gliff, I realised, when I was well up the road. But I had seen him before, fortunately, so I knew who he was. He had come calling at Netherside, making the acquaintance of Mr Davidson and Angus, the grieve.

Donald Maclean had been walking from the direction of Blackrigg. My conversations with Sarah and the scene at the Big House on the night of the fire when Mr Maclean got injured came into my mind. I remembered Miss Fraser on the ground beside him so I wondered if he had been visiting her at the manse.

I was grateful when the hedgerow thinned and a huge blue sky opened up above me. The road wasn't quite as steep where the muir spread out in every direction, shimmering in the heat of the day. Snipe thrummed in flight. Crickets hummed in the grasses. Buttercup and spotted orchid dotted the greener hollows by the roadside. Soon, I passed the place where the path to the shieling wound off through the heather. No one seemed to be about. It was a baking hot afternoon so that was no surprise. I imagined the Grahams at home, seeking shade in our small cottage with the door and both windows open to let the air in; Jean resting out of the sun; the men at the allotments watering the vegetables, necessary work that was permitted on the Sabbath.

Then something metallic, reflecting the sunlight, caught my attention. Glinting from a peat hag, a short distance off the road, was a lady's bicycle: green and silver, with a basket nestling between its handles. It stood half-hidden, propped up awaiting its owner's return from a visit to the shieling on the muir maybe. I shaded my eyes with a hand but saw no one. I felt completely alone on the muir but knew somebody must be about.

I had passed the start of the footpath to The Law and was almost at the first bend in the hill road, when a scream from behind, followed by a screech of brakes, warned me to get out of the way. Yet another fright! Three in the one day! I leapt to one side but had chosen wrongly. A green and silver bicycle, with a basket on the front, went the same way and both me and the rider ended up in the ditch.

'I'm terribly sorry,' said the woman as she rolled into a sitting position free of the bicycle. 'Are you still in one piece?'

I soon came to my senses. 'Miss Fraser! I'm fine. Are you?'

'I'm fine, thank you.' She looked embarrassed. 'I'm not too experienced, I'm afraid... especially on the steeper hills.'

I remembered the bicycle half-hidden from passers-by. And Donald Maclean's smile when he passed me on the road. How happy he'd looked.

'Have ye been for an outing, Miss?'

She readjusted her straw hat before speaking. 'Yes, I was walking across the muir. It's so quiet and peaceful just now. I had it all to myself.'

I was surprised at her reply. I wondered if Miss Fraser had really been by herself but I couldn't imagine her telling a lie. We pulled the bicycle out of the ditch together.

'I hope it's no broke an' ye get hame a' richt.'

She lifted the back wheel and wound the pedals round. The chain had come free of the sprocket but Miss Fraser soon pushed it back into place.

We brushed ourselves down, straightening our skirts, then agreed that walking might be safer on such a steep road. Miss Fraser started to guide the bicycle downhill, pumping the brakes when it threatened to run away from her. We blethered about my work at Netherside, the Graham family, and how well Sarah was fitting in at the manse. It seemed an odd conversation somehow – stilted, forced. I noticed that Miss Fraser said nothing about herself but it would have been rude to ask her anything directly, even though it seemed fine for her to ask dozens of questions about me and my family.

In the field below the final bend, several ponies grazed the long grass behind the wall. I leaned over to stroke their backs. A distant group charged the length of the field towards me.

I thought they were bonnie and I said so. I couldn't mind ever seeing such wee horses before.

'Look at their wee, short legs,' I said. A caramel-coloured horse shook the long blonde hair of its mane out of its eyes. I stroked the thick furriness along its long back. Worn patches of hair formed stripes down its flanks but the animals looked strong and healthy, and well looked after.

Miss Fraser joined me by the roadside, stepping across a dried-up ditch to get close. She pulled a handful of grass and a tiny white horse charged over in her direction. It bumped into her hand, misjudging the distance. It was almost blind which shocked me.

'They're friendly,' I remarked.

'Shetland ponies,' she said.

Miss Fraser opened her hand right up, surrendering the grass to the warm lips and huge yellow teeth of the small white horse.

'They're pit ponies, Minn. They've brought them up from below in preparation for shutting the pits.'

I must have looked puzzled. 'Shutting the pits?'

'Because of the dispute. The men and the owners can't agree about wage rates and the owners are dead set against a four-day week. It's happening everywhere, right across the country. They've threatened to lock the men out if they don't withdraw their notices of intention to only work four days. The Union's told them not to work on Wednesdays and Saturdays from the end of the month. The pits may be shutting indefinitely to force the union's hand. It's not looking good, I'm afraid.'

I was worried. I stroked the heads of several eager ponies as they jostled each other out of the way, their noses up, sniffing the air for signs of more grass, knowing it was always greener on the other side. Miss Fraser leaned over the wall until she was almost horizontal, doing her best to share out two handfuls of grass and flowers but failing miserably in the face of the onslaught of many hungry mouths. The bolder animals at the front took it all and the meek were left wanting, looking on from behind with sad eyes.

We continued our walk in silence. Everybody would be affected by the dispute if it wasn't settled, and the sight of the pit ponies grazing in the field was proof that a long, difficult time lay ahead for the community.

At the end of the lane to the manse, Miss Fraser stopped to take in the view.

'This must be a welcome sight when you return to your family each week, Minn.'

'Aye, it is, Miss.' I shielded my eyes against the brightness of the sun. I could make out the tall lines of the chimneys amongst the square sheds, the round wheels of the winding gear, and the pit bings that seemed to grow out of the moss like enormous pyramids.

'There's nae better sicht onie place. Its ay guid tae come back.'

I saw Miss Fraser staring at the back of the Smiddy which nestled at the bottom of the hill road and I wondered what was going through her mind.

'Mr Tennant will feel the same when he comes back fae Canada, Miss.' The words were out before I could stop myself.

She turned, quite stunned, and stared at me. 'Mr Tennant?'

'Mr Neil Tennant, Miss. Ma sister wrote tae me fae Canada. She wrote she'd met him.'

Miss Fraser's face was a picture.

'He telt her he was comin' back tae Blackrigg at the end of the summer, Miss.' I took a deep breath before going any further but thought I might as well be hung for a sheep as a lamb.

'He said he had unfinished business here.'

'Unfinished business?'

'Aye, Miss. He has business tae attend tae. I hope it was a'richt tae tell ye.'

I pictured the bicycle on the moss and Mr Maclean when he had passed me on the road earlier, looking so happy. I bit my lip.

'Of course it was, Minn.' She stared hard into the distance. 'I'm glad you told me. Thank you.'

I watched her shove the bicycle along Manse Lane. And I hoped sincerely that Miss Fraser really did want to hear that Neil was coming back to the village, in spite of any new feelings she might have had for Mr Maclean. If there was one thing I was learning about life, it was that decisions had to be made with all the facts in front of you. Otherwise, you might get the wrong idea and make a big mistake that you would have to carry with you for the rest of your life.

As Miss Fraser finally disappeared round the corner of Manse Lane, I prayed I had done the right thing.

Chapter 15

John

When we went back to Stoneyrigg after the camp, it was as if a new chapter had opened in my life. Although we'd grown up together in the Rows, a different sort of bond had formed between the friends because of our time together in the hills. I knew that I'd never be able to describe to anybody who hadn't been with us just how rare the experience had been. It was like I'd joined a secret society with Jim, Dan, Bert, and Sandy – a society with a language that only we could understand. Afterwards, when we spoke about all manner of things, our understanding was coloured by our time together at the camp. My love for the countryside and everything it contained had been nurtured that week though I'd always loved wandering the paths and roads around Blackrigg enjoying the fresh air after long days down the pit. I became determined to pursue that delight in whatever free time I had from then on, not just in the Blackrigg area with which I was well acquainted, but also further afield in the Highlands and Border country where, as I now knew, there was so much to explore.

For the first time in my short life, a question arose in my mind about what I did for a living. In all the years of growing up, I had accepted that my fate was to work below ground. In fact, I'd looked forward with almost unbearable anticipation to the day when I would join the men surging down the pit road at the start of that first early shift. Maybe a life as a colliery worker wasn't for me after all; maybe I could work above ground, out in the open. It was a strange and heady feeling that came with the realisation that life might contain choices about such things though it challenged all of my experience until then. I'd watched a generation of boys follow their fathers down the pit as if fated to do so by a greater power and I'd never questioned it until then.

At the end of the holiday period, I joined the long stream of workers leaving the Rows on the first day back at work. A small army of men and boys made their way towards the pitheads, boots crunching on gravel in marching time, and conversations hushed by the early morning mist that hugged the blanket bog like a shroud after the cool of the night. The silver disc of a low sun, newly risen above the eastern horizon, pierced the whiteness that would lift and melt soon after everybody had sunk deep into the ground. I had already served my time as a drawer and filler. Now I was working at the face with two skilled facemen, learning the ropes as I took my turn. I had a lot to learn but I was strong and smart enough, and willing. That morning, I was anxious about returning to my usual employment when I would step into the cage with a dozen others and drop to the depths, then wait for the bogeys that would take us down further to the dook, to the underground roads leading to the coalface. After the break in routine brought on by the holiday, I was feeling sick at the memory of the accident that had robbed me of my finger. I was no worse for the loss of it – the wound had healed and my workrate would not be affected – but it would take some doing to go back to the face again with the memory of the roof collapse still clear in my mind.

But there was nothing else for it that morning. *Maun-be*, as my mother often said.

With Jim, Dan, and Bert, I caught up with Rob on the road and said hello. We'd barely set eyes on him for nigh-on two weeks. Although we'd been kicking about the village for several days, Rob had been keeping his head down, staying out of our way. He seemed to be glad to see us but I wasn't so sure. A discussion about Saturday's football matches around the district started up. We regaled him with tales of our time at the camp, when we'd slept under canvas in a meadow by a burn, waking to birdsong and lambs bleating in the fields. It was braw. We'd gone swimming and fishing and hiking, we said; climbed Ben Venue and Ben A'an to admire the views of lochs and mountains; cooked over campfires; played football a million times. The weather had been mixed but it hadn't stopped us.

What a pity Rob hadn't been there, we agreed.

Rob said he had heard all about it from Sandy.

Maybe Rob would be able to go next year, we said.

Aye, maybe, agreed Rob.

Maybe.

Conversations about the dispute over the daily rates came to us through the crowd, reminding us of the coal masters' latest request for a further reduction in the daily rates from what they had already secured. Because word of the coal masters' refusal to accept the four-day-week had come at the start of the stoppage period, much of the heat had been taken out of the men's reaction. Some had left the village for the duration and others were caught up in family plans for day trips and outings to visit family who lived elsewhere. Some debate had taken place when they'd congregated at the steading or in the allotments but there was little that could be done about it until everybody was back at work again, after the stoppage. Even in our house, with Alex and Davy so closely involved in the union, without new information there was barely a mention of the situation.

As my mother had remarked, there was little talk of the mischief along at the Big House and the attack on the pit manager's son. Anything that was being said was spoken in low voices but mostly folk were keeping their own counsel. In light of the dispute with the Coal Company, it was understandable that feelings were running high and some ill-folk had gone too far in letting those in charge know how they felt. The laying of tripwires, followed soon after by the fire, had folk thinking the two had to be related. Two were in gaol and another had died – a heavy price but maybe they had got their just desserts. If everybody kept their heads down things might blow over. Nobody wanted that kind of bother, no matter how sorely the masters might be treating them.

I noticed that Davy was spending more time in the house and less roaming the streets till yon time like he had in the past. I couldn't have been the only one who'd seen him in the company of the three miscreants in the weeks before they had come to grief but his name didn't seem to come up in connection with any of the crimes in question – otherwise Constable Mackay would have been at the door. If anything, Davy's ability to command an audience was growing. Men sought his opinion along at the steading and listened when he explained a point of view about what needed to be done to make things better.

The line of men streaming down the pit road for that first early shift soon became a throng as we got nearer the pits. Something was blocking the way up ahead. We were still some way back and no one at the front seemed to be moving. Those who were taller strained to discover the nature of the delay. Voices complained that we needed to get a move on since we weren't paid until we got to the coal face. Why should we be done out of wages because of the company's inefficiencies in getting us down below? Questions went forward and information was relayed back until it soon became clear what was amiss.

A crowd had congregated around the main gates to the Broadrigg pits where a notice was pinned.

A simmering agitation – groaning and mild cursing that stopped this side of the wailing and gnashing of teeth – filled the bright mistiness of the morning, rippling outwards as if a stone had been dropped into a dark pool.

Alex barged his way through.

He turned to the men, his face almost black with fury, 'They're threiten a lockoot, boys. If we dinnae tak back oor notices aboot workin' the fower days, it'll be a fuckin' lockoot!'

'The bastards,' muttered Dan's father, a Christian man who wasn't inclined towards bad language.

But overall, the response seemed muted, a restless whisper dampened by the mist. *Maun-be*. The men moved in the direction of the winding sheds.

I forgot about my fears as I lined up for the cage. The injury to my hand did not enter my head, nor did rock falls or flooding or choking dust, nor the absence of daylight and the smell of the moss. I was eager to get down below with the rest of them, down into that netherworld of tunnels and shafts. The men stood in line, eyes fixed ahead, jaws set, heads held high. These were the men who won the coal and I was never so proud to be one of them.

We were living through a time when the dispute in the mines was developing so fast – with regular meetings of the British as well as the Scottish executives of the Miners Federation – that it was nigh on impossible to keep the men up to date except by hastily organised assemblies, notified at the last minute by word of mouth. New questions arose all the time such that conjecture and rumour were soon presented as fact, creating a clamour for truth and hunger for debate. An impromptu meeting started up at Craigpark later that day, in the early evening. The warnings posted at the entrance to the pits had everybody's dander up. The masters meant what they said – the talk about the pit ponies having been brought up from below over the weekend was confirmed. Surely, this was proof of their resolve. They were getting ready to shut the pits to get their way.

John Doyle and Joe MacNab stood unsteadily on the rim of a horse trough and called for order. Steeny and the others would arrive shortly, they said.

'It's a'richt for Mister James Doonan tae command fae oan high,' said an angry voice, referring to the county union official. 'The agent's income isnae gonnae be affected b' a fower day week, is it? Last I heard he was askin' for a rise o' ten bob for himsel!'

'Aye, bloody parasites, the lot o' them,' agreed another. 'Staun thegither, boys, we're telt. But it's no gaunae come oot their pocket, is it?'

'The miners have got a'body livin' aff their backs!' shouted Jimmy Broadley.

'A'richt, boys. Haud oan,' called John Doyle. 'Jist mind whau we're takin' oan here. It's no the Union we're fechtin. They're oan oor side.'

'Supposed tae be.' Several voices together.

'Aye, they're takin' their time makin' up their mind ower this business,' said another in more reasonable tones but clearly frustrated. 'We jist want tae ken whit's gaun oan. It's no like we've been asked oor opinion. We've no been balloted nor nuthin.'

'We dinnae want tae be hung oot tae dry for havin' oor notices in, supportin' the fower days. We could be oot oan oor necks wi' nae place tae bide forby.'

Calls of 'hear, hear!' resounded round the assembly.

'The Executive Committees in England and Wales arenae keen tae support the fower day policy. Is thon the wey o' it?'

'That would appear tae be the case,' confirmed Joe MacNab. 'But I wouldnae like tae say *aye* or *no* for sure. Best haud oan tae Steeny comes by. He'll avail ye o' the facts.'

'If we drap the fower day week, it'll be a strike then?'

'Aye, maist likely,' called out Steeny from the edge of the crowd. He pushed his way to the front. Alex and Davy followed in his wake.

Silence.

'The fower day policy has been drapt,' he confirmed. 'A telegram was sent tae the Coalmaisters' Association at their meetin' in Glasgae. We've threatened a strike if they dinnae see sense an' agree tae negotiate.' He held up his hand for calm. 'The Federation in England and Wales werenae keen tae support Mr Broon an' the Scottish delegation on the fower day week.'

'Why no?'

'Aye, why no? They should be backin' us. We've backed them in the past.'

'They're offerin' tae support a strike should the owners persist in their ettles tae tak wage rates doon ablow seven bob,' stated Steeny.

Alex explained, 'The British Federation have their ain agenda and the current Scottish dispute doesnae fit in wi' their plans. Negotiations inside the Federation are ettlin to keep the union sooth o' the border on board but dissent is apparent in several regions there. They're no ower keen tae back a strike in the Scottish coalfield that'd compromise the Federation's financial position, no when a national dispute, alang wi' the ither big unions lastin' several months might be oan the cairds, come the back-end.

'Mebbe we should dae for oorsels,' somebody shouted. 'If they dinnae back us a hunder percent, the Scottish union should split.' The idea had many supporters.

'Thon micht jist be whit happens. A split's been mooted an' a'body will be balloted.' Steeny allowed a moment for the crowd to come round and realise that their opinion in these matters counted with the leadership.

'There's plenty at stake here, lads, in mair weys than yin. But we'll just have tae wait for a bit an' see what happens.'

When the crowd had decided that Steeny had no more to give them, men started to leak away, heads down, and their representatives watched them go. They began to discuss how desperately the Scottish union had tried to avoid a strike. The four-day week was a better policy from their point of view. It had given everybody a feeling of power, the possibility of control over the price of coal which the coal owners insisted should be the reference point for wage rates.

The men had argued for long enough in the past that prices – the market – were nothing to do with them since they didn't sell the coal. They sold their strength and skill to the employers and produced the coal in return. Surely their labour amounted to the same one day as it did the next? But the owners would have none of it. The four-day policy had been a stroke of genius – the men could act to manipulate the market in their favour and keep wages high. But that hadn't pleased the owners. And they held all the cards. A lockout or even a strike of limited duration would put up the price of coal, so profits for the owners would rise. Yet still they would argue that wages had to come down at the end of the day.

'Mebbe we should be gaun oor ain wey, richt enough,' said Alex. 'Staun up fur oorsels here at hame. Ye've tae strike when the iron's hot an' it's burnin' somethin' fierce the noo, in ma opinion. Tae hell wi' the union doon sooth. They're no happy aboot supportin' a strike here cause it's interferin' wi' their plans. It's enough tae be up against the coal maisters an' be ill-done b' them. But when ye feel ill-done b' folk ye thocht were oan the same side as ye... weel, it maks ye sair.'

Hands in pockets, with little left to say but plenty to think about, the five men ambled the few paces to the roadside together where some of us were standing, wondering where to go, what to do next. They dawdled and we dawdled as well, staring across the road at the works half-hidden in shadow from the great heap of spoil above Stoneyrigg Pit, closed long ago and left to rot by the Coal Company. The Glasgow train chugged out of the station in a puff of smoke and steam. The place seemed suddenly deserted where minutes before a large crowd had assembled. I noticed how quickly the swallows reclaimed the steading, dipping and diving as the insects returned. Swifts came back from nowhere, circling high on the warm air, arrow-like against a blue sky, while cattle lowed lonely and long in the nearby fields.

Davy was the first to see the horseman coming from the west. He narrowed his eyes, the hairs on the back of his neck rising, like a fox smelling a rabbit. Alex followed his gaze along Main Street and we all latched on. The rider was coming closer, staring straight ahead, moving rhythmically with his mount. He was tall in the saddle, holding the strong brown horse tightly by the reins, keeping him in check, letting him know who was in charge. Soon we were able to make out his cap and his uniform. He was brass-buttoned and leather-gloved, long leather boots pushed into shining stirrups. He saw us all standing but he didn't flinch. The horse walked on, steady and composed like his master. But when they came to the Smiddy, the rider gave a yank on the rein and dug in his heels. The horse took off at the gallop, up the hill road and out of sight.

'Somebody's missing their fancy motor,' said Davy. I could see how he wanted to laugh, sure the others must have seen it too.

'Mr Melville's lookin' awfy smert in his uniform,' said John Doyle.

'A Terrier,' observed Joe Macnab. 'Reservist.'

'Comfortin' tae ken we're bein' looked efter b' the gentry,' said Davy. 'I'll sleep soond in ma bed the nicht.'

'A European war's on the cairds, they're sayin',' sighed Joe.

Steeny agreed. 'Aye, accordin' tae the papers there's nae wey roond it.'

'We're in the middle o' a war the noo. Oor ain war wi' the coal owners,' said Davy.

'An' no jist us... workers a' place are battlin' the same. We've naethin' against ither workers, foreign or itherwise,' said Alex.

'But we're no the yins callin' the shots. Nae maitter hoo fell we micht protest, it's no in oor hauns, is it?' said Joe.

'Aye, an' gie us a uniform an' a merry tune, we'll fa' in ahint the flag, quick as a wink,' said Alex. 'Mark ma words.'

'Funny thon,' said Joe, hands in pockets.

'Aye, funny peculiar but no funny ha ha,' said Alex.

'Let's pray it'll no come tae pass,' said Steeny.

We watched him leave for another union meeting in a neighbouring village. I held onto the small lifeline he had thrown to us, hoping that simple and earnest prayer might avert the conflicts predicted. But deep down I realised that if prayer was the answer, then we'd already be living in a much better world than the one we knew to be true.

Elizabeth

I remember how I wrestled the bicycle through the gate into the manse garden after that encounter with Minn Graham. It was such a great heavy machine when it wouldn't go exactly where I wanted. I leaned it against the wall under the pantry window and eased my shoulders back, glad to be rid of the weight of the thing. I removed my straw bonnet, wiped the sweat from around the nape of my neck with a handkerchief, before entering my personal domain at the back of the house. The kitchen was cool and shaded after the onslaught of the afternoon sun up on the muir. I was glad of it: the cool and the shade; glad of the silence, all bar the ticking clock and the ashes settling in the range; glad that Sarah had the afternoon off; especially glad of Richard's absence. I felt my throat tighten and my head swim. Why did the mention of Neil Tennant's name still engender such feelings? To hear of his intention to return to Blackrigg, that day of all days when I had gone back to the shieling on the muir for the first time in four years! I reached for the table and stared at the pattern in the wood. The grain wove and wound around itself in a way that was sickening till it became a blur before my eyes.

In the middle of the journey of our life, I came to myself in a dark wood where the straight path was lost. Darkness was beckoning.

Then it came to me, how that wood was borne of nature, wild and free, strong and enduring. Each curve and whorl, one against the other, was a season of vernal growth, cut short by winter's icy blast.

I spoke quietly to the empty room, took a shallow breath and then another, closing my eyes against the wave of panic that threatened to wash me away.

No!

I would not be cast into the inferno again. I only needed time. Time would see it all straight, as it was intended. And I breathed deeply once again.

At last, I went to the window and looked out. My garden looked splendid in the hot colours of late July, its brightness glorified from my perspective in the cool shade of the kitchen. My arms and legs felt weak – I will admit – but I filled a glass with water from the tap, picked up my drawing book and walked out into the sunshine.

I remember how I placed a potted pelargonium on the garden seat, carefully moving it this way and that. It was an excellent subject for drawing: striking scarlet flowers in various stages of opening, a deep crimson red flowing like blood into the green of every leaf, and the aged terracotta pot encrusted with white salts. I would fetch my paints later, after the pencil outline was done. Little gave me more pleasure. I had complete control over the outcome and it left me with a sense of satisfaction – so unlike my dealings with people. I racked my brain for the secret meaning conveyed by the scarlet flower. It was on the tip of my tongue but I couldn't quite grasp it. Then I spotted a tray on the old rustic table over by the greenhouse – two cups and saucers, a teapot, and a plate with a scattering of crumbs, cushions on the wooden bench. Richard had been there earlier, with a visitor.

I was drawn to it, wondering. The teapot was cold.

'Ah! Elizabeth!' his voice called out from the lane.

Wrestling with the latch, he invaded the peace of the garden like a bull at a gate. He was wearing his white cotton jacket and a panama hat, family heirlooms he had been happy to rescue from our late father's things. Whenever he had the chance to wear them, he was delighted, not just because it meant that the weather was fine but because it vindicated the care he took where money was concerned. He looked very pleased with himself and that put me on my guard.

'You decided to return to the fold,' he said.

'You make me sound like the prodigal son, Richard. Whatever do you mean?'

He perched beside me on the wall, a little too closely, invading my space. I moved sideways as far as I could without falling off the end and into the pond.

'You've been away for hours. Gallivanting. You barely gave me time to say the benediction at the end of this morning's service before you shot out of the door, off on one of your jaunts on that ungainly contraption you insist on pedalling around the village.'

'You know perfectly well that I went to visit Rose and her father. I'd been invited for Sunday dinner. I told you.'

'I know what you told me, Elizabeth. But you left the Mathesons at ten past two, did you not? And I was here until at least four o' clock, yet you still hadn't returned.'

I wasn't about to give him the satisfaction of hearing me ask how he knew exactly when I had left the Mathesons. Gossips were attracted to my brother like flies round a dead dog. Instead, I waited for an interrogation but what he said was unexpected.

'Well, whatever you were doing was your business, I suppose.' He knew he had disarmed me. 'Pity you took so long, however, because you missed having tea with our visitor.'

I added a few more pencil strokes to my drawing, and a bit of fierce shading for good measure.

'Yes. Well, when I say our visitor, I actually mean YOUR visitor. He clearly didn't come to see me.'

I studied the tray, set for two. 'He?' I began to draw more cautiously. 'And who would that be?'

'Who do you think?'

I could feel the heat rising through my cheeks and was in no mood for games.

'For the Love of God, Richard. Grow up and tell me who it was.'

He paused a while longer, exacting the maximum amount of pain from the situation.

'Donald Maclean, of course. Who else could it be?'

I was glad that my face was already red from the sun. 'Donald came calling?'

'Yes, he did *come calling*. You know, it's really not on. Is it, Elizabeth? To have Donald Maclean arriving at the door uninvited, on a whim. Pretending he just happened to be passing this way on a Sunday walk... all the way from Whinbank. What will people think?'

'People will think he happened to be passing and called to say *hello*.' Though I knew the gossips would be having a field day.

'And meanwhile, you were where?'

'I was cycling. And walking on the muir.'

'Hoping to bump into Mr Maclean on the high road perhaps? Did you have a liaison somewhere and missed one another?'

'Certainly not!'

'Yes, that's exactly what he said. In any case, I put him straight. I told him if he had honourable intentions towards you, my sister, then he should come out and say it. I made it clear that he was putting your reputation at risk and should make up his mind about what he intended. Either he makes a decision or doesn't come calling again. And I sincerely hope you follow suit.'

I could hardly believe my ears. 'You did what?' I didn't wait for an explanation. 'How dare you provoke such ideas in Donald Maclean. We are good friends, and nothing more.'

'Now, now. Tut, tut. You know perfectly well that young men and women cannot simply be *good friends*, Elizabeth. Such nonsense. I do believe I may have done you a favour and that you will find out very soon what Mr Maclean's intentions towards you actually are.' He looked extremely smug.

I got to my feet, barely able to speak, and threw my precious drawing book onto the ground.

'How dare you organise my life and manipulate my friendships! You are the most infuriating brother a sister could have! Do you know that?!'

Richard looked as if he did know that, and was perfectly pleased with himself because of it.

I swept my arm round. The pelargonium went flying. The terracotta pot broke into a dozen pieces. 'Stupidity!' I shouted at the plant, suddenly remembering its secret meaning. 'I should have known!'

Richard hadn't expected such an extreme reaction. 'Rather childish, don't you think? Completely unnecessary, I'd say.'

'I don't care what you or anyone thinks or says,' I erupted. 'Why don't you all just leave me alone! All of you!'

I stormed into the house, mounted the stairs two at a time, slammed my bedroom door and threw myself onto the bed. Hot tears pricked my eyes but I was really too angry to cry. I glared at a long crack across the ceiling. 'Stupid, stupid, stupid!' I ranted. Oh, I felt such a fool! 'And as for you, Neil Tennant,' I said out loud as if he was there, 'You have business to attend to. Am I your unfinished business? I'll unfinished business you! Not a word for nearly four years and you suddenly decide to come back here and, no doubt, expect me to be grateful that you finally found time for unfinished business!'

In the days that followed I sought solace in the company of women, especially the women of the Rows. I assisted the nurse where I could; helped a new mother through her first confinement which proved to be lengthy and not without its difficulties; supported overworked mothers with their children; and paid particular attention to Mrs Pow whose physical and mental health were going downhill rapidly. Her ulcerated leg was no longer healing and she found the least amount of walking excruciatingly painful but she still insisted on her daily walk down the pit road to ask if they had found Jamie after all this time. This expedition was not possible without assistance and I was glad to help her on what would prove to be the last she would make before her passing at the end of the month.

Though I knew that I was helping these women, I felt that so much more could be achieved in other ways and that is why I invited several members of the Co-operative Women's Guild round for tea at the manse later that week.

Unfortunately, Sarah and I were in the garden when they arrived. The brass bell must have sounded over and over and over again. Silence would have been restored only briefly before each new bout of irritable clanging started up. I still giggle as I picture Richard prising open the study door, looking peevishly over the top of his half-moon spectacles. He was writing a sermon and the racket would have come at the wrong time. Once he had embarked on a discourse based on Scripture, he had to get on with it or the flow of creativity might be turned off for good. He would have seen that the house was deserted and, judging by the shadows on the other side of the stained-glass window, that a number of people had arrived at the same time. It wasn't his job to open the door, you see. He had a sister and a maid to do that for him, to deal with any visitors, prioritise them according to need, sort them out, and advise the regulars to return at another time. On that particular occasion, I remember, he had left strict instructions that he wasn't to be disturbed. Somebody should have been on hand to deal with such matters. As the church warden often said, *there's nae guid keepin' a dug an barkin' yersel*. Richard always found that expression amusing. He was calling out for me when I came in through the back door.

But without an immediate response, he'd had no option but to answer the door himself.

'Yes?' I heard him say. He would have recognised Mrs Broadley from the Sunday morning service and Mrs Duncan's name might have come to him though she had stopped attending church after the death of her husband some years back.

It was the one commonly known as Highland Mary who stepped forward. Everyone in the village knew her but he had never had the pleasure of her acquaintance, always managing to avoid it. She was a strong woman with grey hair pinned back in a small bun. She had a purposeful look about her, a face that was not unkind but she was clearly someone who did not take any prisoners. She introduced herself and her companions.

'We're here tae see Miss Fraser. She's expectin' us.'

'I'm afraid she's not in,' he replied, too busy to find out where I was at that precise moment. He was engaged in important work, he told them, and needed to get back to it.

'We'll wait then, if ye dinnae mind. It's a waste o' oor time tae gang hame jist tae come back oan anither occasion.'

Rather forward for a woman, he probably thought.

'It is not convenient. I am rather busy.' He felt flustered and couldn't hide it.

Highland Mary was irritated and was in no mood to hide it. 'We have an appointment,' she stated. 'It was arranged.'

I could not eavesdrop any longer and emerged from the kitchen to relieve my brother of his discomfort. I beckoned my visitors into the parlour. Richard was still standing in the hallway when I reappeared briefly to pass on an order for tea to Sarah in the kitchen.

'Aren't you getting back to your writing, Richard? You know how the creative juices dry up when you're disturbed. Don't hang about on account of us.'

I could tell he wanted to know what business had brought the women to the manse but he couldn't ask because the parlour door was open.

He backed off reluctantly but he would grill me later, I was sure. It wasn't my place to have meetings on church property. And three women from the Rows? A parishioner would have told him, no doubt, I was still going there. Whatever I was up to, Richard had already decided he did not approve.

The women were admiring the parlour when I returned, at last, with a tea tray. Mrs Broadley was remarking on how comfortable the upholstery was; Mrs Duncan thought the porcelain planter containing the aspidistra was a fine thing but it would block out all of the light if it sat at her window; and Mrs Birse had just finished saying they would have to come a bit closer, she would hardly be able to see or hear them across such a big room.

I thanked the women for giving up their valuable time to come and see me in their capacity as members of the Women's Guild of the local Co-operative Society. Meetings normally didn't take place during the summer but I had an idea and felt it was too important to wait. I expressed my admiration for the wonders of the Store on Main Street which sold good quality food at reasonable prices, whilst returning a dividend to each and every member. As a widow with a family to feed and clothe, Mrs Duncan was keen to sing the praises of the divi. But the Co-op had been a boon in other ways too, she explained. The Women's Committee, or Guild, was involved in providing social benefits for its members. Thirty young men, including her younger son, had spent a week on one of the many Co-operative camps held across the country. They had benefitted enormously from the experience, learning woodcraft and cooking skills whilst living under canvas. Sandy, apparently, had returned from the Trossachs looking refreshed thanks to the mountain air and the sunshine, and a hundred midgie bites hadn't dampened his enthusiasm for the place; whilst she had been able to visit the seaside for the first time in her life, on one of the day trips, along with her small daughter. The women related their adventures on their visit together to Dunoon. They had taken the train then the steamer, stopping in at Helensburgh en route.

What a fine day they'd had sailing down the Clyde, taking in the sea air and the beautiful scenery, commented Mrs Broadley. Even the weather had been laid on to their satisfaction. They had saved hard to pay for the trips, contributing weekly payments recorded on a card. It hadn't been cheap, right enough, but thanks to the Cooperative they were getting opportunities that would otherwise have passed them by. And as the three women were the mainstay of the committee, they had plans for more – dances and lectures, all sorts.

'That's precisely what I wish to talk to you about,' I said when I got the chance.

The women nodded, waiting, open to ideas.

'I was wondering what the Guild would think about including a specific class I have in mind, in their winter programme of events.' I caught Mrs Birse by the eye. 'I believe a neighbouring Society holds classes in *Nursing the Sick at Home*. Don't you think that would be a boon to the local community?'

'It would need the cooperation of the nurse,' commented Mrs Duncan.

'Dae ye think she'd be up for it?' Mary obviously feared she would not.

'Leave the nurse to me. I don't see how she can refuse if I approach her in the right way. And where the actual classes are concerned, you'd help too, Mrs Birse. As well as making the participants feel at ease, your experience would be invaluable.'

The women nodded their approval. Helping people to help themselves was at the heart of the Co-operative Society's philosophy. It had attracted them to the organisation in the first place. Passing on some basic knowledge and skills relating to health care had to be a good thing and they were all for it.

Mrs Duncan admired the china cups more than once as we drank our tea and chattered about families and fears for the future, bearing in mind developments in the miners' dispute. The possibility of the families being evicted, should it come to a strike, was an ever present worry they said, and it made them grateful to have a roof over their heads despite the shortcomings of the accommodation provided in the Rows. I pointed out that a Parliamentary enquiry was being made into the condition of housing in Scotland's industrial areas with a long period of information-gathering, inevitably, before the report was published in two or three years' time. It would be a crucial step in the process of improving housing conditions for working people.

'Mr Doonan, the miners' agent, has reported on conditions hereaboots, oan oor behalf,' said Mary.

'Yes,' I agreed. 'But why should you have to wait so long for decisions to be made. Pressure should be brought to bear on the landlords, leading to improvements in conditions sooner rather than later.'

'New raws are put up oan a whim,' said Mary, 'An' they never seem tae be much better than the last lot.'

I decided there and then that I would investigate how the women's lives might be improved through better housing. It was the beginning of an idea though I didn't quite know how I would proceed or what I would do with the information once I had it.

'Surveyors have been seen oan the Rashiepark side o' the village,' said Mary sipping her tea. 'There's rumours Melville's puttin' up raws for the Back o' Moss workers.'

Suddenly I knew how I might proceed and I'm sure Mary Birse knew too, judging by the hint of a smile on her face. Despite the differences in our circumstances, it seemed we had much in common.

Richard was hovering when it came time to show the visitors the door, keen to see the back of them and have it out with me. But I couldn't resist the temptation to tease him further. I explained to the women how I had been in the garden earlier when they'd arrived. There was a lot of watering to be done and would they like a tour? My onions were coming on a treat, would be just about ready in time for the Blackrigg Horticultural Show. Mrs Birse and Mrs Broadley seemed particularly interested since their husbands, who kept allotments, would be entering produce for judging as usual. It wouldn't do them any harm to report back on the competition being lined up at the manse, they admitted. Richard was left fuming as I trailed my visitors through the house and out of the back door.

I visited Rose the next day, late in the afternoon. She had not looked in on Catherine Melville and the new baby though she had been staying with her father for some time by then so I offered to accompany her to Parkgate. Wouldn't

Rose feel better if she took the bull by the horns and put in an appearance? She was interested in the progress of the baby, wasn't she? Rose said that she was. How could I think that she wouldn't be? But it wasn't straightforward, if I thought about it, she said. I did think about it, as I had done so many times since my friend had first revealed her secret to me. I knew from my own experience how complicated and confusing affairs of the heart could be. My stomach churned when I thought about my own situation. But thanks to the Stoneyrigg women, I now had an ulterior motive for visiting the Melvilles and I hoped that Rose would soon give in to my pestering.

After supper with Dr Matheson, Rose packed a bag of overnight things whilst I inspected the garden. A lecture on Women's Suffrage was being given in the public hall later that evening and we were both keen to attend. It would be easier all round if Rose stayed the night in the manse rather than having to make her way back to Rowanhill afterwards. Besides, we would be able to talk well into the night and we both had plenty to talk about.

Dr Matheson's garden was well tended so I was full of admiration. It stretched down-slope to where the Red Burn flowed through a deep gorge. I could hear the rushing stream in the bottom of the chasm on the far side of a tall beech hedge that marked the end of the garden ground. Productive vegetable patches and pretty flower beds, with an aviary half way along, were separated by a grassy path that led into a fair sized orchard. I sat on a wooden bench tucked into one corner beside a painted metal gate that gave access to the burn below. It was a sheltered corner and still bright in the early evening sunshine though cloud was building. I closed my eyes letting the birdsong and insects calm me but rustling beyond the hedge soon put me on edge.

I heard him before I saw him – which was strange given that he was sitting on the back of an enormous great horse. I had the feeling that he had been there for quite some time, watching – not me but the house. The beech hedge was dense, impenetrable, but I carefully manoeuvred into position beside a small gap, big enough to see, with an eye on the path back to the safety of the house should that be required. The rider sat breathing hard with his hands on the pommel, whilst his mount took a rest. Ears twitching, alert for the small sounds of a quiet evening, the horse gave a shiver and a snort. Flies were out for blood. He flicked his tail back and forth, head down in a patch of clover.

'Is someone there?' the rider said at last.

I cursed myself for a fool. Why could I not stay at peace? I took a deep breath.

'Dr Matheson?'

Silence.

'Rose? Is that you?'

It was David Melville's voice.

I swallowed hard, walked over to the gate. 'Good evening, David,' I said, shielding my eyes with a hand against the brightness of the sky.

He looked startled.

'Lovely evening for a ride-out,' I remarked.

'Indeed, Miss Fraser. Such lovely views around here.'

You didn't come for the views, I thought.

'Next time I see him, I'll make a point of complimenting Dr Matheson on his garden. As the warm summer has unfolded, I've noticed how the fruit has developed and the flowers have bloomed in an endless succession of colour.'

He sounded awkward.

You come by often, I surmised, but did not reply. Too many thoughts were rushing through my head.

'Such a delightful place yet so close to the industry that has transformed the community hereabouts,' he said, filling the gap created by my silence.

Delightful not only because of the garden, I guessed.

'Well hidden from the brickworks, pits, and ironworks of Mr Imrie's domain,' I said quickly, the words out before I knew it.

My remark, reminding him of his father-in-law, seemed to hit him like a sledgehammer. He dug his heels into his mount, much harder than he meant to. The horse took off, galloping furiously along the old coach road until they were out of sight.

I stood, gripping the cold metal gate with both hands.

When we arrived in the village later, Rose and I joined the women at the back of a crowd that had formed in Main Street. A large group of men had collected around the speaker who was a smartly dressed, rather elderly man with a large moustache and a Glasgow accent. A caravan with the word *Forward* painted in big letters along each side, had parked up on the pavement and the horse grazed a nearby patch of grass. Periodically, a round of applause and *'Hear, hear!'* sounded out.

An onlooker might assume that Mr Maxwell was speaking to the converted when he set out his stall as a representative of the Independent Labour Party but many were yet to be swayed, like the worker who complained that they had let the Unionists in by taking votes from the Liberals in recent bi-elections. And another who said that people like him were funded by underpaid miners who had a fight on their hands. Mr Maxwell was undeterred, he

284

had come to bring a message of hope and support to the mining villages of Scotland, engaged as they were in their struggle against the tyranny of capital. He explained that the Labour Party was behind them in their battle with the coalmasters for fair recompense. It was difficult and valuable work they did, work that kept the fires and furnaces of homes and industry lit across the land. Greed was at the heart of the owners' request for an overall reduction of one shilling in the miners' daily rates, he raged.

'*Hear, hear!*' called the audience.

Their struggle hadn't been lost on the people of Glasgow, the speaker assured them, where workers were demanding a living wage and decent housing, just like them. Had they heard about plans in the city for £8 cottages? That got a cheer from the crowd, especially the Stoneyrigg women who were there in some number. Mr Maxwell acknowledged the presence of the women, perhaps mindful of the need to gain their trust and support in the furtherance of the Labour cause. They had been ignored for too long. So he stayed with the housing issue for a while before changing tack.

Why was so much spent on armaments when workers and their children were in such need, he asked? Weren't the workers of Germany in exactly the same position in their own country? Hadn't miners across Europe supported the British miners during the 1912 stoppage when they had agreed to resist any moves on the part of the foreign mine owners to flood the British market with their coal, and in so doing they had prevented the miners' cause here from being undermined, in the best traditions of International Socialism? At the same time, the Liberal government had sold the miners down the river, claiming they were taking a neutral stance to bring the 1912 dispute to an end but, in point of fact, they had come down on the side of the capitalists, acceding to their demands so that nothing of any note was gained by the Federation as a result of the strike. Why had the Liberals' social reforms taken so long to be passed? The Liberals were merely using reform to protect the status quo!

'Hear, hear!' agreed the crowd.

What the working classes needed was more radical measures not reform, he continued. Nationalisation of land and resources, not kowtowing to the landowners.

'Hear, hear!'

This was also a government that was taking the nation to the brink of war, a war that suited the arms manufacturers and who else? *Not you! Not me! Nor our counterparts in other nations! We have no quarrel with the workers of Germany! But we are led by imperialists, whose greed takes them around the world to conquer small nations and peoples who cannot resist, whose riches they seek to plunder; imperialists who compete for trade routes and see conflict as a means of realising their vaulted ambitions. It does not suit them to work for peace for our sakes, when war might bring them greater reward.*

'Hear, hear!' People in the crowd looked at their friends and neighbours, all nodding in agreement.

A small number of women began to move away from the crowd leaving behind the powerful words of the speaker. Mr Maxwell spoke a great deal of sense, that much was true. He seemed to have the crowd wrapped around his finger and, I have to say, I felt excited by his plea for good sense and social justice, articulated in such a positive and hopeful manner. However, the problem for the women, and many of the men too, was one of means: the means to an end that was satisfactory from their point of view; action that would not jeopardise their ability to put food on the table and keep a roof over their heads, even if that roof was presently damp and invested with vermin. That was the worry. Fighting talk was all very well. But at the end of the day, in spite of Maxwell's protestations in favour of peace in Europe, fighting talk usually resulted in exactly that – a fight. And always in a fight, someone – usually the weak and defenceless – got hurt.

Women gravitated towards the public hall where another lecture was due to commence. Rose followed them whilst I ran back to the manse with her overnight bag. I eventually took a seat beside her at the front of the hall but in good time for the start of a lecture about the Women's Movement. I must have looked hot and flustered – I certainly felt it. When I caught my breath, I explained that Richard had kept me talking longer than I had anticipated. It was almost as if he had been trying to keep me back, deliberately, knowing how much I wanted to hear the speaker.

He had been in a frightful mood since the evening of the visit by the Cooperative Women's Guild and had argued vociferously against any further involvement with them. He had stressed the importance of the kirk remaining neutral in the political sphere. The role of the church was spiritual. Temporal matters should be left to others. It was especially important to avoid being tainted by any hint of socialism which, in his opinion, was the devil's work. It went against the natural order of things which had been handed down through history from God.

In respect of the classes in *nursing the sick at home* which I was seeking to instigate, Richard had been stuck for an answer when I asked if he agreed that since it was the family that bore the responsibility for nurturing and caring for its members, the family should be well-informed on such matters. Also, the prevention of ill-health in the first place made practical common sense. How could such a notion be against the natural order of things? Perhaps, I had suggested, when he had thought up one of his convoluted arguments backed up by Scripture, we could resurrect our discussion at some time in the future. Also, if he could explain to me how the subject could be construed as a political one, far less a wholly socialist one, I would be very grateful. Wasn't good health a goal that everyone aspired to? And something that true Christians could not deny another human being? Helping others aspire to good health could be seen as a manifestation of God's Love through the work of His church in the community. Yes? Therefore, how could the spiritual be seen as separate from the temporal? Weren't the two inextricably linked by the human condition? Didn't the church have views about how people lived; how they were treated by their neighbours; about morality and good and evil? Yes, it most certainly did. And wasn't the Cooperative Movement a logical development that sat well with temperance and personal responsibility, regularly preached from the pulpit? In fact, I had added finally, he would do well to reach out to the Cooperative Guild and offer them the use of the church hall, free of charge, for the classes. It would reflect well on the church and on him personally, as a man of the cloth, would it not?

My questions often came too quickly for him and he would retreat into his study to construct a sermon full of carefully crafted arguments and answers, at which he was very skilled.

Rose had listened patiently to my rant. She patted my hand to show support and admiration for my perseverance with Richard. Rose and I increasingly discussed matters of social and political importance, when we had the opportunity. Later, we would discuss what we had heard at the Forward Van. It was a pity the two events had been organised for the same evening but our ears pricked up when Miss Mutch appeared on the stage ready to deliver her talk about the history of the struggle for women's suffrage.

The audience was rapt from the very start as the speaker gave an historical overview of women's struggle for freedom, beginning with the loss of rights in earlier times that had resulted in the female sex being regarded as frivolous and having no opinion worthy of merit. This had induced prejudice and inequality in education, opportunity and inheritance, a situation that had proved very difficult to remedy.

Miss Mutch followed with a long list of the advances already made by brave women who had challenged such obvious injustices, standing in the face of ridicule and vested interest. This was what was being called *the season of silent growth*, essential groundwork that made *Votes for Women* possible. Although parliamentary bills and amendments had been defeated repeatedly since the 1860s, it was only a matter of time before legislation was enacted for women's suffrage, claimed Miss Mutch. In addition to the progress already made, women would continue showing their capabilities in many fields and *Votes for Women*, when granted, would open the floodgates giving access to all spheres of social, political, and commercial life which had been deprived of the opinion and experience of the female sex for far too long, to the great detriment of society as a whole.

'We merely wish to take our place in the world,' concluded Miss Mutch, an hour later. 'Free to be citizens of our country, to contribute to the society we live in, to use our talents – and we have many – for the greater good of all. Who could not agree?'

Miss Foulkes agreed wholeheartedly, starting the applause with a cheer. Her colleagues from the local branch of the Women's Freedom League joined in. Rose stood up in the front row provoking others to follow, including the handful of men present. I felt compelled to join them. But the response from many in the audience was simply cordial, the more enthusiastic tempered by the more sceptical. Their lack of passion confounded me.

There were few questions. Miss Mutch had spoken a great deal of sense, certainly. Some did not wish to disturb the clarity of her argument with awkward questions. Others, who had been left with a sharp dislocation within their sense of self, when all that they had come to believe about their sex had been deconstructed by the lecture, were left too confused to articulate their thoughts in such a public place. They would pick holes in the woman and her arguments later when they had had time to think, behind closed doors. But Isabelle Melville felt riled enough to put in her tuppence-worth about the methods employed by the suffragettes. The message of the women's movement, which did have some merit in her opinion, was lost in the outrage felt by right-minded people. It had been such an inconvenience to Lady Moffat when all of the telephone wires around Blairhall had been cut earlier in the spring and wasn't such anarchy a threat to social order, something to be resisted by us all? Also, the bomb hoax that had delayed proceedings of the Bo'ness Town Council had been an attack on local democracy when one thought about it, she added. She was delighted when Miss Silver shouted

Well said! Isabelle did not require a debate from Miss Mutch and swept out of the hall.

'How good was that?!' said Rose, when it was clear proceedings had ended. 'It's what I've been thinking for some time… and it was splendid to hear it put into context. What do you say, Beth? Women are taking control of their lives!'

'I'm astounded at how much I could relate to myself,' I replied, feeling that nothing could stand in our way of progress if we put our minds to it.

'Pity you didn't bring Richard,' Rose said with feigned innocence.

'Phee couldn't have put it better! Behave!' I had to suppress a loud snort.

We left our seats and made for the door, laughing at Richard's expense.

A huddle had developed at the exit and we soon found out why. Cloud that had been boiling up since late in the afternoon had developed into a thunderstorm. Rain fell like stair rods, so fast that the pavement and roadway were already awash. The people at the Forward Van were running for cover as lightning flashed and thunder rumbled around the heavens.

'Let's go!' I cried out, too elated by what I had just heard to wait for the rain to pass.

We pushed through the crowd, past the comfortable ladies of the church tea committee who were hanging onto Isabelle Melville's every word about the day she had met the King. We edged between Mrs Gow and the Widow MacAuley who were discussing the likelihood of the thatch in their roofs holding out against the downpour; stepped in front of the nurse and the lady schoolteachers; and the members of the ladies' choir contemplating the distance home in the wet, hoping their summer outing at the weekend would not be affected.

Arm-in-arm, we ran out into the hissing rain. We were drenched to the skin within a few steps which made us laugh. We had no defence against the deluge as raindrops kissed our faces and ran down our necks. It felt wonderful. We were free like the rain, unrestrained by manners and restrictions, feeling good in our own skins.

Barely visible through the downpour, a uniformed horseman was advancing along the road towards us at a fast pace so we had to wait before we could cross the street. There was nothing we could do but stand there, let him pass, and let the deluge take its course. He galloped closer through a stream flowing down the middle of the road. Muddy water splashed from the thundering hooves of his horse. The rain stung our eyes as we focused on him. He was taught in the saddle, his head bent low against the onslaught. Rose looked up at him as he approached but she did not smile. He saw her and touched his cap with a leather-gloved hand but kept riding. Her eyes followed him as he disappeared into the mirk.

I pulled at her arm.

'Let's go, Rose. We're soaked to the skin.'

Rose pulled back for a moment, staring along the road to Parkgate. She wouldn't move or speak. She seemed rooted to the spot, helpless against the onslaught of heavy rain.

'For the Love of God, Rose! He's gone! Let's go!' Then she let me lead her across the road and up the lane to the shelter of the manse.

Chapter 16

Elizabeth

The thunderstorm left devastation in its wake. A small landslide on the south-facing slope of The Law had come to a halt in the field above Craigpark Farm, leaving behind a permanent reminder of the power of Nature to be witnessed the following day when people emerged from damp homes to assess the damage. All night, it had been relentless, battering down onto thin slates and pouring out of gutters too fast for the slope of the land to carry it away. No one could remember thunder and lightning like it. The storm had remained overhead for what seemed like an age, sending down wave after wave of unforgiving hail and rain onto villagers who could do nothing but sit out the tempest, praying to God for an end to it, asking Him what they had done to deserve such a fate.

The Stoneyrigg Rows came off worse than any other part of the district since they had been built on a bog. With Irish labour, the Coal Company had drained the land, a wide flat terrace on the side of The Law. Just two parallel ditches leading into the Red Burn, had rendered unproductive ground suitable for industrial housing. The channels could dispatch the worst of it on a day when the rain wasn't heavy but they had never been designed to cope with much more. Even a normal Scottish winter had not been considered in the planning process, the cost of labour being uppermost in the owner's mind. During the night of the storm, the Rows were inundated within a very short time as the dry closets overflowed and a temporary pond formed. Householders were up all night, armed with cloths, pails and brushes, doing what they could to remove stinking water from their homes.

The following morning, Dr Matheson arrived at the manse under cloudless skies having witnessed the aftermath of the deluge. The people of the Rows, he explained, were busy lugging pails of putrid water to the edge of the road where they were tipping it over the fence, out of harm's way. Meanwhile women lined up in a pool of filth to draw water from the spigots in the street.

'As long as there are places like Stoneyrigg,' he declared as he came into the parlour, 'There will be no end to my work and the work of every other doctor. I've put the word round about boiling the water before it's used for washing or drinking, of course.'

He looked disapprovingly at Rose, wrapped up in a shawl, her dark hair unkempt and tumbling over her shoulders, looking as if she had been up half the night.

'Come along,' he said to her. 'I must get along to Parkgate straight away to telephone the authorities. I'll have someone come out to assess the situation. The Medical Officer of Health should know about this... and so should Charles Imrie. He bears some responsibility for his tenants and needs to get a man down there to organise the clean up.'

Rose hesitated. She was tired out from our long discussion into the night and reluctant to accompany her father to Parkgate for reasons that I now better understood.

'The water is full of disease,' Dr Matheson said, raising his voice just enough to communicate the gravity of the situation. 'Action needs to be taken. The nurse will go round to reinforce the message but time is of the essence, I'm afraid.'

Rose suggested that her father go by himself but he was having none of it. She was being quite unreasonable, in his opinion. Did she want to find out about the work of a country doctor or did she not?

I came to my friend's rescue, offering to accompany her to Parkgate.

She followed meekly.

'We were up quite late,' I explained as we climbed into the doctor's motor car.

'That much is obvious,' he said, his eyes on the road once more. Puddles and potholes punctuated the way ahead. 'I don't know what young women find to talk about,' he added once we were well on our way.

'You'd be surprised,' said Rose.

Jameson appeared at the large oak door, irritated by our urgent ringing of the bell. When he saw the good doctor had come to visit, he changed his tune however, inviting him in without hesitation then rushing him off to the study in order to use the telephone.

Rose and I stood waiting in the semi-darkness of the hallway: a grand oak-lined corridor hung with ornate mirrors and portraits in gilt frames. Dressed in a plain black skirt and a striped blouse of pink and white, Rose whispered that she wished the ground would swallow her up. There was no place on earth she would rather not be, and she prayed that her father would return soon, allowing a quick escape back to the village. A door banged and a voice could be heard in the distance. A servant was receiving instructions from the housekeeper. We relaxed as we studied the ceiling, the ornate plasterwork and the shimmering glass of the chandelier which was modest compared to others we had seen in the main rooms during former visits. The house smelled of beeswax and lavender, and money. A far cry from the cottages in the Stoneyrigg Rows.

'Penny for them.' His voice was deep and rich, like his pockets.

I saw how Rose stiffened.

David Melville stood at the half-opened door into the drawing room. He looked fine in his military uniform. His skin glowed from days in the sun; his eyes shone at the sight of her. He made no pretence at how he felt. His smile said it all, so glad to see her standing there, for a brief moment, staring across the chasm between them yet close enough to touch, had I not been there. He held out his hand, inviting her into the room with him.

She stood firm, made to explain her presence: her father, the telephone, a public health situation of some importance.

I began to speak about the problems that ensue when the wrong site is chosen for housing as might be the case if the rumours about new rows for the Back o' Moss workers were correct. Then I stressed the importance of wash house provision and indoor plumbing for improving the lives of the women; the benefits of investment in the health of workers and the spin-off in terms of output for the employer.

He stared at me as if I was mad. There I was playing piggy-in-the-middle, in the hallway of his home where he was master, and daring to lecture him about how to house his workforce.

He nodded, *Yes, of course. It would all be taken into consideration when the final decision was made about where to build the new rows.*

I was not about to be dismissed so easily. I said that the field on the west side of Blackrigg was clearly unsuitable given the flooding along at Stoneyrigg. The western site was similar in many ways and drainage would be a problem. A sloping site would be better.

He seemed relieved when Dr Matheson appeared from the study and he listened more intently as the doctor reinforced my message. I was grateful for his support but quietly seethed that my opinion was not as credible as the doctor's and had not merited the same degree of interest.

Then Catherine Melville joined us, abruptly ending our conversation about matters relating to the housing of the labouring classes.

'Why don't you come to the nursery while you're here.' She turned to Rose, 'Perhaps you'd like to see how baby Clive is doing, since you brought him into the world, Miss Matheson.'

'I'd love to. Thank you.'

Dr Matheson went ahead, enquiring after everyone's health whilst I followed on behind.

Catherine led the way up a sweeping staircase lit by a long stained-glass window to the floor above.

'Have you recovered after the birth, Catherine?' he asked. 'Has Dr Lindsay been looking after you and baby Clive?'

I wondered what the doctor was making of Catherine's red-rimmed eyes and how drawn she looked.

She climbed the stairs ahead of us in silence, continued along a corridor, before stopping at the nursery door as if she couldn't bear to go inside. Her face was as pale as the expensive dress she was wearing.

'Things haven't been easy since the birth, doctor.' She placed a hand on her lower abdomen. 'My husband says it'll take time to get over it, that things will get back to normal, eventually. But I don't think so. I really don't think so. It would be difficult to go through it all again. Do you understand?'

I hung back a little, not wishing to eavesdrop on what had become a confidential discussion between patient and doctor. I looked round for Rose but the corridor was empty, retraced my steps to the staircase and looked down. The sight of David Melville taking Rose in his arms shocked me beyond belief and I must have gasped.

They looked up at me in alarm and parted suddenly. David disappeared into the corridor below.

Rose soon joined us in the nursery, her cheeks as pink as the blooms I had seen in her father's garden. Baby Clive lay sleeping in his crib, tucked up in pristine sheets and a blue, embroidered blanket. The room was festooned with toy boats and books, tin soldiers and building blocks all brightly coloured and brand new. They evidenced an outpouring of love from doting parents and other relatives, delighted by the arrival of the newest addition to the Melville dynasty. A large rocking horse stood by the window. Like the other toys, way in advance of the child's stage of development but part of the furniture, signposts to his future life as the heir to Rashiepark.

We admired David and Catherine's son. He was filling out nicely, we said, a credit to the care of a loving mother.

'So like his father,' the doctor observed.

Catherine praised the nanny, describing how she weighed the baby regularly to monitor his weight gain. She was an experienced nurse who knew what to do and helped her to get as much sleep as possible in between all of the feeding. In fact, the nurse was so capable that Catherine felt superfluous when it came to the child's care, even though she was his mother. It was a flippant remark, meant to be light-hearted, but it gave away much of her insecurity.

I surmised that the loss of her first child had, perhaps, taken its toll on Catherine Melville.

To my horror, after what I had just witnessed from the top of the stairs, she looked forlornly at Rose.

'I can't seem to talk to Dr Lindsay about how I'm feeling. But I feel that I could open up to you. There's so much I'd like to discuss. So much rattles around in my head, sometimes I think it's all too much but I keep it bottled up.'

'You really should speak to Dr Lindsay about how you're feeling, Catherine,' Rose insisted.

'You're a doctor...more or less... and a woman... I feel you would understand. Will you visit again soon? Call in from time to time?' She looked so sad and lonely.

'If you think it will help, Catherine, I will come again. I promise. I'll visit very soon,' Rose agreed.

'Will you come again tomorrow, Rose?' Catherine asked nervously as we took our leave.

'Glad to,' Rose replied, trying to sound like a friend. 'Perhaps we could take Clive for a walk, and a picnic, if the weather stays fair. The air would do you good.'

Just getting out of this house would do you good, I thought to myself, descending the grand staircase and glad to be going.

'Yes, a walk and a picnic luncheon,' Catherine agreed, with forced jollity. She frowned. Here was something else to worry about. 'I'll tell nanny to have everything prepared.'

'Will you come too, Elizabeth?' asked Rose, searching my eyes for support and, perhaps, understanding.

I glared at her. 'I'm sorry,' I replied curtly. 'I'm busy tomorrow.'

I was not going to be a smokescreen for Rose and David, assisting in the rekindling of a love affair under the very nose of poor Catherine Melville. In fact, I looked forward to the moment when I would be able to give Rose a piece of my mind.

We were met by David in the hall as Jameson showed us the door. Dr Matheson studied his uniform, the insignia of rank, the epaulettes, and the brass buttons. He enquired about army matters. What was the word in army circles about the likelihood of war? Most unsettling that an assassination of one man on the other side of Europe, even if he was an Archduke, could have repercussions for everyone across so many countries. The matter should have been sorted out through diplomacy, the doctor insisted. It should not have been allowed to escalate, drawing so many nations to the brink. In his opinion, he explained with regret, the acceptance of war as a method appropriate for settling the arguments between powers would always lead to conflict, eventually.

He shook his head. 'I'm praying for a miracle. But I'm not holding my breath.'

David laughed off the doctor's fears. 'The army's not too concerned at the moment so don't worry. Though there's not much time for diplomacy to sort out the impasse.'

Rose had made her way towards her father's car and was standing some way off.

'It was a pleasure to see you,' David called, looking at Rose directly. 'You must come again. And soon.'

Catherine joined her husband to wave off the visitors. She linked her arm in his.

'They will be back very soon,' she said to him, looking more at ease. 'Or at least Rose will. She's returning tomorrow for a walk with me and the baby. I'm quite looking forward to it.'

David said nothing but walked off abruptly, to Catherine's surprise. He disappeared inside the study and banged the door behind him.

A few days later, I sat at the bottom of the stairs avidly reading a letter that had only just dropped through the letterbox. I loved to hear Phee's news from the Borders, soon to be her permanent home after her marriage to Eric, at the end of September. Plans were being drawn up for a church service followed by a grand wedding breakfast in the North British Hotel. Visits to the capital for dress fittings had already taken place. The cake and other essentials had been chosen. I realised long ago that Phee wasn't the type to hold back and take her time. She had fallen head over heels with her captain and wanted to be married as soon as possible. She would have been happy to elope into the night with him, just the two of them on the back of a strong white steed, but Isabelle had put the brakes on that idea, persuading her younger sister that the romance of a society wedding was worth waiting for. Often, Phee wrote in her letter, she tossed and turned till dawn tortured by the promised passion of her wedding night. I blushed as I read the letter. There were times when Phee was just a little too candid but I wouldn't have changed her for the world. In truth, it filled me with hope for my own happiness when I learned of how head over heels she was for her dashing cavalryman.

As I folded up the letter, I realised a hurried post script had been added. The news that Phee was returning home at the end of the week delighted me. The news that Eric had been sent for by his regiment gave cause for concern. He had left hurriedly one morning, leaving her upset. Then I smiled. *Parting is such sweet sorrow,*

Phee reflected, longing for the day when she would see him again.

I was brought rudely back to the real world of the Blackrigg manse when the doorbell rang, my heart fluttering with a mixture of hope and dread at who it might be. I hesitated before answering, praying that it wasn't Donald Maclean dropping in to ask for my hand in marriage after his encounter with my brother that awful Sunday afternoon. I still smarted when I thought of Richard's interference, without any pretence at subtlety. I had avoided visiting Whinbank even though I knew Mrs Maclean would be missing my company and I found it impossible even to write with excuses that might have explained my absence. A peak through the stained glass window let me know all was well.

Richard opened the study door asking if the post had come, only to find the schoolmaster, looking rested after a holiday in France, grinning on the doorstep.

I followed him into the study before Richard was able to exclude me. Here was an opportunity. Mr Black might prove useful in fighting my corner.

'I've asked Richard to put his name to a report I'm compiling about housing conditions in the village, Mr Black. I want to send it to our Member of Parliament as a contribution to the parliamentary enquiry.'

'Splendid idea,' he agreed. 'The flooding along at Stoneyrigg was horrendous. As if the design of the houses wasn't bad enough, they've built them in a bog. Every time it rains heavily, it's a quagmire of mud and filth.'

Richard grimaced. Mr Black had said the wrong thing.

'Yes, splendid idea,' Ernest continued. 'Your name, Richard would add a degree of credibility to such a report.' He turned to me, embarrassed by what might be perceived as insensitivity. 'No offence intended, dear Miss Fraser.'

'None taken. A submission from a mere woman would not be as well-received as a report from a minister of the church.... other churchmen are speaking out about such things.'

Richard sighed. He didn't feel like arguing with me in the company of a witness, especially one such as Ernest Black who was clearly intent on currying favour with me. I guessed that Richard probably wouldn't have the schoolmaster round for dinner again anytime soon. Meantime, he would humour us both then refuse to sign the report when I was by myself.

Ernest decided to capitalise on the situation, sensing that he had caught the minister on a good day.

'While I remember, about that matter we were discussing before I went off on my travels.... the matter of the school board feeding the children of the miners should the strike go ahead... as seems increasingly likely.'

Richard looked grave, preparing to quash the man's misplaced enthusiasm for a lost cause.

Ernest continued. 'The loss of income from the government grant to the board, should the children be removed from the school by their parents, would be a set-back for the school.'

'As happened in Lanarkshire during a previous dispute,' I added in support.

Ernest again. 'That's right, Richard. Someone might let it slip to the Blackrigg miners. Despite our best efforts, news gets around. It wouldn't look good for the school to lose much of its pupil roll overnight, due to your lack of support for innocent children caught up in a situation not of their making. It would be a tragedy so early in your tenure as chair of the board. Would it not?'

Richard looked daggers at us both, knowing he was defeated, and backed off into his study.

'Good decision, Richard,' I called after him just as the door was closing. 'And I'll have a full report on housing conditions for you to sign within the month.'

Ernest raised his eyebrows. 'Well done, Elizabeth.'

'Well done to you too, Mr Black, and thank you for your help, most sincerely.' I thought for a moment. 'Don't you feel that change is just around the corner? There is so much to be done but change is coming, we can be sure of it.'

Ernest doffed his hat and took his leave, less buoyant than I had expected after his visit to the near continent with his good friend, Mr Muir.

I found out from him on another occasion that he hadn't wanted to crush my optimism at the time. It suited me so well, he told me, and he loved me for it. He had kept to himself the scenes he had witnessed whilst on holiday, images of military vehicles and the build-up of troops in the quiet countryside of Northern France. He had decided not to mention the latest gossip about the Lithuanian worker who lodged with Mrs Duncan, about how Constable Mackay had come for him in the middle of the night and put him into a cell until his nationality could be checked. Nor did he mention that David Melville had been seen leaving the village early that morning, driven by Billy Dodds to the barracks in Edinburgh by all accounts, by order of his battalion.

Change was most definitely coming but perhaps not of the kind that I was hoping for.

Minn

I only went home the once in all the weeks after the fire at the Big House. When I did, I was reminded of my father's displeasure at my behaviour and his disapproval of Rob.

Though he'd been released from the police station without charge, and despite testimony from no less than the laird himself, it was a case of no smoke without fire as far as my father was concerned. How could I tell him that Rob had come looking for me at Parkgate House that night? I found out from Annie that he'd turned up at Netherside asking for me and she'd told him where I was. Before he managed to leave, the grieve found him at the back of the steading and shouted on the ploughman. They gave him what-for, thinking he was up to no good. That explained the cut and the bruising on his face when I saw him later at Parkgate.

Jean was pleasant enough when I went home but I felt that the door that had opened between us was well-closed again. And though it had always been normal for Uncle Peter and Uncle Gavin to be quiet in my company, now their silence seemed filled with unspoken condemnation. In fact, the absence of any talk in the house about the dispute in the pits, the trouble in the community and whether or not these things were connected, infuriated me. It made me want to scream that I wasn't a child and should be party to everybody's thoughts and accusations. Instead, there was only a running commentary about the weather, the allotments, and occasional tittle-tattle about this one and that one in the village. A remark about Peggy Duncan and her foreign lodger that was worthy of Bessie Morrison and the gossips in the queue at the Co-op, had me running for the hills. My admiration for Peggy merely grew in the face of such small minds.

I worried that it all might chip away at my feelings for Rob which were already confused. My dreams of the early summer and schemes to run away to Canada with him seemed hopeless. And so, it was easier to stay away from Stoneyrigg and get on with life at Netherside.

One evening in early August, I was with Annie, leaning against the back wall of the farmhouse at lowsing-time, another hard day's work behind us. I shook my long hair free of its cotton scarf and breathed in the cool air. Past the midden, the kye grazed lush green grass in the middle meadow. I could have watched them all night. There is surely nothing as peaceful as a herd of cattle with their heads in a field of pasture on a sunny evening after milking is over. The shepherd's ancient mother had warned that such a pleasant summer of weather – apart from the odd downpour – was likely to be followed by a harsh winter. It was Nature's way of seeing to things, of evening it all out: the good and the bad, plenty and scarcity. She'd lived long enough on this earth to have seen it all before, she told us. But we were young, Annie and me, so we didn't pay heed to old wives' tales when it suited us. Whatever lay ahead, we would face when the time came. We lived in hope and, in many ways, life lay in the future rather than the here and now. It was what we worked for, what we wished for, what kept us going through the present, convinced that our dreams would come true and might be waiting for us just around the corner.

A cool breeze blew in from the shadows, finding us where we rested on the sunny side of the house.

'Did ye see Rob thon time ye were hame?' ventured Annie, expecting me to say that I hadn't, shutting down any talk of Rob right there and then as I had done often in recent days.

I took a while to answer. 'Aye, I did.'

Annie gave a start. 'Spill the beans then....'

'He was at the bottom o' the hill road.'

'Ye niver said! Whit happened? Come oan!'

'Nuthin happened. He was wi' the usual crowd... Sandy, Bert, Dan, Jim, and John, Wee Geordie... Billy Tennant...'

'And?'

'They were talkin' aboot the Highland Games... I came on them near the steadin'. The pipe band and the fitba' tournament... sounded fine... sic a shame we missed them.'

Annie raised an eyebrow. 'Did Rob need a' his freens aboot him tae pluck up the courage an' wait for ye, kennin ye would be comin' hame?'

'They were jist hingin' aboot.'

'Whit happened?'

'Rob was there, an' I was there. He looked at me an' I tried no tae look at him. But I couldnae help it.'

'An' then whit?'

'Whit dae ye mean?'

'Is that it? He looked at ye?'

'Aye,' I said remembering how Rob had looked straight at me, unsmiling, his eyes as dark as the Mill Pool on the Red Burn. 'Aye that was it.'

A deep voice suddenly boomed from an upstairs window.

'Minn! Run up tae the tap field, quick. Mrs Davidson forgot tae shut in the hens up by. Dae ye hear me? Minn!'

'I hear ye, Mr Davidson!'

Annie fell in behind me as I took the path up the hill. 'Dirty auld bugger,' she said.

I glanced round at the bedroom window from where the command had come.

'Annie!'

'Mrs Davidson was oan her wey oot tae the hens when he geid her the nod.'

'The nod?'

'They must think I'm blind or stupid or baith,' she said. 'Jist cause I'm up tae ma oxters in the washin-up, disnae mean I cannae use ma een or ma heid. I ken when they're up tae houghmagandie. He gies her the nod an' she gaes runnin'. It's yin bairn efter anither wi' them, fower an coontin', nae sooner yin's drapt but they're at it again, a new bairn every year near enough.'

Annie thought for a bit. 'Must be somethin' a dae wi' bidin' oan a ferm. Fornication. It's a'place ye look oan a ferm.'

I felt my face burn.

Annie laughed loud. 'I ken whit yer thinkin', Minn Graham! Yer thinkin' ye'd like Rob Duncan tae gie ye the nod!'

'I am not!'

'Aye ye are!' Annie chased after me as I ran off.

She caught up at the open gate to the top field where a hen hut nestled in a hollow behind the dyke. I mind staring at the ground where a thousand small brown feathers littered the grass. Hens lay scattered, all dead or nearly so. Inside the coop further carnage awaited. The sound of panicked birds, fluttering wings, and desperate crawing had barely died down – it was still there in the cloud of feathers settling in the dusty air.

'The fox,' whispered Annie. 'He got here afore us.'

'Aye,' was all I could say. I knelt down beside a hen, its neck long and distended from the attack, a smear of blood on the ground. I watched the wind ruffle its feathers, lifting them in wee waves, like flooers rippling across a meadow with the summer breeze. I saw how its eyelid was shut over a once-bright eye; scaly legs and feet, poised to run but now still, caught in its stride by the teeth of the fox. The hen was soft to the touch and still warm.

'Hoo does it have to tak them a'?' I asked, a lump in my throat. 'Is yin no enough? Hoo does it have tae tak sae monie?'

'When they taste blood there's nae stoppin' them. It's in their nature,' explained Annie, matter-of-fact.

We began lifting them by their feet, three in each hand, for carrying down to the barn. Dochie and the bothy lads would come up for the others. The birds would be hung and plucked the next day, ready for the pot and the market, making the best of a bad situation.

'Ye ken whit they say aboot a fox,' said Annie. 'It's a sign.'

I shivered, 'Dinnae.'

We started down the hill, dejected. Shocked.

'Hey!' came a voice from below. 'Have ye heard?' The ploughman at Blackhill was running along the road. 'It's stertit, the war's stertit.'

'The war?' I said, stopping in my tracks. 'We're at war?'

Annie marched on, her eye on the steading. She was thinking about how the news of the rout by the fox would be received at the house.

'We're at war?' I stood staring at the view; the patchwork of fields where the harvest was barely started; the woodland and the farms; and the blue hills on the far horizon. I felt the weight of the dead hens in my arms, as the words lingered on my lips. And the full force of their meaning weighed heavily on my breast.

Chapter 17

SUMMER 1918

John

Summer's come to this valley where I am a prisoner. I can do nothing but wait for the war to end and regain my strength in the meantime. I manage a walk to the river most days and regular food is helping my body to recover. Mostly, I find a place to sit and let my senses fill with the beauty of what is before me. At first, I couldn't see it. I saw only terror and death after a long struggle. But several weeks later, as the sun has grown warmer and brighter, my mind has opened up again to the possibilities of the future. It had been closed for too long, shut down by anger and resentment because of what had befallen me and everybody I held dear; closed by memories of the horrors I'd seen, memories that blocked out the good things that happened along the way.

In times of plenty, these things might not amount to much, dismissed as everyday, but in lean times they make the difference between life and death, sanity and the abyss. The touch of a stranger's hand on your back. The offer of a brew when you're thirsty and cold. A listening ear when you're lonely and far from home. Sharing a cigarette and a joke on a frosty night while the noise of hell rages, barely a mile away at the Front.

Or when a soldier grasps your hand for a moment longer than he needs to before going over the top, letting you know he's terrified, just as you are, and that he's with you.

The look in a man's eyes and the smile on his face when he uses his last breath to tell you that life, in spite of it all, is good.

I cannot make sense of war because it is senseless. So many have had their lives cut short but mine has been spared. I will go on because I must and, one day, I might see the purpose in it.

When we first heard that Britain had declared war on Germany, a strange excitement hung in the air where boys – and some men – were concerned. Several from the village left at the first opportunity, worried hostilities might cease before they'd had a whiff of the great adventure. My mother said she was glad that me and Jim were too young for service and my father's hatred of the warmongers dampened my elation, leaving me with a troubled agitation for pastures new in the company of friends. When the pals got together on the football field or went walking or fishing or poaching, the excitement mounted as we told tales of derring-do, turning each outing into a risky exploit against the enemy. Wee Geordie was ay on the lookout for German spies! In truth, we imagined army life to be a version of the summer camp with guns and bayonets, and medals for valour.

By the end of the first winter, it was certain that the war was going to last much longer than we'd been led to believe at the onset. After those early heady days, when large numbers of men downed tools and took off for recruiting offices, news of casualties and a dip in recruitment led to calls for men to enlist. The dispute over wages that was coming to a head just as war was declared had initially been put to one side in the interests of national security. It fizzled out like a damp squib but the call for a fair rate of pay simmered under the surface and soon came to the boil once again. Of course, folk who'd nothing to do with the mines and had no idea what it was like to work underground, nor bring up a family on a miner's wage, had plenty to say about our selfishness and lack of patriotism in holding the country to ransom at a time of national emergency. Regular meetings at the steading kept us informed about the progress of negotiations and gave us an opportunity to debate the issues amongst ourselves. The cost of living was rising and pay needed to take account of this. And though there was increased demand for coal and steel, this hadn't resulted in higher wages for the workers. Having argued for so long that miners' pay rates should be linked to the price of coal, the coal masters did a volte face, refusing to increase wage rates accordingly, looking to keep any increased profits to themselves. It was blatant profiteering, according to my father.

On a dark night huddled against a biting wind, the threat of rain never far away, we assembled at the steading waiting for Steeny to come with news. Opinions were traded about what was at stake, how we had got to where we were, and what the motives of the employers and the government had been in the latest negotiations. The union wanted a 20% rise – the owners had offered 10%. Somebody said that even in wartime, employers drove a hard bargain, reluctant to hand over a single penny piece if they didn't have to. The Miners Federation wanted national negotiations, the employers didn't, preferring local agreements. Divide and rule was the name of their game as we all knew. We also knew the Scots mineworkers were in a good position to achieve a favourable settlement, since we'd been negotiating almost continually on our own behalf for a whole year and were united more than ever before.

All winter, the government had made noises about wanting a settlement sooner rather than later. Asquith supported the owners' offer of 10%, with local talks for anything over and above, which didn't go down well with the workers. On the other hand, the government was encouraging the employers to cooperate with the unions to avoid stoppages. It had surely dawned on those in the corridors of power how important the mining industry was to the economy, especially during this period of national emergency. Maybe, said an older voice, it was dawning on everybody how important the workers were to the production of coal and, at last, folk were seeing the justice of a decent living wage in return for hard labour. But he'd barely made his point when a loud groan started up, a voice said they'd heard it all before, and we had.

Then finally, Steeny arrived with good news. The negotiations had ended in our favour. They'd agreed on a rise of 18½%. Not the 20% we wanted – but a very good compromise, from our point of view.

A mild round of applause started up as the rain began to fall. Men were happy at the prospect of being able to go home with news of a substantial rise, something that could offset recent increases in prices.

Dan Potts turned to me and Jim. 'Yer faither's the yin man no lookin' pleased at the settlement.'

Bert and Rob laughed.

'Whit dae ye expect?' I said, keeping my voice low. 'He's no happy bar he's fechtin.'

'He'll be riled we didnae get the 20%. Faur as he's concerned, oniethin' less is capitulation,' Jim added.

Steeny wanted a final word before the men went on their way. He slowly read out the names of fellow workers who had appeared in the lists published in the local paper.

'That brings the Blackrigg number to twa men killed, yin missin' in action and three wounded. An' we're barely six months intae the war.' He continued with an important message.

'As ye'll ken the number o' men enlistin' fae the mines has been considerable an' has had an effect on production. The government wants pitmen tae refrain fae joinin' up for the foreseeable future. Oor job is tae bring up the coal. There's nae shame in bidin' at hame, mind. Winnin' the coal is essential for winnin' the war, we cannae a' be expected tae put a gun in oor haun.'

Sandy caught up with us as the meeting came to a close and driving rain had most scurrying for shelter in any case. He'd come from the library. Books were tucked into the front of his jacket, his collar was up and his cap pulled low over his eyes.

'Whit's up wi' you lot?' he asked. 'Has somebody died?'

'As a matter o' fact they have,' replied Bert who proceeded to tell Sandy about the casualties of war and the government's concern about too many colliery workers joining up.

'They dinnae want onie mair frae the pits,' explained Dan.

We didn't need to discuss the matter because we were all thinking the same and it left us downhearted. Sandy fell in behind our group as we made our way back to the Rows. He caught the arm of my jacket, pulled me back from the others.

'I'm no the fechtin kind,' he whispered. 'But there's somebody needs tae get whit's comin' tae them, an' no afore time.'

I looked round to see who he meant, following his gaze along the road. Davy had cornered Rob back at the steading. It was dark but the two figures were recognisable, silhouetted against the faint glow of the gaslights along Main Street. Another two men were hiding in the shadows.

'Are ye comin', Rob!' I took a few paces into the middle of the road, making sure they could see it was me. 'Rob!'

He pulled away and hurried towards us, a forced smile on his face, pretending all was well. Sandy caught my eye and a hundred questions went between us in that look. The idea that he might be considering a confrontation with Davy sent a shiver up my spine.

On Saturday afternoon after work, we assembled on the washing green at the end of Middle Row. We jumped up and down to keep warm, anticipating the long walk for a cup tie and a couple of hours on the terracing at Rowanhill which was not for the faint-hearted. Bert was the last to arrive, apologising for keeping us waiting. There had been a family argument about whether Geordie should be allowed to come with us. Everybody in the village knew that Geordie had a weak chest. His mother paid particular attention to any signs that her youngest son might be coming down with something. It wasn't unknown for her to seek him out from the park, the burn, or the steading as soon as the rain came on, then march him home by the scruff of the neck – which was embarrassing for a fifteen-year-old boy. We'd asked Bert more than once if his mother was ever going to allow poor Geordie to grow up. That day, Geordie had lost the argument about whether he was to accompany us to the game. The wind was getting up and rain threatened, according to Mrs Broadley. It was bad enough that the boy spent part of his working day at the Cooperative out in all weathers, delivering messages to folk that were too lazy to collect their own from the store. At the weekends, he should rest at home in the warm, and take it easy. But Geordie was not to be outdone. He soon appeared, puffed and out of breath, his tear-stained face flushed with both the cold of the easterly wind and the heat of exertion after his escape to freedom.

The queue for the east terracing stretched along one side of the football ground, down a rutted track and out as far as the road. It was the cheapest end and, therefore, the most popular. We stood in line, 4d at the ready. Recruiting posters decorated the outside of the stand and had us gauping. Geordie pointed at a big cartoon of four kilted soldiers, fine strapping men in step with each other, smiling broad white smiles as they marched off to defeat the enemy. Bert could see what his brother was thinking – the spirit of adventure shining in Geordie's eyes.

'Dinnae be daft, yer ower young and ower wee an a'. Forget it.'

'They widnae hae ye,' we agreed, laughing.

'Whit wid yer maw say?' asked Sandy. 'She'd hae yer guts for garters.'

But Geordie wasn't to be put off so easily. Another poster caught his eye.

17th Service batt., The Royal Scots (Rosebery Bantam Battalion)

Wanted, 200 Linlithgowshire Men

To join in order to make up a county company

Recruits May Now Enlist at any Recruiting Office

Height – Minimum 5 feet Maximum 5 feet 3 inches

Chest Measurement – 38 inches expanded

Recruits need not give up Employment meantime but will receive Army Pay from Date of Enlistment

Special Recruiting Meeting for above at the Finish of the Rowanhill Football Match (Saturday)

2/4 Royal Scots Band (late Broxburn Public Band) will be present

Geordie stood tall. He could manage 5 feet. But he wasn't so sure about the chest measurement. He filled his lungs as far as he could to puff out his chest.

'38 inches? Aye that'll be the day,' said Rob.

'There's no a pick oan ye,' Sandy chipped in. 'Ye'll hae tae put oan some beef.'

'See's yer muscles,' said Dan.

Geordie took off his jacket, pushed up the sleeves of his jersey. He held up his arm like a bare-knuckle boxer, fist clenched.

'Jist as we thoucht,' said Sandy sadly. 'Knots oan threeds. Ye've nae chance.'

'Yer jist a wee smowt,' pronounced Jim.

'A rickle o' bones,' I piped up, me who barely surpassed Lord Rosebery's stipulations myself.

Geordie stood despondent. He would have to wait for Nature to take its course. But that would take time and, at fifteen years of age, a single day could feel like an eternity when you wanted something badly enough.

The football match did not disappoint. It had been a much-anticipated event in the football calendar, two local rivals pitched against each other in the later stages of the Eastern League Cup. The standard of play was high in front of the packed crowd of working men and boys. The roars and sighs of two thousand voices carried far, rising and falling on the biting wind until the final whistle blew, the score 3-2 in favour of the visitors. Post-match discussion conceded that the game could have gone either way, disappointment amongst the local supporters tempered by the knowledge that both teams had given their all. On this occasion, the terraces did not empty immediately as was normal, the crowd lingered to the sound of a band marching in from the road.

Two dozen men were led by a sergeant with a shining staff and a serious frown, and three officers in attendance. Rob and Sandy pointed proudly. Archie, their sister's man, was playing in the back row. Everybody knew the story, about how the Broxburn Public Band had joined up en masse and became the military band for the Royal Scots, paraded far and wide for recruiting purposes. It was surely a fine thing to fight for your country and we watched transfixed as the band formed in front of their bandmaster to deliver notes that were sweet and touched our hearts – the rousing song of the weavers, the stirring tune of the Garb of Old Gaul, the gentle notes of Annie Laurie, and the sadness of the Skye Boat Song. We knew the words and we heard them in the silence of our thoughts. Every man and boy felt the tug and pull of the music. It reached deep inside, pleading for our help in this new hour of need for the sake of our country, our folk, and all of the folk that had gone before us.

We were too young to enlist and quiet-like we left the ground whilst a queue formed to sign up and take the king's shilling. That music and the sight of the band in their uniforms, playing perfect notes in the cold wind, stayed with us all the way home and every day thereafter.

If the war lasted long enough, we would have our chance. And it did.

Elizabeth

Phee and Eric were married within a few weeks, as planned. They feared the worst though, as it transpired, Eric was not sent out to the front immediately. However, he spent weeks at a time with his regiment, transforming the yeomanry into a first-rate cavalry unit so Phee often visited Parkgate House in search of solace in a familiar setting. I was glad to be able to spend time with her, walking, talking, or saying nothing at all. It is most comforting to have company when one is troubled and not feel one has to speak or hear platitudes.

One frosty morning, we took a walk in the garden, just after the news had come in that Arthur Moffat had been killed in France. Lady Moffat was bereft and Phee was taking it hard. War had no respect for class and privilege. No one was safe. After a while, she decided to change the subject and asked me to accompany her to Whinbank. Mrs Maclean was long overdue a visit. She must have noticed how tense I became.

'Did anything come of that matter with Richard? You know, when he confronted Donald, telling him to make his intentions clear or to clear off?'

I explained that nothing had been said, not in so many words at least. The war intervened and seemed to throw everyone off course momentarily. 'It's difficult to know what you think sometimes with all of that going on overseas, and so much to do at home. All the usual activities carry on as before but it's as if normal life is on hold at the same time. I know Donald spends a lot of time thinking about whether he should be enlisting or not, though common sense tells him he should stay at Whinbank and make his contribution there. Anyway, we're good friends. Just good friends.'

'Would you come with me in the car sometime soon?' Phee persisted.

'As long as you're not match-making.'

'Me?'

Phee's feigned innocence was unconvincing.

I took a while to answer. 'There's something I have to tell you before we go anywhere near the Macleans.'

Phee was intrigued.

'Last summer, just before war was declared, I convinced myself I'd moved on with my life and I finally managed to visit the shieling on my own. It was like breaking a spell.'

Phee squeezed my hand to let me know how glad she was to hear me say those words.

'By some sort of strange coincidence, that very same day I discovered that Neil Tennant was coming back to Blackrigg from Canada at the end of the summer. I don't know why he was coming back or for how long. Obviously, the war has interfered with his plans because he didn't return. The other day, I was in conversation with some of the local women, about men from the area who are fighting in Europe.' I turned to my friend. 'Neil has joined the

Canadian Army apparently. He's in France with the Canadian Expeditionary Force.'

We sought out the ladies' parlour, looking for warmth and a nice cup of coffee and, hopefully, an escape from the dire consequences of war but, as we discovered, there was no escaping it.

I was delighted to see Rose with Catherine when we entered the parlour. I had not laid eyes on her, nor heard from her since our last visit to Parkgate when I had been so judgemental about her relationship with David Melville. As I entered the room, her broad smile told me we were still friends.

'It's always lovely to see you when you're in the area, Rose,' said Catherine. 'You don't visit often enough and we miss you. Please promise to come more often when you've graduated and are in post.' She rose to pour some coffee for Phee and myself, then offered cream and sugar from a silver tray.

'It depends where I end up,' explained Rose. 'I've always seen myself in town, working with women and children, but the war has everything up in the air at the moment. Doctors are in high demand with so many serving abroad in the Army Medical Corps. The Scottish Women's Hospitals have set up abroad, at the request of both France and Serbia. I could apply for war work there.'

'Oh, isn't that dangerous?' asked Catherine. She moved a long string of pearls back and forth around her neck with a nervous hand.

'Not any more than it is for the men. Women are doing their bit.' Rose looked determined.

'Isabelle says that Lady Moffat's going to turn Blair House into a hospital for the wounded, with the help of the Red Cross,' said Phee. 'In memory of Arthur.'

'The Marquis has done the same at Hopetoun,' remarked Catherine.

'And the Edinburgh War Hospital is set to open its doors very soon, along at Bangour, now that the asylum patients have been decanted elsewhere,' said Phee.

'They'll all need doctors.' Catherine looked at Rose.

'And they'll need nurses,' said Rose pointedly. 'Trained and untrained. You'd make good VADs, all of you.'

'The village needs a doctor and a nurse. We've lost both to the Army Medical Corps,' I said. 'Don't forget the people here at home in your rush to help the army.' I must have blushed severely and could barely look at Phee or Catherine. 'I didn't mean to sound heartless... please forgive me.'

'You're right,' said Rose, coming to my aid. 'The civilian population can't do without medical services just because there's a war on. Their need doesn't go away overnight.'

'No, but everyone has to make some sort of sacrifice in time of war,' said Catherine. 'In our different ways we're all making do.'

I surveyed the comfort of the ladies' parlour where we sat drinking coffee from fine china edged in gold leaf, a fire burning brightly in the hearth, needlework created by generations of pampered women decorating the walls. I liked Catherine but I couldn't help being annoyed by her remark.

'Some sacrifice more than others,' I said, rather boldly.

'Beth!' exclaimed Phee. 'Remember Catherine is missing David terribly. And baby Clive's virtually without a father at the moment.'

'Yes, I know it must be difficult. But ordinary people who live and work in places like Stoneyrigg endure as it is, often unable to afford basic services. They're doing their bit all of the time, and many such families have a father or brother at the front now too.'

I felt my heart race, picturing the new cottages being built by the Melvilles at Back o'Moss Pit to exactly the same plan as Stoneyrigg: no proper sculleries, no indoor tap to make women's lives easier, but the same freezing cold wash houses, spigots in the street, and dry closets at the end of each row.

'Things will improve when the war's over,' stated Catherine.

'Will they?' My eyes were wide. 'Nothing was changing before the war in that regard so why should it suddenly change after? The new Melville Rows are just the same as all of the others.'

'There's a war on.' Catherine bristled 'They'll just have to wait till the war is over.'

'Why should they? Things should be changing now!' I looked at my friends for a sign of understanding. Only Rose looked back, nodding.

I could tell how Catherine viewed me, the interfering do-gooder who did not understand the least thing about business. How dare I criticise. One day she would hint at how strapped for cash the estate was, and that she had been the one to secure the loan from the bank for the building of Melville Rows, with her father acting as guarantor. But even then, I would have little sympathy for her plight. The Melvilles and the Imries of this world seemed to have more than enough whilst working people had very little to spare.

Rose suggested a walk to break the impasse and Catherine left the room in high dudgeon, making for the nursery.

'We're all finding this hard, Beth,' said Phee. 'We've all got people we're worried about. Catherine thinks about David all of the time and hardly ever sees him. He doesn't seem to get away as much as Eric does, and that's not often. They're not at the Front yet but we know they will be, sooner or later. It could happen at the drop of a hat.'

I looked across at Rose who stared back, her face a blank canvas. I wondered if David Melville still haunted her dreams. Did she wonder where he was and pray that he was well? Had they rekindled their affair? Perhaps they met up from time to time – his regiment was stationed in town, after all. How carefully Rose hid her secret.

Perhaps it was the brightness of the sky, or the keen wind blowing cold on our faces, but we felt instantly cheered as we left the house. We strolled through the rowans at the back of the house, Catherine pushing her infant son in his perambulator whilst we took it in turns to chatter to him, ooing and cooing in that strange language specially reserved for babies.

Two gleaming vehicles, newly washed and polished, stood by the open doors of the garage as we passed. The stable yard seemed deserted but an elderly figure, hard at work, could be seen through an open door.

'I heard Billy Dodds has joined up,' I said.

'That's his grandfather in the stable at the far end. Says he'll help out when he can, till Billy comes back,' said Phee.

'We miss Billy,' remarked Catherine. 'But one of the gillies helps out with the driving when required.'

'And I lend a hand in that department, when I'm here!' Phee reminded everyone.

'You're a wonder,' said Catherine with a smile.

'Is old Major around?' I scanned the stables and the paddock for my favourite pony. Taking a couple of sugar lumps from my pocket, I went over to the stables, examining one empty stall after another until I found him. He pushed his nose into my hand in search of what he knew was there. Phee gave his neck a long, firm stroke, rested her cheek against his head.

'At least they didn't take you, Major,' she said.

The stables looked desolate when it dawned on me that all of the horses, except old Major and a foal, had gone. They should have been in the paddock, clad in winter blankets against the cold April breeze after weeks indoors, enjoying the freedom of a canter, sniffing new growth and longer days on the air. Catherine explained how men had come from the Ministry, with papers and money to purchase horses for the army. Phee said she was glad she hadn't been there to see Prince and Fergus, and the two mares, being led off to be loaded into wagons with dozens of others, shut away from the light for the rail journey south to the Channel ports.

We strolled down the track to Redburn, hoping for happier prospects and feeling the need to get moving on a day that was becoming chillier by the moment.

'We can't go all the way, I'm afraid,' warned Catherine.

The sound of woodsmen at work was immediately obvious: the loud thwack of metal on wood, voices shouting words of warning as trees were brought down with a crash of branches in the undergrowth.

'Prices for wood are at a premium. It's needed at the Front, for building trenches and the like. They'll take anything they can get their hands on, except beech,' explained Catherine, shushing Clive who was starting to complain.

'We'll retain some for the mine, of course. The manager is developing the seam as fast as the men are able. Thank Goodness we can do our bit here on the estate. It does give one some comfort.'

Her brows knitted and not at all comforted, Rose stared at the wood as it succumbed to the woodsman's axe. Phee's hand went to her throat when a gap on the skyline appeared. The landscape of her earliest memories was changing before her eyes. A feeling of dread surged through my being. The loss of the wood was terrible to contemplate. Was there no end to the devastation being wrought in the name of freedom?

Courtesy of the war in France, Richard and I called a truce at home. Or at least, I managed to bite my tongue and walk away rather than face up to him as before. That is, until one day when we were discussing preparations for a dinner to which Ernest Black had been invited. Richard insisted I attend and would not accept my refusal. I knew that anything my brother suggested had an ulterior motive so I dug in my heels but he was not about to give in either. It took a whole hour in the garden before I managed to calm down.

Later, I came upon Sarah arranging the minister's tea tray exactly as he liked it: tongs beside the sugar bowl, to the right not the left; a small jug of milk, only half full, no more no less; a silver teaspoon with his favourite china cup and saucer; a piece of fruit cake on a matching plate with a mother-of-pearl handled knife to the right; and a small tea pot covered by a tea cosy, embroidered by our late mother. I watched the girl move the teapot half an inch to the left, adjusting the position of the other items with precision until the arrangement seemed satisfactory.

'Careful, Sarah. They say you get like the people you work with,' I teased.

I swiftly halved the piece of cake before Sarah was able to take the tray away.

When she returned, we settled down with our own tea and began a conversation about what was happening in the village, as always slow and stilted at first till she warmed up, a necessary prelude to our discussions even though we had worked together quite happily for nearly a year by then. Sarah soon updated me about her family: who was working where, what the marriage prospects were for her sisters – Marion and the footman at Rowanhill House; Nell and a miner who lived in the next row; Minn, the farm servant, who was sweet on a lad yet nothing seemed to be coming of it; and the minutiae of life in a miner's cottage with a host of younger children of dubious parentage, all looked after by Tom and Jean Graham and two uncles.

I asked her if she hoped to be married one day and she said, of course, it was common knowledge that marriage was what every girl wanted for herself. It was only natural and better for all concerned in the long run. But she thought it was only a good thing if you could marry somebody of your own choosing which I wholeheartedly agreed with. It would be terrible, she continued like a tap that wouldn't turn off, to marry somebody like Bobby Cherrie who lashed out at his wife with his fists and was well known for spending his wages in the Village Inn, leaving nothing to feed his ten children; or Harry McGonigle who up and left his wife and child for big May Heeps, her with the bright red face because of her work as a setter in the brickworks.

When she eventually stopped talking, she looked at me expectantly as if I should carry on where she left off but I was not about to give away my heart so I nodded and simply said, 'You'll know when the right one comes along and if he doesn't... there's plenty to keep a woman occupied and let her live a useful life.'

A useful life! Was that my fate? By then, in addition to my work at the Sabbath School and on the committees at the church and in the village, I was helping to fundraise for the Red Cross, encouraging everyone to knit warm socks to put in the parcels that were sent to the Front. I also spent a lot of time helping Highland Mary, since the district nurse had gone off overseas immediately after the outbreak of war. A replacement had been found very quickly but only lasted a month before she was dismissed for drinking gin on duty and charging ten shillings for delivering babies when the service should have been free to those on the books. I did all of that whilst keeping house for my brother who gave me nothing but grief.

'Ma Uncle Peter's enlisted, Miss Fraser,' Sarah confided eventually. 'Mind how I telt ye that Bessie Morrison fae the Co-op was tellin' him he should join up?'

I remembered. 'They go dancing together, don't they?'

'Aye. Ma Uncle Peter's fond o' the dancin'.'

'And fond of Bessie Morrison by the sounds of things.'

'Aye, he is. But Jean disnae like her. Weel, she did but she got fair mad when she heard that Bessie was sayin' Uncle Peter should join up or she widnae be seen at the dancin' wi' him again.'

That made me very sad to hear.

'Jean says there's ower monie folk gaun tae France. She says Uncle Peter should stey in Blackrigg where he's needed to bring up the coal.'

'I expect he's thought long and hard before making his decision. It has to be a matter of conscience at the end of the day.'

'Aye, Miss. But I'm inclined tae agree wi' Jean. It's a' richt for Bessie Morrison tellin' folk they should gang tae France when she disnae have tae gang hersel.'

I could think of a few people just like that as I recalled my brother's recent sermon and how certain individuals had lapped it up.

'Well this isn't getting the work done,' I said, feeling the need to get busy. 'We've a pot of soup and a stew to prepare for dinner. Would you mind setting the table for three, please?'

Sarah couldn't hide her surprise.

'Yes, three. Mr Black, Mr Fraser and myself are eating together tonight.' I guessed some of what was going through the girl's mind after the shouting match between Richard and myself earlier.

'And when you're finished, you can get off home to help Mrs Graham with all of those children. And you'll take her the rest of that cake with you when you go.'

Richard could do without for a day or two, I had decided.

Later that evening, he sat in his usual place at the top of the table, the warm glow of the fire playing on his back. 'Do you have any plans to enlist, Ernest?' he asked, once the soup had been served and grace had been said.

'Lovely soup, Miss Fraser. Cock-a-leekie, my favourite.'

'Are you avoiding my question, headmaster?'

'Richard, really!' I was aghast.

'A valid question in these times of peril for our country, Elizabeth,' Richard countered.

'This is neither the time nor the place for such questions. He is our guest.'

Ernest tried to interject but it was almost as if he wasn't there.

'We are at war, Elizabeth. I was merely asking.' Richard took a loud satisfying sup of his soup.

'Ernest's work is extremely important for the future of our country,' I countered. 'What can be more important than the education of young minds? That work doesn't suddenly become unimportant because we are at war. His work prevents him from enlisting.'

'Thank you, Elizabeth, for making that point,' Ernest interjected. 'It is a matter of conscience and duty, of course. To enlist or not to enlist? That is the question.' He looked very serious, a deep frown on his forehead, as if the question was a source of torment. 'But I do feel that my place is here, with my pupils.'

'Precisely,' I said. 'Not everyone can go to the Front, surely? You cannot abandon people here who need you, Ernest. What are we fighting this war for, if not for the children, our future?'

'Ernest is right, Elizabeth. It is a matter for each individual to search his conscience about the best action to take. The war is, of course, part of that timeless struggle between Good and Evil, the never-ending battle for Man's soul. It is there in our daily lives, in the mundane, the everyday and now in the most extraordinary circumstance of war with Germany. The Kaiser, devil incarnate, has come to test our mettle, our nerve, and we must rise against him.'

'And we do that in our different ways,' offered Ernest.

'And by remaining with your pupils, that is your way?' probed Richard. 'Whilst their loved ones lay their lives on the line for their country, their teacher remains here in safety. Is that a fine example to set children grieving for their fathers?'

'I cannot condone the violence of war by volunteering for action, I'm afraid. I do not believe that the war is just, or was necessary from the beginning. Diplomacy at the highest level could have prevented it, had the parties involved truly sought to avoid bloodshed. The foreign policy of the main protagonists has, over many years, brought us to this point in history.' Ernest stared at Richard, forcing him to look away.

Ernest continued, 'I can hardly believe what is happening at this very moment to the beautiful countryside of northern France. Such humble and hospitable people as I have met on my visits, caught up in a conflict that was none of their doing.'

'And you will not lift a finger to help them?' Richard persisted.

'As Byron would have it, is not the conscience the oracle of God?' asked Ernest sadly. 'My place is here in Blackrigg. This is where I can do my best work.'

I turned on my brother. 'You, of course, are prohibited from enlistment by your calling, Richard.'

'I am indeed,' he sighed. 'I must follow the path the Lord has laid before me. It is my calling and my duty.' Richard sat with his elbows on the table, his hands interlinked, as if he was thinking great thoughts.

How convenient, I thought. You preach from the safety of the pulpit, using God's Word in support of enlistment, provoking others to put themselves in the firing line.

I rose to clear the empty plates and remove the tureen, still half full of soup. It crossed my mind to empty it over my brother's sanctimonious head. In order to avoid such a calamity, I quickly made my way to the kitchen, blinking back tears of frustration brought on by Richard's hypocrisy, his rudeness towards his guest, and by the enormity of the peril that faced the country at war, especially the plight of those at the sharp end: the men at the Front. The horror of it was almost too much to bear. When I thought about it too deeply, it threatened to overwhelm me, to suck me under. I had my own way of dealing with such thoughts and took a deep breath. Best to keep busy. That was my saviour.

I retrieved serving dishes from the warming oven, began the dash through the cold house to ensure the main course remained hot. But I was drawn up short at the door of the dining room. Richard had mentioned my name. They were talking about me. The heat of the dishes burned through to my hands but I persevered. However, they had heard me, were suspicious, their talk suddenly reverting to the spring weather and nesting birds of all things. I entered the room saying I would be back with the plates, then ran to the kitchen and back again in case I missed something of the conversation.

'Mind your fingers, they're terribly hot,' I warned. 'I'll be back with the stew.'

I lingered outside the door. They said nothing for a while. When Richard began his voice was low.

'The Mission have said there is great need at the Front, well, not at the Front exactly but behind the lines. So I've indicated my interest meantime. Told them I cannot go immediately. But once I have made arrangements then I will be in a position to go and do my duty: providing spiritual support to our men, who have seen the horror of war at first hand.'

I swallowed hard. Richard seemed to be contemplating joining some sort of church mission abroad. For the troops. It put our earlier discussion into a new perspective entirely. Perhaps I had misjudged him. I craned my neck to hear a little better.

'Do have more potato, Ernest. There's hardly enough there to feed a sparrow.'

'No thank you. What will happen to Elizabeth in the meantime?'

'Well, she can't stay here on her own. It wouldn't be seemly, especially if the Kirk brings in another minister on a temporary basis until I return. I'll have to make arrangements. She is entirely dependent on me.'

'Mmmm.' Ernest was thinking. 'Yes, more turnip, please. Mmmm, very nice with the butter and a little pepper, thank you. Elizabeth is a very good cook, I must say. So, what do you have in mind for her exactly?'

'That's where you come in, dear Ernest. That's what I want to speak to you about. Make sure to tarry a while over the coffee later on, will you? We'll continue our discussion later when Elizabeth is clearing up.'

I ran on tip-toe to the kitchen, my eyes and mouth open wide. I nearly dropped the dish of stew when I removed it from the oven. My cheeks flushed bright red as I took in the enormity of what I had just heard. What was Richard planning for me and what did it have to do with the village schoolmaster? I could barely contemplate the possibilities. I brushed down my skirt and breathed deeply before returning to the dining room where both diners seemed to be eagerly awaiting my return.

Chapter 18

John

My father didn't know what to make of things when the war first started. The differences between the employers and the unions were initially set aside in the national interest. The plans of the triple industrial alliance of miners, railway and transport workers' unions for a major confrontation over pay and conditions disappeared like autumn leaves in the teeth of a gale, and the Scottish miners' dispute evaporated into nothing overnight. The coal owners announced their intention to drop their request for a reduction in wage rates below seven shillings but maintained their right to resurrect the policy as soon as hostilities were over. At first, Alex near lost his reason for getting out of bed in the morning. It was as if the rug had been pulled from under his feet. He'd go quiet for long periods, sulking like a spoiled wean. My mother, who'd endured many years of his moods, took the brunt of it. She could give as good as she got but soon learned to hold her tongue. This was a different Alex, one who seemed to have lost all hope for a better world, who could see no light at the end of the tunnel of injustice. Even during the negotiations that ended so well for the union with a pay rise of 18½%, his mood was black. His anger at the iniquity of sending men from the mining villages to fight other workers overwhelmed him. He called it a capitalists' war. Innocents were dying and children were being left fatherless because the rich and powerful on both sides wanted more than they already had.

The usual litany of problems and mishaps continued at the pits – a fire at the coalface of Broadrigg No.3 left two men badly burned; a man was electrocuted by new lighting underground; a runaway hutch rendered a lad unconscious. I was some way behind Alex on the pit road the day he found out about Stoneyrigg Pit, the one the Company had closed down years past. As ever, his haversack was slung over one shoulder, the frayed collar of his woollen jacket turned up, scant protection against the wind that whipped round the sheds and through the bare branches of the hedgerow beside the track. I watched him stride out ahead, and in every step, I saw the anger that burned inside of him. He seemed to linger at the top of the hill, in spite of himself, studying new activity around the entrance to the old pit. A pile of wood and iron sheeting had appeared in the yard by the old winding shed. Men were busy around two big trucks, removing tarpaulins, emptying crates. *Baird and Sons, Pit Sinkers*, written along one side. So, they were opening up Stoneyrigg. The rumours had been true.

I knew he would not take it well, his fury ready to choke the life out of him. The sounds of heavy boots advancing up the road from behind got him moving, the last thing he wanted was a cheery word. I hurried on after him but thought better of it, hung back for my own sake. I didn't go home straight away, in spite of my need for a seat in a warm room, but lingered in the street instead, hands in pockets, just out of sight but close-by for the sake

335

of my mother. When she appeared in the street with a knife in one hand and my father's mud-caked trousers in the other, ready to scrape away the grime, she saw me, indicated the door of our cottage with her head and gave me the merest hint of a smile. *Thanks, John,* she was saying.

Something that did cheer my father was news of the industrial disputes rumbling on around the country that first year of the war.

'Tae be expectit, when prices are gaun up an' employers are cashin' in,' he said.

The men on the Clyde were speaking up. Engineers were complaining about profiteering by companies that were bringing in skilled men from America and non-union labour, including women, to depress wages. The leaders of the strike at Fairfields were put in the gaol, showing the lengths to which employers were prepared to go. The stakes were high. Closer to home, shale miners in Broxburn were prepared to strike for an increase of 4d a day, and the oil workers were threatening the same; same story at the Bo'ness woodyards, over non-union labour; women at the Regent Works in Linlithgow, doing the work of men away at the Front, had downed tools in March over low levels of pay. And women were at the vanguard in the fight against profiteering landlords in Glasgow who were capitalising on the rising demand for accommodation from labour doing war work. Families were even being threatened with eviction, whilst their husbands and fathers were fighting in France!

'Aye, an a' the press has tae say is *there's a war oan,*' complained Davy.

Davy took it all in, passed the information onto men at the steading or at the pit head. He was starting to sound like the font of all knowledge. When others were quiet, unable to speak the names Loos, Neuve Chappelle, and Gallipoli, Davy spoke them loud, lecturing about armaments, profiteering and injustice. Whilst his star continued to rise, he fell into his old ways and was seen in the Village Inn, staying out till late as it suited him, in the company of shady characters or lassies with reputations that went before them. I could tell how it vexed my mother but she could not say anything to him directly. Alex would always take against her, in spite of her warnings that it would turn out for bad in the long run. And it pleased Davy no end to see our mother put in her place.

One day, we came home from the pit to find her absent, the house like the Marie Celeste floating on an uneasy sea. She had left two pots of warm water on the hearth and the kettle whistled loudly on the swey. We wondered why she wasn't there by the fire as usual. It riled my father but it worried me profoundly until Mags Cherrie stuck her head round the door to explain that Chrissie Brown was in labour and things weren't going well. The doctor had been sent for from Rowanhill. We were glad that she left before saying any more. Davy marched off in a temper to the public baths in Main Street, a towel tucked under his arm, whilst Jim and me, and our father, took it in turns as usual to bath in front of the fire. We were surprised that we managed by ourselves, and when we placed the tin bath for drying outside the door, it was done with a degree of self-congratulation. But who was going to make our dinner? I spotted the ingredients for brose soaking in a bowl high up on a shelf and rolled up my sleeves. Nothing ventured, nothing gained.

I made a cup of tea while we waited but there was no sugar any place though I searched high and low. Alex complained bitterly, as if I had removed all traces from the house by myself. He sucked up the bitter liquid with a face in danger of curdling the milk and he had to force himself to have two more cups to finish the pot.

After what seemed like an age, I dished out the brose. The smell wafted up and Alex raised an eyebrow. Things were improving. He blew hard on a spoonful, breathed in the steam. We watched as he tasted the first morsel. His nose wrinkled up, his mouth turned downwards. He almost spat into his plate but held back, slavering peas down his chin.

'Ye niver put saut in it, ye stupid arse...! It needs friggin saut!'

'There's nae saut either,' I explained. 'I've looked a' place an' there's nane.'

'Nae saut!?'

The door opened. Mother stepped in from the rain. She took the wet shawl from her head, carefully hanging it up to dry on the string above the fireplace. We watched her in silence.

'There's nae saut,' Alex said.

'I heard ye when I was oot by.' She reached into her basket and took out a small packet, filled the salt cellar before handing it to me.

She sat on a low stool, her back close to the fire to get dry, and ate her portion of brose straight from the pot, all the time watching us tuck in.

'Or sugar,' Alex said after a while.

She took a few more mouthfuls before answering. 'If ye'd been wi' Chrissie Broon thur three – fower 'oors past, ye mebbe widnae be complainin' aboot the want o' a wee bit sugar for yer tea, Alex Birse.' Mother worked intently with her spoon, removing every last morsel of brose sticking to the bottom of the pot.

'She had her bairn then. Lad or lassie?'

'A wee boy, the spit o' his faither. She cried him Duncan afore she passed.'

'She's deed?'

'Aye, she is that, puir lass. A helluva time she had bringin' thon bairn intae the wurld. An' he'll never know her.'

'Spare us the gory details,' growled Davy, coming in through the door just then.

She shook her head and sighed. 'A hell of a price for lying wi' a man.'

'For the Love o' God, Mither,' insisted Davy.

'The doctor cam late but said there was nuthin that could've been done onieweys. A' he could dae was sign the certificate.'

She took the sugar bowl, went to see if Mrs Duncan could spare a few spoonfuls till Friday. We were quiet as we chewed over the last of our brose.

At first, I could not get that picture of Mrs Brown out of my head, her lying in the back room of a damp cottage with my mother in attendance, giving birth to her first child. I've begun to think of her again, these several years later after the horror of the battlefield. There is blood and pain in that image of a woman writhing on a white sheet, screaming and grunting like a wild thing, biting down on a piece of leather, scant relief from the horror of her predicament. It makes me think of what I witnessed on the battlefield and behind the lines in casualty clearing stations, men screaming and cursing and pleading for God's Mercy. Yet all the time, it went on in my street, the cottage next door, and I had never given it a thought at the time, never at all. It was part of the natural order of things, something men did to women. Duncan Brown was still an infant when I left for the Front. His mother brought a fine, strong lad into the world for her pain. I have seen many like him, though older, blown to pieces by the war machine. They were all bairns once and they still cry for their mothers. What kind of world is this that sends men, borne of women, to kill and maim each other across a stretch of muddy ground in a land that is not theirs? What kind of world will be wrought by our struggle and sacrifice, at home and abroad, when we come to our senses and the guns stop?

Elizabeth

Though I feared that he might, having been put up to it by my unscrupulous brother, Ernest Black never quite plucked up the courage to broach the subject of marriage when we were alone, briefly, on several occasions over the following months. As I have often said, Ernest was a man of principle and conscience. He understood, without my having to say the words, that marriage was out of the question, if not forever, at least for the foreseeable future. I do believe he was very fond of me and, though I cannot be sure of how far his feelings ran, I often saw sadness in his eyes when he looked at me. As for Richard, I am sure he was quite frustrated with Ernest at times, as much as he was with me since my presence in the manse was preventing him from joining the mission in France. Eventually, a solution was found however.

Much later in the year, Rose was sitting in the kitchen with Sarah when I emerged from the study and my latest confrontation with Richard. Our elderly relative, whom he had hoped would look after me for the duration, had passed and he had decided that my reluctance to live with her earlier in the year had contributed to her demise. Had

I not been so selfish, the old woman might have survived a while longer, he claimed. The sounds of our raised voices from behind the closed door of the study must have horrified Rose but Sarah was sure to have explained the situation in her own inimitable way.

By the time I showed face, she was giving Rose a detailed description of her extended family. This included the details of Uncle Peter's latest letter from Gallipoli, though as always, his letters didn't give much away about what was actually happening to him, except that he was well in spite of the heat and was thinking about everyone back home. Sarah said that Uncle Peter's sister – that's Mrs Graham – had told her that letters from the front had to be read with care. You had to read between the lines. You couldn't just take what they said as the truth, the whole truth and nothing but the truth. But they were a version of the truth, sent by somebody who cared about the feelings of the person they were writing to, and Jean had to content herself with the knowledge that her brother was fine at the moment he had written to her. As the days and weeks passed till his next letter arrived, she had to believe that he was still fine, though it didn't stop her from wondering and worrying in the quiet moments of the day about what he wasn't telling her.

'Mrs Graham is a very wise woman,' said Rose. 'And you must be a great comfort to her, Sarah.'

News of the rout and retreat from Gallipoli had shocked the nation. Rose surmised that the letter must have been written in the heat of the summer of that year, 1915, when dysentery had been as deadly an enemy to Uncle Peter as the Turkish forces in the opposing trenches. Newspaper reports of conditions and casualties had made for horrendous reading, an unsuitable topic for discussion in the warm kitchen of the Blackrigg manse and it was a relief when Sarah got up to answer the door bell.

She returned to say that Mrs Hyslop was in the parlour.

We rushed to hug Phee before asking her how it was possible to look so composed having battled with the rain and wind of a Scottish winter's evening to get there. Phee said that a motor car, and the ability to drive oneself wherever one wished, must have something to do with it. She told us that David and Eric had arrived in the Balkans with their regiment and both had written to say they were safe. Rose turned to me – flushed after my latest encounter with Richard – and suggested that there was plenty to talk about. We positioned three chairs around the small fire crackling in the grate and settled down for a long chat.

When the tea tray had been brought in and Sarah had retreated for the night, Phee produced a silver flask from her bag. She poured a small amount of whisky into each of the cups.

'For medicinal purposes,' she explained. 'To keep out the cold.'

I tried to make excuses but my friends said 'Drink!' so I did.

I began my long sorry tale, starting with Richard's approach to the schoolmaster and the need to remove me from the manse whilst he joined the mission in France. In the beginning, I had wondered if I'd imagined it: he couldn't possibly be encouraging someone to consider marrying me, just because he wanted to go away for a time. Could he? But it made sense on many levels. As long as I was there, I would be an embarrassment to him as a minister of the Kirk; what with my history of association with, first Neil Tennant, and then Donald Maclean, not to mention my insistence on helping Highland Mary in Stoneyrigg, and my letters to the authorities about housing conditions in the area. Richard continued to stress the importance of staying out of temporal matters. Charity was all very well but it could be misdirected, according to him. The poor must come to us, he would say, not the other way round. We are here in the House of the Lord and they must make their choice. The Scriptures tell us so.

'But even if you were married, you would still be living in this village, in the schoolhouse.' Phee faltered, '... with Ernest... virtually next door to the church.' She was trying hard to get inside the minister's head, to understand things from his point of view.

'Yes, but then I would be a respectable married woman, the wife of the local schoolmaster.' I explained.

'Ahh! No longer the young temptress, ready and willing to snare any man who comes along.' Phee nodded her understanding of the situation.

I squirmed. That was exactly what the village gossips, including my own brother, probably thought of me.

'Your past sins would be forgiven,' said Phee. 'But not forgotten, I'll wager!'

'You would be defined by your husband's role and standing in the community,' continued Rose. 'Rather than your brother's role, as you are defined now.'

'And as soon as any children came along, I wouldn't have time to associate with the poor or to interfere with matters that didn't concern me, especially political matters.'

'And did Ernest propose?' Phee's eyebrows were raised in anticipation.

'He came to see me more than once. He started in a very long, roundabout way but I was forewarned. I steered our conversations away from the possibility of a proposal from him.'

'He is a rather sweet man,' offered Rose.

'Yes he is. And a good friend. Eventually, I confided that I loved someone else. He understood my point of view. He did not press me further, said that he would be eternally grateful for our friendship.'

'Thank Goodness,' said Phee, taking another sip of the whisky.

'I am glad. There are many who would take exception to rejection,' Rose said before asking, 'So the matter of your accommodation remains unresolved?'

'Ernest has been good enough to ask the lady schoolteachers if there is room in their lodgings for me but, unfortunately, there isn't. He has two spare rooms in the schoolhouse but, of course, it would be completely out of the question for me to stay there.'

'There's plenty of room at Parkgate,' announced Phee. 'You're always welcome there – I wish you'd said about all of this before. I would've offered!'

'But you're not there that much anymore. I couldn't possibly live at Parkgate without you. Isabelle scares the life out of me. And Catherine.... well, she can be terribly sweet but...'

'You could work on her, Beth. Get her to spend some of her father's money on decent housing and so on.'

I wasn't convinced. 'I've gone through all the possibilities in my head: working somewhere else for the Red Cross, going to stay with a relative for a bit. Actually, that was what my discussion with Richard was about. Our elderly cousin, twice removed... has just passed away...' I gave my nose a loud blow.

Rose had been quiet. 'I have a plan.'

I looked in her direction, hoping.

'I'll come and live in the manse with you.'

344

I was thrown. 'How?'

She explained that she had visited her father in Rowanhill earlier in the day. She had been shocked at how tired he looked, sitting in the kitchen all alone, with his head in his hands.

'He's been trying to serve Blackrigg like he did in the past, in addition to Rowanhill. Dr Lindsay will be with the Army Medical Corps for the duration of the war. The population has soared since the old days when one doctor covered the whole area. There are far too many people for him to cope with on his own and it's killing him.

'He kept going on about a birth he'd attended in Stoneyrigg recently. You were there, Beth, weren't you? The mother died. He said if only he'd been able to get there in time but he'd been delayed at the brickworks – an accident – a man lost his hand and a boy was badly burned. He said he probably couldn't have saved the woman in any case but he'd never know either way. And a child will grow up without a mother.

'He shouldn't be thinking that way, don't you see? It's the tiredness taking its toll. He's losing confidence in himself, starting to blame himself for things beyond his control. When a doctor does that, he's finished.'

She paused staring into the fire. 'My father is very dear to me. I can't stand back and see him suffer through overwork when he has so much left to give. So, I've made up my mind... I will be taking over the Blackrigg patients for the time being.'

She waited for my reaction.

'And I need a place to stay. I don't have a vehicle so I will have to stay in the village. Why not here with you, Beth?'

'What about Spittal Cottage?'

'No. It's damp and run down. Dr Lindsay's ordered renovations in his absence so the place is uninhabitable... for a while, at least.'

'What about the visiting ministers? They'll need a place to stay. Could they live here too?'

'Not here with you two! God, no!' gasped Phee.

'I'm sure Mr Ernest Black could be persuaded to put them up in the schoolhouse if he was approached.' Rose had all the answers.

'Perfect solution,' agreed Phee. 'Richard cannot possibly be seen to prevent the new doctor taking up her post by denying her accommodation in the manse when there's nowhere else. And Mr Black will happily accommodate men of the cloth, if only to assist his dear friend, Miss Fraser.'

She replenished everyone's cup from her flask and we toasted the new arrangements.

'How soon can we pack Richard off to the mission?' she asked.

'He's going in a fortnight,' I said, cheered by more than the alcohol.

'Good Health!' said Phee.

'Cheers!'

We hooted with laughter as the evening wore into night. If Richard was aware of the raucous story-telling taking place in the parlour, he paid no heed. Inevitably, however, mirth fuelled by strong drink descended into melancholy as Phee reminisced about her first year of marriage with Eric. She began to wonder about where he was at that particular moment, asking whether we thought he was safe. Of course, he was safe we told her, and she had to remember that he was with David and they would both be looking out for each other; which had her in floods of tears, crying for the two men in her life that she loved most dearly.

'Such a wicked state of affairs,' she declared. 'How ever has it come to this?'

Rose must have been worried too but, as always, she kept her feelings hidden whilst she comforted our friend.

I could think only of Neil Tennant far away in the mud and the cold of a wet winter's night, somewhere along the Front with the Canadians. 'Sometimes life is really... awful,' I slurred.

Phee was disappointed that her flask was empty. No amount of shaking could produce a single drop

'We've barely had a sip,' I said. 'But I feel quite... mellow...'

'Yes, what we need is... more,' declared Phee. 'But I guess we're in the wrong place for that!' She rolled her eyes around, making me snigger.

'You may laugh,' I said holding up my hand. 'But I know where there might be a bottle.'

'Here? Really?!' said Phee and Rose together.

I toddled over to the door – I did feel a little strange – then put a finger up to my mouth.

'SSSHHHH! Richard's wardrobe!'

We peeped into the hallway, listening for noises that would tell us where Richard might be. Surely he hadn't gone to bed this early? The sounds of paper rustling and a chair creaking in the study told us we were in luck. Egged on by my friends, I tip-toed across the hall and gingerly climbed the stairs. Phee waved me upwards, telling me to get on with it. When I disappeared from sight along the top landing, they kept watch on the study door. I had no idea how much the manse floorboards creaked and the doors squeaked until then. But very soon, I reappeared, carefully treading downwards from the top step. They dashed back inside, trying hard to stifle their giggles.

'This is ridiculous,' whispered Phee, before another bout of laughter started up.

I carefully closed the door behind me, a bottle of malt whisky in my hand and a shoebox under my arm. Phee took the bottle, which was already opened and only half full. She poured three drams.

Rose saw the look on my face. 'What is it, Beth? What's wrong?'

I placed the box on my lap and opened it, took out a letter, then another, and another. There were about a dozen, maybe more. None of them had been opened and they were all addressed to me.

'What is it? Beth darling, what is it?' asked Phee.

'I know this writing,' I said.

'Who sent them?'

I looked at the postmarks, the dates and the places from where they'd been sent.

'They're all from Neil.'

'But how?' asked Rose though it was obvious. 'Who....?'

'They were in the back of Richard's wardrobe... they must've been there all this time.'

Chapter 19

John

Though voluntary recruitment encouraged many to enlist in the army – including one fifth of Scottish mineworkers – it was soon clear that the numbers fell short of what was needed as opposing sides dug in, preparing for a long battle of attrition on all fronts. When the government passed the National Registration Act in July of 1915, every male between the ages of 15 and 65 had to register giving details of their trade. It was done to provide information for military planning but it also concentrated minds on the subject of enlistment and the importance of doing your duty. The spectre of conscription loomed, except for those in skilled and essential employment.

By mid-October, the Derby Scheme was rolled out by a peer of the realm of the same name. Men aged 18-40 were told that they could enlist on a voluntary basis as before or attest under the Group Scheme, to be called up in the future, if and when the country required it. Should they fail to attest by the cut-off date, they faced the possibility of conscription which had never before been deemed necessary in the long history of the British Army.

On a raw December day, we stood in line with hundreds of others, a line that stretched down Linlithgow's High Street from the recruiting office in the army drill hall. We could see Andrew Brownlee further up the queue, standing with his father. Bert called to him and he waved back. We stamped our feet to keep the blood moving and huddled together against the cold blast. We had already tried to attest in Bathgate the previous week but had been turned away after several hours in the cold, such was the length of the queue, swollen like a river in spate by men desperate to have their names recorded before the deadline. We waited with the lave, dressed in our best, in recognition of an occasion that ranked alongside weddings and funerals in terms of importance.

'If they dinnae hurry up, they'll have brocht in conscription afore we get tae the front o' the queue!' somebody shouted.

'Dae they no ken there's a war oan? Some o' us would like tae get there afore it's by!' said another.

I suppose there were many who would have been happy not to reach the front of the line before the end of hostilities but they kept quiet. Nobody wanted to be branded a coward. To wait and be sent to the army as a conscript was a sign of cowardice, bringing everybody out to attest in large numbers. You might never be called up when it came to it but under the scheme you'd get an armband to wear, proof that you were willing and ready to go.

Alex had been in two minds about the scheme. One day he would say he didn't want folk thinking the Birses were fearties, the next he would rage about capitalists benefitting from the war – the only winners at the end of the day – and he made us swear on the Bible not to go, no matter what. So, me and Jim went along to attest with our friends, without asking permission from our father. We stood in line, watching men leaving the Recruiting Office, excitement and pride on our faces, keen to find out about the process going on inside. The wind cut us in two and the rain soaked through to our skin but we never once thought to translate that discomfort into a state of war when a warm seat in front of the fire and a plate of our mother's broth would be so far away. In fact, we couldn't think past the medical examination that was part of the process.

Was it true what the rumour mill said about you having to show the doctor everything you had?

Aye, that was the worst thing about it.

And the horror of it swept up and down the line.

Geordie was glad of his knitted balaclava and thick gloves that were permanently attached to a long string, wound round the back of his neck so that he wouldn't lose them. He ran after us older lads as we walked briskly back to Blackrigg. It didn't matter how fast he ran and how often he caught up, he always seemed to fall behind right away then face another exhausting gallop to regain lost ground. It was all the more upsetting that we seemed oblivious to his plight, caught up as we were in the possibilities of adventure opening up before us. The long wait in the freezing cold had borne fruit. Every one of us – except Geordie who was still too young – had been accepted for service. We were chilled to the bone but nothing could dampen our spirits or cool our enthusiasm. We would be sent an armband, proof of our manhood, in due course. We would wear it with pride for all to see. By the time Stoneyrigg was in sight, we were full of bravado, feats of heroism playing out in our heads. The sight of Jenny Campbell and her sister on the road up ahead had us daring each other to prove our manhood in other ways too. Rob told us all to grow up.

I followed the Duncan boys home to their door for a look at a library book that Sandy had been recommending.

'Cheerio!' shouted Bert from further along the Row. He disappeared inside number 24, hauling Geordie in with him, knowing full-well that their mother would have something to say about the weather and the long walk home.

'Cheers, Bert!' we called back.

Then the mood suddenly changed. 'Whit's this?' asked Sandy, as he bent down by the entrance to their cottage. He held up a short piece of wood which had several nails hammered through from the other side like a giant comb.

'Could dae somebody an injury,' Rob said, pressing the sharp ends of the nails into his palm.

It looked like an instrument of torture and made me uneasy.

'And these,' added Sandy. He struggled to his feet.

We examined what was in his hand – an assortment of tacks and six-inch nails bent over in the middle to an angle of ninety degrees.

Sandy looked upwards. 'Has Imrie finally sent somebody to work on the roof? No afore time if he has.'

'Beats me,' said Rob.

'C'mon, let's see if Ma's got the kettle oan. I've some drouth oan me,' said Sandy, his mind turning to more pressing issues. He took the piece of wood from Rob and propped it up against the wall by the door.

I thanked Sandy for the library book and left them to their tea and a game of cards with their foreign lodger who'd been released by the authorities after the start of the war once they'd verified his nationality as Lithuanian, and not German after all. When I'd reached the end of the row, loud rapping at the Duncans' door stopped me in my tracks. It was a loud, insistent, threatening thump rather than the gentle knock of a friend. Not Mags Cherrie out to borrow a cup of sugar, I guessed. I turned in the dusky gloom to see Constable Mackay, his uniformed bulk filling the doorway, the nail-studded wood in his hand.

'I'm lookin' for the owner o' this,' I heard him say as he went inside.

Sandy told me later how he'd explained they knew nothing about it. Mackay was suspicious, apparently. He'd stared at Rob in particular, waiting for him to answer. It didn't help make their story any more believable when the lodger stated that it hadn't been there when he'd come in barely an hour earlier. It helped even less when Rob took the handful of tacks and nails from his pocket and described how they had been on the step with the piece of wood.

'Richt. Get yer jaiket oan, Mr Duncan,' said Mackay. 'Yer comin' tae the station for questionin'.'

Sandy spoke up, explained how they'd come upon it together with me, John Birse, after our visit to the recruiting office where dozens of folk could testify to our presence. Mackay decided to take Sandy for questioning along with Rob even though Peggy was protesting that he surely didn't have the right to cart folk away on a whim.

Mackay leaned right into her face, letting her know that he could do whatever he liked, cart away whoever he saw fit, and that it wasn't her place to question his actions. He said there had been bother up at Stoneyrigg Pit the previous night. The road had been littered with such-like, causing damage to vehicles going about their lawful business. He said it was peculiar how they had landed on the doorstep of Rob Duncan of all people. They'd had words before, he reminded her.

'An' you keep yer trap shut or ye'll be in yin o' they workcamps afore ye can blink,' he shouted at Joe, the foreigner, when he tried to protest for Peggy's sake.

Rob stood up without argument and Sandy was ordered to do the same. They left their mother and sister to be comforted by the lodger.

I was at home, sitting at the table by the window after supper, only half an eye on the library book – though it was proving to be a great adventure story – wondering what had transpired along at the Duncans' and my imagination was getting the better of me. I chastised myself for thinking the worst of Rob. Surely he knew nothing of the material on the doorstep – I had seen his reaction for myself. He was often with the pals in those days, though sometimes he was nowhere to be seen, and even Sandy couldn't say where he was on occasion. I studied Davy across the room. For once he wasn't out and about which was unusual for him on a Saturday night. He sat hunched, staring into the fire, blowing smoke from his cigarette into the flames because my mother hated the smell of it.

I don't know how long Sandy had been outside, lurking in the shadows, flailing his arms like a tattiebogle on a windy day, and mightily relieved when I finally looked up. He beckoned me urgent-like before stepping behind Middle Row out of sight.

As it turned out, Sandy had been released after questioning, told to go home. There was little point in waiting for his brother, they'd said. He could be a while yet. We wandered into the village as we talked, stood in the cold street, staring at the light coming from the police station windows, hearing the ladies' choir at the fundraiser in the church hall singing *In the bleak mid-winter*. Aye, that was about right. Things weren't looking good for Rob,

Sandy explained. I offered to go in straight away and speak to Mackay, to back up what my friends had said but we agreed it would look like I had been put up to it. The police would come for me if they thought I had anything worthwhile to say. We talked about Rob's reactions when we'd arrived home earlier in the day. Had he something to do with sabotage at Stoneyrigg Pit where his father had worked many years before? Some of the older men had condemned the reopening of that pit because of what it represented. They refused to be employed there but hadn't tried to stop others working the coal. Everybody knew the importance of coal to the war effort, including Rob. There were times when Sandy couldn't make him out, he said, and Rob had been out somewhere the previous night though he didn't say where. But vandalism didn't fit with the brother he knew. Besides, Rob was too smart to leave evidence on his own doorstep. He wasn't stupid. It had to be down to somebody else and we both knew who that might be.

Sandy shivered in his jacket without a scarf or a cap, his nose like a bright red poppy. He had an idea, and a plan of sorts. It might not help Rob in the short term but it was something that had to be done, he said.

We went for Bert, told him to bring a piece of paper and a pencil and as many balaclavas as he could lay his hands on, then to meet us at the wash house in five minutes flat. He was to make something up about where he was going, for his mother's sake, but under no circumstances was Geordie to come along. Jim came out of the house on his way to the closet, spotted us crossing the washing green so he had to be involved as well. That grieved me but I figured he could stand in the background without actually taking part, help make it look as if there was a gang of us, enough to intimidate. In the end, he was the one who slipped the note under the door of our cottage.

The night wound on, bitter and interminable whilst we waited. Then we saw Davy skulking his way up Manse Lane, out of the puttering light of the street and into the shadows. He came to the gate into the park, taking stock, glancing back and forth, his eyes getting used to the darkness. He rarely went anywhere after nightfall without a sidekick, preferably two. But the note had said he was to be alone, or else. I could see how he gripped the top of the gate till his knuckles went white as he peered through the pitch black.

Hello! Hello? Nervous-like.

No reply.

I could almost hear the loud noise in his ears, his thumping heartbeat above the sounds of the night. Nobody there. Just the black outlines of walls and trees disappearing into blackness. But we were there.

Suddenly, there were footsteps in the lane, a figure approaching, quickly, head bowed. As Davy turned for a better look, a hand grabbed him from the other side of the gate, pulled him into the park. He was on the ground before he knew it and a kick was delivered between his legs.

Bastard! His hands went down to shield himself leaving his face unprotected. Two swift punches connected perfectly with his jaw.

'Malky?' he gasped. 'Whit ye daein', Malky? Is it you?' Davy curled up on his side, holding his hands over the top of his head. His attacker did not reply in words but delivered another punch.

A second figure was grabbing him by the collar, yanking him onto his back, leaving him exposed to the feet of the first assailant once again.

'Huey? Fur the love o' God. Is it you, Huey? I didnae mean ye tae tak the blame. Whit could I dae?' Davy whimpered after another fist connected with his face. 'It wasnae ma fault ye were caught.'

I despised him for that sound in his voice, that pleading whine of a bully who'd suddenly found himself alone, without protection from his followers.

He lay there on the freezing ground waiting for more but no more came. He rolled over against a wall and cowered, his hands up in front of him, in surrender. He was feeling his jaw, spat out blood and saliva. He got onto all fours like a dog, holding his side as he got to his feet. He watched his assailants walking away, hurrying down the lane, and disappearing out of sight. *Bastards,* was all he could say.

It was long past midnight when Rob was released from the police station without charge. Sandy was standing with Bert, me and Jim, waiting for him.

'Thanks, boys,' he said. 'I'd nuthin adae wi' thon business the ither nicht.'

'We ken,' said Sandy, though we still didn't know where he'd been.

'It was guid o' ye tae speak up for me, tae gie me an alibi.'

'Nae bother,' we said together.

'Let's get ye hame,' said his brother.

Minn

I can count on the fingers of one hand how often I visited Stoneyrigg that first year of the war, so I didn't set eyes on Rob in all that time but I thought of him night and day. I lived in a world where we were together, a future

357

world full of children and laughter and tenderness. I didn't mind where my life would be as long as I was with Rob though, in truth, I hardly knew him. I thought I did, after all those years of seeing him in the schoolroom every day, the years of knowing his family who lived in the next row, and watching him across the distance between us. I suppose it was his kiss on the night of the dance that did it because I couldn't forget how he'd made me feel. So, with scant evidence to go by, I created an imaginary world, a Garden of Eden, with him – handsome and loving and mine – at the centre. Sometimes that world was in Stoneyrigg and sometimes it was in Canada, near to Meg and Will.

I have a photograph of Meg beside the cabin that Will built on their farm. She's holding a rifle and two huskies are sitting to one side in the snow. They were to spend the winter in Dawson and go out to their farm when the snow started to melt. Well, that's how they planned to live until Will enlisted and was sent to France. Though he'd put thousands of miles between himself and his country of birth, the ties of family and childhood had not been severed. Unlike Canada, Scotland could not provide him with any opportunity for advancement but his love for his homeland remained. When I see the geese return in the autumn and leave with the spring, I think of all of the men from the colonies who've made the long journey home to fight for a country that squandered their youth and let them go in the first place without so much as a by your leave. It is surely a terrible foe that made these young men decide to come back and put their lives on the line for old Scotland. I have prayed for Will these years past, that his life will be spared, and Meg will have him back with her soon.

The younger men left Netherside in turn. First it was Dochie, then the three lads from the bothy one by one.

The work was harder for those who were left and older men did what they could. Annie's mother had died by then so the farm became Annie's whole life. She spent time out in the fields with me and Mrs Davidson managed inside with the help of a pensioner. Gradually, women were encouraged to come back to the land and take the place of those at the Front. In January, a mechanised plough came to the county and Mr Davidson said it could do the work much faster, it was the future whether we liked it or not. The army paid a visit as soon as the ploughing was done in the spring and the two mares were taken away hastening the future our way. I would often go into the stable and speak to the last remaining horse, Hector, who was too old for army service. I'd brush down his long tail and plait his mane, rest my cheek on his warm brown flank, telling him that Bess and Ella were fine because they were together, pulling munitions and other supplies for the troops, and that Dochie would be back one day when the fighting was over. Hector listened to every word of it, turning his head and pricking up his ears, looking at me with his big brown eyes when I stroked his nose. I spoke to him about what was on my mind, asked him what I should do. He was always the same, constant, his eyes fixed on mine, listening but never giving anything away. Horses are wise but they keep their thoughts to themselves.

It was late springtime when I went to Rob that first time. I had been thinking about him all day, a Saturday, after the grieve said that somebody had been seen, and not for the first time, on the road by the east march. He'd been seen before, in all weathers, on the hill above the farm, sitting, just looking, not doing any harm but a concern nevertheless. I got it into my head that it was Rob, convinced he had come for me at last so I stole out of bed when Annie was asleep and I went to find him. The road was still wet though the rain had stopped and the gale had eased to a light breeze. It was pitch dark but the moon appeared now and again in the cloudy sky, enough for me to see him standing by the wall. My heart was pounding in my breast.

'Minn?' he said.

'Aye.'

'Hoo did ye ken?'

'I just did,' I replied.

He reached out his hand. I will never forget how it felt when his fingers touched mine.

We found a dry place along at Eppie's Mill, off the road, away from prying eyes, and we sat together. He was shy at first, drew my shawl up when I shivered, put his arm around me and I laid my head on his shoulder. He said he was glad I was there but he didn't say why and I didn't ask him. He was warm and his arms were strong. I heard the rush of the stream outside and the wind in the trees, and his breathing close to my ear. He didn't say much that first time but his hand on my cheek and his lips on mine were all of the words I wanted to hear. Then suddenly he stopped and he took my hand, kissed it like a gentleman might kiss a lady. He said I should get back to Netherside before I was missed so I smiled shyly and kissed him on the cheek.

'Will ye come again?' he asked when we parted at the east march.

'Aye, I will. But I cannae get caught.'

'The morn when ye lowse,' he said. 'Oan yer road hame tae yer folks. Meet me at the mill.'

I hesitated. 'Aye.' Then I pulled myself away, ran up the road knowing he was watching me, a strange mixture of joy and fear in my heart.

Annie was surprised when I began getting ready for the walk home the following evening because I visited Stoneyrigg so rarely by then. She sat on our bed with her knitting and reminded me to take my mother's hat. I always took that hat though it was daft to wear it off the farm. But I left it on the nail behind the door and I think Annie could read my mind. She asked me if I knew what I was doing and I said that I didn't know what she was talking about. She told me to be careful and I said that I would.

I went to the mill and Rob was waiting for me. He'd made a small fire and spread out a blanket on the floor, assured me any passers-by would think it was tinkers, I wasn't to worry. I didn't go home to Stoneyrigg that night or any of the nights I met him there. I couldn't go. I couldn't face my father because of what I had done.

Chapter 20

John

They finally took the bandage off my right hand today and I can't help but marvel at the sight of it even though it looks like a piece of scrag end in a butcher's shop window. The wound where the bullet went through has knitted together well and I can still move all of my fingers. I touch the wound on my neck, careful-like, relieved to be able to feel the scar, how it snakes across the sinews and muscle, from my jaw into the dip above my collar bone. The injury to my hip is healing too, under the dressing. All in all, I'm on the mend. I hold my injured hand up against the sun, imagine the dark collection of bones encased in light-filled flesh, and ponder how complicated a man is. The merest interruption to his proper function, the slightest hurt, can be ruinous but he has to learn to live with it, adapting his movement and his thinking to the new situation. Just like Davy Broon's dug, I suppose, when it lost a leg down a pothole and had to make do with three.

It pleases me that I may be finding my sense of humour again.

I mind how this hand felt after I'd punched my brother's face that time in the park. He didn't know it was me which somehow made it worse. Even though he was bleating and asking for mercy, I hammered the punches home on behalf of my friend and all of the others who might have gone before him, in the hope that none would come after. But experience tells me a leopard never changes its spots. I'd never used my hands with violence before, beyond a scrap in the school playground – which was a way of life rather than an inclination to cause harm. I can still feel the way my knuckles jarred against Davy's jaw, can still hear the sickening crunch of bone on bone. I hadn't thought these hands were capable of such brutality again and promised myself I would not repeat what I'd done. But the truth is, these hands have done much worse since.

I was a Lewis gunner in the first months after I arrived at the Front. I trained like everybody else for the infantry then was put with a group in charge of a light machine gun. It was a technical miracle devised to deal death and destruction, and me an extension of it. For hours on end, I took my turn on a firing step dug into the side of the trench, directing bullets at the enemy, intending to kill.

Kill or be killed, the sergeant had shouted in training. *Keep it up*. And that's what I did: killed men and boys younger than me, over and over again, dozens of them. I watched the mud between us splatter upwards, a stinking fountain of filth, red with blood and pieces of human flesh. I may never make sense of war but, it seems, I am perfectly suited to it and carried out orders without question.

An officer calls out my name. I hold up my hand so that he can see where I am, curled up out of sight in a deck chair, hidden from the rammie of team sport behind the pavilion. He puts a letter in my hand and tells me not to cry, somebody loves me after all.

88 Stoneyrigg Rows
Blackrigg
21st May 1918

Dear John

I was glad to receive a letter from Major Howe informing me that you are alive and recovering from your wounds. I had begun to fear the worst and could not believe the good news but then your own letter came and I decided it was alright to believe it after all. So, you are being looked after by the Red Cross, in Switzerland. God bless them for their good work. I hope you are making a full recovery and will be back here with us soon. They are saying the war can't last much longer.

You will be glad to know that I have heard from Jim. He is still in the German POW Camp where you were both taken earlier in the year and is in good spirits.

Mrs Broadley has heard recently from Bert. Dan Potts is with him by all accounts, still at the Front. Mrs Duncan asks if you have any information about Rob, she would be grateful for it. He has been posted missing these several months past and there is no word.

Father and Davy are doing fine. I will write again soon, at the first opportunity.

God bless and keep you, John
With love
Mother

At last, I have good news from my mother who is happy that I am alive. Many mothers are not so fortunate thanks to me. My twin brother is alive and well, thanks be. My memory jolts to the POW camp where we were taken and other memories begin to surge in, like a cold draught when the door is opened. Rob is missing. I am seeing pictures of Rob in my head, piecing together a story of what happened. But the feeling is not good and I try to close the door again, pushing back against the stench of panic as it coils a festering hand around my throat.

Elizabeth

Towards the end of 1915, I walked with Sarah across the muir because we both had visits that had to be made and were long overdue. We parted at Eppie's Mill, agreeing to meet up later for the walk back to the manse. Dark clouds were gathering on the horizon though the sky still showed a hint of brightness. We couldn't take too long if we were to make it back to Blackrigg before the storm. I asked her if she needed some company for the rest of the journey to Netherside but the answer was no, she was fine. The thought of seeing Minn again was a comfort to her, she said. We set off in opposite directions and I couldn't help but take a final glance back along the road to her lonely figure, diminished in size by the huge trees lining the roadway, as she pushed her way doggedly into the cold north-westerly wind.

Sarah told me later about how she had stood at the door of the farmhouse whilst Annie hurried off to find Mrs Davidson. Then she was shown into the scullery and asked to wait whilst they fetched Minn from her work. Annie reappeared with a chair and two cups of tea, leaving

Sarah in the gloom, a cold wind whistling under the door to the yard, and downwards from the hatch in the ceiling that led up into the loft. Motes of dust hung in the shaft of dim light filtering through the snow on the skylight above.

Minn appeared through a door in the corner concealed behind a layer of sackcloth. The smell of the byre came with her. Sarah thought Minn looked heavy in her layers of winter clothing, dark shadows under her eyes, and her lovely, long black hair hidden beneath a washed-out scarf.

Worse than Teeny-fae-the-Neeps, in Sarah's own inimitable words.

'It's Uncle Peter,' she said to her sister. 'I thocht ye should ken.'

'How's Mrs Graham... how's Jean...?'

'She puts a brave face oan it for the sake o' the bairns.'

'Aye,' was all Minn said. Then after a while she asked after the rest of the family.

'Aye. They're fine.'

Minn forced a smile

'We never see ye, Minn – it's why I came by – and tae let ye ken aboot Uncle Peter's demise.' Sarah had searched her face, said she looked tired.

'It's the work,' Minn began as if she might be about to unburden herself. 'It's hard, hard work.'

Sarah studied her elder sister and dearest friend. She could see the mark of a difficult year on her, the tea cup held in calloused hands, nails dirty from her work in the byre and in the fields. Her cheeks were ruddy from the wind and the cold, her lips dry. Her skin was pale, almost bloodless and her eyes were full of weariness.

Breaking the silence between them Sarah said, 'Ye've haurdly come visit, Minn, even in the summer.'

'Ye cry yon a summer? The muck was thick like glaur, sair work wi' the rain it was. The harvest wasnae a patch oan the year afore an' it was hard gettin' it in.'

Sarah hadn't been asking about the summer and it hadn't been as bad as Minn was suggesting.

'I thocht ye micht've been ower tae see Rob at least,' she said.

Minn seemed to stare at nothing in particular.

'Have ye seen him?'

'I have.'

'That's guid, is it no?'

'He cam by. No for a while though.' Minn looked down at her empty cup, smoothed out the large hessian apron she wore for her work with the cattle.

There was another long silence.

'Will ye come an' see Jean, Minn? She'd fair like a visit, so would Faither.'

Minn stood up, ignored the question, just gave Sarah her cup saying it was good of her to visit but she had to get back to work, the kye had to be fed. They couldn't wait.

'Tell Jean I'm sorry aboot Uncle Peter,' she said as she opened the door into the byre. The sound of animals shifting and snorting in their winter stalls and a loud bellow drowned out her final words.

Annie was in the kitchen, making scones at the big table, her back to the fire.

'I dinnae ken whit's up wi' her, neither I dae.' She had answered the question before Sarah could ask it. 'But never fear,' promised Annie. 'I ken whaur ye bide if needs be.' She glanced out of the window where flurries of snow rose and fell on the air swirling around the farmyard.

'Ye best get yersel hame, Sarah. Ye dinnae want tae get caught in the storm.'

Meanwhile, I was being shown up to Mrs Maclean's bedroom by the housekeeper who suggested that my visit be kept short, doctor's orders. I found the elderly patient lying peacefully in a bed festooned with thick quilts. The room was bright, although the curtains were half-closed against the glare from the snow on the ground, and a small fire crackled in the grate. I pulled up a chair for myself and settled down beside her, reached out for her time-worn hand with its band of yellow gold. I studied her face, the skin like taut, thin parchment over bone, wrapped up in the comfort of sleep. Mrs Maclean opened her eyes. It was a moment before she recognised me.

'How lovely to see you, lass. Kind o' you to visit.'

'I got your letter and came as soon as I could get away. I'd no idea you were poorly.'

'A lot of fuss about nothing at all,' whispered Mrs Maclean, trying not to provoke the cough that had laid her so low for so long.

'You'll be back on your feet as soon as you're able,' I said.

'Nothing truer,' agreed Mrs Maclean. 'I'll confound them all, if the Good Lord lets me.'

'As long as you do what you're told, you probably will.'

Mrs Maclean made the mistake of trying to laugh which started a bout of furious coughing. I raised her up and put a glass of water to her lips. When the coughing subsided, she lay back on a mound of soft pillows.

'I'm glad you've come, lass,' Mrs Maclean began. 'There's something I need to speak to you about.'

'Are you sure you're up to it?' I asked. 'I can come back when you're feeling better.'

'But I micht no get onie better,' came the reply. Mrs Maclean was suddenly full of realism. 'Dinna fuss, lass. Dinna fret.' She looked into my eyes and admired my neatly pinned blond hair. 'You're a bonny lass, right enough, Elizabeth.'

I blushed, conditioned as I was not to take compliments well.

'What did you want to speak to me about, Mrs Maclean?'

'It's Donald.'

I swallowed hard. 'Donald? What about him?'

'This is a lonely life, Elizabeth, here on the farm with an elderly aunt for company. You can be surrounded by servants and workers, all busy doing the master's bidding, and yet never feel lonelier.'

'He's been here nigh on two years and he's getting to know people,' I said quickly. 'Through his dealings with the merchants, the journeymen and ... he's joined one or two societies, I hear.'

Mrs Maclean held my hand tightly. 'But do you not see what's right in front o' your eyes, lass?'

'Yes, I do,' I confessed. 'But... the war... I don't know...'

'Och, the war. The war's an excuse for a lot o' things but life can go on.'

'Yes, it can. Life should go on,' I agreed. The war had been my excuse for not confronting the truth.

'I can see you're confused. If you don't feel the same about him as he does for you, will you at least be honest with him. He's a fine young man and very dear to me.' Mrs Maclean drew a difficult breath before settling back in her pillows again.

'I will speak to him, I promise. We are nothing without truth after all.' Neil had written those same words to me a long time ago.

'Let him ken where he stands. There's nothing worse than wishin' for somethin' that canna be, lass. That was all I wanted to say. I hope you understand.'

I understood and promised that I would talk with Donald. Mrs Maclean closed her eyes. She would sleep easy now, knowing that she had said her piece.

I closed the bedroom door behind me and stood for a moment in the quiet of the upstairs hall. I thought about Neil's letters, about the joy and sadness they had brought me when I had read them. Tears pricked my eyes and anger rose in my heart as I thought about the wasted years when I could have been with him. We had been kept apart by my own brother's deceit. I better understood Mrs Tennant's attitude towards me, why she ignored me in the street, and why the Tennant family had joined the congregation of another church in the months after their son's departure. To take such action, they must have been bitterly hurt and angry by what had driven their eldest child away from them. Neil's mother must have written to him, to say that I had visited Smiddy Cottage looking for him the day after he had left the village, and several times after that still looking for news. That knowledge must have rekindled a hope in Neil's heart that I loved him after all, encouraging him to write to me over and over again, even though I had never written back. Having heard from Minn of Neil's plans to return to Blackrigg, I had been disappointed not to find a more recent letter with the others, telling me of this intention. What did that mean? That he had given up on me after so long? That he had been coming home for family reasons that had nothing to do with me? And now he was fighting in France under a Canadian flag without knowing that none of his letters had reached me.

I found Donald alone in the parlour waiting for me. He sat staring into the fire, his work-shirt stretched across his broad back, a strong hand supporting his head of sandy-blond hair. He offered me tea which I accepted. I didn't really want it. The day was wearing on and I would have to meet Sarah for the long walk back over the muir. But he deserved my time. I owed him as much, and an explanation. I asked him to listen to what I had to say. It was better that I was frank with him, after all this time. It was unforgivable to lead him on and not be perfectly clear about how I felt. Then I told him there was someone else, someone I had loved for a number of years. When I had first met Donald, I had decided that us – me and this other man – could never be together. But more recently, I had come to realise that this was still uncertain. And as long as the possibility of a reunion with this man remained, I could not pretend that I loved Donald in the way he might wish, though I admired him greatly.

'I am sorry, Donald,' I said. 'Please forgive me.'

As we stood up, he said, 'It is for the best. Do not worry about me. I am unsure of my own feelings, in any case.'

I was grateful to him. He was trying to make it easier for me, so that I would not feel his sadness though his face could not hide it. I felt a profound respect for him and a deep affection that could easily have turned to love, in other circumstances.

'Please feel free to visit my aunt at any time, Elizabeth. She enjoys your company very much.' He half reached out to me but he stopped himself. 'Can I see you safely home? The weather is taking a turn for the worse.'

I shook my head. 'I'll be fine.'

He stood at the window and watched me go away from him, up the long track to the road where Sarah was waiting for me. I knew he would wait until I disappeared into the distance, and would long perhaps for my next visit, in spite of what I had just told him. I felt sick with the torment of it, his and mine, for weeks afterwards.

Turning in the direction of the hill road, I linked arms with Sarah. We bent into the wind blowing hard against us as she related her conversation with her sister. Snow was beginning to fall, small icy flakes borne on a cold, relentless blast.

Chapter 21

Elizabeth

Within months of the outbreak of hostilities, the War Office acquired the Village Hospital at Bangour, creating the Edinburgh War Hospital out of an asylum for the feeble-minded. Built to a German model on a sprawling site in the heart of the Linlithgowshire countryside, wards were housed in large detached villas scattered around communal buildings such as the recreation hall, the shop, the laundry, and the power station. To all intents and purposes, a village community had been created where patients worked their way to wellness or an equilibrium of sorts, on the farm, in the gardens, and in the workshops. The first ambulance train arrived in June of 1915 on a new spur from the national rail network that allowed wounded soldiers to be transported from the hospital ships arriving at Southampton. Plucked from the killing fields of Europe, the men woke up surrounded by green fields and woodlands where the peace was undisturbed except by the birdsong in the grounds, the memories of what they'd seen, and the hospital siren intermittently signalling the departure of another train load of wounded men from the main station in the city, twenty miles away. The small towns and villages of Linlithgowshire took the soldiers to their hearts. Those who lived nearby volunteered for nursing duties, or as medical orderlies and ambulance drivers. Every community hosted groups of convalescents in the afternoons for tea and entertainment or, in the evenings, for concerts arranged to raise funds that provided small comforts sent off to the men who were still far from home, at the Front. On Wednesday afternoons, Brogan's Vehicle Hire transported Bangour patients the short distance from the railway station to the public hall where the women of Blackrigg awaited their arrival.

The day we heard the news from the Balkans, late in 1915, I remember how Miss Silver breezed into the hall with all the charm of the north wind, cold and biting. It annoyed her severely that the rest of the Church Tea Committee had arrived before her. It annoyed her even more that several members of the Co-operative Society Women's Guild were in attendance. According to her, they were too ill-bred to understand the notion of a rota that stated which organisation was in charge of arrangements on which week. And that particular week was most definitely the Church Tea Committee's week. She, on the other hand, could not acknowledge the compassion that drove women from their busy lives to reach out a hand of friendship to damaged men who could so easily have been their brothers, husbands, and sons.

Miss Silver hung up her wet coat and surveyed arrangements in the small kitchen off the main hall. Every kettle was full and on the boil, tea pots were charged, and plates of pancakes and scones waited to be served. She added her own contribution of half a dozen pale specimens. In the hall, no one acknowledged her presence. A large knot of women, each with their allocation of wool from the communal supply, had formed around Mrs Gow and the Widow MacAuley who were demonstrating the art of knitting fingerless gloves – for inclusion in Red Cross parcels. The creation of the cuff was straightforward enough, everyone agreed. The first problem lay in making the opening for the thumb then developing the hand sufficiently for the fingers, without losing stitches or creating extra holes where they weren't required. The Widow MacAuley stressed the importance of sticking to the pattern and counting the number of stitches. Miss Silver told everyone it was simply a matter of common sense and basic logic but she peered over my shoulder with great intent nevertheless.

Movement around the room soon distracted her attention from the knitting lesson. The women of the Co-op Guild were busy at the tables, already set for afternoon tea. She watched carefully, shielded by Mrs Gowans who stood next to her. In Miss Silver's eyes, the Co-op Guild was the haunt of lowly Stoneyrigg women, the wives of mineworkers who inhabited slums and bred large families of unwashed children. Their husbands were pushing for a further increase in wages, after all of the concessions made by the government earlier in the year. She often complained about unpatriotic workers taking advantage of a national emergency and pressing for pay increases. Everyone had to contribute to the war effort, she would fume. It was shameful that miners were capitalising on the situation for their own ends when so many brave men were fighting in dreadful conditions, laying down their lives at the front, for King and Country.

'What are you doing with that sugar bowl?!' she suddenly demanded of Highland Mary, her nemesis from the District Nursing Committee, an upstart who called herself a nurse and midwife but was trained for neither profession. 'Put it down!'

Mary turned round, momentarily startled, then continued with her task.

'Put it down, I say!' Miss Silver advanced across the hall.

'Whit's yer problem?' asked Peggy, busy at another table.

Miss Silver took in the enormity of Peggy's new coat – a fur coat acquired from the pack woman for a shilling. The coat had seen better days but Peggy seemed to revel in it. Miss Silver could not hide her contempt.

'You're stealing sugar! How dare you!'

A collective gasp came from us knitters, and newly arrived members of the ladies' choir.

'They most certainly are not stealing sugar.' I called out, coming to their aid.

'I saw them with my own eyes,' said Miss Silver who was always right.

Mary and Peggy stood, hands on hips, glaring back at her, bags of sugar on the tables in front of them for all to see. Mary picked hers up and held it aloft.

'This bag was fu' when I brocht it here,' she stated. 'If I'm stealin' it, whaurs it gaun?' The bag was less than half full.

'I can vouch for that fact,' I said.

'We're putting sugar intae the bowls, no takin' it oot,' declared Peggy.

'If ma man kent why there was nae sugar in the hoose b' Wednesday maist weeks, there'd be hell tae pey!' said Mary.

A snigger went around the company like a ripple on a pond. Miss Silver stood stock still, her mouth open like a big fish out of water, suddenly looking very green at the gills.

'Ye were mistaken, ma'am,' said Ellen Broadley. 'Sugar is gey dear, an' we can ill-afford it but we've brocht it for a guid cause. Mebbe ye should open yer e'en in future, raither than seein' whit ye want tae see.'

Miss Silver turned on her heels, made for the kitchen to spare her blushes and to avoid having to eat humble pie. In her opinion, the Stoneyrigg women had too many other faults to merit an apology for such a small mistake on her part.

A contingent of Bangour patients arrived at the hall, not a moment too soon. We bustled around them, with plates and teapots, refilling milk jugs and lighting cigarettes. The fracas of moments ago was laid aside in a flurry of activity for men who had sacrificed so much. They smelled of tobacco and disinfectant. Between them, they carried a variety of wounds, had different parts of their bodies wrapped up in bandages or were missing limbs altogether but all smiled broadly, grateful to be out of the confines of the hospital, and grateful for our hospitality. They settled down to conversation that was animated for some and quiet for others. They were happy to have female company, to talk with women who reminded them of their mothers, their sweethearts and their sisters who lived in other parts of the country or in the colonies. I have to confess I paid particular attention to the Canadians for my own sake. They described where they came from – country villages and busy towns, cities thick with grime and smog, or landscapes of mountains and sea where people were waiting for them. They talked about letters they had been sent with news of their children, taking dog-eared photographs from inside their jackets, pictures kept warm in pockets close to their hearts. It meant a lot to them that we listened to their stories, studying the images of people who meant so much to them: brothers and fathers, mothers and wives, new born babies they had never held, fiancées and sweethearts they hoped to marry, one day, when it was all over.

The ladies choir soon struck up a medley of songs that ranged from the cheerful to the melancholic, with me picking out the tunes as best I could in the absence of a more experienced pianist. If anyone was subdued by the entertainment, they did not show it, smiling throughout and generous in their applause. There would be plenty of time for sadness when the songs had been sung and they were back in their hospital beds. When Richard arrived to say a prayer on their behalf, the men were accepting and polite in their response, taking the opportunity to give grateful thanks to the Lord for His Mercy and to the ladies of Blackrigg for their kindness.

Richard stayed long enough to let everyone in the room know that he would be leaving the following day for France, having responded to the call for chaplains to administer to the spiritual needs of the troops. He quoted Byron, having learned the words from Ernest of course, the part about man's conscience being the oracle of God. He explained that he was leaving the village with a heavy heart but he had to heed the call of duty. He looked pointedly at me when he reminded everyone that he would be back in six months' time, and that he expected to take up the reins exactly where he left off. Then he left as quickly as he had appeared, mindful of the soiree being held later that evening on his behalf.

By the time the last of the men had said their goodbyes, clearing up was well under way. The Stoneyrigg women took over duties at the kitchen sink, revelling in the joys of indoor plumbing and a spacious kitchen with yards of shelving where everything had its place. Peggy washed, still clad in her fur coat, stacking clean dishes on the draining board for Mary and Ellen to dry. Miss Silver was thankful for the opportunity to stay out of their way in the hall. Time for reflection over her earlier gaff had her dander up and she needed to restore her reputation. She was looking for a victim. When she spotted her arrival, Miss Silver's eyes narrowed. She watched Rose intently as she entered the hall, seeking me out by the piano. We had begun finalising arrangements for her move to the manse the following day when the viper struck.

'Good day, Dr Rose,' said Miss Silver in clipped tones.

'Dr Matheson, if you please,' I corrected her.

'I'm not sure that I can call her that.' She turned to Rose, 'There's only one Dr Matheson in my book, a man of impeccable character and great learning, a pillar of the community.'

Rose smiled in gratitude for the compliment being paid to her father. 'I'm sure he won't mind if you call me by the same name.'

'It's not as if we would get the two mixed up, Miss Silver,' I said lightly.

''Oh, we wouldn't. Would we, Dr Rose?' she continued. 'You're quite a different creature from your father, altogether very different.'

Rose cast her eyes down over the curve of her dress and held out her hands. 'You've noticed.'

She turned back towards me, clearly disliking the older woman's tone, sensing a challenge based on her gender. She had learned how to deal with such attitudes over the years though it irked even more when expressed by a woman.

'You see, I think impeccable morals are essential in a practising doctor.' Miss Silver gave one of her superior smiles.

Rose met my eyes before turning her gaze on her assailant.

'How is Captain Melville, Dr Rose?' The question struck like a knife.

'I am unsure of your meaning? Captain Melville is with his regiment, in the Balkans, I believe.'

'And you haven't heard from him?'

'No. Should I?' Rose was trying hard to look calm. Eyes and ears were trained on her from around the hall.

'Aren't you acquainted with the captain, Dr Rose?'

Rose knew she had to crush the woman's mischief. But she wasn't allowed much time to give rebuke. 'Of course...'

'Didn't I see you with Captain Melville in the summer?'

'Really, Miss Silver,' I interjected. Several other women agreed, tutting their disapproval loudly.

'In Edinburgh, Dr Rose. Don't you remember? Late June as I recall.' Miss Silver turned to her audience then lunged back at Rose. 'One Saturday afternoon. You were walking together.'

'I do remember bumping into Captain Melville in June,' said Rose. 'In fact, I helped him choose some birthday gifts for his son on that occasion.' She turned to me again, tried to continue our conversation, hoping that the woman would back down.

Miss Silver pulled herself up to her full inelegant height. 'Really? You were not carrying any gifts when I saw you emerge from the North British Hotel late in the afternoon and proceed up the North Bridge together. I had a very clear view from the top of my trolley bus.'

The audience of women gasped but not only because of Miss Silver's revelations.

'That's quite enough.' Catherine had entered the hall and was standing by the door; a beacon of respectability in her blue velvet coat with its large sable collar. She placed a gloved hand on top of her abdomen, emphasising her latest pregnancy which was fully six months in the making by then.

'What are you insinuating about my husband? My dear, dear husband who is fighting for his country, at this very moment.'

She glared at the insufferable Miss Silver before sweeping her stare around the hall at everyone present.

'Dr Matheson is a very good friend of the family,' Catherine continued. 'As she has already explained, she gave assistance to my husband when he went looking for birthday gifts for our son. He is a wonderful husband and father but hasn't the slightest idea when it comes to buying gifts. In point of fact, knowing she was in town at that time, I asked Dr Matheson to give him some help.'

Miss Silver looked horrified, clearly wishing the ground would open up beneath her. It would have appalled her to have been caught spreading malicious gossip about the local gentry by one of their own and, worst still, here was the betrayed wife herself hearing the awful truth for the first time. Regardless of Mrs Melville's protestations, the truth was out. Doubtless Miss Silver was already dreading her next encounter with the family after the Sunday morning church service. She bowed her way out of range and fled to the kitchen to help the Stoneyrigg women with the washing up. The rest of the audience drifted away on a tide of embarrassment, their memories imprinted forever with Miss Silver's insinuations about the new lady doctor and the laird.

Catherine smiled a sickly-sweet smile, kissing Rose and myself each on the cheek but her mask soon crumbled.

'Thank you, Catherine. Thank you for your timely intervention,' said Rose in a quiet voice.

'I did not do it for your sake but for myself and my husband.' Catherine's lips hardly moved, a mixture of emotions in her voice. She was having difficulty comprehending the enormity of what had been revealed by Miss Silver's mischief-making but she was making a valiant effort to hide it.

'I have come with dreadful news,' said Catherine, unexpectedly.

Rose held her breath and I gasped.

'About Eric,' said Catherine. 'The worst news possible, I'm afraid.'

Nothing was said about Neil's letters before Richard left for France. He knew he had been deceitful. Some might argue he was a thief, having stolen letters intended for someone else, but all of that was justifiable from his point of view. Still, he could not bear to discuss the matter with me, to see the hurt in my eyes even if his betrayal had been – in his eyes – for my own good. To have to apologise simply because he had been found out, would have seemed very unfair to him. He left on his journey early in the morning without a word of affection for me. I wished him *God Speed*, watching long enough to see him wrestle his heavy valise along the path and out of sight behind the church hall at which point I rested my forehead against the closed door. Then I called for Sarah to put the kettle on as I ran upstairs to strip the sheets from his bed in preparation for a spring clean of his room even though the old year had not yet fully run its course. Later that day, his study was converted into a temporary office and consulting room for Rose, until the renovations at Spittal Cottage had been completed.

In spite of the relief I felt at my brother's leaving, the difficult task of tackling Mrs Tennant lay like a dark cloud on the horizon. I knew that my sudden appearance at Smiddy Cottage would not be welcome but I needed to try and make the woman understand how I felt, and had always felt, about her son, enough to provoke her into writing about me in her next letter to him in France or, better still, to let me have his address so that I might write to him myself. Though how I could do that without revealing Richard's deceit in hiding Neil's letters was hard to fathom. Needless to say when the time came, Mrs Tennant refused to grant me an audience. She kept me waiting out in the cold and barely heard my enquiries about her son's welfare, before closing the door in my face. But there would be other opportunities. I would make sure of it.

For Rose, the move to the manse and the other arrangements necessary for setting up her practice kept her busy. I hoped she would open up to me about her affair with David but she studiously avoided the subject leaving me to wonder how her next encounter with Catherine Melville would go. In the event, a call in the early hours to an ailing Clive, suffering with a high temperature and a persistent cough, passed without incident. Miss Silver wasn't mentioned. Catherine acted as if nothing had happened, only too grateful for the medical attention her friend was giving her son.

Would Rose return in the morning to check on his progress? Could she discuss her latest pregnancy with the good doctor at that time?

Of course, Rose agreed.

Perhaps, on reflection, the wife was convinced of the husband's fidelity. But Rose was too much of a realist to believe that and it irked her profoundly that she found herself in a situation of her own making, one that had spiralled outwith her control.

A week later and two days before the close of the year, Rose and I were able to make arrangements to leave Blackrigg in order to visit Phee. The train journey into Edinburgh and along the Waverley Line would take a while but, with luck, we would be able to return the same day, though that would depend on how Phee was bearing up. We boarded the train, glad at the prospect of seeing her, but fearful of what we might find. The journey was taken quietly with little said between us, just an occasional remark about the weather, the sky, and the number of servicemen evident at stations along the route. In cold, grey Waverley Station, where the east wind whipped along the railway tracks, soldiers and sailors crowded the platforms, each with a warm smile on their face and a girl on one arm. Whether they were arriving or departing, lovers did little to hide their feelings for each other and, more than once, we were forced to step around couples who seemed oblivious to the outside world. It only served to highlight our own situations and gave us much food for thought on the journey south.

Her arms folded, Phee was leaning against a large green motor car when the train finally rolled into the station. We ran to her, saying how sorry we were, how lovely it was to see her and to be able to visit her in her new home at last, if only the circumstances had been different. Phee did not respond, just ushered us into the car. She said her feet were like ice and her hands were about to drop off so we bundled into the rear seat drawing a tartan rug around our knees for the journey. She studied the sky, grey and cold, said we had better get a move on, the signs weren't good and her father-in-law hadn't been keen to let her drive his automobile in the conditions.

A brief break in the cloud brought a sparkle to the snow-covered trees that lined the winding road to the Hyslop family estate. Blue-white hills rolled down into wooded valleys; hedgerows and stone walls criss-crossed dormant fields, green in places where sheep crowded together for food and shelter. Nothing was said in the car as we sped along and the clouds gathered once more, gloomy grey and monotonous. An elaborate stone gateway marked the beginning of a gravel driveway that quickly disappeared between two lines of tall beech trees. Somewhere on the hillside was the family seat, handed down through the generations but Phee drew up beside a small gatehouse, just off the road. The main house, it seemed, was not our destination.

The embers of a small fire glowed red in the tiny parlour when we entered. It was a modestly furnished room with a brightly coloured carpet and a painting above the fireplace. Photographs in elaborate frames stood on the dresser: Eric and Phee, the happy couple on their wedding day; David, Catherine, and Clive in a rigid pose with David looking particularly severe; Isabelle looking softer and more kind than her real-life self; and a host of others, two extended families brought together in marriage. Phee invited us to sit by the fire whilst she brought us tea. *No, she did not need any help. Thank you.* She would manage fine by herself and she disappeared into the kitchen. We hadn't managed to thaw out by the time she returned.

'I hope you don't mind,' she began. 'I spend most of my time here and rarely venture up to the main house.'

'We didn't come to see the house. We came to see you,' said Rose, accepting a cup of tea that steamed in the cold air of the parlour, the fire having all but died.

'This is a lovely cottage.' I glanced at the wedding photograph on the sideboard. 'Is this where you and Eric... live?' I realised my faux pas too late.

'Yes. This was our little nest, our hide-away. It was supposed to be temporary whilst Burnbank House was being prepared for us. Along the valley a little further,' she explained, pointing in the direction of the road. 'It has a beautiful view down to the river.'

'When will it be ready?' I asked. 'When will you move in?'

'I don't think that will happen now. Not now that the eldest son and heir lies dead in a foreign field.' She sat, rigid, as if all of her tears had been shed already.

We didn't know what to say.

'The thing is,' she continued. 'I was blissfully happy here... when he... was here. I didn't need a big house with servants and acres of parkland. He was all that mattered.' She shivered, 'Burnbank will be reserved for Eric's younger brother now, for when he marries. As for me... it's not as if I produced a child when Eric was alive. I thought... well, I thought there'd be time for that... in the future.' She studied her hands, twisting the band of gold round and round on her finger. 'Who wants a childless widow hanging around, even if she was once married to a dearly loved eldest son? Got to be pragmatic about these things and move on.'

I wanted to say something comforting but couldn't trust myself to find the words.

'The family haven't said anything to me about it, of course. Not yet. They'll be biding their time, waiting for a suitable and appropriate juncture; when best to bring up the thorny subject of my future. What will there be here for me? A grace and favour cottage like this one, for the rest of my miserable life? As long as I don't marry again, naturally. A role in the family firm or in the Big House? Highly unlikely. Without Eric I am... an outsider... a stranger... actually, an encumbrance.'

Rose leaned over to the fireplace and poked the small pile of glowing embers in the grate. A momentary burst of heat soon faded. She added several lumps of coal.

I wanted to know about Eric. How had he died? What had happened and how had Phee found out? Where was she when the telegram came? But, of course, I couldn't ask. I sat in silence, just stared at the fire, wishing it would come to life, to bring some cheer to the room.

Phee broke the gloom, asked if we would like to see the cottage and the garden, not that there was much to see, she warned. She led us into a small hallway where she indicated her bedroom opposite though did not open the door. Next was a bathroom and a toilet under the stairs. Steps led upwards into the roof space where a small room with sloping ceilings had been created. A north-facing window gave a view of snow-covered fields and hills beyond a high wall. Phee picked up a pair of binoculars from the floor and offered them to Rose.

'I used to come up here and study the view, how the colours changed with the time of day or the seasons. I would drink it in... the horses and the farms, the birds and the gun dogs. I watched and waited... waited for him to come home. What plans we had.'

A smaller window overlooked an overgrown kitchen garden, and at the far end, a tiny orchard with a double row of what might have been apple trees under the snow.

'You could have a field day,' she said when she saw me looking.

'I'll come and stay if you'll let me,' I offered. 'And help you lick it into shape.'

'If I'm still here come the spring, I'll let you know.' Her voice was dull.

We returned to the parlour where the fire had sprung to life, making the room a little warmer. It wasn't cosy. Phee headed for the kitchen, leaving us to assemble a small drop-leaf table and whisper about her lack of emotion, the detachment in her voice.

Over a thin soup, Rose broached another subject.

'Have you heard from David?' She broke off a small piece of bread, eating slowly.

'He has written to me, yes. He is well. Shaken, I imagine, after the loss of a friend.'

'I only wondered.'

'You could go to him, Rose.'

'Go to him? What do you mean?'

'You could join Dr Inglis and the Scottish Women's Hospital. They're out there, where he is. You know Dr Inglis, don't you? It could be arranged.'

'I've worked alongside her, that's true. But I'd have no influence...'

'You could arrange a posting and be near him. You could look out for him. I'd be able to sleep if I knew you were nearby... looking out for him.' Her eyes wide, Phee leaned towards Rose.

'I have my duties here,' said Rose calmly. 'I've promised my father...'

'If you loved him, you'd go to him! I know about you and David. Everyone knows!'

Rose stared at me with the look of a rabbit caught in the headlights of Phee's car.

'Catherine knows about you and David,' scolded Phee. 'She suspected for long enough and she's no fool. All those visits of his into town, early on in their marriage, staying with friends that he couldn't name, just *old friends from the university*. And that Saturday in June when he didn't appear for dinner, she was worried. She telephoned the barracks and had some corporal scour the place for him, only to be told he was on leave with his family – 48 hours the man said. An officer confirmed it.'

Phee's eyes were full of fury.

'When he finally arrived home that Sunday morning, laden with presents for Clive, he claimed he'd had to return to the barracks. Confirming what Eric had already told Catherine – *a matter of some urgency*, he'd said. We all knew it was a lie. He was with you. Wasn't he?'

'Did Eric... say anything to you?'

'No, of course not. He's too loyal to my brother. But he was pulled into your murky little affair whether he liked it or not and that wasn't fair.' She repeated her question, 'Was David with you?'

'Yes, he was.' Rose breathed deeply. 'And thanks to village gossip, Catherine's fears have been confirmed in the most public of circumstances.'

'You can make amends,' implored Phee. 'You could go to him. Look out for him for all our sakes.'

'That's impossible,' said Rose.

'Really, Phee. What you're asking is out of the question,' I said.

Phee wasn't listening. 'If you really loved him, you would go to the ends of the earth for him.'

She stood up suddenly, hurriedly cleared the dishes from the table, clattering dishes and glasses onto a tray. She returned from the kitchen, muttering all the while about the weather, how she was sorry but we would have to go. She was sorry we had come so far for such a short visit but didn't want us to get caught out. Better to catch an earlier train rather than risk being stuck half-way along the line in the freezing cold. The roads would be filling up too. The drifts could reach ten feet high in those parts, according to the family.

We made haste; aware we were no longer welcome; aware that Phee needed time to come to terms with the loss of Eric, and the new situation she found herself in. She had barely mentioned Eric beyond what was necessary, which wasn't a good sign. Perhaps, in our absence, she would be able to grieve, once she was alone in the small cottage where she had spent so many happy days and nights with him. Phee drove swiftly, without slowing down for the corners, no time for pleasantries and conversation.

Rose retained her composure until the train had left the station. Through her tears, she stared out at the leaden sky, snowflakes turning to streaks of rain on the window. I watched her intently, waiting for her to speak. But she didn't.

'I suppose it's quite preposterous, this idea of Phee's that you should join Dr Inglis in Serbia,' I said at last.

Rose took a while to reply. 'I do love him, you know.' She blew her nose loudly. 'It was never just a sordid affair between us. Not on my part. Nor, I believe, on his.' She watched the countryside flicker past to the rhythmic sound and motion of the wheels on the line. 'Had Rashiepark not come to him, had one of his brothers survived to take the reins there, we would have met at medical school. I know we would have. Then nothing could've come between us.'

'Isn't it strange how the fates can conspire to keep us apart?'

'And bring us together.' Her eyes were full of sadness.

I felt myself welling up.

'It's what we do with the situations that arise from Fate, that's what matters. That's what's important.'

I thought about it and nodded.

Rose continued, 'David made his choice when he married Catherine.'

'So going abroad to work with the Women's Hospitals... it's out of the question?'

'I've made a promise to my father, Beth. I'll administer to the Blackrigg patients for as long as he needs me.' Her eyes were fixed on the falling snow.

Then she leaned across the table and gripped my arm. 'How can I desert my father, the one man I know will never let me down, to set off on a wild goose chase across Europe for one who has already broken my heart?'

John

We weren't surprised when we heard that Rob had left home just after the turn of the year. He was often absent – in body and mind – thinking about something else when he was in our company or away some place and never saying where. We would rib him about who the unlucky girl was. Jenny Campbell or Sadie Murphy? Or Janet Cherrie who had a fine pair of lungs on her, just like her mother. I feared in my heart it was Minn but she was at Netherside so I contented myself that it was too far away for Rob to visit of an evening. Sandy was averse to say anything against him but, eventually, he confided that Rob had been coming home drunk and it grieved his mother something terrible. He told me about Rob's nightmares, how he would wake in the night, sweating, shouting that he had seen a ghost, babbling about their father who was killed down the pit when they were lads.

Rob hated the lodger, it transpired. He'd never gotten on with the man. At first Sandy thought it was because he didn't like foreigners who took jobs from local men. Then he saw how Rob watched Joe – sleekit-like – whenever Joe was near their mother; how Rob followed their every move, seeing their glances across the busy front room, brushing past each other even when there was plenty space to get by.

There were arguments about nothing; everything about his mother irked Rob; he was ay disapproving. *Who was she tryin' to impress with her stupid hat and that big maukit coat that had seen better days? And her la-di-da china cups... was the queen coming for her fuckin' tea? How come she'd cash put by in an auld tea pot when he'd barely twa ha'pennies to rub thegither?*

The night before he ran off to enlist was the worst. He came in at two in the morning, the worst for wear, covered in glaur, a braw keeker on one eye. Peggy was sitting waiting for him and he hauled her out of her rocking chair, the one Joe had made for her in the workshop at the pit. He smashed it to smithereens on the floor and that had Maggie screaming in terror on her hurly bed. Sandy and Joe tried to intervene.

Rob slavered, 'Aww! Here comes Josef Danieliwicz...' Rob slavered, 'Says he's Joe-fuckin-Daniels, yin o' us. Fuckin' cheek!'

Peggy told Sandy and Joe to stay out the way. It would only make things worse, best let him be. Rob calmed down at that – more or less – was left to sleep it off on the floor. In the morning, they had to step over him to get to work because he was still out for the count. Then came the talk. He'd been seen the night before, found blind drunk face-down in the snow, by men coming off the back shift at Back o' Moss. When the gossips heard that Rob had enlisted, their spite turned to Peggy. What kind of mother would carry on with a Russian under the same roof as her dead man's bairns? *See her in yon fur coat, flauntin' herself, mair limmer than leddy,* they said. No wonder young Rob had run away to enlist – a fine lad just like his faither.

Conscription was brought in at the beginning of 1916 just after Rob left. Men were called up by age group, single men first, married men after and, although the pals were age to go, the authorities didn't come for us straight away because we worked in starred occupations. But after the scale of the losses out in France, we were soon called up to serve our country.

Geordie was left bereft by the news of our leaving. Who would help him patrol the village looking out for German spies? Sandy, being younger, had to stay behind and the sight of him looking glum with his hands in his pockets, unable to make a joke out of the situation, was a sorry sight. It suddenly struck us what we were leaving behind, and that what awaited us might not be the great adventure we'd been longing for.

When it came Dan's turn to leave, his father shook him by the hand. Davy Potts looked his son straight in the eye and handed over a small bible, telling Dan he would pray for God to keep him safe. When Bert was ready to go, Jimmy Broadley put his arms around him and told him to keep his head down, he wasn't to worry about the family but he was to write to his mother as often as he could to let her know he was well. Jimmy walked with him to the railway station, waiting till Bert had boarded the train. He stood on the bridge till long after the train had snaked its way between the pitheads and spoil heaps and disappeared over the horizon. The whole village said what a sad sight he was. As me and Jim got ready, Alex sat at the table chewing crusts of bread that were proving hard work for his few remaining teeth. He looked out of the window and spoke about the situation in the mines with so many men away. Me and John stood in our Sunday best, waiting for him to notice us. When he did, he nodded towards neither in particular and said, 'Aye, aye.' We picked up our bags then said a final farewell to our mother. As I closed the door and Jim went ahead of me, I heard Alex take a long sook of tea. 'That'll be that then,' was all he had to say.

Chapter 22

Elizabeth

On a wild night in February of 1916, loud banging at the door had me hurrying to see who it was. Billy Dodds' grandfather stood ankle-deep in snow asking for the lady doctor. She was needed along at Parkgate by the mistress and she was to hurry. There had been such a palaver trying to dig the motor out of the garage, and now it was stuck in a hedge. They couldn't move it. But the doctor was needed urgently at the Big House, and a lot of time had already been wasted. I began dressing for the outdoors, insisting I should go with Rose, whilst she collected her doctor's bag.

We struggled through the drifting snow that had fallen all that day and the previous night. Snowflakes propelled on the gale stung our faces and stuck to our eyelashes, deep snow caught our skirts dragging us down as we struggled out of the village, helped along on the old man's arm. I was glad to see the avenue of beech trees marking the way to the front door where Jameson stood waiting under the portico holding a lantern aloft, a beacon of hope in the night. Inside, Rose was greeted by Isabelle who looked uncharacteristically shaken. She led the way upstairs, glad to hand over responsibility for a situation she knew nothing about before rushing off, promising to send dry clothes and a hot drink. A servant was on hand, in the absence of a nurse.

I made for the fireplace, stoking up the fire to make the room warm enough for the new arrival. The wind blew relentlessly, whistling down the chimney with an eerie moan that put me on edge. Even when I am warm and safe inside, that sound reminds me of the netherworld that lurks outside in the dark with all its temptations and dangers.

Catherine clutched at Rose's hand, thanked her for coming over and over again. She groaned with every contraction, lost in each long spasm of pain, recovering her composure for a few short seconds before it started up again. Rose said the baby wasn't far away.

Breathe, nice steady breathing, she ordered. *When did the contractions start exactly?* She said it would be over soon, the baby was in a rush to get into the world and wasn't going to be stopped. It was a good sign. There didn't seem to be any danger.

Catherine was determined to say that the baby was early – too early – before letting out a long scream. It wasn't due until March, late March, she stuttered when the contraction subsided.

'Conceived in June, late June,' she cried out. 'Just before my son's birthday. You'll understand what that means, doctor.'

Rose remained calm.

Catherine became quite delirious, rambling on about David and how much she missed him. He was far away on the edge of Europe; it would be cold there too, perishingly cold. She prayed that he was warm, in a cosy billet out of danger; imagined him stern and strong, dressed in his great-coat and high leather boots, patrolling a border on a faithful horse. Then the contractions came with a vengeance. Beads of sweat stood out on her forehead, mingling with tears that ran through her hair and down her neck, saturating the fine cotton sheets.

'Where are you?!' she yelled. 'Why are you never here when I need you? Why?!'

Rose did not expect a complicated birth but it took much longer than she anticipated and both mother and baby were becoming tired. She reached for the forceps when she felt there was no other choice, though the procedure wasn't without risk for both mother and child. But first, she felt for the umbilical cord again, pushed and prodded as far as she could at the baby's shoulders, helping it into a better position for delivery. Whatever she did made all the difference and the baby emerged into the world. She was a good colour, breathing well, and not noticeably smaller than might be expected. Catherine looked down on her child as she suckled at her breast.

'Hello,' she said softly, caressing a finger across the delicate pulsing down on the baby's head. She looked at Rose directly. 'Her name is Davina, after her father, my husband,' she said. 'Davina Catherine Melville. Such a perfect name, doctor. Don't you agree? David will be delighted when I write to him.'

'A beautiful name,' replied Rose. 'Her father will be proud.'

'Yes, a fine name,' I agreed, marvelling as always when a new life comes into being.

The dawn was still an hour or two away when we took our leave. It was dark, no moon or stars to light up the way, the sky heavy with more snow. Jameson accompanied us with a lantern. We followed the tree-lined way to the road. The brown-shrivelled leaves on the beeches rustled loudly on swaying branches that creaked in the biting wind. Jameson hobbled slowly, making heavy weather of the drifting snow. When we reached the gates out to the road, he faltered.

'Don't worry about us, Jameson,' Rose called over the sough of the wind. She refused his offer of the lantern – he would need it to get back to the house.

'Mind how ye go, doctor,' he cautioned. 'It's a grand thing ye've done this nicht, bringin' a bairn safe intae this world. I'm sure the mistress is gratefu'.'

Rose grimaced.

'The Melvilles an' the Imries wield a wheen o' influence in these pairts, as I'm sure yer aware,' he warned. 'Tak tent, Doctor Matheson,' he warned. 'Safe hame, Miss Fraser.'

I watched the small light disappear between the trees, the lantern waving wildly in Jameson's trembling hand. His words left me chilled to the bone, even more than the deep snow seeping cold into my boots and freezing my toes; even more than the biting wind that lifted swirls of powdery whiteness up into the air ahead of us. A bright moon was visible for a brief moment as broken cloud raced across the heavens, coalescing back into inky darkness, building for the next snowstorm. One hand on her hat, the other clutching her bag and her skirt, Rose slogged into the storm ahead of me. It was coming straight out of the east, from Russia where thousands were perishing from hunger and cold; from a fractured Europe, where the bodies of dead men lay frozen in the soil, unclaimed by the families who loved them and had lost them forever.

When the next blizzard came, snowflakes stung our eyes, almost blinding us as we fought through the storm to the safety of the manse barely a mile away. Everything was white: the hedgerows, the fields, the air, the road beneath our feet; muffling all sounds except the faraway wind in the trees and the creak of our footsteps in the snow. I wondered, was this what it was like to die? To lose the senses one by one: the feeling in fingers and toes; the softening of sound; trading bright colours for mere black and white; to trudge on with every breath through a blue-whiteness, seeking comfort and release in a calm place away from the difficulties and complexities of life, leaving behind sorrow and pain for everlasting peace.

I thought of the new life Rose had brought into the world, a little girl warm in her mother's arms. She would bring joy to her father when he had news of her, should he be spared long enough to read the hastily-dispatched letter announcing her birth. I prayed for him, for his children and his wife, for Donald, for Phee, and even for Richard somewhere on the French coast where he read the scriptures to lost and weary boys who wanted home to their mothers and fathers. But mostly I prayed for Neil, dearest Neil, who had opened his heart to me, writing me beautiful letters that were never acknowledged.

Sarah was surprised to see that the range was already lit and the kitchen warm and snug when she appeared at six o' clock. I had a cup of tea waiting for her, and the oatmeal was already bubbling away in the pot. Sarah loved her work, especially now that the minister was away at the mission. The house must have seemed much brighter, the atmosphere still purposeful but much more relaxed with just me and Dr Matheson around; and the morning surgeries, held in the minister's study, added a new dimension to life in the manse. When patients arrived for a consultation, they were asked to wait in the parlour until the doctor was ready to see them. If I wasn't able to deal with them then Sarah would step in. There was only one patient that day, possibly because of the snow. Sarah was collecting the post from the doormat just as Rose was making ready to leave for her morning rounds. The hand-writing on one of them had me excited, though I was perplexed by the postmark. I tore the envelope open.

'Someone I know?' Rose asked as she picked up her bag.

I began scanning the first page. 'It's from Phee.'

'At last,' said Rose, relieved. 'It's been ages since she got in touch. Perhaps she's on the mend...' She studied my face as I read through the letter at great speed.

'Is everything alright? Please tell me.'

I took a few more moments, enough to finish the final page then handed it to Rose.

'I don't believe it,' was all I could say.

Rose read quickly, soon realising why I had looked so taken aback.

The letter hadn't been sent from Hawick but from London. Phee was apologising for not keeping in touch but it had taken her some time to come to terms with her situation, she wrote. She expressed regret for her last two letters which had been written in haste and in anger. She was particularly sorry for things she had written to Rose. *Did I think it was a good idea for Phee to write to her again? Would Rose accept her apologies? She hadn't meant what she had said and she hoped to be forgiven by both of us.* We were her dearest friends and she hoped we understood. She had been *out of sorts, hadn't been thinking straight, had been full of anger and spite* and she was *thoroughly ashamed.* But having had time to come to terms with the loss of Eric, she was now beginning to see things more clearly and put it all into some kind of perspective.

I studied Rose, waiting for her reaction. She began to read out loud, as if the sound of the words might help her to understand them better, and make sure she wasn't mistaken.

'So that is why I decided to contact the Scottish Women's Hospitals myself, to offer my services in support of the wonderful work they are doing. Rose turned to the final page. *They took some persuading of my motives. I cannot pretend that I did not lie a little here and there in order to be taken seriously and not dismissed as some mad woman who has been recently bereaved. With persistence on my part, they have agreed to give me a posting, not in the Balkans as I requested, but in France at the Abbaye Royaumont, north-east of Paris. I am to be employed as a driver, transporting wounded soldiers from the clearing stations near the Front to the hospital for treatment. Although it is not exactly what I set out to achieve, I suddenly feel alive again, knowing that I will be doing good. By the time you receive this letter, I will be on my way south. I will write as soon as I can with an address, Beth. I hope you will write soon. Please understand why I could not write till now. Let Rose know my news – her friendship means much to me.*

With love and fondest regards,

Your dear friend, Phee'

In the parlour later that evening, we settled down in front of the fire. The wind had abated but a soft light penetrated the room from the snow outside, hard with frost brought on by the cloudless sky. Shadows danced around the walls as the flames licked upwards from the coals in the grate. I looked up from my book to see that Rose had forsaken her medical text and was staring into the fire.

'Penny for them.' I stood up, lit the candles on the mantelpiece.

Rose leaned over to prod at the coals with the poker. 'I was just thinking that women are prisoners of their biology, more or less.'

I raised my eyebrows though I shouldn't have been surprised, Rose was a deep thinker.

'I cannot imagine going through childbirth myself,' I admitted. 'I was truly horrified the first time I attended a delivery with Mrs Birse. It still seems a daunting process though I've helped on several occasions since. To be honest, that first time made me realise the whole truth about... you know... intercourse... I hadn't fully thought through what was involved. I was naive, had no one to tell me all about it, to describe the mechanics of it.' I must have blushed a bright pink. 'What a silly girl I've been about all of it – love, marriage, children. Blind to the realities of life... as a woman.'

'Childbirth is a difficult and dangerous process,' said Rose. 'So many risks, even in the best of homes where the mother is well-nourished and the possibility of infection is much reduced. Yet some women go through it time after time.'

'Did it ever worry you that...' I was having difficulty expressing myself. 'You would... might become... you know...'

'When I was with David? No, it didn't.' She stared into the coals. 'In the heat of it, nothing of the sort crosses one's mind. Well perhaps it does but only for an instant. It's all-consuming, believe me.'

'But what if there had been a child? Think what it would have meant...'

'There was little risk of a child. There are ways of avoiding such. Not foolproof, granted, but good enough if one is careful.'

'I'm not sure what to think of such actions... it sounds... so... so premeditated, so devious.' I regretted the words immediately, not wanting to appear critical or take the moral high ground when I knew so little of such matters.

'What you actually mean is that it sounds immoral.' Rose had already encountered the same reaction in others.

'No, I didn't mean it like that,' I replied, though that was exactly what was in my mind.

'Why shouldn't women find pleasure like men do, without the dire consequences?'

I gasped. 'Pleasure?! Goodness, gracious! Perhaps immoral is the right word!'

'But why? Is only the man to have pleasure?' she challenged. 'Is that what the sister thinks or the brother?' Rose had a fire in her eye I had rarely seen before. 'Why should the church, and the conventions it perpetuates, be allowed to condemn women to pregnancy and childbirth, almost as a punishment for her sins.'

'Hardly a punishment! A child is a wonderful gift!'

'Yes, I agree. One or two children, at the time of a woman's choosing, is a blessing. But not otherwise. Certainly not one every year until she drops with exhaustion or a medical complication.'

It was my turn to stare into the coals. I could see her point. 'Do you advise patients of such?' I ventured. 'Do you pass on your knowledge of ... of avoidance?'

'No, not exactly, not unless the woman's life is in danger should another pregnancy occur. I have to be careful. Wider society is not quite ready for such knowledge, and certainly not here in Blackrigg. But the time will come.'

I thought of some of the women in the Rows and in the farms who were Rose's patients, tired before their time.

'The very same women who would be most helped by such knowledge would be the ones to condemn me for it, not to mention the Miss Silvers of this world. Besides, what would Richard say if he knew I was advocating such behaviour whilst living under his roof?' Rose raised her eyebrow at me.

'He'd probably say we were well suited, you and I. One encouraging immorality in the female population – that's you – and another encouraging immorality in the male population – that's me!'

'We'd better mind our Ps and Qs, in that case, Miss Fraser. We don't want the manse to get a reputation as a house of ill-repute in his absence, do we?'

Our laughter masked the sound of the parlour door opening. When we eventually noticed her, Sarah was standing in the doorway looking as if she had just seen a ghost.

'Please come,' she pleaded. 'She needs help, please.'

'Who needs help, Sarah? What's wrong?' I asked, immediately brought back down to earth.

'Ma sister.' She beckoned towards the kitchen. 'It's ma sister. Please, she's through by.'

It was a long dark night, as cold as anyone could recall. The temperature had dropped severely as night had fallen and a raw, angry blast blew across the snow fields, tainted Nature concealed under a cloak of unadulterated white. Trees swayed back and forth in the gale and windows rattled in their casements. Slates lifted in waves, then clattered down onto the roof timbers. Fearful, I stood in the half-light watching at Richard's bedroom window which gave a lofty view of the churchyard and the village. Ferny patterns of ice had spread across the glass so I melted a circle with the heel of my hand, a woollen blanket around my shoulders – the warmth from the fire did not reach far into the room. The clock in the hall sounded out six discordant notes as hunched figures began to make their way along Main Street, each one glimpsed only for an instant in the gas light at the end of the lane below the church. The early shift was heading off to Back o' Moss Pit. The world was coming to life in spite of the weather. The Grahams would be up and about in the Rows, thankful Sarah was safe and warm along in the manse, glad she had not tried to venture home on such a wicked night.

Sarah sat in a basket chair, bathed in a pool of yellow lamplight, beside the bed where Minn lay sleeping. She listened to her sister's breathing, no longer shallow and rapid, but slow and steady since the shivering had subsided. She touched her hand – still perishing cold – and pulled the covers up around her shoulders, studied the soft sweep of Minn's eyelashes over her closed eyes, and the way her thick black hair spread out across the bolster. She repositioned the hot water bottles up close to her and placed her own blanket on top of the quilt, an extra layer to make her warm. She placed her head gently against Minn's chest, hugging the covers snug around her, then weeping because of what her lovely sister had borne on her own for so long.

Rose appeared shortly, still dressed in her night attire, wearing the dark shadows of interrupted sleep. She put a thermometer under Minn's arm then placed a hand on the sleeping girl's brow; took her pulse, gently rubbing heat into the hand before returning it below the covers. She watched her breathing before putting the stethoscope in her ears.

Rose studied the thermometer. 'She's still a little cold but she's improving. Lucky she came to us when she did, very lucky. She needs rest. We'll let her sleep for now and she can have a hot drink in an hour or two, perhaps a warm bath later in the day if she's up to it. Try not to worry, she's strong.'

Sarah couldn't speak.

'The baby's well advanced, fine for now though these things can change suddenly. Minn will stay here until she is well. No one need be told until she's in a fit state to decide what she wants to do, who she wants to see.'

'Do you think the father knows?' I asked.

Sarah shook her head, huge tears welling up in her eyes. 'Oh, Minn,' was all she could say.

Minn

The old mill was our meeting place that summer. We found a dry corner in a room where the roof was complete and gave shelter from the rain then made a bed with straw from the fields, carrying whole stooks under cover of darkness, trying not to laugh and bring attention to ourselves. He would light a small fire with kindling he collected, adding coals from a bag and we would lie together in the darkness watching the shadows dance across the walls while we listened to the rain spill from broken guttering and drip splattering from the trees. I placed an old china jug I'd found in the farm midden on a windowsill and filled it with flowers from the hedgerows. I could tell by the way his eyes lit up that he liked that and he would ask me the names of the flowers, covering my mouth with kisses as I tried to say each name in turn, making me laugh, telling him never to stop. Once, when the night was clear we lay together in a hay ruck out in the open, staring at the starry sky, wrapped in each other's arms until the first glimmer of light woke us and tore us apart. I could not wait to see him again and thought of little else but his smile and his kisses and the way he made me feel when his hands caressed me. I was like a moth to a flame. I couldn't get enough of him, nor him of me, in the beginning. We were like children wrapped up in a game of make-believe but we did not do childish things.

Gradually, we spent more time talking. He would ask me about life on the farm and in the countryside and I would tell him about calves and heifers and cows in milk; about ewes at lambing time and how special it was for the farmer when twin lambs were born; how those lambs would be chosen to mate the following year to breed twin births into the line. I told him all about ploughing, sowing, and harvest, about singling neeps and about tattie howking, though he knew about that already and said he hated it when his mother had sent him to do it as a boy. A dark cloud passed over his face at the mention of his mother. When I asked him about what it was like working underground, he would go quiet, tell me a few facts about the lie of the coal and different jobs that had to be done but he wasn't keen to elaborate. I didn't like it when he clammed up so I didn't prod or provoke and knew when to leave well alone. Rob was deep and mysterious and I loved him all the more for it. He didn't like to talk about his family either so I didn't ask him, waited for him to open up but he never did. One time, I told him about my sister in Canada and asked him if he ever thought of going to live in the colonies. I began to speak about the mountains and the harsh winters, and promised to bring along the photograph of Meg with the huskies next to the cabin Will had built, the next time I came to him.

I remember how he looked at me, how cold his eyes were, his mouth suddenly cruel.

'And what makes ye think there'll be a next time?' he asked.

I was confused. Had I misunderstood what we were to each other? His voice was different. I studied his mouth trying to make sense of what he had said then gave a small nervous laugh when his smile didn't come.

'Do. Not. Presume. There. Will. Be. A. Next. Time,' he snarled into my face, his teeth clenched.

He wrapped his hand in my long black hair and drew me roughly towards him till our mouths were close. I told him he was hurting me, asked him to let go but he wouldn't. Instead, he pushed me hard against the straw and threw away the blanket shielding my nakedness. I tried to reach for it but he laughed and told me to leave it be. I said I was cold and he told me to stop bleating, that I'd never complained of the cold before. There was no tenderness that time and I felt like a beast in a field when it was over and he'd slumped in a heap by my side. I was too shocked to cry, that would come later, so I lay quite still, too frightened to move for a while. Then I heard his breathing, deep and long and I knew he had fallen asleep. I dressed quickly, doing my best to be silent, felt around desperately for my shawl. I pulled it around my shoulders and picked my way out of the ruin, stumbling over broken masonry, my feet sliding on cracked slates. When I was out on the road, and was sure that he wasn't following, I took to my heels, sobbing like my heart was broken.

I didn't go back the following Sabbath, nor the next, or the next but I couldn't stop thinking about him. I wanted him at the queerest of times, day and night, and soon convinced myself that whatever had happened between us – to change him – had been my fault. Maybe I had been wrong to mention my sister and her husband, and their life in Canada. Maybe we hadn't known each other for long enough when I had begun hinting about marriage and emigration though that hadn't been my intention right then. It was just a thing that was in my head so I'd said it. Rob was the main breadwinner in his family, he had responsibilities. It was too much to expect him to think about such things. But I knew by then I was having his bairn. The signs were there and had been for a while. All the time we were courting I'd assumed he was mine and he would be there for me. We both knew the consequences of our actions. I remembered when I'd first gone to him, how sweet and gentle and tender he had been, telling me how long he had wished for me, how much he needed me. I longed for that Rob to come back; prayed he'd come back once I told him I was having his bairn.

As autumn wore on, the weather worsened. Sarah came to see me one bleak day when the first snow arrived. It saddened me to hear about Uncle Peter but I could offer no words of comfort. She couldn't hide her shock at the sight of me, dirty and unkempt. I could see she was worried and she said how much I was missed by the family but I didn't want to see her or anybody just then. I had to sort out my predicament before I could go home.

A few weeks went by before Rob came looking for me. Annie was first to hear him tapping on the small window that lit our sleeping space under the stairs. She gave a yowl loud enough to waken the dead but I told her to calm down when I saw it was him, recognising the dark shape of him in the moonlight. As soon as I opened the window, his fingers sought out my hand and I was his once again. I agreed to meet him along at the mill and he slipped off in the night to wait for me.

As soon as I got to the mill we were in each other's arms, seeking our pleasure like there was no tomorrow. He told me he was sorry and asked my forgiveness. He couldn't explain why he had acted so mean to me, his beautiful special Minn whom he'd wanted for so long. Everything was fine when he was with me, he said. I didn't tell him about the bairn, not then nor the next time we met. First, I had to be sure the old Rob was back, the one who would welcome the news.

It was late in the year when I decided I could not put off what had to be said any longer. Our lovemaking was as ardent and passionate as ever, and though even a blind man would have recognised how my body was changing, Rob didn't seem to notice.

He wasn't there when I approached the mill in the dark of that December night when I knew I would have to tell him. There was no warm fire waiting for me, no candle lighting up the corner where we lay together. I edged my way in through the undergrowth and sat in the straw listening, watching for shadows. The minutes passed, then the hours. I don't know how long I lay there in the cold, the blanket damp with the winter's chill wrapped around me. I must have fallen asleep. The noise of his feet scrambling through the ruin woke me up with a start but I smiled sleepily that he'd come at last, just as he'd promised.

He made his way towards me on all fours, breathing heavily like a dog on the prowl. I caught the whiff of whisky on his breath straight away, sour and hot. He said he'd attested and couldn't wait to be called up. Then he would be able to get away from this piss-rotten place and sluts like me and his mother. We were all the same, he said, and he used words that I had never heard before, that made me try to cover my ears so I wouldn't have to hear them again. He pulled me out of the corner and tore at my clothing. I tried to get up but I was much less agile than before. I rolled over, got onto my feet and he pulled me back, slapped me hard on the face and warned me that if I cried it would be worse and all my own fault. I wanted to get away because of the bairn but he was too strong for me. He told me to stop pretending, knew I wanted it. Only a bitch like me would want to do it in a hovel like this. Did I think he was stupid? Of course, he knew about the bairn, he said, but there was no guarantee it was his.

He was too drunk even to unbuckle his belt so he staggered to his feet and threw the blanket at me. He said he was leaving and wouldn't be back. Nobody walked out on Rob Duncan but he was walking out on me, for good. He spat on the ground, wiped his mouth on the back of his hand and disappeared like a ghost in the night.

After he'd gone, I shivered in a black pit of desolation. Loud in my ears, the sounds of the burn awakened me to my predicament, heightened my despair. The bairn was the only part of me that was warm, that seemed in any way alive and I drew my trembling hands over the round curve of the small body growing inside mine. Had it not been for the bairn, I think I would have lain there all night, let the frost take its grip on my heart and given myself up forever to the cold.

Annie comforted me that night when I got back to Netherside but I was inconsolable. She said she had known about my condition for a while but wanted me to be the first to say. She urged me to go home to my family. My father would be raging, she said, but Jean would stick up for me and help bring him round. After all, I wasn't the first and I wouldn't be the last lassie to get myself in the family way outside marriage. Besides, there were worse things in this life than a bairn.

In spite of her advice, I couldn't bring myself to admit what was happening far less do something about it. Annie helped to cover for me, helped to bind up my belly so I didn't look so much like a heifer in calf but my condition was not going to be hidden forever.

Mrs Davidson noticed how heavy I looked and she confronted Annie. Knowing the truth would have to come out, Annie told her I was having a bairn but she didn't know who the father was because I wasn't saying. We sat in fear and trembling in our space under the stairs that fateful night, knowing that Mr Davidson was being told. As it turned out, his rage knew no boundaries and he shouted to high heavens that he was a God-fearing man and no *hure* would have refuge under his roof. He sent his wife to order me off the farm – she came to see me with tears in her eyes. Annie looked out at the freezing night and asked if I could at least be allowed to stay until morning but she said no, she could not be responsible for Mr Davidson's actions if I was still in the house longer than was necessary. Annie put on her coat to help me over the hill road but he came down the stairs right at that moment. He told her if she so much as put a foot over the door, she was not to come back. I understood that Annie could not come with me. She was alone in the world since her mother had died. Her employment at Netherside gave her a roof over her head as well as her daily bread. Her face was wet with tears and her shoulders shook with her sobbing as I went out alone into the darkness of that bitter night.

And that is how I came to find myself in the minister's bed with a warm fire crackling in the grate and my dear sister fussing about me with beef tea and hot water bottles. The terrible journey through the snow played out in my head like a bad dream but I learned to let it go and be thankful I had come through it. Miss Fraser was kindness itself and she brought Jean to see me a week later. It made me sad to think of how my father would take the news when she told him but I had made my bed and I had to lie in it. Try as I might, I could not reconcile the two Robs I had encountered but I saw him in the eyes of the son I bore him in the early spring of 1916 and was glad.

In a confusion of fear and longing, I have wondered if Rob will ever come home. I am sure that his heart would melt with joy at the sight of his beautiful son and he would fall in love with me again for my part in giving the boy life. Whenever a whistle is heard on the line, whatever I am doing, my eyes are drawn to the station road and a smile appears for a moment on my lips as I picture Rob stepping off the train and coming home to where he belongs.

As the months and the years pass, I know that this will never be and that, after all, it is for the best.

Chapter 23

Elizabeth

It was almost nine months before Richard returned from the mission. He didn't say so in as many words but he was overwhelmed by what he had seen though he was nowhere near the Front, and had volunteered to stay on for a longer stint. Eventually, overworked and emotionally drained, he was forced to retreat across the channel to recuperate. It was several weeks before he felt well enough to make the journey home. I was quite taken aback by how thin he'd become. The haunted look in his eyes suggested a profound change had come over him. He was a much quieter, more subdued individual initially, but he soon became fractious, irritated at the slightest thing but, thankfully, less interested in the day-to-day goings on in my life than before.

Of course, his return meant that Rose had to move out of the manse, but the renovations at Spittal Cottage had been completed giving her a pleasant living space above a surgery and dispensary. I visited her often when my own business allowed and we talked endlessly about all manner of things but more and more about what we might do and where we might go when the war was over. One day, she handed me a letter she had received from Phee.

Scottish Women's Hospital
France
May 1917

Dear Rose,

Spring has come at last! I have been able to cast off my rubber boots which were such a God-send this winter past, and can feel the cool grass between my toes as I write to you from a pretty meadow by a river near the Abbey. The sunshine on the water and the flowers that dance around me in the soft wind lift my spirits after many months of frost and rain. A boy is fishing for perch in a large pool upstream whilst his female companion sits on the riverbank with her book. It is such a happy scene, yet only a few miles away, the mayhem continues. The youthful innocence of the sweethearts gives me hope that one day soon all of this will be over. Being here has been my salvation. I spend nearly every waking hour with my mind on the present so I have little time to dwell on the past and what might have been. In odd moments – like this one – when I am allowed some respite, my thoughts turn to the future and the many possibilities life holds. I have seen death at such close quarters for so long that I feel immense gratitude for my own life and know that I will live it to the full when the time comes, when the war is over, should I be spared.

Although they have little time for the likes of me, I have great admiration for the work that is done in the hospital by the medical staff – all strong women like you, dear Rose. They strive ceaselessly for the sake of their patients who arrive, day and night, from the clearing station. I cannot give details, as you will understand, but there is never enough equipment or time. They make do, improvising with what they have, and go without sleep until the job is done. I can see that they have the same spirit that you have. That same determination and resolve, that same self belief and, dare I say it, bloody-mindedness. I am proud to be your friend!

I have heard from Isabelle that David is well. He has been promoted to major, and mentioned in dispatches. Clive and little Kate are thriving by all accounts. I am homesick at times for Parkgate and the horses – I remember the days when the stables were full of horses. I do love Rashiepark at this time of year. There is something so uplifting about the springtime, don't you think? The drab colours of winter sloughed off for the bright green hues of new growth.

You and Beth are often in my thoughts. I imagine what you might be doing but I am hesitant about wishing I was there at this moment. I have to remember how much has changed since that beautiful summer of 1914. Not just the people who are gone and the effect this has had on those they left behind, but how much we have all been changed by the knowledge of what has passed in the last three years. We are none of us the people we were but one day we must pick up where we left off and move on. I am not so sure it will be easy, though it is what we long for.

In answer to your query, the majority of the patients here are French. We have Canadians from time to time. On occasion, when things are quiet, I am ordered to transport soldiers to one of the camps nearby. I have made enquiries at the large Canadian camp about a Scotsman called Tennant but the response is always negative. The men are very understanding but they cannot hide the pity in their eyes, assuming, as they probably do, that I am a deluded lover who is desperate for news. As you will appreciate there are many Canadian soldiers in France and I do not hold out much hope for a successful encounter. The old saying about needles and haystacks comes to mind.

I must go now, Rose. The lovers have wandered off hand in hand along the river bank, and I am left alone in the sunshine with my thoughts. I hope you are well. Please give my best wishes to Beth and your father,

Much love,
Your dear friend,

Phee

Rose must have seen my colour rise. 'What do you think?'

'Good news,' I said.

'And the bit at the end?'

'It's kind of you to think of me though I am a little embarrassed... the deluded lover... is that me? It's like Phee says, a needle in a haystack.'

'Everybody in this village knows you still hold a candle for Neil Tennant – except his mother. Who knows what someone, somewhere, might turn up?'

417

'Dear God! Does everyone know? Anyway, I'm sure he'll have given up hope, a long, long time ago.' I did feel deluded and quite stupid.

'Well, don't you give up,' she said. 'Not unless you want to.'

Rose was always the pragmatist.

Summer soon merged into autumn and the days became shorter as another year of war drew to a close with no end to the hostilities in sight. One morning I left the house to make a few visits that were nothing out of the ordinary. A mother was poorly and needed some help with a child down with measles. A consignment of wool had arrived for distribution to the knitters – I would put word around for people to collect it. We had to get a move on if each of the Red Cross Christmas boxes for the troops were to contain a pair of socks. And I wanted to visit Miss Shanks at the Post Office, to find out if her throat would recover in time for the next afternoon recital for the Bangour patients. As I walked down the church steps, Mrs Gow and the Widow MacAuley were nowhere to be seen so I lingered, pretending to look at something on the ground. I wanted to give the women time to come out of their homes, to engage me in conversation, should they have any news to convey that might include something about Neil. I hadn't given up and still lived in hope. A curtain twitched at a window across the road but the doors remained firmly shut.

My heart skipped a beat when a dark clad figure in the distance caught my eye. A man was coming towards me, from the direction of the station. He walked at a snail's pace. I stared for the longest time.

'Ernest,' I greeted him at last. 'I hardly recognised you.' He looked smaller than before, huddled up inside a thick woollen coat, his hat pulled down over his eyes.

'Elizabeth,' he replied. 'Forgive me if I do not remove my hat.'

'Of course.' He looked drawn, his eyes sunken, his clothes a little dishevelled, not his usual dapper self. I asked how the tribunal had gone.

'Not well, I'm afraid. I believe I gave a good account of myself but there was no one to speak on my behalf.'

I wanted to sink at his feet and apologise, though not for myself. As Chairman of the School Board, Richard had refused to support Ernest's appeal against conscription.

'Did they give their verdict?'

'They did,' he said. 'It would seem that men of conscience are to be removed from the society they serve. Their presence might influence the minds of others, especially in my case, in my role as schoolmaster.'

My heart went out to him. He had already endured months of taunting from his pupils and several of the villagers had shunned him. Miss Foulkes had plenty to say about his refusal to join up when conscripted. She was prime suspect as the perpetrator of the white feathers pinned regularly to the door of his study for all to see.

'I am to join a work camp,' Ernest explained. 'That is my sentence: to cut down trees in the absence of the forestry workers away at the front. Timber is much needed.'

I could not imagine Ernest wielding an axe. How ever would he cope?

'I am not inclined to decline such work, even though it contributes to the war. But I understand why others refuse and why they are prepared to go to prison for their ideals.'

'I've heard the camps are just as harsh.'

'Punishment is not meant to be taken lightly, dear Elizabeth.'

I studied his face seeing his gentleness but also a great strength that others failed to see.

'I will have the companionship of other like-minded fellows,' he assured me. 'Perhaps our shared beliefs will see us through. A local man from the Church of Christ was similarly refused his appeal at the tribunal today: in his case, on the grounds that he is too young to have developed the intellect necessary to come to a conclusion about weighty matters of conscience. Yet they could not see the irony of their assumption that the same man is not too young to fire a gun in order to kill another human being. Such is the madness of war.'

'I am sorry, Ernest.' I put my arms around him.

'Why thank you, Miss Fraser,' he said when I released him. He seemed quite overcome as he readjusted his hat. 'Please be careful. Think carefully of your reputation.' He looked back and forth as if every window in Main Street might have eyes trained on us. 'You mustn't be seen cavorting with a coward.'

I looked at him with profound admiration. 'You are no coward, dear Ernest. You are the bravest of men. Perhaps if there were more like you, this terrible war would never have come to pass.'

'I will remember those words in the months ahead.' He gave a short bow. 'I mustn't keep you out in the cold, Elizabeth. And I must pack some things as I am to report for duty tomorrow. I have a journey ahead of me.'

I watched him, a dejected figure, make the long walk across the school playground. I waited until he had disappeared from sight around the side of the building as he headed for the schoolhouse. It saddened me to see a proud and principled man so mistreated and misunderstood. Even if he survived the rigours and privations of a forest camp, Ernest Black might return a broken man, unable to take up his position as schoolmaster again with his authority so undermined.

I wrote to him weekly; long rambling letters about the wintery weather and whatever thoughts I had about the books I was reading. He rarely wrote back and when he did his prose was short and stilted, his thoughts poorly articulated with very little detail about his life at the camp. I was shocked but, in the end, not surprised when his good friend Mr Muir appeared at the door one day in the spring of 1918.

Mr Muir sat in the parlour clutching a box to his knees like a gaoler guards a prisoner. Richard sat opposite holding the man in the strong grip of a treatise about sacrifice and suffering, practising for the following Sunday's sermon. His parishioners were restive for the war to be over, he explained to the visitor. They needed constant reminding of the need to endure, for the sake of the country. They were sinners who were weary of conflict but they had given their savings to buy war bonds and given their sons to the slaughter, worked hard to bring food and fuel to the nation. They had even raised money to buy weaponry for the front: a howitzer, as it turned out, not as great a contribution as the towns had been able to make but little acorns from great oaks grow, it had to be remembered. Richard was delighted – he could barely contain himself – to impress on the man his ability to inspire. He stressed the importance of a sermon in giving the flock sustenance, enough to keep them going from one week till the next. Fire, passion, and the Holy Spirit were a formidable foe in the fight against the devil and immorality which came in many forms. I am sure the visitor could see that Richard would not recognise either when they were staring back at him whenever he looked in a mirror.

Mr Muir was sitting like a coiled up spring, rigid and tense, his teeth on edge, and a grimace fixed to his face when he noticed me standing in the doorway.

I extended my hand. He fumbled to retain his grip on the box which I could not help but stare at. It seemed to be important to him.

'Do sit down, Mr Muir,' I said. 'I have heard of you from Mr Black.'

Our gaze fell on Richard who backed out of the room, finally, calling for Sarah to hurry with the tea.

When the door was closed, I sat down. My eyes went from the visitor's face to the box.

'I am sorry that I could not come sooner, Miss Fraser,' he began, taking care over his diction. 'I have not been well.'

'I hope you are much recovered.'

He nodded. His collar seemed stiff. 'It was Ernest's dearest wish that you should have these.' He tapped the sides of the box.

'You are most kind to bring them.' I could not hide my sadness.

'My brother... he brought me here today, in his automobile from Glasgow. It would have been impossible otherwise. We have cleared the schoolhouse of Ernest's things and will take them to his mother.' He pushed his spectacles up against the bridge of his nose with a long finger.

'May I?' I reached out. He stood up to give me the box.

'They are mostly poetry. He specified certain ones... those he knew you would like.'

I examined the first two or three volumes and agreed that I would like them very much.

'There are also one or two texts on the subject of botany. I believe you are well read on the subject.' He smiled, hesitant, not wishing me to think I had been discussed, not wishing to allude to the private conversations he had had about me with his good friend.

'I will cherish them,' I promised, now close to tears.

Mr Muir nodded quickly.

'I had not heard from Ernest for some time. I did not realise... I knew nothing of his illness.'

'No.' He stared at the floor, remembering. 'He did not look for pity.'

'Pity? Not pity... concern for a dear friend... and... most definitely not pity.'

'He was a proud man and knew he was gravely ill, Miss Fraser. Believe me, your friendship meant a great deal to him. He often spoke of you.' He looked into my eyes, let his gaze drop down to the books on my lap. Then he stood up all of a sudden, straightening his jacket at the hem as if his life depended on it.

'It is best if I leave you now. But please permit me to write with any details that you may wish to know. Perhaps I might visit in a few months when we have both come to terms with Ernest's passing.'

I did not trust myself to speak, just followed him out of the parlour into the hall where Sarah was standing with the tea tray. He apologised profusely for any trouble he might have caused but he could not stay.

Hesitating at the door, Mr Muir fumbled in his pocket. 'I almost forgot the most important thing!' he exclaimed.

'Please forgive me for the delay in bringing this to you.'

I took the envelope he proffered, recognising the handwriting straight away, though it looked a little faltering, much less confident than in the past.

'It was a pleasure to meet you, Miss Fraser. I am glad you were his friend.'

I stared at the letter, remembering its author. Against the onslaught of public opinion fuelled by government propaganda and the need to justify so much death and violence, Ernest had fought his own battle for Good over Evil but would be condemned by history as a coward. So many men had shed their blood on the field of battle for freedom and honour and peace. Had Ernest Black not stood tall for the very same things, in his own quiet, measured way? Was the wholesale slaughter of a generation of its young men, the only answer the nation had to the Kaiser?

I remembered Ernest's mild manner and his timidity in my presence. I smiled at memories of him tripping over the rug in the hall and slipping on the front step as he nervously took his leave. He had a gentle sense of humour borne of intellect, extensive reading, and a deep understanding of the human condition. I remembered his friendship with Murdo Maclean, imagined the discussions they might have had about Greece and Rome, about education in its broadest sense, and the pace of social and political change. Unlike Murdo, Ernest would not fulfil the potential of his early life. He would never come back to the school or to any school to pass on his considerable knowledge of many things: his love of Latin and literature, of geography and science; to encourage excellence in his pupils, or frighten the living daylights out of the timid ones and give much-needed guidance to the bold. What sort of nation would squander such a life as Ernest Black's?

It occurred to me that he had been spared a life made difficult, perhaps intolerable, by his objection to the war on the grounds of conscience. As the troops returned home, triumphalism would inevitably grow if the war was won. Duty and sacrifice had already been exalted above all else by people like Richard who justified the carnage and bloodshed in adulatory terms for King, Empire, and God – together, the embodiment of all Truth and Reason. I feared it would only get worse. Whilst the men came back home to what? A struggle for a fairer share of the wealth of the country they had fought for? To overcrowded homes, to poverty, and to the possibility and iniquity of unemployment?

I opened the letter. There was a single page and a flower, delicate, fragile – its delivery much delayed by Mr Muir's illness. I extracted it carefully and laid it on my lap. A message without words. Blue flowers in a cluster, sepals blunt, small three-veined leaves. Linum usitatissimum – Common flax.

Your kindness reaches me.

My heart was fit to break.

I saw that the single page had been folded over concealing another flower, this time much more robust, encased in large broad leaves, a spike of tiny, creamy-white, bell-shaped flowers. Convallaria majalis – Lily of the valley.

Return of happiness.

How strange, I thought.

With trepidation I opened the piece of paper and in Ernest's faltering hand was written:

2nd Lt Neil Tennant 03462, 1RC, 4th Canadian Division, British Expeditionary Force, France

Chapter 24

John

Eventually, the Germans moved their positions east to make a shorter line that was easier to defend, leaving us with miles of abandoned trenches full of sewage and booby-traps, in a sea of stinking mud and bomb holes. There was hardly a blade of grass anywhere and the trees were barely recognisable, broken shadows of what had been. The battalions of the Scottish Division were together and there were Canadians too. Many were Scotsmen by birth and we got on pretty well together when we had time off for rest and recreation. We talked about the old country as if it was a land of milk and honey. That made it worth fighting for – that and the folk we held in our hearts. Our comrades were like a family to us, without the baggage of years spent under the same roof. Even though friends we'd joined up with were not in the same company, we had folk to look out for, folk you put your life on the line for, and you knew were doing the same for you in return. I was glad Jim was in the same company as me. It was comforting to wake up in the morning and know that he was there beside me. One time he took a bullet in the leg. They sent him to one of the field hospitals and he didn't come back for three weeks. It felt like a burden had been lifted from my shoulders when he was away and I didn't have to worry about him but I missed him just the same.

After weeks when I felt like I'd had a shovel in my hand more often than a gun, we were given some respite, sent well behind the lines for a rest. Even the army recognises that the human body has its limits. The long march out was begun in twilight and my company soon had to take refuge in an old farmstead. It was stripped of any comforts but the barn offered shelter from the freezing rain outside. That's where I came across Rob for the first time in over a year. He'd been made up to corporal and was sitting against the back wall with his small group of men. He was smoking quietly, staring at nothing, as if faraway in another place. I was overjoyed to see him and bounced him into a conversation of sorts. They'd had a rough time of it, by all accounts, so I put his reticence to speak down to that. Looking forward to picking up where we'd left off the following day, I settled down for the night feeling comforted that I'd found my old friend. When we woke, though it was barely light, Rob and his men had gone. He'd left without a word.

As I marched along the road north, Rob's demeanour the previous night weighed heavily on my mind. He'd become distant long before he'd enlisted but the bonds of friendship, forged in the formative years of youth, ran deep as far as I was concerned so I felt hurt by his indifference. During my company's week in the camp, I looked for him everywhere but he was nowhere to be seen. I asked men from the same regiment if they'd seen him. Most shrugged their shoulders. They didn't know him. The few who did were suspicious and only one had something to say.

'Whau kens whaur thon yin is? I'd leave well alane if I was you.'

The words made my flesh crawl.

Weeks and months of war take their toll on a man: the shriek of shells exploding into the mud and the booming thud of the big guns; the rattling of the Lewis gun in your hands, vibrating through your body till your nerves are shattered; the sights and the smells of war that haunt you day and night. I saw all of it in Rob's eyes the next time I met him.

My company had dropped back from the front line for a few days after some heavy pounding. We passed tattered groups of men, what was left of whole companies, taking rest in bombed-out farmsteads and villages that were barely recognisable as such. Officers in vehicles sped up and down, sometimes stopping to take details and give orders, amalgamating remnants of shattered units, bringing order out of chaos, getting ready for the next push at a time when the enemy was in danger of getting the upper hand.

We stopped by the roadside after a long spell on our feet, sat down for some rest and a bite to eat. A group of men and officers from another regiment had settled themselves around the ruin of a farmhouse some way from where we sat. Our sergeant ordered me and one other to find out if there was fresh water available. That was where I came across Rob for a second time in as many years. He was sitting propped up against a pile of rubble, all by himself, shivering like he couldn't help himself. When he saw me, a glow of recognition swept across his face and he grinned. I offered him some chocolate but he refused. He reached inside his jacket, handed me a half bottle of brandy. I said no – I'd never been one for the drink. Rob took a swig, began asking questions about the pals and about people he'd shown no interest in before – weel-kent faces in the village, or men down the pit. He didn't ask me about Davy and, though I was tempted to bring up the subject, decided I'd better not. I did mention Andrew Brownlee's name, said he was in the Black Watch. I saw a cloud pass over Rob's face and he was quiet for a bit.

He'd had the best part of the bottle and was fair maudlin by the time we got onto the subject of his family. His language was foul. He didn't have a good word to say about them, not even Sandy. He was soon cursing his mother, proud Peggy Duncan with her airs and graces who lived like a hure, granting favours to a piece of foreign shite who knew a soft bed when he saw one.

I asked what difference it made that Joe was foreign and he said all the difference in the world. I said it was common enough for widows to get married again, especially when they had young children to look out for. I told him he should be happy she had a bit of security. Apart from anything, didn't it mean he would be able to get on with his own life when the time came.

I let that sink in then said that Joe had moved out. Sandy had said so in a letter. Didn't Rob know? Hadn't he heard? Since Archie had been killed at the Somme, Lizzie and her children had moved in with Peggy, Sandy, and Maggie. They were all looking out for each other and were getting on fine.

Rob took a long slug of brandy and drew his hand across the drool that spilled from his mouth. Then he began to laugh, loud and coarse, before it petered out into a fit of coughing that was rough from too much tobacco.

'I'm no gaun back tae yon shit-hole when this is a' by,' he slurred.

'There's worse places in this world.'

'No monie. I'll never gang back. Naw, I'm better than yon.'

My hackles rose at the cheek of him.

'They're guid folk. *Buirdly chiels and clever hizzies*,' I said, quoting the bard.

'Nane as clever as me but. Rob Duncan, tap o' the class, eh?'

I leaned away from his stale breath.

He thought for a bit before havering on about a girl he'd been sweet on once upon a time, telling me about how it hadn't taken him long to get his way with her, how he used to meet her in secret and what they did together.

His filthy talk repulsed me. When I realised who he might be talking about, it made me want to throw up.

'Whiles, ye want somethin' for lang enough an' it torments the hell oot ye richt tae the soles o' yer feet, till ye think ye'll gae aff yer heid for the wantin' o' it... then ye get it oan a plate an' find oot it's no worth havin',' he said. He put his head back, stared up at the sky, his eyes swimming in his head. Then he began to laugh again. He elbowed my side, slurring his words as he spoke, 'Ye'll mind her frae the school... a richt piece...'

I don't know what came over me as I laid into him with both fists even though he was too drunk to defend himself. I called him a worthless shit, an arrogant pathetic self-centred coof as I rained blows on his head. I would have started in with my feet had Billy Nairn not grabbed me, warning me I was a private hammering into a corporal and that was a no-no. My anger knew no end but I managed to step back and see my handiwork for what it was.

Billy motioned for me to take Rob's arm whilst he took the other and we half-carried him back to his men. As we rounded the roofless shell of the farmhouse, we could see a group was trying to start a fire to make tea. The wood was refusing to light. We dragged Rob towards them, left him in a slump clutching his empty bottle but nobody said a word. They'd seen it all before, no doubt. A couple of officers appeared on the scene so we began to walk away, quickly, but I couldn't resist a last look round at my old friend and what he had become. He was on the ground, curled up like a bairn, vomiting brandy and bile into the mud.

Nearby, the fire had begun to take hold to everybody's delight then all of a sudden, WOOOOSH! A huge explosion sent everybody up into the air. I felt the hair on my face singe and everything became red before I fell backwards and the world went black.

When I came to, I had a bandage round my eyes. I tried to take it off because I couldn't see a bloody thing but a man came to my side, told me to leave it be for my own good. He asked if I remembered being in an explosion and I said *aye, more or less, somebody was trying to make the tea.* He told me the fire had been lit over an unexploded shell buried in the ground, just below the surface. It was a common enough danger when land was gained from the enemy. Six men had been killed so I was lucky to have been walking away from it. I had some burns to my face but they were superficial, he assured me. The pain was a sign that the damage hadn't been too deep. But my eyes had been affected and the doctor couldn't be sure how bad the damage was. They were going to take me to a hospital as soon as transport was available. I'd be there for a while before they would know. So I lay there in the darkness at the mercy of men that I did not know. They cared for me, helped me wipe my backside, fed me and told me what time of day it was. While I could only see black and red and, in my mind's eye, a big white explosion sending bodies and limbs and mud flying into the air.

Elizabeth

The Manse
Blackrigg
1st May 1918

Dearest Neil,

I hope you will give me the honour of reading this letter which has taken me so long to write. I can understand if your inclination is to cast it aside and I ask forgiveness for my lack of response to the beautiful letters you wrote to me so long ago. I hope that one day you might find it in your heart to allow me the opportunity of explaining the circumstances that have prevented me from writing back to you. For the moment, I ask you to believe that these circumstances were not of my making and, had they been otherwise, nothing would have given me greater pleasure than to tell you of my profound love and admiration for you. I understand that your feelings towards me might have changed and, if this is the case, I wish you every happiness though my heart will break for my own sake.

I sincerely hope and pray that you are well wherever you might be. I pray that the war will end soon and you may come back to those you love and who love you in return.

God bless and keep you, dearest Neil

All my love

Beth

It is many weeks since I wrote my letter, opening up my heart to someone who might be a stranger to me should we ever meet again in the future. I have written once more since with never a word in return – which is hard to bear – but I understand why Neil's heart might be turned against me after all this time. Now that the summer is here, I try to face each day with optimism. The better weather is always an antidote to gloomy thoughts, I find, and even when the postman does not bring the news I crave, I find comfort and happiness in my good friends, my garden, and in the people of this village who, in good or bad weather, face life with great fortitude.

Today, I have the Bangour patients to look forward to. Sarah has made some of her scones for the afternoon tea and we spread them with a little butter and a generous layer of raspberry jam, the first of this summer's batch. Although food rationing limits the amount we may purchase of certain items, I have saved a small amount of sugar every week through the winter and spring months so that we can make our preserves as usual. Sarah declines my invitation to help out in the public hall and I leave her in the knowledge that she will work her fingers to the bone in my absence in order to get home as soon as possible. She dotes on Minn's child like he was her own. As I expected, the Grahams took Minn and her son into their big brood with open arms and he is much blessed. The father, whoever he may be, is nowhere in sight and I wonder if he will ever face up to his responsibilities. But as they say hereabouts, it is his loss if he does not.

When I go in through the main door to the public hall, I can see that everything is laid out ready for the arrival of the patients but no one seems to be about. The place is deserted, as if a ghost ship has grounded right here amongst the coal pits and cottages of Blackrigg. The ante rooms by the main door are unoccupied and no one is in the kitchen, though three large kettles boil furiously on the stove and plates piled high with the purvey cover a table. Voices draw me into the hall and out of the back door where several women are engaged in a heated discussion.

'We can haurdly feed oorsels, nivermind the patients, is a' I'm sayin',' says Mary Birse.

Miss Silver looks apoplectic with indignation. 'Had I not heard it with my own ears, I would not have believed it! Are you suggesting we abandon these men who have given so much?'

'We're sayin nuthin o' the kind,' counters Ellen Broadley. 'We're jist sayin' the rations we get are gey sma'. Ye cannae feed a workin' man oan whit we're allowed b' the government.'

'It's no jist the quantity either,' continues Mary. 'The quality is a disgrace. The oatmeal tastes like sawdust.'

'An' the tea's nae better than sweepin's aff the flair,' adds Ellen.

'It's gantin'!' says Peggy from behind, having only just arrived.

'Is a'body gettin' the same or is it jist us in the minin' districts that are gettin' short-changed?' asks Mary. 'I cannae see the ladies o' Morningside or Kelvinside bein' content tae serve up whit we're gettin'.'

If looks could kill, Miss Silver would be six feet under.

'I might have guessed class would come into it sooner or later,' sighs Miss Silver. 'I'm sure we are all treated the same by the ministry at the end of the day. The best food must go to the men at the Front who are putting their lives on the line for their country.'

Mary is furious. 'We dinnae need a lecture fae yersel aboot the sacrifice o' the men at the Front, yer majesty. We've got boys in service.'

Ellen looks as if she might burst into tears. The news that Geordie has enlisted, and left without telling her, has hit her hard. He is but a boy, barely out of short trousers.

I speak up quickly. 'Let's keep to the point, Miss Silver, please. The war is being fought at home and abroad. Remember how important coal is to the war effort. The miners must be properly fed if they are to do a hard day's work. If their wives are saying the food rations are insufficient in both quantity and quality then the ministry must listen.'

Peggy gives a cough. She is holding the plate of pancakes she has brought to the tea. 'The train was jist comin' intae the station as I cam alang the road. The patients'll be here onie time.'

Mary takes the plate from her. 'Thank you, Mrs Duncan,' she says. 'Yer kindness will be much appreciated b' the men.' She glares at Miss Silver whose own contributions are known to be frugal. 'C'mon, hens, we better get the tea made.'

The afternoon seems longer than usual. It is hot in the hall though we have doors at both ends open to get the air moving. Mary and Ellen leave early, rushing off to prepare bath water for their menfolk due in from the early shift. Peggy and I see to the last of the clearing up.

Only women and children live at the Duncans' these days. It saddened Peggy when the time came to ask the lodgers to leave, she said. She knew that Joe Daniels held a candle for her. When he was leaving for a bed in the lodging house in Main Street, he asked her to keep the new rocking chair he had made for her, said he would be honoured if she would. She had been flattered by his interest in her but had made up her mind, she'd told him. Family had to come first.

When word came through from France that Archie had been killed in action, Peggy pleaded with her daughter to return to the Rows. It had taken a long time before Lizzie was persuaded to leave the home she had made with Archie. Since his body had never been found, there was always the possibility that he was still alive and he would walk through the door one day looking for his dinner, ready to give his children a birl in the middle of the front room. When the letter finally came from a sergeant to say that he had witnessed Archie's passing, and to offer his sincerest condolences to the widow of a fine and brave soldier, Lizzie relented. She sold their furniture, such as it was, and put everything else she had into a pack made from a blanket, slung it over her back and, heavily pregnant, walked the twelve miles to her mother's house with a child clinging to each hand. With only Lizzie's war widows' pension of 2/11d and Sandy's wage from his job in the pit office, things would be tight without rent from the lodgers. Peggy had taken employment on the picking tables at the pit and Lizzie took in washing to make ends meet. Between them, they looked after the children and lived as a family, just the Duncans, altogether under one roof, praying for the day when Rob would come back to them. It had been fine and they'd been happy. Until Sandy was called up and had to leave in the spring.

Peggy is studying the view of the pits out of the window as we work together.

'I wonder what Robert would've had to say aboot it a', Miss Fraser. Tae think o' a'thing that's happened since he died in the accident.'

I put my hand on her shoulder.

'Hoo could it've been allowed to happen, Robert?' she asks him as if somehow, being on the other side, he has the answers, knows the reason and the purpose behind all of the injustice of this earthly life.

She shakes her head and removes her apron, says she has to be getting home. She asks if I've heard there's to be a big meeting up at the brig tonight at seven o' clock.

'Folk have got their dander up aboot the food situation,' she says. 'But keep it to yourself if ye would, dinnae let the authorities ken in advance.' She taps the side of her nose.

I agree and decide that I'll go along to hear what's being said.

After supper, I manage half an hour in the garden before the meeting is due to take place. There are very few flowers in evidence this summer, the flower beds having been sacrificed two years earlier for the growing of food. The village allotments have become more important than ever as a source of sustenance. Everywhere, land that was used for less intensive forms of agriculture have been put to the plough, where possible, to grow vegetables and cereal crops. The country has never truly recovered from the bad harvest of 1916 and merchant ships face constant danger en route to Britain with supplies from abroad. Women were recruited to the farms in large numbers to replace the men who left for the front, and I see myself in my garden as part of that great land army tasked with feeding the nation. Richard has never been able to thank me for my foresight in developing the garden, though he benefits greatly from its bounty. His plate is always laden.

I see him standing watching me from an upstairs window when I leave by the back gate without telling him where I am going.

A long trail of people is heading east between the Rows. As soon as I reach the Rowanhill Road, I can see a large crowd forming up ahead on the Burnbank Brig. A steady stream coming from Rowanhill is swelling the numbers. The main players are already positioned on the brow of the bridge, ready to take control of proceedings. Mr Doonan, the miners' agent speaks intently to his counterpart from Lanarkshire. Meanwhile, the Food Controller and the local shopkeepers are in a huddle. The women, and there are many in attendance, stand at the back of the crowd, giving the men their usual place at the front.

Alex Birse is ready to start proceedings in the absence of Steeny Simpson. We were surprised when he was conscripted – him being a skilled face worker – but Alex believes that the British state would have Steeny as a marked man, a man too dangerous because of his union activities and the esteem in which he is held locally. He could not be allowed to escape a spell at the Front. It is a notion that many would find far-fetched but I am not so sure. I am inclined to agree with Mr Birse.

A train pulling a dozen empty wagons, heading for the pit at Allerbank, rumbles under the bridge. As the steam and smoke dissipates, Alex has his hand raised against a blue sky. He introduces both Mr Doonan and the Food Controller from Bathgate who had agreed at the last minute to attend the meeting and address the community's concerns. Together, they explain the situation regarding food supplies and the discussions that have already taken place locally. A meeting has been arranged with the Scottish representative of the Food Ministry in

Glasgow, they say, and two miners are to be tasked with taking the community's concerns about the quantity and quality of food allocated by the government. When the officials hand over to Alex Birse, the crowd become agitated, having listened intently for, perhaps, half an hour to the officials. It is time, it seems, for the ordinary folk to have their say. It takes a minute or two and much remonstrating on the man's part to bring the meeting under control.

'Aye, aye, dinnae shoot the messenger! We ken whit's wrang. That's why we're here.' Alex raises his hand, appealing for calm. His voice subsides into a bout of coughing and he can only shake his head as the crowd continues in full voice. I pray he isn't coming down with the dreadful illness that is laying people low in villages across the county.

His son, David, comes to the rescue, his voice loud. 'Hoi! We've had this discussion afore, have we no? We're a' in agreement an' we've found a wey furrit. If ye'd a' jist haud yer wheesht we'll get oan wi' it,' he bellows.

Silence.

I am impressed.

He turns back to his father.

Alex asks for two volunteers to attend the Food Ministry in Glasgow at the weekend.

'Nominate Davy Birse,' says a youngish voice, immediately.

'Seconded,' pipes up another.

A low groan can be heard. David Birse, it seems, is not universally liked though he certainly has a presence about him.

'Nominate John Doyle,' says an older man.

'Seconded.'

'Grand,' says Alex before any more names can be put forward.

'Can I ask a question?' says a lone female voice.

The crowd seems bemused.

'I'd like tae mak a point,' she insists.

The men erupt into mirthful laughter.

To his credit, Alex holds up his hand. 'Come oan noo! We'll hear her oot. This is as much a woman's affair as a man's. It's the women that have tae eek oot the rations an' see their men fed.'

'It would be wise tae let twa women gang tae the Food Ministry,' the woman suggests. 'They could gang wi' the men an' explain the difficulties fae their point o' view.'

Several heads nod their approval whilst others aren't so sure. A sizeable number find the notion to be ridiculous.

'Fair enough,' concurs Alex. 'Onie dissenters?'

No one seems prepared to openly condemn the idea.

Alex casts his eye across the women congregated at the back of the crowd, their appointed place since time immemorial.

'Ye cannae feed the menfolk oan whit we're allowed,' shouts one.

'As if we didnae ken,' says Alex, his colour rising.

'Last bit ham I bocht had mair baird than ma man,' says a different female voice.

The men begin to snigger.

Alex acts quickly to close things down. 'So, we're agreed?' he shouts. 'John Doyle and Davy Birse will meet wi' the Food Controller on Saturday next at the ministry in Glasgow, accompanied by twa weemen. Volunteers, ladies?'

Most keep their heads down; several draw shawls over their hair in an attempt to disappear from view; but one or two look sideways at those they think might be capable of the task. However, this is a new avenue opening up before them, and no woman present, including myself, has considered themselves fit for such a role before.

'Grand. There'll be a meetin' for the weemen the morn's nicht,' says Alex. 'That'll gie them time tae consider their position. Can we have a volunteer tae supervise the election o' the twa weemen delegates?' He looks towards the men.

It does not seem to occur to him that the women might be capable of managing their own meeting.

'That'll be up tae me then,' he says, when no one appears keen to take on the role. 'An we'll reconvene here, same time, Monday next, when the delegation will report back oan the Ministry's response. At the same time, we will turn oor attention to the housin' question, in view o' the recommendations made in the report afore parliament concernin' conditions in the industrial areas. We hae tae ensure improvements are made forthwith, that the landlords are held tae accoont, an' the cooncils stert buildin' as directed in the report. Steeny would expect nuthin less.'

'Hear, hear!' they shout, and the crowd slowly drifts away on a wave of optimism

The following evening, I am cycling with Rose along Main Street. For her benefit, I summarise the discussion that had taken place on the bridge and express my delight at the determination of local people to be involved in housing matters. I tell her about the approach made to the county Food Controller with the backing of the miners' union; about the election of two male representatives for the visit to the ministry in Glasgow and the participation of women in the process.

Rose points out a group of women in the distance. The crowd is growing bigger as more arrive at the steading. They are clearly animated and interested women, already shouting out opinions and listening to each other's views.

'Hurry, Beth,' urges Rose as she forges ahead. 'You'll put your name forward to join the deputation, won't you?'

I bring my bicycle to a halt.

Rose looks back and stops too. 'Aren't you interested in what's going on? Come on, you're well suited to speak up for the local women.'

'No...' I say forcefully, shaking my head. 'They are well able to speak up for themselves and will choose two of their own.'

'But you're perfect for the job.' She is surprised. 'Are you sure?'

'Quite sure. They don't need me to speak for them. And now that they've found their voice, there will be no stopping them.'

'Will you attend the next meeting at the bridge, on Monday? Your knowledge of housing conditions is extensive and combined with your understanding of health...'

'No... I won't. Who better to decide what improvements should be made than the people who endure the very conditions castigated in the parliamentary report? They won't let the landlords and the local authorities put off what should have been done long ago. They've had enough.'

Rose can see my point.

'When the nurse returns from France, I won't be required in that role either.' I have the air of someone who knows that her life is about to change dramatically and is perfectly at ease with the prospect.

'I can't wait to see your father's garden,' I call out brightly as I begin pedalling again. 'It is always such a joy!'

We cycle towards Rowanhill, admiring the countryside, lush and verdant in the evening sun.

'What will you do when the war is over?' I ask when we arrive at our destination.

Rose comes to a halt, her brakes squeaking. 'I'll return to the women's hospital in Edinburgh.'

'But won't you miss...'

'No, I won't. Remember, I came here for the sake of my father. There's nothing here for me in Blackrigg in the longer term – the patients will be well-served by Dr Lindsay when he returns. I do hope the war will end soon, please God.' She manoeuvres her bicycle in through the gate. The spring is rusty and old, making it difficult for her.

'Besides,' she says, after a struggle, 'I cannot stay and deliver another of Catherine Melville's children.'

My heart goes out to her. I know the hurt and the pain she has endured. There are times when I sense something like regret in her eyes, in the quiet moments we share in front of the fire in the parlour, in occasional careless comments made when she is tired.

'I've been thinking too...' I begin. 'I've no wish to live under Richard's roof for the rest of my life. It's intolerable as you well know. In fact, an independent life is what I crave most of all. I've decided I must make my own way.'

Rose sees it in my face. I could have been married by now; made a comfortable life for myself; a happy life keeping house and bearing children for a respectable man. Instead, I have rejected what many women would have settled for long ago, determined to have exactly what I wanted, or not at all. We are alike in that respect, me and

Rose. In private moments, I have often wondered where my need for independence might take me.

'Perhaps I could seek employment in the city... as a lady's companion... or a housekeeper.'

'Or a plantswoman?' suggests Rose.

I laugh at the idea. 'Do you think...?'

'Or a nurse? You are already competent in the basic procedures, learned through experience, and have a wide knowledge of medical matters. But you must be certificated to continue. You could apply for training at the infirmary.'

'There are so many women with experience from their war work. Many will be seeking recognition for their skills.'

'But you have a practising doctor who will be delighted to write references on your behalf. And that doctor might need a companion to share her rooms in the city, until said companion gets on her feet.'

I am delighted at the idea and follow Rose up to the open door of her father's home.

'I do hope the war is over soon,' I say.

Chapter 25

DECEMBER 1918

Elizabeth

It was one of those dull autumn days when the cloud is almost at ground level, shortening the view, closing the world in till it felt like there was nothing out there beyond the straggle of cottages cluttering Main Street. A few trees and shrubs held onto a smattering of yellowed foliage so the scene was not entirely devoid of colour. Mrs Gow and the Widow Macauley were gawping from behind half-closed curtains when I returned from the Store that morning of 11th November. They were in the street in an instant. Each one carried a broom, a perfect disguise that justified their presence and allowed them a full view of proceedings. They tackled a pile of dead leaves littering the pavement by a doorstep. When one had their back turned, the other kept her informed about activity on the opposite side of the street, which for some considerable time had been negligible until I happened by. I felt obliged to cross the road and enquire after their chilblains and other ailments. They were soon distracted when an unknown man carrying a large box returned to a vehicle further up the street and the driver took off: slim pickings in terms of detail but enough to catapult the vivid imaginations of the two women into the great beyond. Better still, soon after, the postman returned to the post office. He had barely gone inside when he reappeared and sprinted back in the direction he had just come from, towards the Rows. Who was about to get bad news we wondered? Next to erupt from the building was the stationmaster's wife who toddled off in the direction of Station Road as fast as her considerable bulk would allow her, followed by Miss Silver. She galloped westwards at such a speed that she missed the church steps by several yards and had to backtrack quickly, almost coming to grief thanks to her big, flat feet skidding on the wet ground.

Mrs Gow and the Widow Macauley barely had time to exchange quizzical glances with me before all was revealed. Miss Shanks was out in the street shouting that the war was over. Hostilities had come to an end at eleven o' clock. The news had come in on the telegraph. Right on cue, the church bell sounded out loudly, over and over and over again, a most joyful and urgent sound, leaving no one in any doubt of the message it conveyed through the still air.

The old women said, *Thanks be, the Lord is Good!* and flashed their toothless grins at me saying, *The men'll be hame soon, Miss Fraser*, leaving me in a quandary about whether to laugh with relief or cry with the sadness of it all.

I remember how angry I became later because it had taken so long for it to end; angry that the war had taken millions of young lives before the armies could lay down their weapons. Women and children were starving on the streets of Berlin but the role of that particular tragedy would feature less than the determination and bravery of our troops in the celebrations to come. Which was understandable, perhaps, after all that the country had been through.

As I wound my way home up the lane, the sound of the church bells was joined by whistles at the pithead and on the railway line, a collective expression of joy. I imagined the news being carried down below, relayed along the underground roads to the men at the coalface who would down tools and make for the cages, taking the rest of the day off without waiting for permission from the gaffers and the masters. Sarah met me at the back door and I let her go home to celebrate with her family.

There was dancing in the street as well as the public hall that night, to make up for lost time, to celebrate the lifting of the brooding pall of care that had weighed heavily on our lives for so long. Richard opened up the church for those who needed to come and give thanks to God for their deliverance. He told them that the people who sat in darkness had seen a great Light, that the fallen were now enjoying celestial glory having surrendered their souls to the Lord. He asked, what greater love hath a man than that he lay down his life for another? And the faithful nodded their heads, blinking away their tears because the minister was telling them, as he always did, that it would all be alright in the end if they waited long enough. The Lord would see to it, as long as you had faith in Him. Those waiting quietly at home for menfolk to return were thankful and allowed themselves the luxury of a small smile but they could not get above themselves, not just yet.

One after the other, ships docked at Leith to the cheers of excited onlookers; families and sweethearts waving flags in hopeful expectation that the one they waited for was somewhere amongst the hundreds of men about to disembark. Sarah had tears in her eyes when she told me the news that her brother-in-law, Will Morton, had survived the war and was on his way back to Meg in Canada. She kept me abreast of local developments in the weeks following the signing of the armistice, as the troops began to arrive home.

Dan Potts and Sandy Duncan travelled on the same train, the latter entertaining everyone in their carriage with some jokes he had learned from comrades in his battalion. Bert Broadley arrived a few days later with a permanent limp from a wound in his leg, grateful he had gotten off so lightly, still able for most jobs in the pit. Peggy found out that Rob would never be coming home in a letter from the army, delivered the same day the armistice had been signed. Nervously, Ellen and Jimmy looked forward to when their youngest son would return. One day in December, they finally received word that Geordie was back in the country. He was in Craigleith Hospital and they were to visit him as soon as they were able.

When the news spread through the village that Wee Geordie Broadley had died within minutes of his parents arriving by his bedside, people were drawn up short. This was the boy who had defied all the odds as a youngster and survived into adulthood, more or less, thanks to a mother's love. The passing of Geordie was like the passing of everyone's son.

By all accounts, an old man at the steading had remarked, 'There's a nation has a lot tae answer for.'

'Whit nation is that then?' asked Davy Birse. 'The German nation?'

His eyes blazed.

'Or the British nation?' he asked. 'Eh? The British nation that niver gave a damn aboot the lad when he was alive.

That thocht it fine he should be brocht up in a miners' raw wi' an ootside cludgie and damp risin' up the wa's? That thinks his faither disnae deserve a decent wage for the work he does doon the pit? That maks him gang cap in haun tae plead for a rise when the maisters live it up oan the profits?'

Trust a Birse to put it all into context.

'But they were quick enough tae put a gun in the boy's haun when it suited them, eh? Is thon the nation yer meanin'?'

'Things will change, Davy,' said Steeny, newly returned from France. 'They'll get better. They have tae.'

Minn

I gave a knock before walking into the cold gloom of the scullery at Redburn Farm.

'Mrs Gowans? Are ye there?' My employer was busy through-by in the kitchen, at the range. 'Mrs Gowans? It's me.'

'Oh, whit a fricht! Come in, lass,' she beckoned then spied the boy clinging to my skirts in the shadows. 'An' ye've brocht the wee lad tae see me at last. Come in, son. Dinnae be feart.'

The boy moved in tandem with me, his big hazel eyes fixed on Mrs Gowans.

'This is Robbie,' I said. 'He's pleased tae meet ye. Aren't ye, Robbie?'

He set his gaze on the strange woman in the flour-covered apron.

Mrs Gowans signalled towards the table where freshly baked scones were set out. 'Tak aff yer coat, Minn, whilst I pour the tea.' She disappeared into the pantry and returned with a cup of milk. 'Here ye are, Robbie. Drink up.'

The fire in the range glowed brightly. I slipped off my coat then removed the child's blue knitted jacket and matching tammie as he took in his surroundings. I offered him a piece of scone spread with butter which he took in a small chubby hand before settling his gaze once more on Mrs Gowans, following her with big eyes as she moved around the kitchen.

'Yer takin it a' in, aren't ye, laddie?' The woman ruffled his dark hair. 'Naethin'll pass you by, eh?'

Robbie glanced up at me for reassurance then, quick as a wink, looked back in her direction.

'It was guid o' ye tae bring the lad tae see me.' Mrs Gowans blushed. She seemed to have something to say, and was finding it hard to get the words.

I told Robbie to sit up straight at the table and I put my arm around him to stop him falling off the big cushion that propped him up in the chair.

'The trouble is, Minn. See, noo oor dairyman's back fae France, there's less need o' ye in the byre. Ma eldest, Ruby, an' her man are movin' intae the ferm cottage – they'll tak ower the worst o' the work inside and oot. Mr Gowans is getting' oan a bit an' the truth o' the matter is the ground isnae whit it was since they taen awa' Paddy's Wood at the stert o' the war. Weel… whit I'm tryin' tae tell ye is there jist isnae the work tae keep ye oan. I'm sorry, lass.'

'I see,' was all I said, turning back to the boy, steadying the cup in his hands as he raised it to his lips. He smiled broadly after the first mouthful. It was full cream milk, straight from the cow.

'Milk,' he said. 'Guid.'

'Drink,' I told him.

Mrs Gowans watched us together then flushed a bright shade of pink. 'Jings! Yon fire's gey hot!' She fanned her face with a tea towel.

'It was guid o' ye tae gie me employment when ye did, Mrs Gowans. Efter the bairn was born. Lettin' me gae hame at nicht an giein me a day aff a week. It was kind o' ye an I'm gratefu'.' I dabbed the child's mouth with a handkerchief though he resisted.

'Ye've been a guid worker, Minn. If ye need a recommendation I'll be happy tae provide it. Mebbe when the singlin's needin' done, or at tattie howkin time, we'll see ye again.' She took my boy's hand and gave it a squeeze.

'I hope ye get somethin' else, lass. For the bairn's sake.' She hesitated, studying the child all the while, taking in the colour of his hair, his eyes, the look of him.

'Aye. There'll be somethin' for us. Whit dae ye think, Robbie?' I took the child's hand from her grasp. 'Ye niver can tell whit's comin' yer wey, eh?' I gave him the last of the milk from the cup.

'By jings! That'll be him comin' up fur three, is it no?'

'Aye, come the spring. Three.'

The boy held up three fingers. 'F-r-ee,' he said proudly.

'One, two, THREE,' I corrected but just as proud.

'Fower, five... nine, ten,' he added quickly, holding up both hands, looking pleased with himself.

'My, yer a clever lad!' said Mrs Gowans. 'Robbie... Robert. A fine name. Is it a faimily name b' onie chance?'

'Thomas Robert Graham. Efter his grandpa and my mither's faither. But we've a'ready a Tommy in the hoose so Robbie it is.'

'Minn, dear,' Mrs Gowans began slow. 'I hope ye dinnae mind me sayin' but I speak as an aulder wuman wi' some experience. Weel, the truth o' the maitter is, the lad needs a faither an' you're a fine lookin' lass...'

I made to go, thanked her for the tea and the scones.

'Guid,' Robbie said. He pointed at the ones left on the plate in the middle of the table, couldn't take his eyes off them. 'Guid scones.'

I began dressing the child for the outdoors.

Mrs Gowans bustled into the pantry, returned with a large paper bag. She filled it with scones and gave it to Robbie.

He took it in both hands. 'Ta,' he said.

Mrs Gowans patted his knitted tammie down around his ears. 'Gie Mrs Graham ma best, will ye?'

'I'll dae that. Thanks, Mrs Gowans.' I was keen to be on my way.

'Come an' see us again,' she called from the doorway, watching us cross the cobbled farmyard.

'Safe hame, the pair o' ye. There's snaw in the air, for sure.'

Robbie stood pointing in the direction of the farm kitchen where he knew warmth, milk, and good scones were to be had. I pulled him alongside me. We started the long walk down the farm track that led past the stable yard at Parkgate House, towards the road into the village. The track was rutted and pitted with large puddles that Robbie found fascinating. I made him walk beside me, along the grassy verge where it was drier, and I thought about what Mrs Gowans had said about the boy needing a father.

Out of the blue, a motor car bounced past, spraying me and the bairn with muddy water. I peered after the vehicle. The driver was Andrew Brownlee, newly returned from the Front, and beside him was his fiancée, Daisy

Gowans, now a teacher at Blackrigg School. They were laughing and blethering to each other. They probably hadn't noticed us in by the hedgerow, I told the child as I brushed the worst of the wet from his knitted coat. He began to cry so I lifted him up for a cuddle. He was heavy but he needed comforting. I brushed away his tears and wiped his nose. Told him everything would be fine.

A snell wind was blowing in from the north and the sky was heavy with cloud. Without Paddy's Wood, there was nothing to shelter Redburn Farm from the weather. I looked back into the teeth of the blast, seeing empty moorland where the wood had once clothed the valley all the way to the Whinbank Road on the northern side of the ridge. I minded what Billy Dodds' grandfather had said when I first arrived at Redburn. The Black Moss was reclaiming the land it had lost more than a hundred years before. The farmland had been hard won from the bog, by dint of the work of generations. It was protected by the trees of Paddy's Wood, planted on the instructions of a laird intent on increasing production in an earlier age. It was a well-known procedure for the improvement of soil, employed by those who understood something of the battle between Man and Nature. Old Mr Dodds reckoned the present Major Melville would have something to say about the loss of the wood when he returned from his army service.

I scanned the parks and meadows of Redburn. The wind whipped along without mercy. Pools of water lay on the flattest land, and threshes grew where rich pasture and root crops had supported a large dairy herd and many sheep in the past. Nearby Home Farm did not seem to be faring much better. The steading was in a state of disrepair, and sat in a sea of trampled mud. As the first snowflakes began to fall, I drew my collar up around my neck and hurried Robbie along, telling him the weather was closing in and we'd better get home.

John

I'd waited so long for the war to end that, when I heard the Armistice had been signed, I could scarce believe it. The Swiss were quick to organise our transport out of the country but there were delays further up the line with so many men being repatriated along the damaged transport system, and Germany was in chaos. The delays as we travelled home gave me time to think about what had happened since I'd come out to France as a naive young soldier with barely a few weeks training under my belt.

Our backs were up against the wall in the early part of 1918. The enemy had the upper hand for a while. But things weren't good back in Germany and morale amongst their troops began to waver. There were many desertions and, by the summer, it was obvious their ability to make progress against us was waning. As we went over the top that last time back in March, I lost sight of Jim when I took a bullet to both the neck and the hand. I was left for dead whilst the rest of my company, and hundreds more besides, were taken prisoner. On another occasion, they might have been shot as an inconvenience but Fate intervened and Jim was taken to Soltau POW camp where he recovered from minor wounds. Meanwhile, I lay in the mud of no-man's land, my throat shot to pieces. It was a German raiding party that came out the following day, found that I was still alive despite my wounds, and a night in the freezing mud. Why those men decided I was worth saving, I will never understand but they took me to a field hospital where a German doctor operated on my injuries. He took cartilage from my hip and repaired my throat. He was also able to repair the blood vessel that had been ruptured in my neck. In the chaos of battle, when their own people were lining up to be treated, they found room for a young Scotsman with life-threatening wounds. Maybe their mothers had given them the same message my mother had given me all those years before. *Life is precious, John.* Maybe they saw past my uniform and saw only the human life inside it.

After but a few days in the POW camp, my health began to deteriorate because of infection, though the doctor had done his best to strip out the dirty damaged flesh around my wounds. That's when an inspector from the International Red Cross found me, half-frozen at the bottom of a dank cell soaked in my own urine, and splattered by the thin soup they sent down a chute at me but which I was never strong enough to eat. That man from Switzerland arranged my transfer to Konstanz where I was nursed back to health before being taken to a camp surrounded by mountains whose beauty is etched on my heart.

I came home in December to what I thought was an empty house. It was evening so I surmised that Alex and Davy were probably at a meeting of some sort. I'd thought about this day many times. Over and over again, I'd lived the moment when I would walk up the Station Road to Stoneyrigg and push open the door of the end cottage in the Back Row where the fire would be lit and the smell of broth would fill the air. It had never occurred to me that my mother would not be there to welcome me and, although the room was warm and everything was in its rightful place, the house seemed desolate at first.

I sat staring into the fire glowing in the grate, hearing familiar sounds like the tick of the clock and the purr of the flames in the coals, and the scrape of a man's boots on the gravel road outside in the street. I was glad to be back, grateful to be sitting there in a warm room – a simple pleasure so many had been deprived of – and my face was soon wet with tears. The rush into my head of what I had seen and done made me dizzy and I wanted to vomit. I shut my eyes, breathing slow and deep, banishing the trembling ache from my arms and my hand, and the dark thoughts from my head. That's when I knew that I had to get busy. I had to get back down the pit and get on with my life. What I had done, what we all had done was in the past, and I couldn't dwell on it or it would crush me. I wouldn't forget what I'd been asked to do but I had to forgive myself and would pray that the boys who came after me would be spared the horror of war.

I heard a different sound just then – a feeble cough and the wheezing breath of someone fighting for life in the box bed behind where I sat. I pulled back the curtain and there was my father staring upwards, fear in his eyes and sweat on his brow. He glanced at me briefly, tried to breathe slow and steady as if trying to banish demons from his head, like I'd been doing only a moment before. But the disease that had ravaged his lungs in all those years down the pit would not let him be. He was soon wracked with the coughing again. It was the kirkyaird hoast and it terrified him. I put my hand under his head then a cup of water to his dry lips, watched as the liquid seeped into his mouth and saw the coolness of it salve his red-raw throat when he swallowed. He mouthed a few words but, to this day, I do not know what they were because there was scant breath behind them and they only brought on further wheezing. As I sat on the bed beside him, looking at his skin, taught across the blue bone of his skull, and his eyes darting beneath closed lids, I felt his hand on mine. I saw in his hand the hard work he'd done all his life, the tons of coal and clay he had shifted each day for forty years, and I guessed that touch of my hand was the hardest thing it had ever done.

My mother saw it as she took off her wet coat. She wrapped me in her arms in a way she hadn't done since I was a bairn and I buried my face in the warm smell of her.

'Yer back, John,' she said and I said that I was.

When Davy burst in through the door sometime later, I was sitting quietly at the table with a book.

'Yer back,' he said taking his bunnet from his head, slapping it into the palm of his hand like a schoolteacher warming up the tawse.

He went over to where our father was lying, told him what he'd been talking about with Steeny and the other union men. He talked about a commission to look into miners' pay and how the masters were up to their old tricks, complaining about the cost of labour and the loss of profit when the war was just by, and some boys were yet to come back from the Front.

When Davy got busy about the fire, I was taken aback. I had been away a long time – my elder brother was making tea! Not only that but he was whistling a happy tune, telling our mother to sit still and rest, he would manage by himself. He even set out the cups, the milk jug and the sugar bowl and put the tea cosy on the pot. He didn't ask anything about where I had been or what I had done. He didn't even mention the wounds to my neck and my hand

457

and for that I was grateful. He poured me a cup of tea, gave one to mother.

As he made for the back room with a cup for himself, he turned to me. 'Ye'll be doon the pit office the morn' I expect. There's jobs for them that's been at the Front. Imrie's kept his word an' for that we are truly thankfu'.'

'Aye,' I said though I must have sounded hesitant. I was just in the door.

'Ye'll want tae pey yer wey noo that yer back,' he replied.

It wasn't a question. But had it been, my answer would've been, *yes*. I desperately wanted to get back to my life in the Rows and move on.

Chapter 26

Elizabeth

Last night went well. We didn't want a fuss, and definitely no gifts, so they tagged *thank you* speeches onto the end of a recital planned some time ago. Richard seemed genuinely sad that I was leaving. He said how much he would miss me when I was gone, how he hoped I would visit often because I had many friends here in the village and was held in such high esteem – in fact, much higher than he had realised for long enough. When it came to the presentation, he apologised profusely, explaining that so many people had insisted my leaving should be marked in the proper fashion and he could not persuade them otherwise. When I made my reply, I told everyone how touched I was, more than I was prepared for, and my voice wavered throughout. But I managed to say that many people had already given me the priceless gift of their friendship and that was something I would keep with me through the days to come.

Rose returned from her new position at the women's hospital in town for the occasion. When he thanked her for her diligent service in his absence, Dr Lindsay told everyone what a fine doctor Rose Matheson was and, if proof was needed that a woman could be suited to the medical profession, then she was surely it. I stood up to lead the applause and the assembly followed in genuine appreciation of her time in the community. Rose wished everyone well before pointing towards the supper laid out at the back of the hall, saying it was time to tuck in and no one disagreed with that. She seemed anxious to get back to her new life and not dwell on the past so she left with her father straight away but not before she put a key in my hand. It was the key to the rooms she had organised on our behalf, the key to my future beyond Blackrigg. She told me there was no hurry, to take my time, and move in at a time of my choosing.

I was excited and nervous in equal measure but mostly I was grateful to my good friend for helping to smooth the first faltering steps on my future path. Though I was unsure of exactly what the future held, Rose had helped me open the door to a new life. Now I had choices, the chance to seek opportunities beyond the four walls of my brother's house, where I would no longer be at his beck and call. As I made my way around the hall, conversing with this one and that, I promised to keep in touch and to let everyone know how I was getting on if they did the same in return. Mrs Maclean had a special gift of her own for me. Did I remember those books belonging to Murdo, the ones about botany and gardening, that she'd shown me before the war? Well, I was to have them all. They were no good to her and Donald had given his blessing. I held out my hand to him and he took it firmly. He wished me well, said I knew where he lived, and I wasn't to be shy about dropping in for my tea. I looked into his eyes and knew I had a good friend in him. I promised that I would take him up on his offer, once I was settled.

Today, the excitement of last night has been replaced by a dull trepidation at what lies ahead. I decide that I have to get on with my packing or it will never be done on time. It is quite incredible how many things even a church mouse like me can accumulate during a relatively short life span. A trunk and one small valise, the latter enough for me to carry on the train journey, stand in the middle of my room. I have packed the heavy things, like my books and mother's china, into the bottom of the trunk and have added the linen and other textiles from my bottom drawer. A single woman has need of such things when setting out on a new life. I open the dressing table and wardrobe and begin filling the valise with essentials for my first few days of freedom until the trunk arrives. My hairbrush and silver mirror will be the last to go in.

I notice Sarah hovering in the doorway and wonder how long she has been there. I feel a sudden pang of guilt. I hope she does not think I am abandoning her to Richard but she knows her job better than he does and will stick up for herself. Besides, I have noticed a handsome young man waiting for her at the bottom of the lane of an evening. She has a spring in her step that suggests he is someone special. I understand it is Peggy's younger son, Sandy. From what I know of him they are a good match for each other.

'Can I help ye, Miss?' she asks at last.

I hum and haw. Actually, I would like this time alone to consider what the coming days will bring and to think about what I am leaving behind. I spot a dress at the back of the wardrobe and pull it out. It is the grey one I wore to Phee's engagement party.

'Would you like it, Sarah?' I hold it up.

Her face tells me she's not keen.

'Mrs Graham could take it to pieces and make something nice out of it.'

'It's kind of ye... but... no thanks, Miss.'

I don't want to force it on her so I put it back in the wardrobe unsure of what to do with it. Sarah stands stubbornly refusing to leave me be so I ask if the vegetables are ready to go into the soup for the midday meal. She nods her head and I can see she has something to say.

'Sarah?'

'It's Neil Tennant, Miss. I thought ye'd want tae ken.'

'Neil?'

'He cam hame yesterday, Miss. I hear he's at the Smiddy the now.' She turns to go and I can tell she feels sorry for me.

'Thanks, Sarah. Thanks for telling me.'

My head is swimming as I go over to the window and notice, for the first time, that the garden is clothed in a blanket of glittering frost. The temperature must have dropped in the night. The view reminds me of those early years when I laid out the garden with so much hope in my heart for a fruitful outcome. And Nature did not let me down. I remember how much that garden kept me sane when I felt that my world had ended without Neil by my side. I have come so far from those days of my youth and I know that I cannot go back there. I am strong and independent and I will not be otherwise. I must make my own decisions.

I go back to the wardrobe where only the dress is left hanging, alone and forlorn. I push it to the back and close the doors. Someone will find it and make use of it one day. I check the drawers carefully. Each one is empty and I close up the trunk. The valise is a little on the heavy side but I will manage it on my own.

John

I visited Dr Lindsay the very next day after I came home and he looked me over, declaring me fit for work but said it would be better if I worked above ground for a bit, to see how I got on, then he wrote out a certificate for the employer. He was fascinated by my wounds and took a long time examining them, especially the one in my neck. He probed me for what I knew about the procedures, marvelled at the skill of the surgery performed under field hospital conditions, and said he had seen nothing like it on the British side. It was fortunate that the enemy had picked me up and not my own people, he jested. He said he would write to the professors at the universities – he was sure they would want a good look and could learn a lot from my case, if I was willing to cooperate.

At the pit office, Sandy took my name and certificate with a big grin. He said Mr Brownlee was organising the names personally and I had to come back at the start of the year to find out where I had been allocated. I thanked him, said it was a shame it was too cold for football, and he said he would be chapping on my door as soon as the conditions improved.

I headed for Bert's house and found Mrs Broadley there on her own. She told me Bert was away for a doctor's assessment but she would tell him I had called round when he came back. I said I was sorry to hear about Geordie's passing, he was a fine lad, and would be much missed. She smiled in a pained but thankful way as she closed the door.

Mrs Duncan said she was glad to see me. She invited me in but I could see she was helping her grandchildren with their reading so I declined. I gave her my condolences for Rob and she said how much she missed him. I think she was meaning the old Rob. She thanked me for being such a good friend to him as I turned to go. She could never have guessed what was in my head at that moment as the memory of my last meeting with him, the manner of his passing, and my part in it flooded into my head. But something in my eyes as I fought for the right thing to say maybe gave me away.

'Rob was lost tae us a lang time ago, John,' she said sadly. 'Mind hoo ye gang.'

I had to pass the Graham house and Minn came to mind, though in truth she is rarely out of it. I saw her in the distance yesterday evening so I know that she's not employed at Netherside anymore. Had she been coming in my direction I would have tarried, made an excuse to engage her in conversation, but it's probably just as well she wasn't. I've often lain in bed at night wondering what I will say to her when the time comes.

I went back to the house and helped my mother where I could. She is hard wrocht with my father's illness and I can see how it's taking its toll on her. He's at death's door but, knowing Alex Birse, he'll make heavy weather of it and fight to the last. My mother was spooning soup into his mouth one day when she told him Auld Nick must have the doors to Hell barred and was probably keeking out from the inside, hoping he would go away.

He managed to whisper, 'I'll slip in efter you,' before another coughing fit sent the soup all over the clean sheets. 'Thon's what ye get for yer impertinence,' he told her.

I miss having Jim in the house but he got home quicker than me and in better shape. He's taken employment in Allerbank Pit at the brushing. It wasn't practical for him to stay in Stoneyrigg, the walk each way to Allerbank being nearly an hour, so he took lodgings in the rows near his work. I look forward to his next visit home, a big smile on my face at the thought of it.

Davy is another kettle of fish and I watch him with interest. I'm struck by the changes in him but they are superficial. He still has the sleekit look of a cat on the prowl and fingers in too many pies. But he is working hard for the men through his position with the union and is well versed on matters of politics and industry. Steeny might be influencing him in that regard, steering him towards methods that can improve things through negotiation but I've known my brother for too long to be sure he won't revert back to his old self. He is certainly more civilised in his habits. He's taken to brushing his teeth and combing his hair. He tells my mother he's changing his underwear weekly whether it's needed or not – which has her in stitches – and he hasn't once been caught spitting into the fire during meal times in all the days since I've come home. It's enough to make me think there must be a woman in his life. I want to like him in the way brothers should like and respect each other but I cannot. I've lived under the same roof for too long, have been hurt too many times to let my guard down. I know that when his anger is up next, and things are not going to plan, I'll be fair game. As soon as my father dies, Davy will be the man of the house. He'll rule the roost and woe betide anybody who gets in his way.

A letter from the professors in Glasgow arrives sooner than expected. I've been invited to visit them today and they've sent me the fare for the journey so that I'm not inconvenienced. Mother has made me a piece – four slices of best plain bread from the Co-op thickly spread with butter and home-made raspberry jam. To think I was longing for this only weeks ago! As I walk along the road to the station, neighbours say *Aye, John* as they pass, men touch their bunnets and I do the same. I have entered the world of men. Women say *Mornin'* and smile. And I say *Mornin'* and smile back. It is the way of a civilised world to acknowledge each other's existence with a simple greeting, to live together, and get along.

I am so enthralled by the pleasure of small things that I do not see who is coming along the road towards me. She is leading a group of children of various sizes and ages but I hardly notice them. My eyes are fixed on her, and her alone. She's a little rounder and fuller in the face and her long black hair is pinned up on the back of her head but she is still the beautiful girl I admired across the schoolroom so many years ago. Her eyes are kind and they crinkle up at the sides when she smiles at me from far away, and I love her for it. But there is a sadness behind the full curve of her lips. It's there in the shadows that fade into her pink cheeks. It's there in the way she holds her head a little to the side, and the way her shoulders are hunched though that might be down to the weather. *I know what happened,* Minn, I say but not out loud. *I know how much you must have loved him but it wasn't enough and that must be a hard thing to bear.*

'Mornin', John,' she says.

I touch my cap, quite dumbstruck.

'Say *Mornin'* to John, Robbie,' she says and that's when I pay attention for the first time to the small child holding her hand.

He looks up from the folds of her skirt and waits a bit before doing as he's told.

It takes a second or two to register. She has a bairn. I hunker down beside him, take his small gloved hand in mine and say that I'm pleased to meet him. He is his father's son and no mistaking it.

'He's a fine lad, Minn,' I say.

She has a hand on his shoulder and brings him in close to her. 'Thanks, John.' And they go on their way with the other children, back up the station road. Then she remembers something and calls out to me.

'I'll see you efter when I come round for ma supper! I've been invited!'

I raise my hand and watch her walking off with her bairn, talking all the while to him.

Supper, I say to myself. Minn is coming to supper at the house.

I am rooted to the spot and cannot move as it dawns on me. Davy? Davy and her? It cannot be, no it cannot be Minn. But why else would you... come for... supper? Surely not! I want to run after her and tell her what he's like. She has suffered too much already to be shackled to him.

Then it comes to me – a plan! I could ask her to come with me to Glasgow and we would never need to come back. We could live like brother and sister and could be happy together. I could give her and the boy a home and work hard for them. Maybe in time, things would change between us, once she saw how much I care for her. But the Glasgow train is coming to a halt in a skoosh of steam and I have to run because the timetable for the Caledonian Railway Company waits for no man and I am out of time.

I take my seat in a fog of disbelief, the truth of it dawning on me. As the countryside begins to move faster and faster past the window, I hurtle towards a future that is quite different to the one I played with in my imagination for long enough. The frosted hills are bonnie in the sunshine, in spite of the pits and the quarries that mark their flanks. There is no more beautiful sight than the hills of home though they may be no match for the spectacular mountains of Switzerland that held me and nursed me back to health. When I think back to the way those lofty peaks encircled me as I healed, I see them only for the prison they were, keeping me from my own place and the people who are dear to me. I cannot help but wish that I had come home sooner but it was not in my power to do so.

My heart is heavy as we approach the city and I know that I cannot live with regret and what could have been. If it is too late to change what might already have been arranged, I have to look forward and make the best of it.

Minn

It is a strange and wonderful thing that connection I feel with the folk I am acquainted with from my years at Blackrigg School. I greet them knowing that they know a lot about me and have a place for me in their memories. They know my father and where I live, the names of my sisters and who they're married onto. They remember me in those years when I was growing up and all of my future was a mystery, and I mind the same about them. We knew the things that went wrong in families but we never blamed each other because we had no say in where we'd come from and who we lived with. Though it's not in my nature to criticise the path that my school friends have taken, I know that's not true of everybody. Some are quick to condemn what other folk have done or blame them for the misfortune that has befallen them. It's hurt me to the core to know how some who I counted as friends carp about me behind my back because I have a child out of wedlock but I've found a strength I didn't know I had before Robbie came along. Only Sarah and Annie know who the bairn's father is and they will never tell. We are the best of friends and I owe them such a debt of gratitude.

When I see John coming down the road towards me, I feel that he will not pass judgement on me for having a bairn and no husband to show for it. John hasn't had an easy time of it and understands that life doesn't always turn out the way you might want. And so it proves. He is genuinely taken with Robbie and I am glad that he will be his uncle soon. There's a sadness about John that makes me want to reach out to him, to protect him like a mother for a son or a sister for a special brother. I feel that we will be good friends as well as sister and brother-in-law when I am married to Davy. I held off from making the decision for long enough but my bairn needs a father and my mind is made up for his sake.

I am walking towards the steading with the children when I hear somebody running along Main Street. We stop our chattering, and even the bairns are taken with the sight of the woman, hurrying in our direction. It's Miss Fraser but she isn't coming to speak to us, as she normally would if she saw us. She's stopped at the door of Smiddy Cottage and is taking her time rearranging her coat and putting a lock of hair back in its rightful place. She is staring at the door as if she has something very important to say and needs to go through it in her mind. She glances back and forward along the street and that's when she catches sight of me and Robbie and the rest of the Graham clan.

I give her the biggest wave and an even bigger smile and she waves back before stepping forward to knock at the door. Whatever has to be said cannot wait any longer. The door has opened and there seems to be a bit of a delay while she's left out in the cold. I take a deep breath as I wait to see what is about to unfold. Her hand goes to her throat and she steps back from the door, her eyes darting across the front of the cottage as if she is wondering what is going on inside and how long she will have to wait, even though she has already waited these many years past. I can see that she's anxious but she's standing her ground. Her mind is set. Then out comes Neil Tennant in his jacket and scarf and a moment later he has taken her hands in his while she speaks to him, saying her piece. He pulls her towards him and is suddenly sweeping her up in his arms, holding her like he's making up for lost time. She reaches up to touch his hair and he kisses her full in the mouth for the longest time. They cannot take their eyes off each other. Then they begin walking up the hill road together, his arm around her.

I watch – entranced – until they are out of sight.

It's a fine bright day with all of the frost about. The children are ahead of me, running and skipping, laughing together, full of stories and fun. We follow them, me and the bairn, hand-in-hand as we make our way towards the Rows.

'Oan ye gang,' I say to him, loosening my grip. 'Catch them up.'

'Robbie! Come oan!' shouts Tommy, right on cue.

The bairn looks up at me, hesitant, and my heart melts. Then he takes off at a run into that beautiful icy morning when the sun is shining and the only sound is the laughter of children ringing out in the frozen air.

The Linlithgowshire County Courant

January 1919   Blackrigg News

OBITUARY Private George Broadley RSF, aged 18 years. In the days following the signing of the armistice, Mr & Mrs James Broadley, 24 Stoneyrigg Rows received the news that every parent dreads. Their youngest son, Geordie, had disembarked at Leith with his battalion only to be taken immediately to Craigleith Hospital in very poor condition. They rushed to his bedside and arrived just in time before their much loved son succumbed to the pneumonia that had laid him low whilst on active service in France. In his letter to the family, Cpt Grieve wrote that Geordie had been a brave soldier who was always cheerful and helpful, a good friend to his comrades, young and not so young. During his short life, Geordie was an employee of the Blackrigg Cooperative Society. He had many friends in the village and he will be sadly missed by all who knew him.

MEMORIAL A committee is to be set up to discuss the funding and erection of a memorial dedicated to the gallant men of Blackrigg and the surrounding area who made the ultimate sacrifice for King and Country in the recent conflict. Enquiries to Rev Fraser at The Manse.

SOIREE The final recital of 1918 saw the Ladies' Choir deliver some 'weel-kent sangs' to an appreciative audience. Before the tea was served, two stalwarts of village life were thanked for their valued service. Dr Rose Matheson, who worked tirelessly in difficult times, is returning to duties in Edinburgh following the return of Dr Lindsay from army service. Miss Elizabeth Fraser is also leaving the village after eight years of dedication to both the church and the wider community. In particular, her work on the District Nursing Committee will be greatly missed, said her brother, Rev Richard Fraser, in his moving speech.

HOUSING SHORTAGE A 'practical steps' report is to be compiled for the County Council to consider the role of local groups such as burgh councils, as well as the employers, in providing new homes. Locally, the owners of Back o' Moss Pit have been praised for the addition of 36 homes to the local housing stock, during wartime. 50 new homes are to be constructed under the auspices of a housing association.

MAJOR DAVID MELVILLE esteemed member of the business community, has returned to a hero's welcome after service on the Macedonian Front.

HOUSING   CONDITIONS The influence of poor housing on the health of the population was discussed in submissions by local doctors to the Parish Council at the start of the month. Dr Matheson said that housing conditions in Rowanhill were the worst in Scotland and it was no mere coincidence that the influenza known as 'Spanish flu' had resulted in deaths during the second half of 1918. Miners in Blackrigg had also been affected and schools were closed to restrict the spread of the contagion. Dr Lindsay pressed for a reduction in crowding as well as improvements in sanitary arrangements and water supply.

MINING MATTERS Mr S Simpson addressed a packed Public Hall on the demands being made of Mr Lloyd George's Coalition Government by Mr Smillie, MFGB President: namely, a 30% increase on total earnings exclusive of the war wage; a six hour day; matters relating to demobilization; and State ownership of the mines with miners and government administering jointly. Should the latter be refused, members will be balloted on future actions. Unemployment and its consequences were discussed at length. As demand has dropped following the end of hostilities, and as men have returned from the Front, the number out of work has already risen to a worrying level.

Author's Note

In the final year of the Great War, my grandfather went 'over the top' with his battalion. As he ran towards enemy gun positions, he was wounded and left for dead in no man's land. It is not known how long he lay injured in the stinking mud of the Western Front but he was discovered alive by a party of German soldiers sometime later. In an enemy field hospital, a German doctor performed life-saving surgery on his throat. Although the details are unclear, this may have involved the removal of cartilage from his hip to replace what had been damaged and, possibly, the repair of blood vessels in his neck. During the weeks that followed, he was removed from a POW camp by inspectors from the International Committee for the Red Cross 'for humanitarian reasons'. They took him, with thousands of others, to Switzerland where he recovered during the final months of the war. The operation, performed under field hospital conditions, was so in advance of anything being done on the British side at the time that, after the war, he was asked to report to medical professors in both Edinburgh and Glasgow that they might learn from his case.

I was aware of this story when I was growing up and was slowly being drip fed triumphalism and the glorification of war by the British state. I never questioned the bravery, courage and sacrifice of soldiers and their families on the

Allied side but, equally, I was never taken in by the wholesale condemnation of the people they faced across the battlefield. The humanity shown by the German working party, the medical staff of a German field hospital, and the workers of the ICRC saw my grandfather's life spared in the midst of a conflict that took the lives of millions of others in the most brutal fashion. Were it not for the humanity shown towards my grandfather, my mother and her siblings would not have seen the light of day, nor the generations that came after. It is no exaggeration to write that, ultimately, I have the kindness of strangers to thank for the life I have today.

It was this story that inspired me to find out more about the life and times of my grandparents and, more widely, the people of the Scottish coalfield. That research led me to write Black Rigg and now its sequel, The Cold Blast. Hopefully, there will be a third in the series. Whilst the characters portrayed are entirely fictitious, the wider historical background is not.

PS Thank you to Billy for his factual account of a deceased West Lothian miner being taken home to his family by a group of his fellow workers after he had been killed in an accident in the pit. Finding no one at home, the body of the deceased was being delivered through a window when his widow appeared on the scene.

Also, thank you to Elaine for her description of her grandmother's fur coat, worn in a group photograph of her family on the occasion of their eviction from their rented company cottage in Cowie, Stirlingshire, following the death of her husband, Elaine's grandfather, in a mining accident.

Lightning Source UK Ltd.
Milton Keynes UK
UKHW011105060421
381511UK00001B/29